'Wicked shards of humor and sophisticate[...] [...]cent of James Joyce's *Ulysses* make up th[...] by Colin Sargent. *The Boston Castrato* ch[...] 20th century Boston's nine circles of hell, led by Alighieri's Dante and Virgil in the guise of an Italian Neapolitan castrato, Raffi, and his guide, a blind dishwasher named Victor. And, of course, there is a Beatrice, and a devil, and all manner of historical Boston figures, both famous and infamous. Sargent's masterful command of the language, his respect for affairs of the heart, and his playful pokes at some of Boston's bad-ass Brahmins combine to make this a rare book, one that will settle into the soul for a lifetime.'

Morgan Callan Rogers, author,
Red Ruby Heart in a Cold Blue Sea

'As a child in Italy in the early 20th century, Rafaele Peach is castrated by a priest who wants to preserve and exploit his beautiful voice. But the practice has fallen out of favor, and Raffi is exiled to the U.S., where he makes his way to Boston and falls in with "a circle of misfits, dreamers, and strays." Raffi's picaresque adventures take him from the highest echelons of society to the mobsters, schemers and charlatans who occupy the bottom rungs. In exuberant and yet precise prose, Colin Sargent conjures a sweeping tale of love, murder, and revenge.'

Christina Baker Kline, #1 *New York Times*
bestselling author of *Orphan Train*

'A musical priest disemballs a Neapolitan street urchin who thus begins a peripatetic journey that takes him to Boston where he becomes entangled in the web of Amy Lowell's Modernist mob and the real one as well. What happens? Just about everything, none of which you will want to miss on the way to a "happy" (?) (!) ending.'

Lewis Turco, poet and
author of *The Book of Forms*

'Antic and episodic, *The Boston Castrato* is as hilarious as it is compassion-ate, intriguing and wise, the prose finely honed, and its metaphoric richness rendering even the darkest, zaniest scenes with a haunting tenderness. Colin Sargent is a fearless and generous writer, and his blend of humor and pathos takes the reader into both the heart of this story, and into the lives of these deeply imagined and unforgettable characters who inhabit it.'

Jack Driscoll, author of
The World of a Few Minutes Ago

About the Author

COLIN W. SARGENT is a novelist, poet, and founding editor and publisher of *Portland Magazine*. *Publishers Weekly* praised his novel *Museum of Human Beings* as "a stylish look at the fate of Sacagawea's baby son, Jean Baptiste Charbonneau." As a helicopter pilot, Sargent was entranced by the slopes of Mt. Vesuvius and the Bay of Naples. A graduate of the United States Naval Academy, he has an M.F.A. from Stonecoast and a Ph.D. in creative writing from Lancaster University. He divides his time between the coasts of Maine, Virginia, and, when possible, the rest of the world.

The
Boston
+ A Novel +
# Castrato

Colin W. Sargent

BARBICAN PRESS

First published in Great Britain by Barbican Press in 2016

Copyright © Colin W. Sargent 2016

Barbican Press, Hull and London
Registered office: 1 Ashenden Road, London E5 0DP
www.barbicanpress.com
@barbicanpress1

A CIP catalogue for this book is available
from the British Library

ISBN: 978-1-909954-20-5

Text designed and set in Goudy Modern by Tetragon, London
Cover by Jason Anscomb of Rawshock Design
Cover photograph by Tilo Gockel

Printed and bound by Totem, Poland

Dear Johanna,
Yes, everything must be a joke to me.

'These are the days of impossible beliefs.'

—R. CORTISSOZ, 1913

I

Quando il vostro diavolo era uno studente, il mio era l'insegnante.
When your devil went to school, mine was the teacher.

NAPLES, ITALY, 1906

This was going to be his day. Raffi seized control of the rail platform, pushing away the other *scugnizzi* just as the gleaming carriage from Rome slid to a stop. As the glass doors opened in the hiss of steam rising to the vaulted domes of Napoli Centrale station, he was encouraged to see it was full of a dressy crowd, all fur and silk ribbons. If he worked quickly, maybe he'd be able to eat more than just moldy bread tonight. He closed his eyes and cleared his mind.

He had just one shot.

Raffi started to sing, very slowly, very controlled. One missed note and he knew he'd lose them. This time he wouldn't scratch the streets; he'd build a tower. He swept into 'Caro Mio Ben' in a lucky way, the soaring notes clear and fine without a hint of sharpness, exploring the sweetest heights of his range. The concourse wheeled slowly around him. He felt a warm rush. This was it. He was transported, all eyes on him.

In the dusty scuff, baggage handlers, vendors, soldiers, even the rats on the tracks—all stopped short. He had them.

His mother's ghost drew near, set down her suitcase, smoothed her skirt, and fell into his music. Raffi drifted out of himself and into her heart. His pure notes curled above the gas globes and gate signs and vibrated across the ceiling, wafting back and forth until the echo seeped into the stones and became part of the foundation.

His captivated audience on the upper balconies held its breath. Even the massive locomotives lowered on their suspension systems as if to put their ears to the ground. Behind them, Mt. Vesuvius leaned into the window. Raffi's final note was a shining arrow that pierced the coal-soot dusk as it rose to the domes, then softly fell.

'*You are my wonder,*' his mother cooed. '*You have such a gift. Don't squander it.*'

Nannies joined the buzz and rewarded him with figs from the tin pails they hung from net-covered carriages.

'How old are you?' asked a lady with a beaver collar as she drew a coin for him from a drawstring bag.

'Old enough,' Raffi said, making people laugh, though he wasn't sure why. He just knew six sounded like such a baby. Bad form to look at the purse. 'Thank you, signora. Thank you, signor.'

'Where are your parents?' the lady asked.

'My father lives at the base of the volcano, where the giants sleep.'

Fathers were luxuries. Who could boast of one? Grandfather Vesuvius knew him best. As long as he could remember, the slow blue slope had followed him—an attentive audience. It roamed with him through the city, into Virgil's Tomb where he sold daguerreotypes to sightseers, down sooty alleys where the dustbins stood, rich with treasures, disappearing and reappearing at the end of sunlit squares to whisper, 'I've got my eye on you.'

The woman watched as he stuck the coins in his pocket. 'And your mother?' she asked softly.

'My mother died two months ago, from the typhus.' He'd thrown himself down and wept beside the Fountain of the Little King.

The wallets and purses opened. Coins spilled and sparkled around him. Raffi looked behind her voice. A dark shape glided to the edge of the throng. A little man in a black robe. Crowded eyes. It wasn't the first time he'd noticed Father Diletti watching.

'Beginner's luck,' the priest said. 'You can only travel through the *zona di passagio* like that if you have no idea what it is.'

Raffi looked for his mother, but she'd disappeared again. He felt a tug on his shoulder. 'That's enough, little stray,' a carabiniere said. 'Get out of this station, now. Stop bothering the tourists. Get out, I say!' Awkwardly, the brute started dragging him. 'A train station is no place for music.'

'Hark,' Diletti said. 'I'll handle this.' In a quick motion he grabbed Raffi's hand and led him away.

Squeezing his upper arm, Diletti yanked Raffi through the series of narrow alleys above via Vicaria Vecchia. Beyond the Archbishop's Palace, a shadow cast a chill from the great gray stones of the Duomo di Napoli.

Inside the cathedral, Diletti soundlessly descended three passageways with a simian grace, pausing just once to light a candle without releasing Raffi's arm. The boy heard water dripping on stone before he saw it in the flickering gloom. When had it started to rain?

'Where are you taking me?'

Diletti turned on his heel, crouched, roughly gripped Raffi's chin with his bony fingers, and stared him in the eye. 'Consider this your baptism.' The monk's upper lip curled back, exposing the rotten teeth of his bulging maxilla. The black hairs in his flared nose were a tangle of snakes.

'Why so close, old man?' Raffi said. 'Are you trying to kiss me? I'm not your girl.'

'So cocksure, aren't you? What a wolf pup I've brought into my choir, pissing on everything.'

'You old queer.'

'That screeching of yours back there might have impressed the illiterati, but to me it was sickening. I almost couldn't watch it. Still, I might make a singer of you yet.'

The black stairwell where Diletti pointed was like looking into a rifle barrel. But Raffi relaxed when he heard the sound of a choir.

'The practice area is in the basilica, above the necropolis,' Diletti said. 'We certainly don't want to offend the angels if we're not ready.'

In the murk, a railing barely saved Raffi from falling into a bottomless cistern from the slippery stairs. The sound of their steps rang along passageways decorated by faded frescoes. A door swam up from the darkness. Diletti turned the lock and looked back. 'I suppose you're hungry.

'Attention,' Diletti said as a dozen boys looked up from their music charts. He pushed Raffi in front of them. 'This boy wants to eat you alive. I commend him to your discretion. Get him some lunch.'

Raffi shrugged and stuck out his tongue.

'Nice,' the priest said.

A moment later, they were scuffling and playing as if Diletti weren't there.

But he was always there, an icy presence. During the next six months, Raffi no longer thought about food all the time, though a sense of uneasiness sometimes stole his appetite. One thing about the Monkey: Diletti knew the music, cold.

He occasionally plucked one of the boys out for a special session. The others were left to hold their facial muscles still while singing into mirrors, so as not to over-emote. The morning after Diletti had forced Raffi to sing trills, scales, and embellished *passaggi* well past midnight—until he cried for his cot—the announcement came.

'Rafaele is my new protégé. After your transformation, you'll one day be *primo solista* at the Sistine Chapel.'

'You promised me!' Carlo screamed. 'I'm the one who earned the *onore e fortuna*. I was the one who got all the applause in the Jubilate Deo.' He turned on Raffi. 'How dare you? You did this.'

Diletti shook his head. 'Talent like this appears just once in a generation.' He disappeared behind the rood screen.

Raffi, asking for it, thrust his chin up and flashed his teeth.

'Lucky stiff,' Carlo shouted. 'What did you do to make him pick *you*?'

'I'm so sorry,' Raffi said. He rubbed a false tear.

'*Bastardo*,' Carlo cried and sprang. 'You'll pay for this!'

'They'll pay *me*!' Raffi laughed, dancing away.

The displaced star raised his fists.

'Aw, come on, Carlo, don't you know the old Monkey just loves to see us draw blood?'

Raffi sensed the swing slowly departing the platform—just a quick shift to the left was all he needed. The punch whistled past his chin. As though he'd dreamed it but couldn't stop it, he watched the big goon slip off the chancel, rattle his foot in a wash bucket, and crack his head against the stone floor. The other choristers gasped, looked at each other for permission, then laughed. But it was no longer funny. He felt a chill, even a pang of regret. Carlo had been one of the hardest to read, but if there were anything Raffi had learned about his fellow singers, it was that Carlo's only certain virtuosity was a gift for recalling a grievance as clearly as one of Aida's elephants. He sure wasn't going to forget this.

The next night, Raffi listened to the pounding rain. The table in the butcher shop felt cold, but the wine was warm and woozy. Through a cracked windowpane he caught sight of the Cathedral tiptoeing across the alley. It slipped behind his volcano, floating through the moonlight. He tried to sit up, but the straps seemed to tighten around his wrists.

'Be still,' Diletti said and poured some more of the Lacryma Christi. 'Just think how good you'll feel about yourself.'

'Will it hurt?' Raffi asked.

Diletti sighed. 'All the others in Monte Compatri greedily received their gift, which opened so many doors while softly clicking the tiniest shut. A passage to lust and dreams, maybe, but not to rapture. You wouldn't want to be chained to a madman like Socrates says, would you?'

Raffi didn't know who Socrates was, but it sounded bad. Was he the devil?

As though the devil had tickled his ear, Diletti reached to check his own privates. 'Surely I'd have jumped at this, little demon, as did so many at the Conservatorio. If the prestige isn't enough, there's the twenty gold *Umberto* coins, a great deal more than your father—if one would claim you—could steal in three years.'

'But will it hurt?'

The door creaked and the butcher's apprentice shuffled in behind a flash of white cloth and green glass. Diletti uncorked the bottle and waved it under Raffi's nose. The vapor was sweet and sharp at the same time. His eyes watered as the room darkened two shades. He was certain Diletti said, 'I'll stop right now unless you beg me to continue.'

With liturgical reverence, the Monkey unrolled a velvet pouch of sparklies near his feet. 'Knives, scissors, *emasculatome*.'

The apprentice shuddered. '*Gesù Cristo*.' He shook his head and backed away. 'Maybe I shouldn't take this money.'

'One more word from you,' Diletti growled, 'and you won't have to worry about being paid.'

'Does it have to be now?' Raffi asked.

'Imbecile. It's now or never. I'm doing it to protect your voice before it's too late. Actually, I might already have heard tinges of something "other" in your *fioritura*. Singing is your one and only grace. I can't stand by and let time take that away from you.'

'Father, what if I change my mind later?'

'Child, are you asking a man of God if he believes in miracles? Anything's possible in science. But from my experience, eunuchs are always happy with their lot. They have no time for trivial reflections.

They're too busy choosing between offers to sing in the greatest basilicas and opera houses in the world.'

'Will it hurt?'

'You won't feel a thing. What did Abelard write to Eloisa? "A long fixed calm of still repose." Don't squirm in the face of lustrous culture. You're not losing much for greatness. Just two tender clams shucked from shells, fresh from the Bay of Naples.'

Raffi struggled. His eyes grew wild. 'Carlo told me I could never be a man, sir.'

'Rubbish. Castrati are the world's greatest lovers. Tenducci married and fathered two children. Did he remember his old choirmaster in all his fame? Bah! But you'll remember me, won't you?'

Feeling a rush of dizziness, Raffi looked up to see spider webs lit by the tapers flickering on the chandelier. He reached to touch them, forgetting something was holding his arm down. He blinked quickly, and the chandelier began to spin.

'Lust is an interruption to pure thought, little sparrow, an erupting volcano—a false urgency that blocks the music of the spheres,' Diletti whispered. 'Who wants a leaping serpent when he's contemplating Saint Thomas Aquinas? Why plod through life grounded when you can soar? Look!'

From the folds of his robe he drew out a smoky photo in a silver-filigreed frame. 'This month the greatest living singer is in Teatro di San Carlo and La Scala. This will be you.'

Raffi studied the supercilious expression on Alessandro Moreschi's face. Cast in chiaroscuro, the singer's cavernous eyes were sunk in deep dark circles of exquisite *tristezza* like two moons over a fleshy lake. With his chins thrust slightly upward, arched eyebrows, and glistening black coiffure, he exuded an exotic air of both focus and indulgence. 'Sing well, eat well,' the Monkey always said. The entertainer's luxuriant wrap, a cloud of cashmere, coordinated carefully with a matching three-piece suit, a flash of white shirt, and a viceroy's striped sash arranged *just so*. Moreschi sure had God by the leg.

'Just imagine the esteem in which the whole world will hold you.'

'But...'

The priest shrugged. 'You'll never be a man if you shrink from beauty. Maybe you don't have the balls for this. Ha!'

Raffi forced himself to conjure the feeling of singing for his supper in the train station to fend off that gnawing hunger that never went away. He could smell the night soils in the alley, his only bedroom. A cusk he'd run into on the little black beach near Castel dell'Ovo after a deadly storm—and considered eating—opened his dull eye to warn, 'Your hands will never be warm again.' He'd caught the fish's twin with his bare fingers just feet away in the silvery waves and marveled at its rainbow scales—its live, golden eye. He thought of his voice, the only thing in this world that still loved him back. Maybe he could stand a little… editing.

'My pay'd better be in gold, not paper, old man.'

He lay still as the Monkey covered his nose and mouth with the hand-kerchief dipped in ether. The ceiling floated overhead as the paralysis bathed him. The priest metamorphosed into a descending black cloud, and Raffi drifted in and out of consciousness. The voices melted away, then grew near.

The apprentice waved a tin of olive oil over a kerosene lamp; Raffi heard the tinkling sound as the can warmed. Diletti poured the oil in a thin stream on his nether regions, and the boy felt the lower half of his body drift away.

'How can something so inconsequent mean so much to so many?' Diletti murmured.

Then he gently pulled Raffi's left testicle, the one that cradled his unborn sons, with the *emasculatome*. With a scope of twine, carmine and cutting, he tied the skin above it until it was barely a hair's-breadth wide. 'Just the smallest snip, and you begin your ecstasy,' Diletti said. He turned to the apprentice. 'Now, the scissors. Cut right here.'

'I just can't. You do it.'

'Oh, why not?' Diletti said, holding out his hand. 'I have to do everything else around here. I'm curious, what did you accept the money for? Is there not a sign on your quaint shop that promises in addition to your wormy steaks and chops, *Qui si castrano ragazzi*, here boys are castrated? You at least have, as promised, his box?'

The apprentice took it out of his greasy apron.

'Well, it *looks* like gold, anyway,' Diletti said.

Raffi stirred.

'His eyelids are moving,' the apprentice said. 'He's not waking, is he?'

'Just a reflex. Maybe he's running in a dream. Don't worry, they're all like that.'

With a smooth movement, the scissors clicked and Diletti dropped in the scrap of flesh. 'See, there isn't so much sensation.' He peered down as a tiny pulse of dark red appeared. 'Humph.'

Measure for measure, 'It looks like a heartbeat,' the assistant said. 'Is that supposed to happen? Doesn't that mean you've nicked a vessel?'

'So now you're the expert?' Diletti wiped it with the back of his sleeve. Then he looked into Raffi's eyes. 'You're almost there, angel.'

Raffi raised his head and was enveloped by a beatific calm as he watched the blood pool against his creamy leg. He tried to speak, but his lips wouldn't move.

Diletti guided his head down and finished with neat, catgut stitches, stealing an admiring moment before swaddling him in a snowy gown. 'It is done. I release you—from the fever of life!'

Suddenly a tremendous thumping erupted behind the iron door until it swung open, nearly off its hinges.

Gasping, Raffi surfaced from his sickly lagoon. 'Hey, Carlo, what are you doing here?' But Carlo, pointing, wasn't alone. He was surrounded by a coterie of priests in white, a cardinal in scarlet.

'Fetch the surgeon!' the cardinal roared.

'Belphegor!' a priest charged at Diletti. 'God help you for what you've done!'

'You've heard him sing,' Diletti shrieked. 'He's like an angel! He'll be the next Moreschi!' He took a step backward and balled his fists.

'You've heard the papal decree,' a Slavic monsignor in a black beard said in basso profundo. 'There will be no further mutilations.'

'That was advisory in nature,' Diletti said, spitting. 'I do not mutilate but celebrate.'

A dark-complected initiate gaped. 'He didn't get the memorandum.'

'Restrain him!' the cardinal said, then touched his ring to his lips. 'You'd better hope this boy doesn't die from exsanguination.'

'Oh, there was never a chance of that,' Diletti said. 'This is a matter of art for me. You can't tell me the congregations won't worship his voice.'

They'd sure better. Raffi propped himself halfway up.

Red as his gown, and athletic from the polo field, the cardinal rushed three steps and slapped Diletti backhanded with his ring.

'Mercy, your serenity! Forgive an old man.' Diletti dropped smoothly to his knees. 'If I thought this was wrong, then all the others I've brought to beauty would be wrong, too. I couldn't live with that.'

'Contemptible toad. You'll roast in hell.'

'I beg for you to receive me in confession.'

'You stink of the ignorance of the province,' the cardinal said, 'which may be the greater shame. This rabid search for the exquisite. The clipping of boys disgusts me. You're finished, old man.'

'No, he is mine to train. His music will be unearthly. He is most precious.'

'You have my word, no one will ever hear him sing. The Church is out of the monster business.' His Eminence took in a purple stain on the filthy stone floor and wrinkled his nose. 'What a foul Bacchanal. We expunged these abominable rites from Florence, only to have to race to Milan. Now it's resurfaced here in my own Naples? How is this possible in the twentieth century? I want all evidence of this destroyed and wiped clean.' He stopped at the door. Fascinated, Raffi watched him examine the mold-blackened ceiling. Scrawled at its center was a devil dancing around a tiny fountain.

'What, more barbarism?' The cardinal seemed to be addressing the painter, long dead. 'Did you think this could pass for art?' He scowled at the worn sign in the window. 'Pull down the walls, if you must. Turn this into a haberdasher's.' He turned to stare at Raffi.

The cardinal's mouth moved—a flicker, like candle flames disturbed by a basilica full of ghosts. 'The worst of it is, I never thought much of Moreschi.'

Raffi looked back at his volcano, encircled in a crown of smoke. He fell headlong into hell.

2

Al confessore si può dire qualche bugia, ma al medico no.
One can lie to the priest, but not to the doctor.

CASAVATORE, 1906

Raffi woke in a blinding white room with a long row of iron beds. A lamp on a stand marked 'Ritter, Port Huron, Michigan' washed his hands in a greenish light when he lifted them to rub his eyes.

'This may amuse you,' he heard a lovely voice call from down the hall.

'Glow little glow worm, glimmer, glimmer' began to spill from a gramophone in the nurses' station. He opened his eyes wider and was relieved to see he was no longer wearing that silly gown, which lay folded on an empty chair. Light reflected from the mother-of-pearl buttons on its cuffs in shades of violet, magenta, and aquamarine. He sat up, and an angel sailed in under a big white hat.

'How do you feel, my child?' She cupped his cheek with her right hand. 'A little warm, I see.'

'No flies on me. Where am I?'

'You're eight kilometers outside of Naples.'

'I've got to get back to the Cathedral. I'm going to miss practice. Where's my gold? I want my twenty *Umbertos*.' He frowned and folded his arms across his chest.

'You'll not be going to Naples. We don't want to get you too tired, dear.'

'I have to get up and sing,' Raffi said. 'Is the rest of the chorus here? In two weeks, you know, I'll be singing from the *Diluvium Universale*.'

She didn't answer. Raffi watched as she spoke into an annunciator. A fanatically groomed Someone in a white coat started toward Raffi, stopped short, and turned away, reluctant to get any closer.

'The boy must be exhausted,' he said to the angel. 'I'll speak with him tomorrow.'

The next morning, Raffi rolled off his cot with barely a note of pain. The angel escorted him outside to an enclosed garden—just a few dozen carefully pruned rose bushes Dr. Someone kept all his own.

As the gate clanged shut, the high roller in a starched white coat put his shears down quickly (covering them with deerskin gloves), took a deep breath, and turned in greeting. At least this time he had the balls to look a guy in the eye.

'So you're feeling better, son!' he said, holding out a manicured hand.

Gold cufflinks floated at the end of the doctor's sleeves. Gobs of black Vesuvian lava sat in finely wrought nests, which by the color had to be at least eighteen-karat. Large as olives, the ancient yet lustrous pearls in the center of each link held within their depths the azure mysteries of the Bay of Naples. As the exotic gems slid in and out, they winked like eyes of the *camorristi*. Someone as powerful as a doctor shaking his hand with such warmth couldn't be good news.

'Sit down, son, right here on this bench.'

Raffi was nobody's son. Mindful he hadn't been paid, he determined upon a tone of matched friendliness until he could tell if the doc was square or had shaved the dice.

'You've been through quite an ordeal,' Dr. Cufflinks began.

'Wasn't much.' Surely the doctor was hiding something behind those kind eyes. Raffi tried hard to guess what he was thinking but drew a blank. 'Say what you've got to say.'

'The first thing we want to do is get you healthy,' the doctor said, 'so you'll be... good as new.'

'I'm all for that. I'm ready to sing now.' When he'd begun an aria in his recovery room, the sisters had rushed in and put their hands over his mouth. It was crazy, as though they'd regarded his first experimental stabs at warbling to be heresies in Satan's tongue.

'That's the trouble,' Dr. Cufflinks said.

'What trouble, sir?'

'What was done to you should never have happened.' He said it like snapping a wishbone.

'What do you mean? Where's Father Diletti?'

A single blink of the eyes. 'I don't know, actually. Your Father

Diletti seems to have disappeared.' He looked above the trees as though searching for something. Then he brightened. 'Say! I have something you've been looking for.'

'So you have my money! It better be all there.'

'It's a great deal more than twenty *Umbertos*,' he said gravely.

'That's… great,' Raffi said. Then he stopped. There was something wrong here. Why the heck would they be paying him more money than what was due, unless what they'd taken was of greater value? An unbidden tear welled up and now drenched the center of Raffi's right cheek. Impossible. He hadn't cried in years. The doctor leaned in to wipe his face like he was a baby, so he backed away.

'*Che cazzo?*' Raffi spit, carefully avoiding the doctor's shoes. '*Vaffanculo, stronzo*–what the fuck do you want?'

'Well,' Dr. Cufflinks said, straightening. 'You certainly are from the street, *scugnizzo*. They told me you were a little prodigy who could parrot French and German lyrics better than the older choristers.'

'And read Latin better than an ancient physician.'

They stared at each other.

'I'm not sure any of those languages will help you now.'

Raffi hawked up another gob of spit and sent it straight into the man's neck.

'Girl whore,' Dr. Cufflinks said. 'This should be good. I want you to know Cardinal Vespati has granted you an audience with him.'

'Will he be coming for my rehearsal?'

'We'll continue this later. He's arriving right now.'

Raffi looked up the lane to see the same red man who'd yelled in the butcher shop. He seemed to have recovered himself.

'Stand up,' Dr. Cufflinks said as he rose to his feet.

'Now kneel,' said a sycophant in a worsted English suit who'd run ahead of the cardinal.

Stand and kneel at once. There's the Church for you. The cardinal approached him, and he felt powerful fingers spider across his head before they bit. He looked up quickly and flashed his eyes just as a thumb dug into his chin and pushed it up.

'Look at me when I'm talking to you,' the cardinal said. 'Your voice has been disfigured by the devil. It is the mandate of my office and therefore a command of God that you never sing again.'

Squirming, Raffi yanked his head to get away, but His Serenity held him fast.

'Not in church or in the society of men, or in the mirror, or even in your mind. There's nothing but darkness there. You have no music. Your song must never be heard. You must never sing, or try to sing, not here, nor in the depths of night, nor in the depths of your heart, upon your word in heaven. Or damn you and Diletti to suffering in eternal hell.'

'I will sing! I must!'

'In the mouth of the Spirit, in the teeth of the Almighty, I command you to silence. *Abyssum ad abyssum*, hell to hell.'

'Keep your head bowed,' Dr. Cufflinks said until the retinue disappeared from view. 'I don't know what's more barbarous, what's happened to you or what's happening to you. I certainly have my reservations about participating further in this ritual, but perhaps it would be worse still if I didn't give these to you.'

He reached into his battered leather valise and held out Diletti's box.

Raffi took it quickly and lifted the lid. He studied the melancholy scraps of flesh that were no more significant than the baby tooth he'd lost during the festival of San Gennaro. Atrophied and shrunken, his flesh was already a lifeless gray. He sucked in a whistle. Two ghosts! Like memories, they were cold, disconnected, and could never be stitched back. He felt a heavy sensation in his penis and then a quiver. This and no singing?

'For those without the *buon allevamento* to say it, I'm sorry, son,' the doctor said.

Another tear escaped and stained Raffi's cheek. He angrily rubbed it off. 'I was ruined to sing. I was promised—'

'Have you no family at all?'

'He promised the church was my family,' Raffi said, recalling Diletti's warmth when he pulled him out of Napoli Centrale.

'Let God be your father now,' the doctor said. 'You must go find your own joy, somewhere in the world where no one knows this… defining situation of yours happened—so you can start a new life. Flee so far from this hell even you won't find yourself preoccupied with what is simply a medical condition. Cheer up! We're going to send you on a great adventure, to the United States of America.' He took a piece of paper from the lining of his vest pocket, unfolded it. 'We've found just the place for you'—he adjusted his glasses and read—'at the Roman Catholic Orphan Asylum, where the Sisters of Charity will give you a proper education.' He hesitated, then laughed. 'It says they even have their own ball field and beach. The Church always provides for its own.' Dr. Cufflinks pressed his lips together, darkened his brow. 'Why has this fallen to me?'

'Doctor, will I be able to sing there?'

'I already know you have no manners. Don't pretend you have no ears. You must never sing again or this will happen to another boy, and that will be your fault.' He shook him by the shoulders. 'Don't just promise the Church or me, promise yourself. Now leave before I have to beg you to get out of my sight. Go.'

Raffi followed his pointing finger past the outer gate to a long black sedan with the angel and a driver standing beside it. 'Is this a new way not to pay me?'

The doctor reddened, shook his head, and rummaged through the contents of his valise as if they were unfamiliar. He grasped a small maroon bag and held it up in exaggerated surprise. *I don't suppose you mean this?* Raffi tore the little sack from the quack's hands and untied the string from its mouth. The coins glinted as he counted them. 'I was ready to blow this town anyway,' Raffi said. 'If I must go to hell, I'll find a place to sing.'

'You're too young to know what you're saying, my son. The world has no ears for you. There's been a horrible mistake, rendering yours the voice of doom. Don't forget I was the one to care for you.'

'I'll remember you as the one who sent me away, *dottore*.'

Dr. Cufflinks winked. 'If my own son were a castrato, I'd want him to act like you. What a thought! Why ponder the unfathomable? Who knows?' he said suavely, and they shared a last smile. 'Remember, in this warm weather, you have to keep clean or you'll develop scars.' He dropped his voice. 'The larvae of flies will settle in. They'll flourish there. I've seen this with wounded soldiers, and early on, when I was an intern, another boy exactly like you. My professor declared over the dying youth, may God strike us dead if we ever witness this again.'

Heading for the car, Raffi looked beyond the stones of the cloister to the domes and red-tiled rooftops falling away toward Lake Avernus. Then he turned and waved goodbye to Mt. Vesuvius before nodding to the doctor. Beyond that, the *tramontana*—a mysterious gust from the other side of the mountains, its icy fingers on the future—lifted the branches of a cedar tree on a hill he could barely make out.

'*Bella fortuna*!' The doctor turned and walked down the arbor path to the hospital. 'Live as a woman or a man—what does it matter in this moral twilight? You're a good little actor. You won't be the only one among us living with a secret.'

'You keep a lookout for your own scars, Dr. Cuffrocks.'

3

Si stava meglio quando si stava peggio.
'We were better off when we were worse off.'

THE BRONX, USA, 1907

The Angel's name was Karen. Over the next two weeks, she took Raffi across the sea in a freighter packed with hopeful souls from all over the Mediterranean. On the ship, Sister Karen told him stories about her childhood in the very same orphanage they were sailing to. Her brio was a lifeboat. It turned out the sweet angel knew the score.

When they arrived, everyone at the orphanage crowded around Sister K. immediately. It was as though she'd never left. Raffi felt welcome when she introduced him around, gave him a tour of the grounds, and showed him his digs.

'So here are your roommates, Raffi.'

'Hello,' a cross-eyed boy said.

'Lo,' said a boy holding one hand behind his back.

After supper, the boys climbed the stairs to their dormitory and bragged in the fading light. 'I can wiggle my ears,' Cross-Eyes said. 'Look.' But no one could see any movement. 'Okay, I can also touch my elbows behind my back.'

'That's just something to get girls to try.'

'I have six fingers,' Hidden Hand said. He spit three times.

'Technically you have five fingers,' Raffi said. 'And a thumb.' As the boys laughed, Raffi shuddered to think they might soon find a similar way to define him. He determined to remember: the cross-eyed boy's name was Aaron. Hidden Hand was Joe.

'What can you do?' they asked Raffi.

'How about sneeze with my eyes open.' He detonated a pulmonary and nasal bomb so explosive and unblinkingly calm the others were startled into silence, then burst into laughter. A sharp voice from the hall said, 'That's enough, boys.' The lights went out.

Blinded, Raffi sat on his bunk and waited until the others' breathing became more even. A red glow began to appear around the edges of the curtains. Sure he couldn't sleep a wink, he stole across the room and looked under the shade.

Across the Harlem River was an enormous billboard sign in letters illuminated by a battery of incandescent lights. Prancing against its stage was a huge red devil entertaining the moon and the stars. Who *was* this *primo huomo* in the footlights of the Manhattan firmament? Raffi marveled at the pointed tines of his pitchfork, his pointed beard, pointed tail, and pointed horns that carried such a grave weight. His reflected glare dipped the neighboring rooftops in red. This must be an American Rigoletto, a juicy part to play—a sure-fire star maker. With luck and hard work, he might one day capture exactly that topliner role. Everything was supposed to be possible here.

Just then a locomotive hurtled through a bridge toward the skyline, slashes of lightning sparkling around its wheels. The Underwood Devil on the sign disappeared. It reappeared, disappeared, reappeared, disappeared for twelve seconds as the train passed through, bursts of light flashing between boxcars as the devil danced.

This was really something. Who needs the Jubilate Deo? He returned to his cot, arranging his pillow so he could keep an eye on the window. As his lids got heavy, he thought he could see the incandescent devil through the shade. A part of Raffi slipped to the river and turned back to his window. Like a fairie prison, the orphanage watched from the top of its palisade. He dreamed he climbed to the top of the brilliant white bridge to see the tall buildings Sister K. had shown him when coming into port.

By the time a few weeks had passed, Raffi had a good many pals among the boys. This was all right. It was like being back with the choristers, just a fistfight or two from a real gang.

Every day after classes, he'd see Sister K. 'Hello, Rafaele,' she'd say. Her voice sounded so much like home.

'In English,' Raffi joked. Then they talked like brother and sister.

Many evenings he'd see her, too, because she worked in the library, which drew Raffi even closer.

After the library was closed, in the fragrant quiet of her room, she let him curl up under her arm while she read *The Emperor and the Nightingale*. 'This is how you'll improve your English, Raffi.'

When they read *Peter Pan in Kensington Gardens* together, the misty tendrils of the story crept in and surrounded the divan. 'There's a place like this I can show you,' she said.

The next full moon, she took him to Van Cortlandt Park. Inside the shiny black gate, a herd of deer stood very still beside a pond that glowed in the nocturnal gloom. 'Get closer, one step at a time,' she said, 'so they won't see us.' At first when he tried it, they scattered like a deck of cards. 'You'll get it,' she said. Walking home, she held his hand.

Night after night, he returned to the park. A month later, he invited Sister K. to Van Cortlandt again.

'That's close enough,' she said softly. But Raffi kept walking, without a sound, to a lost spot of green wakened by moonlight. He closed his eyes, extended his palm with a lump of precious sugar saved from his own tea ration, and a fawn skipped up to him. Slowly, he laid his hand on the fawn's warm back and caressed it. The creature trembled but didn't try to run. Sister K. caught her breath. 'You have a wonderful gift, Raffi. Don't let anyone tell you you don't.'

Raffi grew taller than the other boys. He felt odd late at night when the talk began more often to take a rough, sexy turn, but he did his best to take part. While their voices deepened, his took on a strange, strangled shade that he tried to cover by clearing his throat. Concentrating, he could barely control its squeaky effects, but he wondered for how long.

The boys were starting to turn on him, whether they realized it or not, so he was determined not to become so handy a target. He tried to ease into the shadows below their thoughts so he could stay one step ahead of them. If he sensed they were getting ready to comment on some physical weakness he'd shown, he'd jump in and say, 'Boy, that was girly.' If they were bruising for a shower fight, he'd feign another illness and take sanctuary in the infirmary—though there was a danger in pulling this too often. Before they could even finish crafting their clever boasts about how their bodies were changing, he'd suddenly remember a chore he'd forgotten to complete, slip out the back, and disappear. But he knew he couldn't do this forever.

In the early spring of 1911, it was rumored a circus was coming to Kingsbridge. A snippet of the show would be set up right on the lawn.

It was a three-tent affair, respectable for the Bronx. Real children from real families with doting parents filled the good seats as paying customers. Then the side curtain lifted. Raffi and his friends scrambled into the bleachers for free.

Mala, the Bengal tiger, cut a look at Raffi before leaping from her stand through a ring of fire. Who could take his eyes off the tiny macaque riding on a pony's back, nervously removing its miniature gold-braided hat to applause? Sister K. whispered to a man by the tent flap. A moment later, Raffi and the orphans had bags of peanuts to share. He felt a thrill when Shiva the Elephant from Bombay delicately snuffled one up from the palm of his hand.

After the fire eaters and snake charmers, a murmur. The Skeleton Man jounced in, flashing his black teeth. Nightmarishly lanky and strange of movement, he seemed in danger of blowing over in the wind-less ring. Then Owl Man and Lobster Boy joined him. Raffi rose in his seat, watching. The Mummified Man, alive. Dwarves. The Rajah with a Second Face—a dead twin hanging from his chest. The Human Pincushion seemed perky for someone whose right nipple was pierced through his back by an icy arrow.

As the show went on and more wonders slouched by—men with bosoms, young girls with lush beards—Raffi began to feel his skin get hot as though he were the fawn in the glen. He turned. The eyes of his pals were on him.

'The Fee-jee Woman,' the ringmaster called. 'Discovered by sailors, she has the black face of a langur and the tail of a bluefin.' She invited Raffi's eyes. *Dare you come into my loneliness?*

'No other big top can top Barnum & Bailey's Show of the Human Spectaculars.'

A cart rolled by under the power of not one but two Galapagos giant tortoises, without a driver.

Joe called out, 'Look, Raffi, they've left a place for you.'

Raffi smiled quickly.

Inspired, the boy lifted his voice. 'See the wonders of Empty Nest. All brains, no balls.'

The clowns turned away. The freaks seemed embarrassed and looked down. A cold breeze gripped Raffi from outside the tent flap.

They'd spent so many sylvan sometimes together. Had everything changed?

The next morning, reflected in the white tiles of the locker room, his old friend strode over. A long look. Too late, Raffi realized he'd been distracted and missed the signs. *This is a boy's shower. No girls allowed here.* His new tormentor pushed him down and started punching and kicking. Beaten bloody, Raffi crawled into a broom closet and waited for the others to leave.

Instead of going to class, he went to Karen. He needed to hear that reassuring trill of laughter. He climbed the stairs to the dispensary door but stopped short, hearing voices. Sister Karen was not alone.

'You've been spending too much time around that filthy boy. Don't get attached to any one of them.'

'I apologize, Sister. You always have such a kind manner of speaking.'

Raffi had never heard Sister K. speak sarcastically before.

'You bring him in your room?'

A pause. 'Just what are you implying, Sister?'

'That you're not his mother, or even a mother figure. You would do well to examine your motives in playing favorites among our students. You hurt the Church as well as the child.'

Raffi swallowed. Karen's voice softened. 'Oh, it's my fault. I know I've been getting too close. He has no one else. He doesn't even know how bad he has it yet.'

Raffi reversed his tracks and crept down the stairs. He walked quietly toward the back gate, and then he ran, tearing through leafy branches until he reached the park. But the park was empty. Even the fawn was gone. So he kept going. That night, he slept in the woods. He heard voices calling his name, sensed the lanterns of a search party but far away. He pulled leaves over his body and tried to close his eyes.

The next morning, he crossed the white bridge and slipped past the sleeping devil. But as he drew closer to the tall buildings that leaned into each other, deep in private conversation, he saw the Underwood Devil through the open doors of an empty electric car, leering from a placard above the handrails.

Underwood, so splendidly self-satisfied, was everywhere in Manhattan—in newspaper ads crumpled on the streets, on delivery trucks, reflected in the windows of grocery stores wherever he turned. In the Battery, where he spent two nights watching the Statue of Liberty turn her back to him, busy with new guests, the devil himself tried to entice him with one of the white-paper-wrapped tins from a cart.

High above Columbus Circle and Broadway, as the streets shifted to evening dress, two more billboards vibrated with voltage. Policemen watched Raffi carefully—did they think he had plans to steal?

In the tall evening, the lamps guttered. The tides of traffic grew low along Fifth Avenue. Passing fire escapes and spillways, noble rats and sewer drains, he twice skirted the high stoop of an elegant brownstone garnished with English lattice pulled open at a lower corner. He knew right away this was a place to tuck in for the night. But he also knew he wouldn't be in there alone.

He sensed eyes under the stoop, a shifting sound. The packed-down earth smelled like cemetery dirt. How many fledglings had taken refuge here in the sewers and basements of the unseen?

'Do not drop in,' a sophisticated voice said from under the stoop.

'Have a pleasant evening,' Raffi said.

He floated. Time disappeared as his circles widened and he found himself drinking from water spigots and licking the wrappers of bright trash to keep his strength up.

On Coenties Slip, he sprinted from two mounted policemen who bore down on him, whistles blasting. He jerked hard right and ran down an alley, feeling for an opening like braille. When he closed his eyes two warehouses shifted just wide enough to let him fall through to the other side. Indifferent silhouettes stood up from a burning rubbish can: brigands.

Stink of mackerel. Breaths sharp and cold. Just keep running. He flashed past a fruit vendor and grabbed the two biggest, most scarlet apples.

'Thief!' the costermonger cried.

Raffi stopped. 'This is a loan. Upon my word, I will pay you back.' Bowing, he dashed into the dusk.

Night directed his search for a place to sleep. Wet grass or a park bench had lost their luster. What on earth was pulling him back to the Harlem River, dream-deep? As if entering one of his own fantasies, he re-crossed the white bridge to the Bronx. Making his way to the water, his spirit grew larger and larger in the dark. Surely he could bunk down here. He jumped two sets of tracks, yakked it up with the rum-dumbs, paid tribute to the mossy rivermen with half a cigarette, and climbed around the Chinese gateway that held up one end of University Heights Bridge.

A service ladder lifted him to an iron workman's platform with private views of the great harp. No one could see him up here.

To his left was the New York Highlanders baseball stadium with its soft roars. To his right was Spuyten Duyvil, where the Harlem flowed into the Hudson and the sea. But straight ahead...

The rumble and crash of urban commuter trains raced toward Manhattan through the girders. Above the river's dull root beer, the mad concert set his mind dancing with its shuttling clangs of iron. The red devil was awake now, prancing right above him. Raffi stopped to study his childhood idol, but something was strange.

The more he watched the performer, the more he realized Underwood pointedly had that special nothing—a defining absence between the legs just like his own. Raffi saw the devil wasn't a star at all. He was nothing but a shill, just a hawker. As he watched the devil grinning through the girders, he felt angry at himself for being so stupid. How was it he was only now learning that the most attractive iconography in this new country was no more mysterious than potted meat? Whoever the real Mr. Underwood was, of 'Fulton Street, Boston, Massachusetts,' as the sign proclaimed, he certainly had the devil by the horns.

He dropped to the riverside and saw a few young strangers beside a utility shed must have had the same idea he had about spending the night. Their dark shapes broke the reflection of the wild water. With luck, he might find a friend. He walked over, set down his bag, and fished out his two spheres.

'What's the password?' one of the boys whispered. Two more appeared out of the shed.

'Grub,' Raffi said. When he held the apples up to catch the light, they looked even more dear, a deeper red.

'Come on in,' the shadow boy said. 'If you dare. It's not exactly a hotel.'

'Splendid,' Raffi said. 'I like a rough sleep.'

'First, the fruit.'

He tossed them in.

'Okay, now get your bag.'

But when he turned for it, a black square was swinging toward his face with a small shadow behind it. No time to duck. Somewhere below the floor of his unconscious the sense of *pala del carbone* started to form. Coal shovel.

He woke with a ringing in his head. He reached quickly to make sure he still had eyes, but when he felt them the black squares were still coming toward him. It hurt even more when he moaned. Scrambling back in bed, he blocked his face with both hands. He cracked his fingers to see who was standing over him.

'This is not the way, Raffi,' Sister K. said. 'Running solves nothing. You're going to have to make your own way.'

'Yes, sister. I get that now.'

In 1915, when word came across the Atlantic that the *Lusitania* was sunk, the whole nation shared the grief with their English allies. Raffi devoured the newspapers along with the other boys, even as they grew further apart. The nuns looked the other way when Raffi took to sleeping in the utility closet between the boys' and girls' dormitories, a pile of books rising on his table. Nobody's parrot, he was resolved to master the languages of French and German. He would never feel sorry for himself, and he would never sing a note.

He carried bedpans in the ward for Sister K., his only contact with the world of grown men coming when he wrangled baggage on the ferry docks, polished the Bishop's black limousine, set up deck chairs at the diocese's Long Island retreat in Montauk, or earned tips brushing down the horses at Harlem River Speedway.

When two orphans arrived with tuberculosis, Sister K. volunteered to care for them in the isolation wing. Raffi was ashamed he felt something like jealousy. When Raffi heard she died, it was like losing his mother all over again. Now there was one person less in the world who knew the truth about his condition, for better or worse—the last who'd loved him.

With pity behind their smiles, the other sisters made sure he knew he was provided for, though they only professed love for *Gesù Cristo*. With their pigeonlike voices, they kept him near like a pet and never again made him sleep or wash up with the other boys. Raffi's greatest fear was, he might one day find himself sick of being grateful.

As the years grew beards and his classmates' voices deepened, he studied ever harder to get ahead. When 1917 blitzed in, nobody suggested that Raffi join the line of boys who were examined by the Army surgeon, clipboard in hand. He watched from his lonely window as his former chums rowdily boarded the recruiters' bus to kick some Kaiser ass, a close-knit band of adventurers heading to the great fishing trip of war.

Why wait for the horror to get more horrible? So he graduated and caught a boat to Italy. Not to take revenge on Diletti. Not to find his missing father. Not to recover his old life, but to find a calling and be reborn. He would make a startling success of himself in Italia and then return in triumph to America—as a man, on his terms, to find a place to belong. No one else had to know. Nothing would stop him.

4

Non comprare la gatta nel sacco.
Don't buy a cat in a bag.

EN ROUTE TO BOSTON, USA, 1922

R affi leaned over the taffrail of the *S.S. Ariadne* as kitchen
boys emptied pails into the steamship's wake. It was vaguely
satisfying to watch the rotten potato shavings bob in the
waves.

'I just think that's vile,' a musical voice said behind him. 'The seas
aren't ours to foul.'

He turned. He'd noticed this girl several times during the crossing
and wondered if he were imagining this lucky moment. The first glimpse
was in Naples. Clusters of families clung to their awkward trunks and
baskets as they climbed the ramp. A stevedore whistled slyly to alert his
friends there was something worth a look-see. The world stopped as a
compact bear of a man pulled his two daughters close—one strikingly
tall and smiling luminously, the other's eyes downcast.

Two more times Raffi had caught sight of the bright one below
decks, and now here she was, sweeping into his life like a sunbeam. He
cleared his throat and lowered his voice an octave. 'Not a problem. My
assistants will take care of it for us.'

He snapped his fingers. On cue, a flock of gulls descended and squab-
bled for the remains, the finest of delicacies. In a hail of screech and
braggadocio, they picked the ocean sparkling clean.

His goddess smiled. 'We haven't even reached Boston yet, and you
have connections.'

Watching the birds separate and lose themselves in the blue nourished
the lark in his heart. But as they disappeared over the horizon, a chilly
breeze across the deck reminded him of the wind from sixteen years
before on that green hill in Casavatore.

He stepped closer to the girl and was electrified by her natural perfume—violets in a thunderstorm.

'Raffi Pèsca.' He took her slender fingers in his and brushed his lips against them, a skill he'd honed in Rome. 'I'd be honored to know your name.'

'Beatrice.'

Instead of removing her hand, she allowed it to linger.

'Beatrice,' Raffi said. 'You can be my guide.'

'And you can help me with my English,' she said, giving him a gentle squeeze before letting go.

'English it is, then.' He lit two cigarettes, gave her one, and stopped himself from tossing the match over the side. They both laughed.

A menacing transverse wave slapped across the slighter undulations dancing in the foam of the *Ariadne's* wake. It was a disturbing wave no painter would care to paint and no tourist would ever want to see. Black clouds scudded toward them, their bellies heavy with rain.

'I wouldn't want to get caught in that,' Beatrice said.

'I wouldn't mind it.' Raffi looked right into her eyes.

She blushed. 'Aren't you a bold one.'

'You know, your English really is quite good!' He moved beside her until his shoulder touched hers.

'My sister and I were at the top of our class in school.'

'Were you in the same grade?'

'Dorotea is my twin.'

Beatrice looked away, and her gray eyes refocused on the horizon. Raffi watched as they seemed to catch the mist, too, like the ocean after rain. When she turned back to him he was surprised to detect a cloud below her sunshine. But the cloud had the effect of making her radiance even brighter.

'The two of you don't look like twins. Were you both born in an enchanted forest? And tell me, pray, Beatrice, which of you is the bad twin? I'm hoping it's you.'

'You brute, you've been watching us. I think you're rude not to have said so before.'

He looked toward the ship's bow and saw a solitary figure looking back at him through the drizzle. The silhouette half disappeared the way his fawn used to vanish in the gray approach to dawn.

'Beatrice, up toward the bow, there's…'

'I know.'

That night, as the ship rumbled through the darkness of a restless black ocean spilling around him like a dream, Raffi thought long of Beatrice and fleetingly of her sister. So much of life was hidden behind the drapes of things. He waited on the deck all morning for a chance to be near Beatrice again and suddenly there she was—a warm cloak of stormy violets. His heart swelled as she rounded the corner.

'Can you take supper tonight in the company of our family?' she asked.

'My ticket doesn't include meals.'

'Don't worry. We have plenty.'

He joined her family in the curve of the bow at a small table set with jellied lamb, squab, and cabin biscuits. As the waves rose and fell, the glassware around him chimed, a chorus of F, C-sharp, and A.

'Mother, Father, this is my friend, Sr. Pèsca,' Beatrice said.

'My great pleasure, Signora,' Raffi said. 'It's good to meet you, sir.'

Beatrice's father half stood up. Then he stared.

Mrs. Favi waved her blue knuckles. 'Sit, *per favore*.'

'English, English,' her husband said. 'We're not in Civitavecchia anymore.'

'And, there's no need to guess…' Raffi said, taking in Beatrice's glowering twin, 'who you are.'

'We're crossing the Atlantic to get away from fops like you,' Dorotea said.

'Funny, so am I.'

As they picked awkwardly through their meal, a fly joined the orchestra of goblets, its wings whirring disturbingly between B and B-flat, stopping only to rest on the lamb.

Waving the pest away, Favi offered a second serving of wine.

But sensing a test, Raffi declined. 'Are you looking forward to your move to Boston?'

Favi turned in his chair. 'What's it matter if we're looking forward to it or not? We're already almost there.'

'Where will you reside, sir?' Raffi asked.

'Fulton Street,' Beatrice said, 'with some relatives. Do you know anything about Fulton Street?' She looked to the others. 'Raffi grew up in America.'

'Ah, yes,' Raffi said. 'Fulton Street. It's close to the Underworld.'

They stared at him.

'Just a joke,' he said.

'Not very funny, in my judgment,' Favi said. 'Mr. Underwood is a world-renowned businessman.'

'Papa's been invited by Mr. Underwood himself about a very important job,' Dorotea said, 'at the Underwood Deviled Ham factory. Papa is an industrial engineer.'

'I know of this ambrosia,' Raffi said and smiled. '"Branded with the devil but fit for the gods."'

'So you've been back and forth across the Atlantic before,' Dorotea said. 'You must be running from something.'

He grinned at Favi. 'It's known the underworld over, a very nutritious and popular snack.' Then he leaned closer to the girls and whispered, '"Branded by the devil but fit for the dogs!"'

Beatrice laughed easily, Dorotea in spite of herself.

'I prefer a serious man,' Favi said. 'What business do you have in the United States?'

'Boston is the hub of the world,' Raffi said. 'I'm certain to find something, or something will find me. Do you know of a hotel called The Parker House?'

Favi shook his head. 'Hotels are for people who don't mind wasting money.' He took in Raffi's cashmere jacket and foulard tie. 'Those duds must have cost a lot.'

Raffi flushed. On an impulse, he'd stopped in at the most exclusive men's store in Naples and placed the last of his gold coins on the marble counter with satisfaction.

'But nothing is more valuable than family,' Raffi said. 'If I had two such pretty daughters, I'd be very careful about who they consorted with as well.'

'Pretty words,' Favi said, 'but I've heard gentlemen in business in America don't like flashy clothing as much as they like plain speaking.'

'They say clothes make the man—I hope it's true. I want to make myself useful as a concierge. I have a letter of introduction from when I worked at the Hotel Forum in Rome.'

Still not the right answer. His opponent turned away. He'd have to be more careful with his words. 'And how about you?' Raffi asked, addressing the girls but looking at Beatrice.

'For now, we're hoping to work at Daddy's plant if they'll have us, but one day, I'd like to be a teacher.'

'All the boys will be in love with you, Beatrice,' Raffi said.

Her hand reached below the table and touched his.

'I'd like to be a private investigator,' Dorotea said. She looked past her sister into his eyes.

'That is no job for a young lady.' Favi got up. 'That's it. Time to go.'

'Go along, sister,' Dorotea said. 'I'll cover for you.'

Raffi bowed and took Beatrice by the hand. They climbed two narrow sets of stairs in search of fresh air. When he undogged the hatch and stepped outside, he felt the night rushing along the ship's superstructure.

For a moment the stars looked down on the two of them as though they were at the edge of an infinite dance floor.

'Well, that went well,' Beatrice said.

'I was hoping to have made a better first impression,' Raffi said.

'I think we've seen the worst of it.' She paused. 'Do you have spirits?'

'Who, me? That's illegal.' Raffi winked and slipped a flask from his coat. He drew her out of the wind and unscrewed the cap. 'A little tonic to keep you warm.'

'It smells like some herb... juniper?' She took a sip and coughed.

Raffi touched her shoulder. 'I'm sorry, it's very strong. I should have warned you. I know what it's like to be sensitive to taste and scent. Yours, by the way, is intoxicating.'

'Well, has any girl ever said you have a most pleasant aroma of tannin and cherries?'

'No, but do go on.'

'I love that you're so tall,' Beatrice said, her cheeks flushing in the moonlight. 'It's so nice to be looking up at a boy.' She paused. 'I'm always the tallest in the bunch.'

'Me too.'

For the first time he was thankful a pituitary storm unchecked by testosterone had rushed his height to the upper balconies.

Beatrice looked at him so intimately he sensed she was on a strange journey of her own. As he looked at her loveliest of all faces, the deck of the ship rose up quickly under his feet and then fell away, as though they were both floating above the waves. Could she be what he needed to feel whole, a person who could understand him, forgive him for what he wasn't, and somehow love him for what he was?

He sensed the ghost of her yearning reaching out to him in misty tendrils. He pulled her toward him and kissed her. She sighed, and her perfume embraced him. The wings of the reckless traveler fluttered inside him as he experienced an electrical wakefulness transmitted to him via one of Sr. Marconi's aetheric waves. And he knew it was his stunted libido—which he'd come to nickname Voluptuo, The Traveler—quickening in him like a nightingale flying through a subway. It was remote and touching, lost in an underground network in lurid flashes of purple, green, and black. It caught his eye but then flew down another shaft and disappeared, leaving him alone.

He was cut with disappointment as the beating seemed too distant, and sensed the man he might have been whispering in another room. He knew his second self well, having traveled through other disappointments with him. As the 'traveler' flew away, his lips found the hollow of Beatrice's neck and felt the mortal beauty of her pulse.

Maybe love could exist independently of sex. If he spent his life making her happy, maybe that's all he'd need.

'I wish I could stay out here with you forever,' she said, 'but Father will be looking for me.'

'Yes, I know.' He ran his fingers beneath her fragrant curls, releasing their scent. He brushed her temple with his lips. 'Beatrice, before we go forward, darling, there's something you should know.'

'Shhh,' she said, covering his mouth with her fingertips. 'I think I understand how it is. The mystery is part of the attraction.'

5

Avresti potuto almeno prenderti la briga di inventare una buona menzogna.
At least you could have taken the trouble to make up a good lie.

BOSTON, 1922

Raffi descended the ladders to his third-class cabin under the trunk room. His head had barely touched his pillow when, just like that, he found himself behind the bar at the Hotel Forum.

'Is my mistress here?' a diplomat asked in a low voice.

'Yes, she's waiting upstairs,' Raffi said, handing him a crystal glass and a snowy napkin. 'For you.'

'Does she understand how it is?'

'We're all well versed in our roles. Is the drink to your liking, sir?'

'Singularly engaging, but I just can't place what's in it, actually. Most unusual, in fact.' The man smacked his lips. 'Here's a little something for you. You understand the need for discretion.'

Raffi nodded and melted away.

Well before he'd joined its employ, he'd understood Hotel Forum was known as a landmark devoted to tourists gawking at the ruins, and as a way-station for the sexually adventurous. If all roads led to Rome, all intrigues led to Hotel Forum.

Here he'd developed his taste for cashmere and shown a flair for helping others hide their baggage. The world placed a great value on a fellow who could make things move so easily around him, reducing the sliding friction for all concerned, and it was as though everything around him became dusted with the finest coat of silicon.

'He is a wonder, the soul of discretion,' his letter of introduction began.

But it was more than that: the intelligence quickly flew through the international set that if your desire need be wrapped in a prudent

31

silence, Raffi made sure he was your young man. In time, his bar had taken on the aspect of an adjunct office of the American embassy, the more valuable for his evenness of temper, insight, and calm approach to uproar—a sheltering eye of the hurricane. In subjugating Voluptuo, Raffi discovered a transforming eroticism in making strangers' lives more fulfilled.

Among many special considerations, the hidden corner booth was ready whenever the consul slid in with his inamorata to sip the martinis that had become just one of Raffi's many specialties: ice-cold gin, a whisper of vermouth, and a single lusciously pendulous caper berry.

Knox, the wary bellhop—'Call me Opportunity'—asked him in his New Orleans patois, 'Do you know how to make any other aperitifs, Sport?'

'As far as I'm concerned, my friend, one needs no other cocktail.'

Casting a glance at Raffi's discreet tip jar, always stuffed with lire, pounds, and papiermarks, Knox had finally blurted out, 'How do you manage all of this?'

'This' was what Raffi had made his art. He was a balm, a salve. To the children of local tradesmen he taught English; in turn, the plumber would tend to a leak before a single drop could spoil his bar's elaborate crown molding. If the porter slipped out back for a hand of gilet, Raffi ensured the guests' luggage still appeared without delay in their rooms. If a chambermaid failed to punch in, the guests' marble tubs sparkled nonetheless. The sterling humidors on the gleaming rosewood registration desk were never seen to need replenishing, though the fragrant smell of Havana cigars wafted deliciously in the corridors. Water rings from casually abandoned highballs never appeared on the surface of the bar's luscious marquetry tables. Fingerprints were never left behind on the mirrored telephone stand. And nobody's hysterical wife was ever heard screaming in the lobby. He'd so deftly reorganized the library at the Forum—so as not to offend someone wearing royal blue with *The Red and the Black*—that a number of business deals, including several exquisite trade agreements, had been sorted out here.

It was in the Forum, too, that Stefania, the embassy stenographer, had let it slip to him over drinks when his bar had closed that she'd grown up in Porto Molo Bevellelo, outside of Naples.

When was it she'd not just guessed but relished, even craved to test, the consequences of his secret? Was it when they'd stepped out for a late supper, strolling along via Veneto, and she'd tossed her hair and asked him, 'What planet do you hail from?'

'Ischia,' he practiced lying. 'Have you ever been there?'

'Ischia's too pedestrian,' Stefania said loftily. 'My family prefers Capri. We have a villa on the cliff that looks over the sea. From our private tavernetta there's a staircase to a secret canal that takes us into The Blue Grotto.'

'My family owns three villas,' Raffi said, 'if you don't count the castle.'

'Those truly gentle-born are embarrassed by their castles and never mention them,' Stefania said. 'Leading me to believe,' she said, licking her lips, 'you are an imposter.'

'I am just a babe in arms,' he said, 'compared to the imposter you are.'

'Are imposters impotent? Or is the imposter's post imposing? Can an imposter live a full life?'

An attempt at intimacy with this mercurial girl might very well be a disaster. But to live a full life, should you not upon occasion court disaster, too?

Lights shining through the Colosseum's arches projected an ancient pattern on the sidewalk as they followed the building's curving wall. Slipping behind a crumbling doorway, he pulled her in. 'I'll show you who's full of life,' he said, leading her up a flight of wet stairs into a niche with a stone bench covered with moss.

'I think I love you—tonight,' Stefania said in the dark. 'Where are we?'

'I know this place blindfolded. We're in the Vestal Virgins' apartment.'

'You know, you remind me of my great uncle. He had a wonderful voice. So let's get this show on the road. This tour is beginning to bore me. Take off your pants.' She made a sharp bark when she saw his warm ivory in the moonlight. 'You have no hair—anywhere? Ooh! You are like a little child.'

'Just come closer,' he said, now fully erect. His penis was as narrow as it was when Diletti had molested him, no more than an inch and a half long fully extended. Stefania was enchanted.

'May I touch you, you clever newt?' she addressed his crotch, not his face. 'I have just the sheath for you.' She caressed him.

33

He looked away through a slit in the stonework at the Colosseum's arena floor and Libitinarian Gate, through which the bodies of vanquished heroes and leopards were carried. Above its edge, lights from the modern skyline blinked in the more fashionable districts of Rome. He thought he could detect the soft step of the wolves allowed to roam free in the inner amphitheater to ward off intruders. Neighbors were unnerved by their howling.

He'd been drawn to the cavernous, shadowy building when he returned a penniless teenager from America, and had slept in its catacombs for weeks before earning enough for a one-note flat in the basement of a bakery on viale Lodovico. Beyond the shadow of a doubt, he knew his way around the Colosseum as surely as the *allupata* Stefania knew her way around him.

Why was she so fascinated with the smooth scars where his testicles had once just barely descended? She stroked them with her index finger, then nearly purred as her nostrils widened. 'Maybe you can fuck me after all,' she said, 'since you smell like Taurasi. Of course the consul wouldn't like it. Nor my father. But maybe I would like it. Come closer, little boy.'

He obliged, and a few convulsions later entered her. Or at least he thought he entered her. She could barely have noticed it. All of a sudden, she started writhing and whooping. She gasped and reached her hand down to stimulate the place he knew he'd barely penetrated. 'Move faster,' she said, her hips thrusting. 'You are the most incredible lover. Can I see you tomorrow night?'

'Couldn't you at least have said "hardly credible"?' He grinned, realizing his partner had just made love to herself. Get this! What truly excites you is your knowledge of what I've lost.

Over the next few weeks, in various stages of moonlight, dress, and inebriation, Raffi the infamous Forum roué escorted Stefania back to the Colosseum, but it was more to listen to the howl of the wolves than anything else. One night he heard them squabbling, devouring a stray dog. Trapped in this circus of hunted souls, they circled the starlit enclosure, impatient for the next show.

He began to step away whenever Stefania fell in love with herself to light a cigarette while she masturbated. After the third time she did this, he said, 'Don't let me get in the way.'

'*Ricchione*! You're neither man nor woman enough for me!'

Next day, she told his coworkers he was queer. His education was complete. It was time to move on.

'I just don't like him,' Dorotea said sharply from her bunk.

'Well, you certainly have a funny way of showing it,' Beatrice said.

'What on earth do you see in him?'

'Don't worry, I couldn't make him touch me. He's too much of a gentleman.'

'He's too much of a girly beanpole. You could be his mother.' Dorotea bit her lip. When they burst out laughing, it was too late to pretend to sleep when they heard their father's steps approaching.

Sr. Favi ducked his head inside the curtain. 'You will not see this boy when we reach the shore, do you understand me? If I see him close to you, I'll string him up by the balls. You make that clear, all right?'

'Yes, Papa,' Beatrice said. 'But how can I tell him if I can't see him?'

Raffi dreamed on.

As usual, he found himself running up spirals of stairs in a lighthouse gone dark, only to slip out at the top and fall to the moonlit rocks below. He had yet to hit the ground.

But tonight it was different. The stones became a wet street as he walked through a darkened metropole in the rain, rushing past signs in German to make sure he was on time for his appointment at 18 Luminstrasse. In the greenish light from the streetlamp he could just make out the name Dr. S. Freud. A massive black door loomed at the top of the stairs. He rang a bell, and through a crack that opened he saw a pallid girl.

'Are you looking for my father?' she said in a faerie-light lisp. Her eyes were encircled by a bluish tinge. Behind her, a large Alsatian dog stood guard. 'Not another one of you. What a nerve.'

'Oh, but he'll want to see me,' Raffi said. 'I've discovered the cure for castration anxiety.'

She looked past him down the street, as though she were leaning forward to listen to a distant train. Then she looked back into his eyes.

'Oh! Well, he can't see you now. He's not here.'

'That's all right, I'm barely here myself.'

She closed the big black door. The detonation of the bolt sliding into the strike plate woke him with a start. As the ship rocked back violently and shuddered he realized the *Ariadne* had found the shore.

6

Metti dei soldi addosso a un asino, e lo chiameranno Signor Asino.
Put money on a donkey and they will call him Mr. Donkey.

BOSTON, 1922

Raffi dropped his duffel and rushed to the rail. In a tornado of shouts and pointing, it seemed as though all of the New World were floating while the steamship was standing still. Below the weather decks, he could see Beatrice and her family descending the gangplank to join 'the hopeful tide of immigrants venturing into the Land of the Free' or 'the horde, bearing its contagions,' depending on which yellowed *Boston Post* column you'd read last in the *Ariadne's* lounge.

'Beatrice,' he called out.

'Raffi, Raffi!'

'Meet me by the swan boats. Ask anyone,' he shouted over the hubbub. 'At noon, on the seventh of April.'

'I'll be there.'

The hell you will. It was easy to read her father's thunderous brow.

Taking both girls by the elbow, Favi plunged deeper into the determined crowd. Raffi saw the feather on Beatrice's hat bobbing and then she was lost in the line marching toward the delousing and fumigation chambers, with their mists of hydrocyanic acid gas.

Thank God their date was nearly a month away, so he'd have time to get a fresh start and heal the wounds he'd already made with her father.

'Could you please point me in the direction of the Parker House?' he asked an old man selling beans baking in a large crock of dark molasses near Lewis Wharf. Behind it, the mucky seashore perfume of the harbor plunged the depths of low tide. He stopped, filled his lungs, and drank it in.

The vendor regarded him from stem to stern and shook his head. 'I wouldn't have any business with those high hats, honey. What do you want with that set?'

'Why, I intend to work my way up,' Raffi said, 'from waiter to concierge.'

'I just wish I could be there when they get a load of you.'

You're sure I'll be nothing but a figure of fun. You're probably right. Raffi followed his gesticulations until Faneuil Hall rose on the north side of Quincy Market.

'Is this the turn to the Parker House?' he asked a milkman feeding bits of brown bread to a delivery horse with a coat the color of drizzle.

'What do you think, Otis?' the man inquired of his pal. 'Should we help this lost soul?'

The Flanders gelding shook his head side to side, snorted, and looked Raffi straight in the eye. Then he went back to his oats.

'What did he say?' Raffi said.

'If you really want to be a concierge at the Parker House hotel, you're going to have to work on your mind reading,' the man said.

'So you think I can't do it?'

'There you go.'

Raffi laughed and felt his spirits rising. He reached to pat Otis's snout. 'You're a hardworking boy! I bet you're looking forward to hitting the hay.' At Harlem River Speedway, he'd loved slipping into the low brick building to groom the horses in their stalls.

It was the milkman's turn to snort. 'Hardworking nag, you mean. Otis says, "If you're looking for the Parker House, follow the scent of the rolls." Surely you know Parker House rolls? You can almost smell them from here. There's an alley vent from the kitchen, a heavenly aroma. Sometimes a few precious scraps get swept and wind up in the dustbins outside.' He took a long look at Raffi's thin wrist, which extended from his sleeve as he stroked the horse's mane. 'Something you may want to remember.'

'Thank you,' Raffi said.

'Oh, you're welcome, your highness,' he said, stepping back. 'You're pretty tall for a wop, but be careful—that strut gives you away.'

'Oh, really, then what do you suggest I do?'

The little gnome rubbed his index finger along the top of his lower teeth. 'Unbutton the top button of your jacket. And another thing—get your nose out of the sky or someone's likely to break it. Over here they don't go in for that dandified air.'

'I'll take that advice,' Raffi said.

The man pointed to Raffi's duffel. 'Say, what else have you got in there, Naples? What district are you from, dear?'

By that term of enqueerment, Raffi knew he was expecting to hear the Borgo Marinari district, renowned for its *elegante* cross-dressers. 'The address, please, for the hotel,' Raffi said. 'And I'm not your dear.'

'Keep your shirt on, Mr. Sister! No offense! It's that ritz right there!'

Rising from a hollow on the corner of Tremont and School Streets below Granary Burial Ground and a cluster of smaller, darker buildings, the Parker House glimmered with a white marble exterior finished a bit self-consciously with a mansard roof on the twelfth storey. Raffi brushed off his coat and strode with *guapparia* past the palms curving in graceful arcs inside the front door. What was the big deal? It takes more than marble to make a Vittoriano.

Taking in the walnut wainscoting and coffered ceilings, he joined a crowd of guests below three chandeliers (leaded, cut crystal, not blown Murano) and made his way to the registration desk. 'How do you do,' he said, with careful enunciation. 'I'm Rafaele Peach. Might I enquire if Mr. Addison Saltonstall is here this morning?'

In the orphanage, Sister K. had changed his name to Peach from 'Pèsca,' lest American listeners mistake it for 'fish,' when it really did mean 'peach.' On top of that, in his earliest memories of her, his mother had called him her little peach.

'A person of Mr. Saltonstall's water is not in the habit of chatting with Eyetalians,' the desk clerk said with a phony British accent, 'however elevated they believe their stature may be.'

'I have a communiqué from the U.S. Consul in Rome. I've been instructed to deliver it personally to his friend Mr. Saltonstall.'

When the clerk saw the embassy seal on the correspondence, he sighed and rolled his eyes. 'One moment.' He slipped behind a narrow walnut door which when closed disappeared into the paneling.

Raffi waited. He had a growing awareness of a high-pitched giggle that grew increasingly louder, with a forced gaiety. Three flappers in startling carmine lipstick were perched on the edge of the lobby causeuse.

When he turned to appreciate them, one of the ingénues, designated the leader by a poke on the forearm, caught his eye, stepped up, and strode toward him. Her hair was cut short as if hacked at the nape by a cleaver, the edges of her smile curved in a well-rehearsed smirk.

'Finally, a person of interest in this mausoleum of waxworks!' She tossed a look to her fellow members of the smart set. One of them—her nails manicured so viciously it looked as though she'd just torn a wild hare open with her bare hands—waved without lifting her arm by simply straightening her fingers while the other covered her mouth as her shoulders shook. 'What's lickin', Chicken?'

Raffi studied her with a grin, not wanting to disappoint, as he was certain he was the moment's entertainment. He turned his toe to the right and lifted his nose slightly in the air—precisely as he'd just been advised against. 'I come to your arms from out of nowhere,' he said, sketching a bow as he reached for her hand to kiss.

She jerked it back as if his lips were on fire. 'Well, you're certainly faster than the prune pits around here.'

'It's the foolish lover who lets an opportunity pass,' Raffi said.

'Oh, you are so Continental...'

'But Boston is the true home of my heart. Do you hope to visit Italy one day?'

'This very summer!' she said. 'With the Cabots! How could you know?'

'"One is never a prophet in his native country,"' Raffi said. He looked her directly in the eyes and out of habit held her stare a little too long until he felt her temperature rise a few degrees. Better go, little one. You have hungry green eyes, sparrow. But you don't have Beatrice's power. Time to cut the act short. The new boss wouldn't appreciate this burlesque.

'Mr. Saltonstall will see you,' the clerk said, reappearing. 'In his private office—post haste.'

With a closing bow, Raffi followed the clerk's indifferent directions up a steep, curved stair. With his long legs, he'd long since learned to make a conscious effort not to take, inelegantly, two steps at a time. At the mezzanine, he paused and looked down at the wealthy brahmins gliding across the lobby's marble floor. What a lovely world. Their reality matched the dreamy hotel posters lining the stairwell. To his right, he saw a door marked 'private' in small gold letters. Before he could knock the door drifted open, so he boldly stepped in.

'How do you do, Mr. Saltonstall?' Raffi said, covering a note of surprise that in his aridity the hotelier had elected to have no art on his walls, save a few more of the bland posters. Nor did he offer personal photos of family and friends—the hallmark of a hidden life.

'Halt,' Saltonstall said, raising his hand as the telephone rang. He pointedly did not ask Raffi to sit in the rich leather chair opposite his desk as he listened to the caller for a very long time, avoiding eye contact with his intruder between burning stares. 'No, no, it's no trouble at all,' Saltonstall said. 'Yes, and good day.' He put the receiver down. 'Well,' he said. 'As a matter of fact, that was the Consul, calling most urgently to push along his insistence that I employ you. Most indelicately brought about, if you ask me.' He held Raffi's letter of introduction to the light to ensure the water and chain marks were right-side up. Since Stefania hadn't typed it, they matched up perfectly. 'I suppose you'd call that lucky timing.'

'I hope so, sir,' Raffi said and bowed.

'And you'd be wrong.' Salsonstall slowly lit a cigarette. 'Knew him at Exeter.'

Best not to ask a follow-up question about a boyhood chum. Raffi held his silence.

'He was brusque even then, to the point of bad form,' Saltonstall said. 'So naturally he's the famous diplomat now. Question is, who, or what, are you?' He pulled a nasty grin. 'And what are you to him?'

'I know I have a lot to learn at this world-class establishment,' Raffi said, 'but from my experience at the Hotel Forum, I am hoping I might be of service to you and your staff.'

'We have too much staff by half right now. Your timing, Mr. Peach, is rotten, as they say.' Saltonstall flicked the letter across his desk to him—it fell to a blue Nichols carpet.

Raffi chose not to retrieve it but instead held the manager's eyes.

'What I'm telling you, young man, Parkhurst or no Parkhurst, is we have no work just now,' Saltonstall said. 'Nothing you'd be interested in.'

'Any work you have,' Raffi said, 'interests me. It doesn't matter where I start. I'll be proud to show I can be of use to you in any capacity, sir.'

'I'm talking about the wait staff.' Saltonstall flashed an accusing look back at the telephone, with its ears and eyes. 'You have waited table before, haven't you?'

'I'm ready to begin at this very moment.'

'What? That doesn't shake you? If nothing else, you seem so well turned out. Bit of a flaneur, for my taste. To make it quite clear, when you're not servicing the tables... you'll be pot walloping.'

'Whatever is needed, I'm your man.'

'Good heavens. That kind of grease won't work here.' Saltonstall scribbled on a piece of hotel stationery and then thrust it to Raffi, knocking over a vase holding a single daffodil. Except Raffi seized it midair and restored it to his employer's desk.

'Now you're on the trolley!' Saltonstall said. He clucked his tongue. 'Let them know downstairs. They'll take you to our *tableur*, whose office is just off the bakery. And do tell,' he said, 'what would you have done if you hadn't caught the flower?'

'In a few weeks, sir?' Raffi said before bowing. 'I plan to snap my fingers and an attendant will catch it for me, without spilling a drop.'

'And how do you propose to do that, Mr. Latin Waiter?'

'I'll listen and watch until I discover the one with the best reflexes, and he's the one I'll post at your beck and call.'

7

Le cose proibite sono le più saporite.
Forbidden things are the tastiest.

Raffi entered the kitchen to shouts of 'Zeppelins in the fog!' as a plate of sausages and potatoes floated past him. 'Mike and Ike!' A tossed set of salt and pepper shakers barely missed his head. 'Mystery in the alley!' He started to get the hang of it—hash on the side. 'Flop two, over hard, and drag it through the garden! Where's my shad roe?'

'Down here.' Stanley the bellhop, nearly Raffi's height, beckoned as if they were descending to a slimy *sotteranea* in the seventh circle of the hospitality industry.

They ducked the divide and went down a final set of stairs until they came to an embrasure at the end of a shotgun corridor. A half dozen dishwashers in stiff aprons spurted steaming water at stacks of serviceware emblazoned with a hound, all rib cage and jaws, perpetually disturbing two antlered ruminants above the motto 'To The Faithful, There Is Just Reward.' Raffi thought of the wolves in the Colosseum.

'Heads up. Oncoming,' the bellhop shouted over the din. He held a swinging door open and pointed across the room. 'Victor there will give you the lowdown.' He turned back. 'What do you go by?'

'My name is Rafaele Delfino Lorenzino de Medici Peach,' Raffi said. 'I'm pleased to meet you.'

'Oh, God, not another cake eater,' the bellhop coughed under his breath. He shook his head and left.

'Come again?' Victor said across the room.

'I'm sorr—Raffi Peach, at your service, sir!'

'Well, there's no need to shout it,' Victor grinned. 'For every peach, there's a fly.'

Raffi sensed a kindred spirit. Victor was mulatto—a *bokor*, as

43

Opportunity Knox would say. Natty and well formed, he had a neatly trimmed beard and arrestingly clouded, unfocused eyes. Apparently he didn't have to have sight to see through people.

'If you're hoping to wash dishes, you've come to the right place,' Victor said. 'If not, abandon hope all ye who enter here.'

'Ah, Dante!' Raffi said. '"Happy the man who's been able to learn the causes of things"!'

'Virgil quit last Tuesday. You're my assistant now.' Dressed in a white smock with matching baker's hat monogrammed with a florid PH, Victor stopped polishing a silver salver as though posing for a photograph and leaned his head toward the sound of the bellhop's footsteps growing quiet with his departure. 'Goodbye, Stan.'

'Goodbye, Victor,' the faraway voice said.

All of a sudden, Victor had an Egyptian Prettiest in his mouth, puffing. Raffi hadn't seen him light it. 'Want one?'

Raffi shook his head no before catching himself. 'No, thank you.'

'Do you mind my asking you, exactly how tall are you?'

Raffi smiled. 'Yes, I do mind.'

Victor stuck out his hand. 'Victor White.' After Raffi shook it, Victor said, 'I suspected I wasn't the only freak in Boston.'

'A mistaken impression now corrected.' Even though Victor couldn't see him, Raffi knew his measure was being taken.

'Ah, the ghost of *Peer Gynt*. If anyone else asks you, you're six and a half feet tall,' Victor said. 'And you should take off those street clothes.'

'How do you know what I'm wearing?'

'Cotton scrapes, silk whispers. But cashmere enters the room quiet as a cat. Where was your last assignment?'

'At the Hotel Forum in Rome, but I was born in Naples.'

'Funny,' Victor said. 'I picked up a hint of the Bronx in your speech.'

'This isn't my first trip to America,' Raffi said.

'Everybody's got a cover story. Your English is excellent. How'd you get to be so well-read?'

'The Forum is close to the embassies, so we kept a collection of international bestsellers for guests.'

'Let me get this straight,' Victor said. 'So here's the U.S. delega-tion, in the land of Dante, reading *Huckleberry Finn*? Mark Twain was a frequent guest here, you know.'

'There's a raft in both stories,' Raffi said. 'Though the Mississippi isn't the destination attraction the Styx is.'

'I'll match the Parker House's popularity against your Hotel Forum's any day. We've had to call the police when Emerson, Thoreau, Longfellow, and the rest of the Saturday Club got too rowdy; Edith Wharton tippled here; and the playwright Ho Chi Minh worked in our bakery.'

A white-haired kitchen assistant entered quickly, heels clicking, shaking her head. 'Hot and cold running waiters.'

'Never a dull moment,' Victor said.

'Easy for you to say,' the woman said. 'Twelve new tables to inspect for one turn, monsieur *tableur*. On top of everything else, Miss Lowell and Mrs. Russell are expected, and you know what that means.'

'Just so,' Victor said. 'Luckily we've got backup. Jeanne, this is our new friend Rafaele. Rafaele, you'll take Miss Lowell's table.'

'How do you do?' Raffi said, sweeping up her hand for a kiss.

'You'll do,' Jeanne said and left.

'So I hope your library prepared you for Amy Lowell,' Victor said. 'She and Mrs. Russell are the Yankee Gertrude Stein and Alice B. Toklas. Except prickly.'

Raffi waited.

'But enough gossip from you. We need to go upstairs and check the tables. Just a last run-through before we provide a tea service for the Occidental Club,' Victor said. 'You can take in the show, Rafaele. Or rather, you are the show, as we've had two no-shows in the wait staff today and those still here are spent from brunch. There's only Havelock to help you.' He pointed to a darkened room on the other side of the polishing tables, where a pair of black shoes was visible, extended from the ends of a dilapidated couch. Slowly, they were pulled out of view.

'It will be my honor,' Raffi said.

'Go ahead and get a uniform out of the locker,' Victor said. 'Something in there should fit you. Jeanne can show you.'

As though she'd been listening through the wall, Jeanne reappeared and ushered Raffi to the servers' armoire.

'What exactly is a *tableur*?' Raffi asked her.

She snorted. 'Victor's the world's one and only. He's a maître d' with unmatched vision.' Her voice had a tender depth.

'I see,' Raffi said.

'Make no mistake—he can though he can't.' She smothered a smile. 'Follow along when our crew goes into action, including sleeping beauty here.' She gestured to Havelock.

Upstairs in a private dining room with coffered ceilings, french doors, and a faux Norman fireplace, the troops assembled. 'Ready on the right?' Victor asked.

'Yes,' Havelock whispered. 'Sir.'

'Ready on the left?'

Jeanne pinched Raffi's elbow and lifted her head.

'Yes, sir,' Raffi said.

'Ready on the firing line? Let's have a look, then,' Victor said. With a brisk, economical step, he approached the first table and drew an ebony baton from his pocket, tapping each piece of silver cutlery into place, setting by setting, as lightly and familiarly as Paderewski might have executed Scarlatti on the pianoforte. To assure the tapers were lit, he deftly opened the palms of his kid-gloved hands to feel the warmth, glow by glow. 'Very nice,' he said. 'Fresh linens, newly fold—' He stopped, smiled, and shook out a napkin, reshaping it and gently putting it back in place. 'Salad fork, dinner fork, dessert fork, there's the cucumber server, nut picks, demitasse, and then the bouillon spoons. We'll have the tureens on the sideboard, brought out just before serving so they'll be steaming hot. The menu today will be simple. Haunch of Venison carved on the station.' He whirled to Raffi. 'You'll promenade with a gueridon with gas jets, serving each table in turn with Lobster Thermidor and bullet ramekins of béarnaise. And be careful. Nothing ruins a tea like the immolation of wait staff.'

'Yes, sir,' Raffi said.

'Don't call me sir.' Now Victor walked more rapidly, touching individual pieces of silver at each table with a blur so fantastic it seemed like the silent buzz of a moth's wings. 'Interesting,' he said as he took a little sniff in the air. 'Let's get another fish server. This one's too tarnished for service.' He ventured the smallest of smiles. 'Miss Lowell makes a point of noticing everything. Make sure there are sixteen cubes of sugar in the bowl by her teacup. Her ice-water glass must be kept full.'

Raffi marveled at the masterful performance. Victor was careful to lay his hands on the objects as little as possible, to ensure his braille remained sanitary. How intimately he conducted the unseen. Fairly dancing with a deeply private familiarity, the *tableur* checked the chairs with the toe of his shiny shoe so each was equidistant from the six round tables. Except at the best table, the one centered in the bay window, Raffi saw him pull one chair a jot farther back.

'What time is it?' Victor asked Raffi and Jeanne.

'Two-thirty five.'

'Jeanne, has that soiled section of wallpaper been attended to?' She squinted. 'Yes.'

'Then do you suppose the crew can take that ladder downstairs?'

At the far end of the room, a ladder lay quietly along the floor against the baseboard trim.

'You never cease to amaze me,' Jeanne said.

'And you never cease to abuse me.' Victor continued checking the tables with his spatial whisking. He occasionally talked to himself with his rhythmic, nodding motion. 'The bone vise is still missing, Jeanne. You say it's on the way?'

'With the venison. The steward chose to launch it in the kitchen.'

'All right, aperitifs are served at three. Don't worry,' Victor said when he reached Raffi's side. 'This'll be something. I'll pull the strings from behind the curtain.'

A few minutes later, the chatty dowagers of the Occidental Club breezed in, all dusty tube rose, a clatter of silver-tipped canes.

New brothers, Victor squeezed Raffi's wrist to let him know the show was about to begin. Before the smoke could issue from the lip of the starter's pistol, Raffi was off. Having studied the layout, he brought the soup course to the tables most distant from the kitchen first so he might create the perception that his service was moving ever faster, though in reality his circuits were simply ever closer.

When he reached the table with the chair aired out for relaxed sitting, he found an enormous woman with pixie bangs accompanied by her paramour, who scowled as though she'd just been poked with a pin. The queenly one was upholstered in slacks and a tunic of iris jacquard. The dark circles around her great hazel eyes struck Raffi with their resemblance to Moreschi's portrait that Diletti had seduced him with so many lifetimes ago.

'I'd like—'

47

'Two White Ladies nonpareil,' Raffi smiled, producing the frosty intoxicants in mid-spin while Victor appeared at his side.

'Charming.' She took a sip and smacked her lips. 'To the Volstead Act. It keeps alcohol out of the wrong hands. Well, well, Victor. Looks like we've got a new friend!'

'Miss Lowell, this is Rafaele Peach, new to our employ. This is his maiden voyage here, but he comes to us direct from Italy, where he's had a distinguished career.'

She raised her lorgnette and caught Raffi with an appraisal so warm it was as though the sun had come out from behind a little cloud. When Raffi looked at her sad eyes again, he sensed the youthful spirit behind her knowing gaze.

'Ah, bella Italia. Some of my fondest memories are there,' she said.

'*Sei molto affascinante*, Miss Lowell,' Raffi said, bowing. 'I trust you are enjoying your afternoon here in beautiful Boston.'

'This is much more like it, Victor,' she said. 'Of course, you'll bring him around tonight.'

Now it was Victor's turn to bow.

Miss Lowell's companion eyed Raffi, then cleared her throat dramatically:

> '*And this is good old Boston*
> *The home of the bean and the cod,*
> *Where the Lowells talk only to Cabots*
> *And the Cabots talk only to God...*
> *—Except, of course, the Lowell'ladies*
> *Who chat up waiters.*'

The Occidental Club ushered out, and the linens replaced, Raffi joined the rest of the wait staff in serving dinner. So immediately popular was he with his sections, and so smooth was he in his delivery, there were grumblings of jealous disdain from his peers, quelled only by the generous tips they were happy to help clear from the tables along with the dishes. It was money in the bank to overlook such misdemeanors. As the busboys finished, Raffi followed Victor into the scullery.

'The dishes and cutlery will be washed first. That leaves the Baccarat. I like to care for that last, when things have quieted down,'

Victor said to Raffi, Jeanne, and nearly a dozen Chinese, who whistled and clucked and worked with a will that far surpassed the energy of the wait staff, the last of whom had slunk off to the smoking lounge. 'Not that they care,' Victor said upon hearing the door click.

'I can see why you enjoy the quiet,' Raffi said.

Victor pulled a rolling bus tray of crystal beside one of the long, low sinks next to a Cantonese scholar-bureaucrat with a white beard like an ermine's tail. They each donned a pair of white gloves. 'Jeanne, the champagne glasses first. She'll hand them to you, Rafaele.'

'Please call me Raffi.'

'Very well, Raffi,' Victor said. 'Let's put these two clean ones aside over here. Then dip the others into the soap solution, but the water can't be too hot or it'll cause clouding. Have you got it?'

'Check.'

'All right. Ladies and gentlemen, ring the stemware.'

Raffi kept an eye on Victor as he picked one piece of glass after another without a fumble and made it gleam. The tableur worked easily alongside the dishwashers and even murmured a word or two with them in Cantonese, polishing every centimeter so not a smudge remained.

But Victor didn't say anything—really say anything—until everyone was gone at shift's end, after he'd inclined his head and listened to the scrape of Jeanne's tread as she climbed the stairs to a dream of cool night air. 'Where are you staying?'

Raffi hesitated. 'Nowhere, yet.'

'I have an idea,' Victor said. 'If you need a place to bunk out, there's a way we can discuss dirty dishes twenty-four hours a day.'

'Well, that's very kind of you,' Raffi said. 'Is it far from here? What does it cost?'

'Nothing in gold, but plenty in amelite fittings.'

'I beg your pardon?'

'Elbow grease. I'll show you after dinner.' Victor moved an old hotel sign that had been discarded on its side, 'No Jews, Please,' that he'd been using to conceal a hole in the wall. In its grinning indifference, the sign's calligraphic lettering was remarkably similar to the *Qui si castrano ragazzi* sign in the Naples butcher shop. 'My vault,' Victor said of his hiding place. He pulled out a covered dish and set it beside

Raffi. Replacing the sign, he set out two plates, two forks, two knives. 'Jeanne told me she was impressed with your work tonight. Me, I wasn't at all surprised. I don't need to tell you to keep an eye on the rest of the wait staff. They're likely to be a bit jealous, but you can handle it. Can I serve you a little something?' He lifted the lid.

'Escargot,' Raffi said. '"Where you work, you eat."'

'Okay, now this one.'

'Lobster. I'm beginning to like this job.'

'Have a seat now, Raffi,' Victor said, 'and tell me how it is you've ended up here, in the bottom of the Hub, a Peach in the very pit of New England society.'

'What version of my story would you like?' Raffi said.

'Let's start with the lie,' Victor said. 'That way, I'll believe you. But first, take a few bites of supper, along with this champagne.' He held out a magnum of Berlioz 440 and reached for the pair of glasses Raffi had set aside. 'Nine dollars a bottle on the menu. They asked for it to be removed still half full.'

'I saw it but didn't dare lay claim to it,' Raffi said.

'As I'm the host, I'll do the toast: to who we are and who we might have been. You know, this goes tolerably well with cold snails and lobster, eh, pardner?'

'When I was a young lad, I was born in Arabia,' Raffi said, 'the son of the great sultan Osman. But he died and left me as an orphan in the streets. My evil uncle, the vizier, brought me up, but soon he sold me into slavery.'

'Let's hurry through this material and get right to the castration,' Victor said.

'You know,' Raffi said.

'I'm not obstructed by sight. You're very tall, and you're not exactly a basso profundo, which means you "lost your eyes" before puberty. You're well read and frankly brave to travel alone, though I suspect something beyond adventure has inspired you to wander so far.'

'I was going to tell you I was injured in the war,' Raffi said, 'but it's more a case of pretty larceny. Someday I'll tell you a taller tale.'

'Oh, I see, you're a work of art!' Victor said. 'So am I. Do I entertain you with my fumbling around?'

'Enormously.'

'Had enough?'

'You haven't offered the famous Parker House Boston cream pie,' Raffi said. The lobby cards were everywhere.

'Some things are too precious to be shared,' Victor said and stood up. 'Besides, it's time to go.' He speared the lobster carcasses with his sword cane and with a relaxed motion flung them through the air into a waxed bag.

Raffi took the glasses and plates to the sink and rinsed them off. 'Where are you taking me?'

'To a place in Brookline.'

'Your house?'

'Yes, all blind men are issued houses in the suburbs by the government.'

'What I mean is, have you lived there long?'

'For three years, I've shoveled coal there at night in trade for a place to sleep when I'm not staying in my room here. Your admirer Miss Lowell is a dangerous lady who will help you. You want to talk about a slice of cold-roast Boston. She lives in a soggy French pile her family built just after the Civil War. *Entre nous*, it'll be up to you to work out the details about what she'll expect from you in return.'

'I wouldn't expect quarters to be free,' Raffi said.

'She's a collector of oddities. She's already nicked an ashtray from the lobby. You'll make a perfect souvenir. You go up ahead. I'll turn off all the lights down here on my way out.'

8

La moglie è sempre moglie.
The wife is always the wife.

BOSTON, 1922

Gaspare Messina had a bad feeling about this. His nightclub's renovations had cost him an arm and a leg and his painter had shown up drunk, so he was having second thoughts about the sleazy stalactites in plaster of Paris brushed in shades of *caput mortuum* to make paying customers feel like they'd tripped down the stairs into Hades. He hated how pretentious it was—even for the North End. Maybe this whole dystopia thing had played itself out. Maybe he should have gone 'Egyptian.'

Plus he hated the sinking feeling that the big money was still downtown. Who was going to come out here and plunk down four bucks for a haddock dinner, let alone ten more for a show?

The waitresses were a pain in the ass, too, all artsy-fartsy chicks whose moms were docents at the Museum of Fine Yawns on Huntington Avenue while their husbands took in a ball game at Fenway Park.

No, he hated the makeover, he hated the new name Avernus (though it had seemed so clever at the time), he hated the amount of ass-kissing he'd had to do to turn on the liquor spigot. Worst of all, Johnny Cavallaro was not going to bring the house down as their moony singer on opening night as promised, and the regulars were going to hate that.

Marcello Sprezzatura, Gaspare's manager, was nonchalant as always. 'Cavallaro is parked in New York.'

'New York, my ass,' Gaspare said.

'Not a bad slogan,' Marcello said. 'I'll alert the media.' He took in the limp paper flames blown by a fan and rolled his eyes. 'By the way, boss, the place looks like hell.'

'Not helping. So what other singers have we got?'

'We haven't got nobody. Well, we have got nobody. His name is Carlo D'Amore.'

'You've gotta be fuckin' kidding.'

'I wish I were kidding. You might as well hear him.'

'Before I fire you? Sure. Get me a beer.'

'Yeah, right. I'll send someone over... boss.'

Gaspare tossed his car coat over a zinc-topped table and put his feet up on an empty chair, which was all too easy to find for this soft opening. The swells were a no show, filling every hole in the wall on the block but his. Every chair around him was vacant, with Saturday's big opening night just four days away. Careening toward disaster, he felt no one—no one—rushing in to take his side. Led by his wife.

Vulgara Messina stalked in and pushed Gaspare's coat onto the floor to make room for her farm-raised mink, which she cradled in her arms like a baby. When he didn't rise and pull out a chair for her, she sat down with a big sigh and started in on him. 'My father dies, so the first thing you do is dump the name Blue Grotto and change the restaurant, which always had a crowd, to this—this nightclub? What, so you can be the big man?'

'I have shareholders who believe in me. Just you watch.'

'Oh, I'll be watching.'

'You watch when we pack them in on opening night.'

'Oh, I'll be there,' she said. 'Remember whose money this is, Mr. Bigshot, Mr. Egohead, Mr. "I'll change the face of the North End."'

So no Cavallaro. Wait till she hears that. It was only a matter of days before that thug Ira Stadt would lurk in to call in his investment. And now this kid, never heard of him. 'Tell me your name's not Carlo D'Amore,' he called out to the moon-faced youth who'd just appeared on the black stage.

'Hello, Mr. M.,' Carlo said into the microphone.

'Does he always talk like that?' Gaspare asked Marcello, who'd drifted back with three drinks in his hand.

'Watch. The ladies love him,' Marcello said, sliding onto the last seat at their table.

'Ladies, my ass,' Gaspare said.

'Exactly,' Marcello said. 'He learned his "English" working the cruise liners in Naples, and working some of the passengers, too.'

With a nod from Carlo, the band in the dinky orchestra pit jumped into 'If You Were the Only Girl in the World, and I Were the Only Boy,' but Gaspare held up his hand. 'Not that one. I hate that goddamn Vallee kid.'

Carlo smiled. 'To be honest with you, I know just where you're coming from. Here's a little something from home, where I was taught by the original hoo-doo, the Grand Impresario Diletti.' The young man walked to the lip of the stage and whispered with the music director. Taking three steps back, and winking to Vulgara, he belted out '*A Vucchella*,' Your Sweet Mouth, sans orchestra.

Gaspare mopped his forehead, but Vulgara was radiant.

'This boy is hired,' she said.

'This is a night club, not a bordello,' Gaspare said.

'Nevertheless,' she said.

'Look, kid, can't you pull anything more modern outta your ass?'

'No problem, Mr. M.' Carlo flashed a bright smile which displayed the caps on his six front teeth. The klieg lights shifted on their gimbals and glittered his brilliantined hair. And then, spreading his legs, thrusting out his hips, and singing from the base of his gut as if he hoped to rattle the plaster stalactites from the ceiling, with a sexy bump, and absurdly slowly, he leaned into 'When the Grownup Ladies Act Like Babies.' While he was singing, some of the wait staff came in from the kitchen to hear. Even the barkeep looked up.

When Carlo finished, the room went quiet, 'like a fuckin' cah had run them over,' Gaspare said. 'Jolson wouldn't have ever sung it like that.'

Though the boy sounded like a moaning moose, his warm, mahogany intonations had somehow polished every chair in the room. Gaspare looked at Vulgara, who'd squeezed her eyes shut and swooned face-first into her mink. She crossed and uncrossed her legs. 'Come on, now!' Gaspare raked his hair. 'Am I the only person here with the balls to say how bad that was? Jesus Christ! Since when did music stop having to sound human? Look, I'm all for modern. But this must be a joke you guys are playing on me. I mean—you're kidding, right?'

In the deafening silence, Gaspare started to pace. 'Carlo d'Amore.' He chewed it over. Beyond the jinky stage presence and vapid warbling— such bullshit—this kid was lift-your-leg, three-drink ugly. Was he even wearing underwear? Above his thick neck, the young man's bloated lips lit up the darkness like an underwater pig. He walked a quick little circle before addressing his lieutenant, who was now clap-clap-clapping in the empty performance space as though he'd heard something they could actually use. 'Okay, I'm throwing in the towel,' Gaspare said. 'Honest, Cello, do you think they're really going to like this crooning? You can go ahead and kill the lights.'

9

Chi segue il cieco finisce dentro al fosso.
He who follows the blind will end up in the ditch.

BOSTON, 1922

It was nearly I a.m. by the time Raffi and Victor put on their street clothes and ascended the stairs from the hotel's service catacombs to a world of cool air. Victor pushed open the lead-lined door off School Street into Roll Alley, moonlight glinting on slimy cobblestones.

'This is a bit of a shortcut,' Victor said. 'Hope you don't mind the company.' He bent over, tucked his trouser cuffs into his boot tops, and started a slow prance—like Gloucester in *King Lear*—lifting his knees high in the air with each step.

Raffi heard a rustle and peered into the shadows. Rats, their fur dark as Venetian canals, eddied around rusty barrels and below a vent fragrant with the smell of Parker House rolls. Their lookout stopped and stared at him with red-rimmed eyes before slipping into a drain pipe. 'This reminds me of home,' Raffi said.

'Oh, but this is the really highest-class garbage,' Victor said. 'Thieves, burlesque stars, and merchant princes have wound up face to face here after falling on bad times.'

'Rats included?'

'Anyone's a good dinner companion when you're hungry,' Victor said. 'I've dined here a time or two myself. It's so much more intriguing if you can't see who's sitting across the table.'

Raffi eyed the rusty barrels. 'How often are these emptied?'

'Before the typhus scare, we used to leave them out a couple of days for the pickers to go through, a sort of charity for the world of the great unwashed, and the rats remember. Now the dustmen attend to the cans three times a day. But in spite of everything we do, some precious crumbs of the rolls leave a trail to the door after sweep-up, and a few morsels still drop from the scullery window. The rats know if they wait here they might catch a piece like a penny from heaven. By dawn, there won't be a speck of anything out here but stone. When you think about it, it's a coordinated effort. The rats are our third-shift cleanup crew. The *Post* would call them "our new citizens," stealing jobs from perfectly loyal union members.' Victor winked. 'I think it was Southey who suggested the best way to make rats disappear is to make them a table delicacy.'

'No,' Raffi said. 'Extol their powers as an aphrodisiac.'

Victor paused. 'There's something else about this place. There are other monsters here. That's when taking out the trash doesn't mean taking out the trash. It's a way station for a different kind of rat.'

As a bulky figure slipped among the shadows and out of view, Victor pulled Raffi toward him and whispered, 'That guy works for the real mayor of Boston. Tourists get rolled here, and old accounts get settled. Deposits are made into these cans on their way to the mud flats on Jefferies Point, where they turn cods inside out and dry them on the rocks. Screeching cats won't let the dead sleep. The smell of cod is the only thing strong enough to drown out the smell of garbage and dead bodies.' He resumed his curious walking. 'Maybe the rats aren't after the rolls but the rolled. If I were you, I wouldn't look under those lids.' Victor turned a corner, and Raffi quickened his own pace, mimicking his steps. 'The blind leading the blind,' Victor said.

Raffi stayed close. It was always good to know where an urban oasis of free food was, because one never knows, does one? If nothing else, it was a reason to be cheerful.

Suddenly Victor stopped short at the curb of a wide boulevard, turned his head, and listened for the sound of approaching traffic.

'It's all clear,' Raffi said.

'Take note of where you are,' Victor said. 'Look up. Do you see that golden dome up ahead? That's the State House. In my mind it's something out of *The Arabian Nights*.'

'Have you always been blind?'

'I was four when I fell down a flight of stairs. Ever since, I've been looking for a "black cat in a basement without a candle." Now it's your turn.'

Raffi swallowed. Maybe it would be easier to tell someone who couldn't look him in the eye. 'I wanted to be a great opera singer where I grew up, in Naples. It was what I was trained to be. I didn't have anything else. So I agreed to the alteration, though all the roles for castrati had disappeared. Overnight, the world decided that the sound of a castrato was a horrible reminder of human pain—no sweeter than the sound of your black cat being strangled.'

Victor's Adams apple traveled up his throat like a rodent on a rust pipe as he swallowed. He turned back to the street. 'No,' he said. 'I meant you were supposed to turn here.'

They crossed to the Park Street subway incline at the top of Boston Common. As they stepped up to the curb, Raffi paused.

'Are you looking at the State House again?' Victor asked.

'Yes,' Raffi said. 'I'm sorry you can't see it.'

'Don't sorry me. Just tell me.'

'There's a full moon out. Gas lights glowing around the dome make everything else darken and drop away. That travertine marble wing behind it is precious, even in Rome. To the left is a cluster of brick town houses and streetlights.'

'Do you see the entrance to the Metro?' Victor asked.

'No.'

They walked a little farther. Raffi sensed Victor counting their footsteps echoing against the white marble portal to the underground. Victor leaned to the left, guiding through the unfamiliar.

'What's the best thing about traveling light?'

'I never itch,' Raffi said.

'Now, do you see the stairs going down into the subway?'

'Yes.'

'What are we stopping for, then?'

A dead nightingale lay on the cobblestones, its large eye still bright and illuminated by one of the incandescent streetlights. What could have killed him? Impossible. There were no nightingales this side of the Atlantic. How could he have turned up here? Raffi admired its miniature perfection. Its indigo wing startled with color and fairly throbbed with recent life. So seductive was the bird in death, he felt a strange compulsion to reach down and touch it. Sorry, little one. You're so lovely. What happened to you? He shivered and jerked his eyes away. Madness to court the dead. 'It's nothing,' Raffi said.

Descending the stairs, they reached the platform and hopped aboard the subway. Flashes of black assaulted the jostled pair as they sped west inside the cavernous tube of the Heath Street line, sparks of the electric trolley pole visible from the car's clerestory windows as it scratched and vibrated against the overhead wire. They were moving faster than ghosts, but was it really polite to arrive somewhere before it was ready to greet you? Why did people have to dig to be transported through a lonelier place? 'This is truly extraordinary,' Raffi said.

'The first in America,' Victor said.

'It would be difficult to put a subway in Rome without disturbing all the bodies buried in its path.'

'In Boston, we didn't let a little thing like nine hundred unmarked graves stop progress. We just assumed they were all just wops, anyway.' Victor grinned, but Raffi didn't take the bait.

Raffi welcomed the fresh air as they climbed the stairs in Brookline. Victor slapped his neck as they passed below the sign for Heath Street. 'As much as suburbanites don't like to believe it, rats ride the Metro, too. You don't mind fleas, do you?'

'I adore them,' Raffi said. 'Nothing can give me the bite! I have a job, a friend, a place to stay.' He pictured Beatrice and her congenitally suspicious family, toiling in the shadow of the Underwood Devil. He had a purpose—a chance to prove himself. 'Everything is right with the world.'

'Mr. Peach, you sound as if you're about to burst into song.'

'I'm sorry, but I don't sing.'

'Come on. A ship sails, a blind man taps ahead with his cane. Weren't you any good?'

'I was six years old. I was the Spagnoli Discovery.'

'Which in Boston is like being the Newton Discovery or the Brookline Discovery.'

'Of course I thought I was good,' Raffi said. 'How could I have known? I was very young. I haven't sung in sixteen years. I don't mean to be rude, but I hope you'll forgive me if I refuse, more for my own good than for anything else. Besides, I promised not to sing.'

'Who made you promise not to sing?'

'I promised God.'

They walked a few more paces. 'Which god?' Victor said. 'We have all we can stand in Boston. Hang onto your hat—we're headed up Mount Parnassus.' He pulled a leather-covered glass flask from his overcoat with some brandy sloshing in it. He took a few slugs and held it out to Raffi. 'Maybe you should try some hooch first.'

10

Ciò che fai ti è reso.
What you do will be done to you.

BROOKLINE, 1922

The flask was four fingers lighter when the pair reached the black ironwork gate. Looking past the swashy 'L,' Raffi could barely make out lights hovering high in the rising mist that was quickly becoming an enveloping fog. The peal of a piano vibrated softly through the trees. Victor pushed the gate open and stepped through. Raffi followed the tap-tap of his cane along the gravel walkway, a long curve shrouded by inky gardens. Now this was unusual. There was no sentry on duty. That would never have been the case back home, where such an estate would have been locked against the Socialisti.

The tapping stopped. Raffi could see where the music came from. He stood in the moistening darkness before the grandeur that was Sevenels. Fronted by Corinthian columns, the Victorian pile seemed to rise to fabulous heights from curves and galaxies of Bohemian bushes. Built like Miss Lowell herself, the brick fortress was solidly belted with quoins, its square edges softened by a veil of wild ivy.

As the fog dropped away, Raffi caught sight of the widow's walk cresting the moss-pocked mansard roof like a rusty tiara. The porte-cochère was choked with several motorcars, haphazardly parked. Clearly the house staff suffered from a malaise that was affecting their work. The tall windows of the first two floors were dark, but the third-floor casements were flung open, scattering laughter and voices. Light spilled out in long patches on the lawn. 'Are we going upstairs?' Raffi asked.

Victor nodded. 'Presenting the Sky Parlor. "Sevenels" stands for the seven Lowells who lived here. The Baron, as she calls herself, is Miss Amy—she bought out her siblings. Her brother Abbott is pres of

Harvard College. Percy, a big star-gazer, is a writer, too. He's the author of *Occult Japan*.'

'I've heard of James Russell Lowell.'

'The long-dead Fireside Poet,' Victor said. 'Amy was his favorite younger cousin.' He waved his hand in the air. 'The fog is gone now, isn't it? Is there moonlight?'

'Yes, it's quite bright now,' Raffi said.

'Good, because there's something you must see.' Ticking along a slate path, Victor led Raffi around the breezeway to the side yard, which dropped to a sunken garden twinkling with cast-iron Chinese lanterns.

After the decay he'd witnessed, Raffi was surprised at the sense of order here. Exotic plantings "from anywhere but New England," as Victor put it, were carefully tended, some shaped into fanciful sculptures. 'These are lovely,' Raffi said. 'I've never seen some of these plants before.' Lushly landscaped and blackened with time, a natural rock amphitheater was carved more deeply to create two dozen seats with a flat stage at the base. In the center was a lectern surrounded by white orchids that danced in the lunescence like swaying stars.

'This garden is one of the few family traditions Miss Lowell takes pleasure in,' Victor said. 'Down in that hollow is where she hosts her Devils—that's what she calls her inner circle. She has her regulars, and then there's always someone new—conductors, academics, mystagogues. Last week she hosted the orientalist Ernest Fennelosa and Grueby (just because she loves his vases' shade of green). The week before it was the new Boston Symphony maestro Pierre Monteux and the musicologist Carl Engel. There might be Dr. Pierre Bernard the yoga guru or little Khalil Gibran. If you're a night-blooming hierophant or you have an unpopular idea, you'll no doubt get an invitation to the stones out here. What's stylish now is the breeze from the East—China.'

'I'm interested in that myself,' Raffi said.

'You might meet Florence Wheelock Ayscough. She's working with Miss Lowell on the translation of some Chinese poetry. Then there are... others.'

They circled to the front door. When Victor started to turn the knob, Raffi asked, 'Should I ring a bell?'

'No, that's not necessary. It's always open.' They entered the center hallway, where Victor waved his cane through an arch to the library.

Unlit crystal chandeliers, leather chairs, and mahogany bookshelves rolled to a vanishing point. Victor sank into a chair and put his cane in his lap. 'We wait here. Miss Lowell will let us know when curtain time is.'

Raffi wandered among the bookcases, many of them fronted with wavy glass dotted by bubbles. The brandy was getting to him. For a shadowy instant his library at the Forum floated back. When an open bookcase carved with wheeling bats and writhing dragons veered his way, he ran his fingers along the spines of some of the books it held. He looked closer and saw they were written by Miss Lowell herself. Beside *A Dome of Many Colored Glass* was *Swords and Poppies*. A green volume all but fell into his hand; it flipped naturally to a page viewed many times. He read aloud:

> *'And I wished for night and you.*
> *I wanted to see you in the swimming-pool,*
> *White and shining in the silver-flecked water.*

> *'While the moon rode over the garden,*
> *High in the arch of night,*
> *And the scent of the lilacs was heavy with stillness.*
> *Night and the water, and you in your whiteness, bathing!*

'How long have Miss Lowell and Miss Russell been together?'

'Mrs. Russell,' Victor said. 'At least ten years.'

Raffi went back to the bookcases. *Some Imagist Poets*, Volumes I-III, commanded the second shelf down alongside an embossed black 'Souvenirs' memory book. When it started to slide out on its own, he caught it and scanned the scraps tucked into the pages.

Clipped to the spidery diary entries were keepsakes from two sojourns to London, one in the summer of 1913—including a letter from Ezra Pound full of wild enthusiasms for Amy's 'In A Garden,' which he promised to include in *Les Imagistes*—and then documents from late July, 1914 (tickets from the S.S. *Laconia*, passage for two plus a limousine and chauffer, receipts for a suite in the Berkeley Hotel, Piccadilly). And a chummy note from D. H. Lawrence.

Raffi glanced at restaurant tabs for groups as high as twenty. Some new-found friends. Among the London snapshots was a buff-shaded envelope stuffed with paid receipts of D.H. Lawrence's personal bills—from hot water to Hayman's Old Tom Gin—each carrying Amy's sure-handed signature. She was obviously a devotee of the Palmer Method, the same modern handwriting Raffi had been taught in New York.

On the heels of this was high-spirited correspondence from Pound suggesting his Dear Amy underwrite his editing a French literary magazine for $5,000 a year, followed by missives of escalating fury as she gently declined. A series of letters bloomed as Miss Lowell floated the idea that she herself introduce the Imagists to the American audience with a three-volume anthology.

Then her beheading. Ezra Pound was not going to go so easily. In deckle-edge, a tableside snapshot marked 'Dieudonne, Ryder Street, St. James's, London' showed Pound and his wife Dorothy at the north end of the banquet dais. Amy and Mrs. Russell stared back with daggers from the south. Seated in-between, in threadbare black suits, were 'starvelings' identified as Lawrence; Richard Aldington and his wife, H.D.; F. S. Flint; John Gould Fletcher; Allen Upward; John Cournos; and the sculptor Henri Gaudier-Brzesca—the original Imagist circle.

Raffi noticed the date, July 14, 1914. So while the Great War was exploding in Sarajevo, a tempest was brewing at London's haven for the literati. A good concierge might have been able to deflect some of that.

Sympathetic letters to Amy in the wake of this disaster told the story: Pound openly ridiculed her at Dieudonne by grabbing the tin tub that held champagne and putting it upside down on his head—sending up her bathing poems, which he'd once so admired when he still held out hope Amy's money was coming his way. He did it to make the other poets imagine her naked and flabby, an intruder—not just a woman, but an enormous woman whom he now characterized as a buttinski, and a lesbian at that. Perhaps your Imagistes should be called *Les Nagistes*, he said. Perhaps it was inappropriate for you to have brought Mrs. Russell.

Raffi flipped the page: raves for the first volume of Lowell's renegade Imagist collection. But none from Pound beyond a terse note: 'Surely you don't think you can buy Imagism away from me, no matter who defects to you.' And then another, even more venomous: 'Don't count on that whale Ford Madox Hueffer. He's made it clear there can be only one fat person per movement.'

The next section proved to be from 1915: savage reviews from Pound, who shifted to a new tack—her age, and even worse, her Americanism.

Pound's pencil had sharpened itself into a hate-stick. Beyond 'lowering the standard' for Imagism, Amy's excess stemmed from laziness. The snubs, the slights, his cruel description of her sinking herself into a chair, were circled in Amy's cool blue ink. Raffi closed his eyes, feeling it. Pound had damned her to hell (or Brookline), and naturally all the svelte critics in his sphere of influence had hopped on board. A *Philadelphia Inquirer* caption of her disastrous reading of May 1916 twisted the knife: 'From left to right, Amy Lowell.'

'We have just entered the private chambers of the loneliest poet on Earth,' Raffi said.

'Not the loneliest person,' Victor said. 'Mrs. Russell loves her with deadly accuracy. Technically she's engaged as an employee, to handle manuscripts, submissions, and literary rights. Miss Lowell pays her to cover what she might have earned otherwise, had she remained an actress.'

'There was a Mr. Russell?'

'Barely a year, long disappeared,' Victor said. 'A fellow actor. A marriage of inconvenience, doomed from the beginning.'

'Do you think,' Raffi said, 'there's such a thing as unrequited intellectual love?'

'D. H. Lawrence was Miss Lowell's greatest hope for the British connection. But he's just refused to visit her for the third time, even though she redid this library in old English oak in the hopes of enticing him here.'

Raffi flipped back to the Lawrence letters. The last was chilling, furious she'd used World War I imagery for special effects—the gas, the purple lips. How she must have ached to be included in the ranks of the Imagists' elite, refusing to understand the impossibility of their accepting her. Seduction, then destruction. Was it Pound or Lawrence who'd been her Diletti?

'Is this why I'm here?' Raffi said. 'Misery loves company?'

A bell rang from above. Victor stood. 'I have a theory about why Miss Lowell took such a shine to you. Past that tall bookcase with all the Keats, isn't there a smaller set of shelves?'

Raffi studied the row of collectors' editions, leather hardbacks, fabric-covered weaves with light foxing, some stamped in gold. 'Sixteen copies of the same story. *Rollo in Naples*.'

Victor shrugged. 'She was sixteen the first summer she went to Italy. Rumor is, the number sixteen has a special significance to her, but I've come to wonder, is she just working at being picturesque? In any case, be geographically bewitching and help out wherever you can. Just... do what Rollo would do.'

'Couldn't I just shovel coal?'

From the far end of the library someone coughed. Raffi listened with his eyes. 'Who is that?' A girl with curly red hair was dusting the paintings as she moved down the wall. How odd, someone working so late when it had appeared no one in service was working at all. Was she the only attendant left to take care of this huge house? When the servant moved on to a mirror, she polished it, then swiftly re-covered it with a scrap of muslin.

Raffi sadly realized this measure was taken under Miss Lowell's direction. He could hear her self-deprecating joke: *because mirrors have feelings, too*.

Victor dropped his voice. 'Elizabeth is technically Miss Lowell's private maid, but she gets cranky sometimes because she values sleep, and on top of that she refuses to be one of the Devils' Disciples. So we all chip in here and there in the wee hours.'

Elizabeth headed toward the stairs and turned to them. 'No one should be forced to witness what's going on in this madhouse.' She reached the landing, stopped, sighed heavily, and wiped her forehead with the back of her hand. 'Coming?'

II

Sono italiano. Va bene così.
I'm Italian. That's enough.

Raffi and Victor followed Elizabeth two more flights to the third floor. Victor put his finger to his lips as they paused in the open doorway of an immense room lined with nail-studded leather Chesterfields. A painter's easel stood in the far corner.

At the bar in the shadows along the back wall, three silhouettes—one in a tall hat—nursed drinks beside an ingénue in a short skirt and a willowy figure maybe a decade older. Amid the murmur, a cat slept on an ebony piano, sun-faded to a pearly gray. Center stage, on an overstuffed tapestry couch, their hostess lounged in silken trousers, puffing on an *Ilusione* cigar. Beside her Ada Russell sat stiffly, her face as well as arms crossed, her forked cane leaning against her chair.

'My next piece,' Amy Lowell began, waving away a cloud of blue smoke. All conversation came to a halt, and everyone turned to watch. Amy flicked through a sheaf of papers and showed one to the actress, who shook her head. 'Not that one? All right,' Amy said, shuffling until she unfolded a printed broadsheet.

'Get on with it,' Ada said.

'You're frightfully rude, Pete,' Amy said. 'It isn't called "Get On With It." It's called…'

A Lady

You are beautiful and faded
Like an old opera tune
Played upon a harpsichord;
Or like the sun-flooded silks
Of an eighteenth-century boudoir.

In your eyes
Smoulder the fallen roses of out-lived minutes,
And the perfume of your soul
Is vague and suffusing,
With the pungence of sealed spice-jars.
Your half-tones delight me,
And I grow mad with gazing
At your blent colours.
My vigour is a new-minted penny,
Which I cast at your feet.
Gather it up from the dust,
That its sparkle may amuse you.

Ada batted her eyes. 'Of course, that's a man's poem, however avant.'

'In what way, pray?' Amy said.

'Well, I'm not going to spell it out for you,' the actress said, enlarging her voice so that it spilled across the room. 'Between the My and the I. The vigor and penny and all. Even worse, it's the false protection it promises. But then you'd never notice that, my dear, because with your foul cigar you've always been a man. And by the way, put your smoking jacket on or keep your distance tonight.' A dramaturgical wave of the hand. 'I won't keep company with a cloud of tobacco fumes.'

'This is a night to remember,' Amy said. 'She rarely insults me in private.'

Pointedly disengaging, the others turned back to the bar and slouched over their drinks, putting their backs to the lovers. When Victor coughed, Amy looked his way and her face lit up. She hadn't lost her entire audience. She jabbed the air with her cigar. 'All this acting, Pete, may be a bit much for our new arrivals.' She took a puff, leaned back, and rudely looked Raffi over. 'My word, you are tall, aren't you? For the benefit of those who haven't met you, tell us who you are, good sir?'

Playing his part, Raffi offered a swift bow and kissed her hand. 'My name is Rafaele Peach, recently arrived from Rome and now under the employ of Mr. Addison Saltonstall at the world famous Parker House hotel...'

'Scullery,' Victor said. 'He's working with me.'

When Ada leered from her tea cup, Raffi entertained the notion it might hold something more. She straightened her back and for a shadowy instant was malevolently sexy. Her look gripped him by the throat. 'Ah, you're our evening's representative of the common man, the émigré flagrante. I see how you fit into Amy's collection.'

Amy rolled her eyes and stamped out her cigar on a glass dish. 'Ada, maybe you've had enough giggle juice tonight.'

'He's so new, he doesn't even know what he doesn't know.' Victor gracefully handed his coat and hat to Elizabeth, who took them away.

How comfortable he seemed in this company, so patrician, somehow to the manner born. There had to be more to his story. Not only was Victor not a stranger to the Sky Parlor, he was not a stranger to this class.

'But he can read your deepest thoughts,' Victor went on. 'If you don't mind, Miss Lowell, he's going to be my roommate for a while till he gets a place of his own.'

'I am at your service,' Raffi said.

Sensing it was safe again, the group at the bar rose from their seats. As they drew closer, Raffi realized the central figure among them was not wearing a hat at all but a towering hair arrangement.

Amy nodded and raised her arm toward a blinking figure dressed in pinstripes and a pince-nez. 'Rufus Cloud, magician. He works at S.S. Pierce, making jars of boiled cabbage disappear.'

'Cost accountant, nothing more,' Cloud said, shifting to shake Raffi's hand.

Ada struck. 'Former vice president, before the audit.'

Amy turned to a lanky young man who wore an argyle sweater vest under his coat. He parted his dark hair in the middle. 'This sour grape is my nephew.'

'Ephraim Lowell,' the young man said. Elbows out, he stuck his hands in his pockets and scowled.

'Ephraim is a communist, embarrassed by his family fortune.' Amy patted him on the back, but he pulled away. 'He is recently returned from Russia, where he had an audience with Comrade Stolitski. He told me just this morning he's going to go out and find an honest wage, working with his hands.'

'We Lowells should be embarrassed,' Ephraim said, 'for the shameful way we've earned our wealth on the backs of the unfortunates from away.' He stopped himself. 'Sorry, Tiger Lily—I didn't mean any offense.'

'None taken,' said the tall, plump Mandarin woman with the black coiled pompadour. 'Give me your poor, your huddled messes.' Only her thick-lidded eyes were visible behind an ivory-handled fan. Though she wore a scarlet *qipao* embroidered with a white-capped cobalt mountain and salmon clouds floating over an emerald sea, it took greater effort not to stare at the sparkling gems on each of her fingers, the knuckles stubbled from a not-too-recent shaving.

'This is Miss Lily,' Amy said. 'She looks half dead, but don't let her fool you. She's completely dead.'

'Dead awake,' Tiger Lily said. She lowered her fan to reveal vaguely masculine features and smooth, boiled skin. When she pulled back her painted lips, her teeth sprang forward, blackened with betel juice. 'Beauty's so relative, yes? Where I come from, this is a sign of elegance, not that baring of white fangs you Westerners call a smile.'

The last two guests, a scholarly teacher in gray and a college girl in a jumper, drifted over. 'Don't let Professor Benedict's demure demeanor fool you,' Amy said to Raffi. 'She's hiding an anthropologist under that frumpy frock. Ruth, which of your savants are you gracing us with today?'

'This is Margaret Mead,' Benedict said. 'She's one of the brightest young things at Barnard. I'm trying to convince her to dump the psychology mumbo jumbo and move over to my department, where she can make a real difference.'

'Yes, yes.' Amy returned to Raffi. 'Ruth spends her nights dreaming of the Zuni Indians. In dreams, she compromises herself with an intimate group of gentlemen whose claim to fashion is they implant sacks of sand under the foreskin and finish with a coat of red, white, and blue war paint. It makes their sexual organs all the more imposing.'

'How patriotic,' Ada trilled.

Benedict looked down, red flames flashing high on her cheekbones. Raffi felt keenly that in one fell swoop Amy had dismissed Benedict's entire life's work for the sake of a joke. But that wasn't all. There was something else. Benedict might as well have whispered it directly into Raffi's ear: *I'm also a poet, Amy. Isn't it so like you not to mention it*?

'I'd be honored to hear more of your work, Professor,' Raffi said. He waited. He knew Amy was saving Ada for last.

'You've met my wife, Pete—the actress Ada Russell Lowell, queen to my king of our secret society.'

'Nothing secret about us,' Ada said. 'Everybody despises us, that's all.'

'I find that hard to accept. I think you're swell,' Raffi said.

'That's one of the few American words he knows,' Victor said.

'Swell or swollen?' Ada lifted her chin.

'Oh, but every bit of this is swell,' Raffi said.

'Ah, the puppet continues, without a yank of the string.' Ada's eye narrowed. 'Please do honor us with more of your insightful truths, Guignol. What can you even find amusing here? I'd think you'd be uncomfortable upstairs, away from the servants' quarters, riff-Raffi of the week.'

Raffi stepped to the side with a slight bow. 'Actually, I am most interested in that photograph behind you. It's spellbinding.' He moved closer to a silvery albumen of Virgil's Tomb. An umbrella of a cedar shaded it from centuries of exotic glare. In the background, Grandfather Vesuvius puffed into eternity atop a curve of coast. As an artful dodger, Raffi had hawked similar daguerreotypes in 'genuine gold' frames and seen that the tree and volcano were a couple, keeping their distance from each other but always shown together. Amy and Ada stood beside the crypt, their faces indistinct from bright sunlight. 'Does your snapshot picture the two of you with a tree or a volcano?' Raffi dropped his voice, gently increasing his Italian accent. 'In my mind, the two are inseparable. There are other trees in Naples, but memory summons them as one. What would the volcano be if not framed by its tree? A picture of a rock. And the tree without Vesuvius would be an empty frame.'

The room went silent. Amy put her hands on her hips. 'So who's the mountain and who's the tree?' She quickly touched him on the wrist. 'You know, you are a most romantic young man. Virgil would be proud of such a Neapolitan.'

'No matter that Virgil is not buried in Virgil's Tomb, he wasn't Neapolitan, and he called Naples Partenope,' Ada said. 'Who's the romantic?'

'After a short decade, the tree derides the volcano,' Amy said. 'Remember when you loved my reveries?'

'Aren't you forgetting me?' asked a young woman in a smock with big eyes and lacquered hair slicked back.

...*Again?* Raffi finished the sentence in her mind. He got a better glimpse of her as she leaned into view from behind her easel.

'Oh, yes,' Amy said. 'Our resident visual archivist, Lorna Peabody.'

The painter stared at Raffi. 'I agree with Ada. What makes you think you belong here?'

Ada stiffened. 'Oh, knock off acting the drab. How easy for the artist to play the superior judge by observing and recording rather than participating. I'm sure he'll prove too smooth to reply to your childish attack.'

'How lucky you are to have a talent for painting,' Raffi said. 'An artist's work ensures the rest of us will never forget this moment in time, Miss Peabody.'

'I prefer Lorna,' she said. 'Lorna Doom.'

Footsteps echoed on the stairs. Interesting. Two men, one more imposing than the other. Then the knock, rude and self-important.

'Oh, my, Amy,' Ada said when the pair walked into the center of the circle. 'Be still my beating heart. If it isn't your former beau, "the heavy-booted" swain in your poem. The dashing fiancé who dashed into the arms of another.' She raised her chin and turned to the big-shouldered one. 'Still in love with the Lowell name in spite of'—she ran her hand along her hip—'all evidence'?

'Good evening, Secretary Laughlin,' Amy said. 'Harry. I'm gratified by your sudden interest in poetry. If only I'd known this as a teen, when you whispered sweet nothing into my ear.'

'Give us a buss, girl.' He pointed to his lips. 'For old times' sake. Right here on the kisser.'

Amy recoiled. 'What really brings you here?'

Laughlin pulled a folded document from inside his jacket. 'It was never true I loved you for your name and money.' He smiled. 'Just your name. Sign here to get the campaign started, darlin', and I'll be out of your hair again.'

'Who invited you?' Ada said.

Laughlin looked only at Amy. 'Your brother's already signed. Think of it, the famous poet and the president of Harvard, leaders in the private investment that's so essential for public support. Boston must have an airport, and someday the record will show you Lowells dared to back the future.'

Amy nodded to the second man, Laughlin's companion. 'Hello, Mr. Dawes.'

'Who's this snake charmer?' Ada, now the soubrette, winked.

Dawes grinned. 'If I'm the charmer you must be the charmed, baby. William Dawes of the Dawes and Associates Advertising Agency. Look me up when you want to make a comeback.'

Amy whispered something to Laughlin. Raffi watched the two closely and imagined them, so long ago. She, knowing her parents were disgusted by his crassness but still hoping her Sapphic secret wouldn't get out. He, dazzled by all the opportunities she represented. As a couple, they must have caused quite a stir.

'I'll just be a second, everyone,' Amy said. She walked out to the landing, throwing in a little shake as she looked back at Ada. She and the men dropped to a whisper as they passed the document around. A pen flashed in her hand. 'Here,' Laughlin said, 'and right here. Come on, one more, Aimsie.' He brushed his lips across the top of Amy's forehead.

'Maybe we'll see each other again, Old Beau,' Amy said. 'In another thirty years.'

Amy and Ada descended to their suite, and the other guests excused themselves. Raffi followed Victor down the back stairs to the cellar. Though it smelled of tar and over-ripe apples it was clean and dry, with ivy-patterened floor tiles cut from the modern linoleum.

'Here's our digs, and here's Charon,' Victor said. 'But our ferryman requires coal instead of coin.' He waved his hand toward a great furnace that flapped and hummed with a heart of fire. It was larger than the one at Hotel Forum—a technological tour de force. 'Between the two of us, we ought to make one heck of a stoker.'

'Do I need to shovel any now?' Raffi asked.

'I think you've shoveled enough for one night,' Victor said. 'On balance you got over.' He took off his jacket and rolled onto a cot. 'The other bunk's yours, for as long as you like—when our service room at the hotel won't do. You're welcome to that upper shelf, too.'

Though the furnace door was shut, the flames' dancing light threw patterns into the dim sleeping quarters. Raffi snapped open his leather portmanteau. Putting his few items away in the cupboard, he realized Victor was holding his breath, intent at guessing at their mysterious identity, still fragrant with the tang of the ocean and camphor. This didn't take long, because there wasn't much left of his old life. Raffi sat on the edge of the bed and lit a cigarette. 'Do you want one, Victor?'

'No thanks,' Victor said. 'Nightcap?'

'Thank you, no.' Raffi blew a smoke ring and watched it grow soft and disappear as it drifted toward the ceiling. 'Did you know those two?'

'Secretary Laughlin's a regular at the Parker House. Got here before Paul Revere. They might as well name the bar for him.'

'What's his drink?' Raffi asked.

'Canadian Club. Neat.'

'The other fellow, Dawes?'

'He's drinking what you're drinking, and keep an eye on your glass, too. Never paid for a drink in his life. Got a percentage in everything. For both of them, money's the North Star.'

'Is there a history between Mr. Saltonstall and Miss Lowell?'

'I don't remember hearing anything in particular. She comes into the hotel fairly often. I don't think Miss Amy thinks much of Mr. Saltonstall, because he's a step below her set, his working for a living and all. Since the Saltonstalls are Unitarians, I don't think he cares for 'that Mormon actress.' You know, Ada was big once. When the Great White Fleet of U.S. Navy dreadnoughts sailed into San Francisco, she was billed as The Stunning Russell.'

Raffi leaned over, took off his shoes, and polished the toes. He placed them carefully on the shelf, rolled over on his cot, and closed his eyes. Of all of the disciples, some men dressed as women, some women dressed as men, all costumed—including that painter in her cover-up smock and smirk—it was Ada's physical disintegration with the passage of time that was most crippling. How difficult it must be if your face is your fortune. He blew a last luxurious smoke ring. And what had they intended his role to be? A jester only, with his neutral persona? A grounding wire, a negative charge, a safeguard for the harem. Maybe this was all too expensive. Surely he wasn't that desperate to be part of something. Why did he allow himself to show off tonight? He just let himself get too tired. 'Victor, I'm sorry if I was prying and got too personal earlier this evening on the way over.'

'Forget it,' Victor said. 'I already have.' A distant whistle from South Station pierced the air, but softly, as though traveling through the mists of time instead of fog. Another peal echoed the first, almost impressionistic in its mournful gaiety. 'Do railway whistles sound the same in Italy?' Victor asked.

'They're more shrill,' Raffi said. 'But because I spent most of my childhood in an orphan asylum in New York, some of my recollections of locomotives may be the same as yours. I'd be drifting off to sleep and we'd hear a faraway whistle and feel the softest vibration, barely there. And then it would get closer and closer and louder and louder and the whole ward would start moving up and down and it was the *iron horse*. It was here and it was changing everything. You had to hold onto your bunk to keep from falling off. Slowly you'd feel the vibrations fading away. It was like a bedtime story in the middle of the night. After I finished school, I went back to Italy—that's how I came to work at the Forum. But I found the nights to be too enervating. I missed that melodic lament.'

'Let me get this straight. You came back to America because you missed a certain steam trumpet?'

'Wherever I am, I dream of the other place,' Raffi said. 'While in Rome I dreamed of the summers here. Near the switching station where the train dropped off mail and took on water in the Bronx, there used to be a rotting wooden water tower. Every year, on the hottest day in July—you know what I mean, Victor, when it seemed like it was two hundred degrees and even the dogs wouldn't get up from their shadows—the stationmaster would ring the big bell and we all knew what that meant. We'd run to the platform and stand below the tower. Then he'd pull on that rusty old crank. The bottom would drop out, and all the sun-warmed water would crash down on us in a single, luscious, heavy wet wall, like a transparent tongue—huge as a tidal wave. It had held its silence for so long, Victor. A curtain of warm, piney water collapsed on us with a whoosh!'

'Here we go again,' Victor said.

'It shimmered all around us.' Raffi carefully twisted the end of his cigarette, saving it for later. 'Sunlight picked up the droplets that hit the boards and splashed back up on us in the haze. It happened only once every year.'

Victor lay motionless in his bunk. He rubbed his chin. 'So that was sex as you knew it. I get it now. It's like me, unable to see my skin color.' He pulled the blanket over his shoulders. 'Even though I can't see myself,

74

others can see me and define who I am for me. To them I'm just black and blind, a handicap.'

'Why do you keep referring to things one might see or not?'

'It's dark work taking umbrage against the rest of the world. I shouldn't have to tell you, of all people, there's more than one way to see or feel things.'

Raffi heard the bed creak as Victor turned to the wall.

12

Un corpo sazio non desidera più niente.
The satisfied person has no desires.

QUINCY, 1922

Ephraim Lowell stepped off the trolley at the iron works. With his hat brim turned down and topcoat collar turned up, he insinuated himself into the crowd of workers heading toward 'Fore River Shipyard,' as the sign on the gate said, 'A Division of Bethlehem Steel.' The carefully chosen clothes he wore reflected the tastes of the masses: cotton and denim, in dull blues and blacks—unlike some coffee-house communists' duds. You don't get punched by Harvard's Porcellian club for nothing. He was on a mission, and the only thing to set him apart was his pair of spectacularly expensive Interwoven Scottish guard fancy wool socks. If nothing else, you have to trust in your own socks. Politics aside, who knew when you were going to need machine-reinforced toes?

The universal shuffle continued until Ephraim and his group passed through a long, low set of gates topped by concertina wire. Above a central large sign was the legend 'Through these portals pass the greatest shipbuilders in the world.'

This was bigger than being a Lowell, and quite a bit more than just a St. Grottlesex prep-school thing. Just like the poet William Blake said, people of change fermented in a universal wine. Harvard, with its false protections of 'learning,' seemed so remote now. His fraternity brothers would surely raise their eyebrows upon seeing his raw knuckles the next time he showed up at the Owl Club. He reached one of the sign-up tables and stood still as a clerk gave him the once-over.

'Name?' the clerk asked.

'Eddie Lowalski,' Ephraim said.

'Age?'

'Twenty-five.'

'Married?'

'Good lord, no!' Ephraim said.

The clerk looked up. 'What was that?'

'Eddie' just shrugged his shoulders.

'Injuries or disabilities?'

How often had Aunt Amy complained that being born a well-heeled Lowell kept other writers from taking her seriously. He shook his head no.

'Well, go over there and join that group for orientation.'

Ephraim's noble experiment was working. He'd have no trouble with 'orientation,' because before the weaving mills, his family had earned a great deal of its fortune in merchant trade with the Orient. The early morning Massachusetts sun warmed his neck, and he made a mental note as he slunk into position to cancel his weekly appointment with the barber. He tried to engage one of the working stiffs in conversation: 'It's quite a morning, isn't it?' he said to a burly fellow with iron-gray hair.

'Mmmph.'

'Maybe it is a little chilly,' Ephraim said.

'Outta my way. You're blocking my view,' the slob said in an accent so thick it took Ephraim a moment to understand. He'd have to practice running his consonants together like that. He looked at his seventeen-jewel watch—oops. He'd have to pick up a more modest one at Shreve, Crump & Low the minute the afternoon horn blew. Maybe something with a dark gray band and large numbers as a paean to the practical.

Smelling of wet wool, garlic, and cabbage, the pushing, heaving crowd of oily ruffians started moving, lifting him and carrying him forward, only to stop in front of a dais. Supervisors—apparatchiks all—walked this way and that on scaffolding. Then one tall man with tired eyes and a wool scarf ascended to speak, accompanied by an officer of the United States Navy sporting two gold stripes on his sleeves. Ephraim had met Rear Admiral Crowninshield once after a Havershom lecture in Cambridge, but he'd never been addressed by anything so lowly as a lieutenant before. Maybe he wasn't even an Annapolis man! Perhaps he might make use of that later, in banter with the other workers. He felt himself transforming, changing, as though all the false walls of privilege were falling away. How he'd enjoy telling Aunt Amy and Adder (certainly quicker than any serpent) about all that was happening to him! Because was he not a microcosm for great world events? A real worker now?

A gull swooped up and flung a blue mussel to the macadam, then dropped down to pick its live insides out. Clever little thing, though probably a capitalist.

'Welcome to Fore River Shipyard,' the speaker said. 'The morn-ing horn sounds at eight bells—that's four a.m. You will be paid by the Quartermaster at the end of each Friday at fifteen-hundred hours. You are here to do exactly as you're told, and nothing else.' The speaker paused. 'Our activities here at Fore River are top secret. Understood?'

As if on cue, the men gruffly answered something like *strawberries, raspberries*—that unintelligible sound effect radio swells were using to approximate the murmur of crowds. There were a few *Mmmphs* as well. Ephraim was disappointed—how can the speaker understand our individual replies?

'I call your attention to the destroyer in dry dock behind me, the USS *Saxon*—467 feet of deadly dreadnought. What a lady. She has already cleared her sea trials and has a full coat of primer paint, so she's ready for one final touch.' He waited. 'My question for you men is, do you see any deficiency in her? Is there anything she lacks?'

They all looked past three low administrative buildings and a covered warehouse to see a gigantean Navy vessel looming over the corrugated tin roof, its superstructure a gleaming city of dominance. Sunlight flashed on her bridge, sensitive whip antennae, and menacing four-inch guns. The ship certainly didn't lack... understatement. Awk. The man beside Ephraim hawked up a gob of spit and accidentally hit the tip of Ephraim's new, scuff-tumbled work boot. 'Pardon me,' Ephraim said.

'Anybody?' the speaker asked.

More gulls careered in, whirling over the buildings, free to fly wherever they pleased. Ephraim liked to study songbirds, but not these unprincipled predators.

'If you can see this ship, men, you know that what this ship needs, and does not have, is invisibility.'

So pleased he'd been addressed as one of the men, Ephraim had already looked to his left and right to share in the distinction before he realized that what the supervisor was saying was accidentally interesting.

78

'We're going to give her a coat of camouflage, boys, and not just battleship gray. If only we could permit you to do it, you could all go home and tell your wives you've just been hired as modern artists! Because from my point of view, we're going to take this perfectly yare ship and paint her up like a whore.' He scanned the men and let it sink in. 'Yep, you heard me right. I'll leave it up to the $10-an-hour types to let you know if it ever works. Okay, let her roll.'

A sailor in dress blues cranked a 16mm Kinescope, which clicked and whirred as the foreman stepped aside. Light flickered on the wall behind him, and in the brilliant sunlight the image of a model of the *Saxon* hove into view. It was the *Saxon*, but it wasn't the *Saxon*. She was distorted by, and emblazoned with, crazy rays, starbursts, and zigzags. The only breaks in the lines came on the flat surfaces, where suddenly a different direction was taken and that line would continue unbroken across the hull and up over the superstructure so that it was very difficult to tell where one part of the *Saxon* began and another ended.

Maybe Amy's stodgy 'friend,' the critic Royal Cortissoz, would now declare Cubism had finally earned its place during his regular rounds of the Beacon Hill salons.

A single Mmmph turned into a guffaw which built to a rumble until the whole audience was laughing.

'All right, all right, cut it!' the supervisor shouted over the din. 'It's called Dazzle Camouflage.' He picked up a pointer and walked into the projected ship's rays as they danced and distorted against his arm, back, and head in profile. He became a part of the images on the screen. His pointer actually disappeared amidst the crisscrossing lines, and only through its movement could Ephraim detect where it had been. He shrugged. 'Well, you could lose her in a herd of zebras, anyway.'

When the crowd quieted down, the supervisor dropped to a low and reasonable voice. 'Look, I don't come up with this stuff. I'm only taking orders, just like you. What the eggheads tell me is, instead of making the ship blend in with the sea and specks of white foam and whitecaps from miles away, we're going to paint her with this scheme of great, long stripes so she'll stick out in such a way that her actual length and direction will be a mystery to enemy U-boats. Hide her in plain sight, so to speak. Even if you don't understand the scientific principles behind what you're doing, I want you to understand you're doing something patriotic for your country.'

Still no joy. The speaker looked into the crowd.

'Then let's break into three groups. Those with a last name beginning A through K follow Lieutenant Anderson through this gate on the left. Those with a last name beginning L through R will follow Mr. Vollmer through the center gate. The esses through zees will follow me, to the right. And remember, the Navy Department classifies this as secret, under wraps, an activity upon which our national security depends. What you see here, what you hear here, it remains here when you leave here. Let's make it smart, gentlemen, we have work to do.'

'Mmmph.'

Ephraim looked around. 'Where are the women? Where are the handmaids to our cause? I could stand a spot of refreshment.'

'I wouldn't say that too loudly, bub,' a voice behind him said. 'My old lady could knock your block off.'

Then Ephraim spied a cart laden with glistening crullers and steaming coffee guided by a statuesque girl toward a group of supervisors talking animatedly about a recent sporting event. When she tossed her golden mane, she reminded Ephraim of Rockwell Kent models in his favorite radical journal *The Masses*. She must be quite the hoofer, with that impossibly long neck and broadish shoulders tapering to a long, slim waist a cat could get his hands all the way around. A darker girl, almost invisible, watched the crowd with darting glances as she pulled a second cart, wiping the counter with a rag.

13

Chi non ha nulla non ha che perdere.
He who has nothing has nothing to lose.

BOSTON, 1922

'Secretary Laughlin never makes a move without two baby grands, so we'll need to add some muscle,' Ira Stadt said. He settled into the cushy back seat of Frank Morelli's spanking new Studebaker. Boy, it must pay well to be the head of the Massachusetts arm of the Providence Syndicate.

Morelli turned in his seat and produced a solid gold matchbox. He struck a lucifer with his thumb and lit the Lucky Strike hanging on his lower lip. 'I trust you to take care of things, Ira, because you're smart enough to know the value of cooperation,' Morelli said. 'Boston doesn't need another massacre.'

Stadt, who was something of a student of massacres, longed for the leather wing chair in the corner of his library, where he'd spent many a quiet hour reading about wars that had once meant so much to somebody. He'd often pondered the fallacies of 'the one to end all' and 'never again.' 'Thank you for your confidence in me, Frank. The Syndicate's made its position clear: Secretary Laughlin either goes with our guy or he's dead meat. After the jackass announces his ruling about who gets the aerodrome contract at the press conference, we'll get a call from our man on the *Herald*, and we'll know what to do next. We already know the Secretary will leave the State House by the front steps and head down the hill for his Canuck whiskey at the Parker House. Because he always does.'

'What kind of insurance did you purchase?' Morelli asked.

Stadt permitted himself the smallest of smiles. 'It's a family policy. We've sent some lovely photographs of his daughter walking to school from their mansion in Newton and a few from her bedroom window

81

to show we have access. Quite artistic but nothing smutty—all in good taste. His place is just across the border from Jamaica Plain, not that far from mine.' Stadt paused. 'How ironic it's just this one individual who stands between us and real progress for the Hub. As long as he toes the line, though, we should be all set.'

'Ever have any trouble with him before?' Morelli asked.

'Time was, everything went like clockwork,' Stadt said. 'Our guy Brewster got the nod for the El, the subway, and the commie detention camp for the Feds. But then a bright young alderman started going to the press and talking about open and fair contracts, and somewhere along the line I guess the Secretary got the idea we were vulnerable. Out of the blue the putz got so big for his britches he handed the breakwater repair deal to Melvin Dingle's construction company, as though nobody knew the Secretary's brother-in-law was also a partner with Dingle on Shawmut Ferries.'

'So the real question is, is the Secretary now basing his decisions on blood?' Morelli asked.

'If you want to call money blood,' Stadt said. 'It's my job to make sure his judgment isn't clouded on this aerodrome project.'

'I'm glad you share our vision.' Morelli waved in the direction of Jeffries Point. 'That swamp land out there could be a gold mine instead of a dump full of... gulls. Maybe its use as a storage facility has come to its natural conclusion. What Beantown needs is a longer runway. I know your tribe won't mind the development that'll come from it.'

'Tribe.' Stadt winced. He thought of his parents in their stingy little store in the long-gone ghetto on Jeffries Point, working impossible hours; his father was murdered when he couldn't come up with the monthly donations for the police fund. Alone, his mother lost the store in foreclosure, took to drink, and drowned in an alcoholic stupor in two inches of gutter water. Not one member of the tribe had stepped in to help, though they did attend the auction of the pitiful remaining stock. 'The old neighborhood's gone. The Army's using the land for practice flights, but it could be so much more. To win this race with New York to build the first metropolitan aerodrome, we must stop the Secretary from giving Dingle the contract.'

'Sounds like Dingle's the one we should give the black eye,' Morelli said.

FlashScan System

City of San Diego Public Library
Linda Vista Branch
****

1/4/2017 3:02:51 PM
Title: Rake. Season 1 the b
Item ID: 31336093223049
Date Due: 1/11/2017,23:59

Title: Midnight crossing :
Item ID: 31336100848846
Date Due: 1/25/2017,23:59

Title: The Boston castrato
Item ID: 31336101413939
Date Due: 1/25/2017,23:59

3 items

'Dingle's just out for Dingle. The way he sees it, his ferries will get to take passengers straight to the tip of Jeffries Point to board those commercial rattletraps if they ever start flying. Unless they build a bridge to the runways. Then he'll build that, too.'

Morelli held his cigarette out and looked at it. 'So if the honorable Transportation Secretary Laughlin wants to stand in the way of Progress, he'll wake up as part of the fill under the runway.'

'Speaking of blood, I hope you have no problem that I'm having one of our friends tap Gaspare for a couple of men,' Stadt said.

'Who?' Morelli frowned. 'Nah, I don't want to know. Gaspare will always be part of the family, and he'll always have a place at the Office, but like a dog who's been getting too old, he can only see the bone in front of him. When he had a little spell with his heart last year, he went into the hospital one man and came out another. Now he's mostly preoccupied with his nightclub and his music. He's lost the ability to see the big picture, so we might as well keep it that way. Sure, it's okay to use a couple of his sheiks to help out, but beyond that there's no reason for him to know what this is all about. Let him think it's just a routine shakedown. Less he knows, the better.'

'That's one way to cut off his balls,' Stadt said. 'On that note, I heard an interesting rumor. Gaspare has delusions of bringing that old windbag Moreschi, 'The Last Castrato of Rome,' for a concert here, even though he's on death's doorstep.'

Morelli tapped his forehead. 'Just more proof Gaspare is losing his grip. Who'd pay perfectly good money to hear half of a half man?'

'Never underestimate the power of a horror show to draw an audience,' Stadt said.

'The more I think about it, this could prove useful to us,' Morelli said. 'A long sea voyage for an ailing singer who everyone's heard of but nobody's actually heard—there might just be the perfect cover opportunity we've been looking for. There's a certain *persona* in Naples whose talents make him *non grata* with the Feds. We need him here, but he is, shall we say, between passports.'

'Let me know if I can help,' Stadt said. He got out of the car and watched it disappear in a plume of smoke. He crossed Scollay Square below The Old Howard's flashing 'Vaudeville!' sign and headed for the luncheonette without a name on Charles Street. With unhurried grace,

Stadt stepped inside, took a seat, and nodded as the waiter wordlessly brought him a single white napkin and a seafood fork.

'Will there be anything else, Mr. Stadt?' the waiter asked.

Stadt waved him away and reached into the inside pocket of his jacket. Producing a sealed tin labeled with the S. S. Pierce escutcheon, he delicately pried off the metal key on its side with his little finger, transected the tab with it, and rolled the lid to expose what was inside. He took a silvery sprat from the green olive oil, stared at its still pupil, and popped it into his mouth: if anybody's going to poison me, it's going to be me, myself, and eye.

Compression and substitution. Isn't that what Dr. Freud called the spark and tinder of a good joke? Stadt smiled as he indulged himself with another morsel. Without looking up, he pushed the rest of the tin out of reach, wiped his fingers on the napkin, and felt Joe Linsey, everybody's number-two alcohol supply guy, standing across the room. Stadt motioned Linsey over.

'Take a load off, Joe,' Stadt said, though he didn't like the smarmy Linsey any more than he'd liked Joe Kennedy during their days together at Fore River Shipyard. Kennedy and his business interests might as well have poured the gin down Stadt's mother's throat. Joe Kennedy had had the nerve to offer his condolences when they ran into each other on the docks after the funeral, saying what a great lady his mother had been, 'such a gorgeous dame my wife would be jealous'; could Kennedy have been setting up Rum Row that early on? With a touch of jealousy, Stadt imagined Kennedy's line of freighters fixed like stars outside the three-mile limit, smuggling Wiser's, Old Kilkenny, and Canadian Club along the Eastern Seaboard from Halifax to New York. Too many rats mixed up in this aerodrome, you ask me. No doubt the liquor mob wanted in on aviation: if it galloped or sailed or flew, you could move hooch on it.

'Good old Joe Linsey.'

'How've you been, Ira? You are looking fit as a fiddle. Have you found the secret to the fountain of youth?' Linsey checked the doorway. 'Morelli still around? I thought I saw his car.'

'He's got other fish to fry,' Stadt said. 'How is Gaspare getting along with the help? Frank doesn't want any of the usual guys for the Secretary job.'

'We've got three new guys,' Linsey said.

There were always new guys.

'Perfect chumps,' Linsey said. 'Between you and me, Gaspare prom-ises they're just dumb enough to do whatever you say without asking why. Let's go view the goods.' They walked into the restaurant's adjoin-ing bakery where the new conscripts sat, coffee sloshed around their mugs on the table. Linsey rolled his eyes. 'Get a load of them, my friend.'

Stadt watched as a slick-haired oaf in a tight tuxedo, for God's sake, nicked himself sawing at a piece of bread. Two Ruskis looked on and laughed as the ventriloquist's dummy squealed and stuck his thumb in his mouth. The dummy was a big boy with big triceps and a huge knuckle of an Adam's apple. Bet the women couldn't keep their hands off him. 'What boat did he just step off?'

'The big Neapolitan's name is Carlo,' Linsey said. 'Gaspare told me the moron fancies himself a singer. He looks like he could use his dick as a microphone, singing in the shower.' He addressed the trio: 'Stand up, boys, and show some respect. This is Mr. Stadt. He is a very, very important man.'

'Do all three of you speak English?' Stadt asked slowly. 'That's a requirement we expect of our part-time help.'

'These two speaka pretty good,' Linsey said of the Russians, who appeared to Stadt to speak no English at all, one a crow with a freak beak and the other, the sensitive one, with a white knife slash eye to collar. 'Can you say, "tuberculosis"?'

'Okay, boss,' one of the Russians said.

Stadt and Linsey looked at Carlo, who was twisting back and forth, biting his thumb.

'This one speaks very well,' Linsey said. 'He's got a lot of bounce.'

'I don't want a lot of bounce,' Stadt said.

'Sorry.' Carlo squeezed his thumb into a fist at his side and flashed his *Photoplay* grimace. 'I'm at your service around the clock except Friday nights. Because to be honest with you right up front, I have an important job singing on Friday nights.'

'We'll see about your Friday nights,' Stadt said.

14

La ricaduta è peggiore della malattia.
The relapse is worse than the illness.

BOSTON, 1922

How long had she been awake? Beatrice looked at the ceiling in the closet with twin beds and no window. It was already half past four. If they didn't get up soon, they wouldn't make it to work on time.

Giving her sister a gentle tap on the shoulder, she stepped out of bed and made a quick trip to the necessary, with Dorotea right behind her. Passing her parents' 'room'—a curtained alcove—she saw their mattress was empty.

They took turns combing their hair and brushing their teeth. They shared a runny egg washed down with white powder stirred in water—'the milk that never spoils.' Donning work smocks, they joined the crowd walking the final three hundred yards to their morning factory job. Beatrice enjoyed catching the individual melodies of the shoes, and more shoes, sliding, scuffing, advancing in the name of Progress. A leather rain.

The bulwarks and fenestrated ramparts of The William Underwood Company, 'established 1822,' rose above her as she approached. The factory stacks billowed with purpose and a smoke so redolent with the pong of slaughtered animals she'd unconsciously trained herself to breathe only through her mouth as she entered the processing line in her white cap. She felt the comfort of a governing intelligence here, a luxury of forethought. Carefully planned by an architect, the brick and ivy monster devouring her morning hours was steam heated and surrounded by arborvitae and other fragrant garnishes overseen by, she joked to Dorotea, 'the former chief gardener at the Boboli Gardens, because everyone who's anyone is coming here from Italy.'

Atop the factory tower was the incandescent sign of The Red Devil, erected two hundred feet high so the line of motorcars couldn't miss it brandishing its spaded tail in Boston's night skyline. Even now, in the predawn darkness, the Devil smiled benignly down at her and the other processors of the meat which inspired its ads to trumpet, 'There's No Mystery Here!'

Not that the devil didn't have problems himself, she'd heard from her father. Cans of clams, sealed under perfect scientific temperature control, had begun swelling in Warehouse No. 3 as if they had minds of their own. Holding one of the spoiled cans to your ear, you could almost hear the teeming microbes clamoring to climb outside. A few people had taken ill in Somerville from the clams, even before the newspapers had gotten wind of it and run the headline, 'Canned Cockles and Mussels Alive, Alive, Ooooh,' and a faculty member from MIT had been brought in to have a look. Someone had to take the blame, and clearly Papa had to watch out or he'd be one of the fall guys. 'I hope he got some sleep last night,' Beatrice said of their father. No matter your innocence, bad shellfish was the stuff of nightmares.

'Why shouldn't he?' said Dorotea, who still looked a little sleepy. 'He hasn't done anything wrong. They were canned before we even started here from Italy. They're so old, I think the Pilgrims ran that shift.'

In the breakfast room of his Back Bay brownstone, Professor William Thomson Sedgwood, chair of MIT's Department of Bacteriology and Immunology, slid into his seat after a full night at the laboratory.

'So sorry, Ellie. I had another meeting with Mr. Underwood.' He caught his wife studying his rumpled suit, the dark circles around his eyes.

'You adore a disaster so much, don't you, Sedge? The thrill of the hunt. Did it ever occur to you that it might be alarming to our help that you're bringing filth from that tainted factory into this house?'

'That's uncharitable. People could die from this,' Sedgwood said very softly.

'Charity begins at home.'

Why were some cans of clams actually swelling at Underwood when all of the preconditions for safe, pressurized boiling had been met and similar cans of mackerel, herring, and even restless, volcanic lobster lay quiet on the shelves? Sedgwood was just 40 when he'd solved a similar case back in 1896 and been the hero of the *Boston Post*. Now he was 66.

In his first campaign, he'd identified a single microbe that had 'learned' to become heat-resistant during the sterilization and sealing process he himself had devised. It had risen from the ranks of the perfectly happy bivalves heading to the steam room. Sedgwood had directed plant managers to answer with a superheated 'retort' to this offender, and the mysterious microbe retreated.

So sanguine was he with his triumph, Sedgwood had raised a few eyebrows by sampling the clams at lunch in the faculty lounge to remind his MIT colleagues of his positive association with the practical world. Now, at the request of Bill Underwood, he was rushing into battle again because a variant of his famous heat-resistant microbe had returned, more bold and heroic than ever.

He'd pushed the temperature up, but this second coming of *clostridium perfringens* still had the factory under siege. The situation, perversely romantic to the scientists, was a terrible threat to the businessmen. Why not blast it to Hades with even more heat? Every added degree would cost Underwood another $62,000 across the year, so the art of the matter was to discover the exact temperature that cost the least but got the job done.

Now that the workers had begun to identify with it in spite of the danger it posed to their jobs, the microbe had come, in some circles, to symbolize... resistance. What would it take to isolate this new microscopic 'immigrant' and shut it down? How could anything sealed in a can be so virulent, with a biological 'intelligence' the board of directors hadn't prepared for?

Bright red under a microscope, this jazz-age spore with the extended thermal death time and deadly neurotoxin—the *second* Bostonite to displease the devil since Daniel Webster—had been dubbed 'Belly Blin' by the press, after a Celtic goblin whose arrival gave rise to an affliction nicknamed 'Lucifer's Lick' or 'Satan in a Can.'

Thus far, the 'Lick' had presented itself with diarrhea and watery stools among a concentration of both the rich and not-quite-so-rich in Somerville, Nauset, Methuen, Hyde Park, and three handsome Beaux Arts dwellings on Commonwealth Avenue.

Vomiting, night sweats, and malaise were calling cards for a pinching pain strong enough to keep sufferers up all night. Late the previous afternoon, somebody's daughter had briefly slipped into a coma before recovering.

Sedgwood felt an excitement that bordered on the sexual. His nerves were tingling, his face was flushed, he felt every inch the warrior of science. But how might *anyone* react to something, someone, who makes you feel young again? He caught Ellie staring at him and wondered if she'd looked at him like this in years.

'There's an Italian fellow they have helping me with changes of temperature,' he said. 'A new man, Eduardo Favi. Dirty collars, and all that. He has some sort of degree in thermodynamics, or so he claims, but he doesn't seem to be aware of what's at stake here. He doesn't respect the microbe for what it might mean to science. His only concern seems to be to keep his job.'

'Shouldn't the plant owners be worried about his cleanliness protocols?' Eleanor asked. 'You never know what standards he's brought with him.'

'No, I think it's something more than that. Or, sadly, less,' Sedgwood said. That was the problem with immigrants. No trace of a sense of humor. No time to look beyond the confines of a Monday for the pursuit of knowledge. Not that it was their fault, really—it just made them execrable partners in conversation. 'You know what this fellow does when I talk to him? He just grunts and polishes his greasy glasses. Certainly a communist. I try to make pleasant conversation and what does he do? He just keeps asking me, '*What are "we"*—ha!—'*going to do?*' He's only worried about what he sees right in front of him! Of course I want to make the cans stop swelling! That's what we're all here for!'

'Ooh, but don't make him angry,' Eleanor said. 'Look at what those two Italians did in East Bridgewater. Those people are known for their hysterical tendency toward violence.' She splashed coffee into his cup and took a sip of hers. 'Then there was the waiter at the Parker House at lunch today. So odd looking, so Continental, and much too personal. He may be the most disturbing immigrant I've ever seen. Friendly to the point of insolence. My friends at the table seemed concerned he was trying to seduce me.'

Sedgwood looked up. 'Yes, they can bring a bad element, but when you think of it, you should be grateful for your Sacco and Vanzetti. *The bad creates the good.*' He'd used that phrase in each of the two articles he'd published in *Nature* magazine, one of which (December, 1913) carried the catchy title 'Sleuthing for a Virus.' He'd actually come up with the fireproof answer to the age-old question—predating Pasteur—of whether or not a virus was alive. 'Yes,' he'd written. 'A virus is alive because you can kill it.'

'You're not dishing out some theory to me, are you, Sedge,' Ellie said, holding up her hand, 'because we're not in class anymore, and I'm no longer your student. I'm not just talking in theory, I'm talking about real life.' With a practiced hand she spread some Scottish marmalade on a piece of white toast, then cut the toast into triangles.

Sedgwood offered the ghost of a smile.

'I'm glad at least something is interesting you now,' she said.

'What's come over you?'

'Late for dinner two nights in a row, now you're up all night so you barely make it in for coffee before classes. It's as though you're having an affair.' She sniffed, then laughed. 'When I was your star pupil, I was what interested you. And look at what you've done to me. Our children don't even come for Sunday dinner, and you have your career. Just look at you, gloating about your new "assignment." You'd have to kill me to prove I'm alive.'

Sedgwood looked at Ellie's furrowed brow, her flashing eyes. He grinned. 'Is there more coffee?'

She looked down at her *Boston Evening Transcript*. 'Those two Italians, Sacco and Vanzetti, just shot those poor people in cold blood like Thanksgiving turkeys, and the lawyers are making sure the madness will never end. It's best to stay out of these immigrants' affairs. You never know what an anarchist is thinking—it's his business until he makes it yours.'

Sedgwood bit into a toast point, then turned it over to look at it.

'Why would you care what this man Favi's thinking, Sedge? You could be joking around the way you do in your classes and suddenly you've sprouted a stiletto in your neck.'

This from the woman whose mother was a barefoot teenager in Sicily. Talk about a short memory. When he threw an accusing glance at her newspaper, she flipped it face down and sloshed more black fluid into his cup.

'I don't care a button for that,' Sedgwood said. 'I just want to skin this "Belly Blin."'

15

Chi semina vento, raccoglie tempesta.
He who sows wind, reaps a storm.

The circle of misfits, dreamers, and strays sat reconvened in the Sky Parlor, bored and restless. Clearly, money and registry in the Blue Book didn't ensure happiness. They were on the hunt for the next new thing. Raffi leaned forward in his chair to listen.

'It'll be a leap in the dark,' Ada said, 'the perfect answer to "Come As You Really Are Night" at Fenway Court. I for one am not agin' it.'

Amy glowed. 'We'll "stick it to the pricks" with tango.'

'Even better, *tapette* tango, dear!' Ada said. '"Everyone's queer but you and I, and even you are a little queer."'

Tiger Lily ventured a single blink of her eyes—an alligator lounging on the banks of the Yangtze.

'How your stiff-necked *Mayflower* snobs will hate this,' Ada said.

'Making it that much more delectable,' Amy said. She winked at Ada:

Such fireworks as we make, we two!
Because you hate me and I hate you.

'How delicious. I can just see Belle Gardner swanning around her belvedere-for-viewing-achievements while we strut up a storm. Who knows? Maybe we'll be tapped to dance across every avant-garde cul-de-sac in underground Boston. You can discreetly solicit tips, Ada! Who can't use a little extra scratch in these uncertain times?'

'Spoken like one of Freud's famillionaires,' Ada said. 'So easy to speak of earning money when you don't need it. How the rich love to give employment tips to the poor, as if the only thing keeping them in poverty is a lack of gumption.'

Raffi slid his dishwater-red hands unnoticed to the side of his trousers.

'Really, Auntie,' Ephraim said, 'This may be too much. Isn't it enough if we agree to tango man-to-woman?'

'Why not just carry out the garbage?' Amy boomed. 'Nowadays, audiences will accept nothing less than voyeuristic eroticism. They crave pizzazz, dazzle.'

'Remember,' Ada said, 'you're not supposed to use that top-secret word around your important nephew.'

'What I mean to say is, I feel no personal inclination to dance with boys,' Ephraim said. 'Or men. Not to put too fine a point on it.'

'Dare to live out loud,' Ada said. 'Like all of you who suffer from *homophobia nervosa*, you're just denying your true nature.'

'The gentlemen you'll be dancing with will be young men of the first water, such as he who sits to your left,' Amy said.

'I can dance a little,' Raffi said.

'What would have made me think that blind tango wasn't novelty enough?' Victor asked. 'Will I be wearing false eyelashes? And how about a monocle?'

'Oh, but you will! We'll all be wearing disguises!' Amy said.

'Okay,' Victor said. 'I'll wear blackface.'

'We'll be all the rage as the first Brahmin tapette-tango troupe in Boston.'

'To your knowledge,' Ephraim said. 'Maybe the Crowninshields or the Cabots have already started one.'

'I don't think the Cabots have the imagination,' Amy said, 'but the Crowninshields certainly have the criminal genes. If you think there's that possibility then we must hurry. It just wouldn't do to start the second tapette tango troupe in Boston.'

'Melvina Cabot might be game,' Ada said.

'Oh, no,' Amy said. 'I've tried dancing with Melvina on Cape Cod, and in spite of what you're implying, Melvina just doesn't dance backwards.'

'If you ask me, that dried-up old bitch doesn't dance at all.'

'Well, I wasn't asking you,' Amy said. 'It was so long ago. Maybe we've buried the hatchet.'

'Not a good idea in an old New England home.'

Ruth Benedict took her eyes off Raffi and Victor to interrupt: 'I'll need to practice wearing high heels.'

Amy smiled. 'No, Ruthie, you'll be wearing your insensible shoes and dancing with Lorna Doom. Any objections?'

'Ephraim, you can dance with your own shadow, per your custom,' Ada said. 'Is it *camoufleur* or *camoufleuse*?'

'I must say, you're looking lifelike tonight, Aunt Ada,' Ephraim said.

'Mr. Peach?' Amy said.

Raffi bowed.

'You'll be our dance master, demonstrating the way you tangoed on the Continent.'

'I will be most honored to show you what I learned from a few members of the delegation from Uruguay when they visited the Hotel Forum.'

'Here we go again,' Victor said. 'All roads lead to the Forum. Why'd you leave if you loved it so much? Why don't you just hack your heart out and bury it there, for crissake?'

'Sometimes you sound exactly like your father,' Amy said.

'You have a father?' Ada asked. 'You mean a stork didn't just drop you down the chimney at the Parker House?'

'We'll talk about it later, Pete,' Amy said to Ada.

It was obviously time to change the subject. 'Even Caliban had a father,' Raffi said. He took a deep breath and adopted the air of a Neapolitan guide. 'The sexual undertones of the tango are at the very origins of the discipline,' he began. 'Tango sprang up among the dock-workers below the Tropic of Capricorn. The music is an amalgamation from Italy and Africa, blended by pure accident and transmuted on the journey across the sea. Over time, sinewy stevedores offloading cargo found themselves undulating to the strange, new music with a pretty wench who might drift by...'

'Interesting,' Ruth said. 'In 1914 alone, there were a hundred thousand more men than women in Buenos Aires.'

Raffi smiled. 'A most apt observation. Because until such luck arrived and a girl was in eyeshot, the men generally resorted to dancing with each other.'

'Oh, please, take that bull and tie it outside!' Ada said. 'Particularly with each other.'

In the basement that night, Raffi couldn't stand the suspense. 'Miss Lowell mentioned your father,' he said to Victor.

'I'm trying to sleep.'

'Yes, but who is he?'

'He's just another man,' Victor said. 'If I don't talk to him, why should I talk about him to you?' He shifted in his bunk to face the opposite wall.

'Come on, Victor, you know far more about me than I do about you.'

'Too much, in fact,' Victor said. 'Now good night.'

'As you wish.'

A moment later, Victor threw off his covers. 'Saltonstall is my brother, or at least my half-brother. That is, we share the same ofay father.'

'Why don't you use the name Saltonstall?'

'Because my mother's name was White. Or Half-White, or Quarter-White. Where do you stand on the one-drop rule?'

'Sorry, Victor. I wasn't trying to be insensitive.' Raffi thought for a second. 'Do you use your mother's name as some sort of vanishing cream?'

'It's a habit my brother and I adopted as children when we first learned about each other,' Victor said.

'Did your brother get you the job in the hotel?'

'No, I'm there in spite of him. My only pleasure is, he thinks I'm spying on him for our dad, though I haven't spoken to the bastard in over ten years! The Greeks got the story wrong. Oedipus wanted to kill his father so he wouldn't disappoint him.'

'So Miss Lowell was right in saying I'd be teaching an all-Brahmin tapette-tango troupe. Who's your mother, then?'

Victor rolled halfway back over. 'She died when I was pretty young. Tell you what. I'll tell you more when you sing for me.'

'How very operatic,' Raffi said. 'With my dying breath, I'll sing a few notes, you'll drop to your knees, confessing she's the Queen of Sheba, and the curtain falls. Speaking of drama, I'm escorting a young lady I met on the ship for a walk in the park tomorrow. We'll stop at the Orpheum and get tickets for a show late next week.'

'You mean somebody actually responded to your smarmy European advances?'

'Yes. Her name is Beatrice. I fell into the depths of her gaze like the sea at night.'

'This is making me seasick!' Victor said. 'How were you able to look into her eyes, you're so tall?'

'She's quite the willow herself.'

'Why haven't you made a date with her before this?'

'I wanted to establish myself first,' Raffi said, 'so I might court her in a way that will be considered responsible by her family. Her father isn't an easy fish to land.'

'Oh, you're taking him to the opera.'

'In a way. They're all very close.'

'How very foreign,' Victor said. 'What's playing?'

'*L'Orfeo*,' Raffi said. 'At least, I think that's what's on the menu.'

16

Col mal tempo di mare il cefalo diventa caro.
When the seas are rough, the fish are expensive.

BOSTON, 1922

Raffi finished serving dinner. It had been a slow evening, no doubt due to the storm outside, so Victor closed the main dining room early and sent him upstairs to help out in the lobby bar, just in case some poor souls still showed up hungry. Glancing outside the window, he saw a young couple he'd served earlier standing outside the revolving doors. The husband, with the stooped shoulders of The Forgotten, stood in the rain, sheltering his winsome bride. Something in the veteran's look told Raffi that too solicitous a gaze would embarrass, so he returned to brandy-and-cigar service as the man hailed the jitney that offered night tours.

But when Raffi stole a glance at the couple again, he noticed a convention of thaumaturgists had already boarded ahead of them, so the omnibus splashed by without slowing. Raffi watched through the window at the movie playing silently outside in the deluge. He stepped closer and put his palm on the glass. He felt his heart open, and he could hear them as clearly as if he were standing next to them:

'*Don't worry, dear,*' said the veteran of the War to End All Wars. '*There'll be another in no time.*'

A gust of rain carrying half of dreary Boston Harbor with it whooshed below the hotel's canopy and darkened her new shoes.

'*Would you like to go inside?*' the shadow of a man said.

'*No.*' She smiled bravely. '*I can handle anything. You're looking at the president pro-tem of the Springfield Rossini Club! When do you think the next one will come?*'

'*Every fifteen minutes, according to the concierge.*'

Raffi stepped back from the window. Perhaps this was too personal.

After twenty-five minutes, he allowed himself a look at them again and began to feel concern. The sheer silk sacque she'd so carefully picked after scrimping for three months on the grocery bill was bewitching beyond its intended translucence.

'*You're shivering,*' the shadow said. '*Let me give you my coat.*'

'*I wouldn't put on that smelly woolly if I were on the North Pole,*' his wife said.

As another bus splashed by, the shadow looked down at the tweed trench his mother had proudly given him when he went off to Princeton. '*Maybe that was the wrong bus.*'

'*How can one tell?*' she asked.

The man turned his head as if suffocating, searching for breath. A little raindrop that had followed the soldier back from the Argonne Forest landed on his check, as though to whisper, 'You had such high hopes, and now you can't even please your bride. Could four years have passed already?' What was happening to his life? The last time he'd felt this particular splash of rain he was standing on the banks of St. Quentin Canal with Col. Winstel, counting floating bodies.

'*It was painted differently. I don't know. It doesn't matter, does it?*' He looked down at her and smiled. '*Besides, I'm already taking in the sights.*'

Out of modesty, she folded her arms.

'*No, no, no! What I mean is, in this light, your eyes look "blue-after-a-rain."*'

'*Why won't they stop for us?*'

'*Maybe they can sense we're from out of town. Shall I go in and talk with the concierge? He arranged for this clambake. "See the Sights of Beantown!"*'

The rain-swept breeze lifted the hem of her dress, which she pressed down with her hand. '*I guess I really am getting… cold. I feel like even my slip is sopping. Do you think the management of the famous Parker House knows we've been left out here like this?*'

He jingled his keys, checked his watch, lit a cigarette—the secret handshakes of insufficiency. When she wasn't looking, he even stole another look at the schedule. '*We've been out here an hour and fifteen minutes. We might as well go in.*'

'*You have to go in,*' his wife said.

He craned his neck and looked through the glass doors. '*The concierge hasn't been at his desk for an hour. Very poor service if you ask me.*'

'*Who'd be asking you? This is our honeymoon all over again. This is your doing, your plan. Surely if you cared anything at all about me you'd have looked into these tickets, checked on the arrangements. Just look at my gown, these stockings, my hair. These shoes are ruined. I'm soaked to the bone. Don't worry. We'll celebrate our anniversary next year.*' She closed her eyes.

Raffi closed his eyes. He was afraid the soldier, too, knew what she was thinking: you knew how much I wanted this. Bus after bus went by, and were you even man enough to lift up your hand to stop them?

She walked a few paces. '*Can't you help us?*' she asked the door-man, who shrugged and started flipping through the brochure he was handed.

Raffi saw the concierge station was still unmanned and made a note to check it again in a few minutes. But a tall, thin sort walking with a malignant elegance stopped him near registration. He leaned on the desk. 'So where's the sign? Don't worry, I'm not going to check in. You know the man who calls himself Secretary Laughlin? I've got a very important message that needs to be delivered to him, and to him only. Here. You just make sure he gets it. And I'm not asking you, I'm telling you.'

The sealed envelope was inked with crosshairs instead of a name.

Secretary Laughlin was holding court in the bar with his body-guards. Sprawled in a leather club chair, he was red-faced, boasting loudly, the remains of the whisky Raffi had poured for him before he'd thought to ask at his elbow. Raffi gave him the envelope and turned to go when the Secretary called back to him, 'Who gave this to you, boy? Is that Jew still in the lobby?'

Raffi didn't know how to answer. All the color had gone out of the marked man's face, and his hand was shaking. 'The gentleman left without leaving his name.'

Laughlin stumbled to his feet, and the three quickly slipped out the back exit.

So odd. Did this have anything to do with Laughlin's turning up at Sevenels? Raffi felt the hairs standing on the back of his neck as he headed back to the concierge station. Again finding it empty, he inquired at registration, interrogated the bellhops, and dashed out through the lobby doors to rescue the couple in the rain, the lady now in full distress, the gentleman no longer her lord nor master.

'Madame and monsieur,' he said. 'May I be of service to you?'

'You!' the husband said. 'Where's the concierge? For that matter, where's the manager? Your hotel sold me these counterfeits.' He waved the bus tags, which Raffi recognized immediately as ducats to a service that ended promptly at sundown. 'Assurances were made'—he dropped his voice—'to me.'

'I'm here to help you,' Raffi said. 'Come inside and we'll sort this out. Let me offer you this wrap.' He tucked a cashmere blanket around the lady's shoulders.

'Don't you touch me,' she said as he led her by the elbow to the lobby, her husband following, his neck red. 'You're not the concierge. I remember you, you imposter. You're our waiter!'

'Tell me what's happened.' He listened intently as the words spilled out of their mouths, showering in the undischarged voltage of their fury so that it sparked about him and they could see the impact of each syllable as he demonstrated his understanding. He gasped, somehow without overreaching, at each mention of the rain. He seemed modestly to take in her ruined garments without focusing on anything so intimate as to be forward. He frowned with lovely gravity at the most 'important' parts of their story—without ever appearing to be amused. He telegraphed that he was prepared to take over her cold and wetness, even the embarrassment she might have felt seeing her outfit, so carefully planned, and her hair, so carefully coiffed, so completely drenched. He looked deeply into each of their eyes so they could see all the way down the corridors of his sincerity—beyond the letter drop and the fire stairs to the single open window at the end of the shaft.

For a flash Voluptuo flew past the shaft, more a shadow then a fully imagined bird, as Raffi stood there, rebuilding the silence in his head until his thoughts were clean and clear.

Breathing evenly, he stopped time. In the gentleman's shoes, he marveled, how deeply a little rainstorm can cut you, and how completely. Don't worry, I'll restore you. He called on his gift again and slipped into her thoughts. This is your one night in Boston. How you've looked forward to this, and how ashamed you are for being angry and for letting me see your anger, which makes you angrier. The wetness and the lost tour are surface wounds. But more deeply, you and I both know I've got to save you from how you're about to behave. 'This is entirely our fault. I can't tell you how shattered I am,' Raffi said. 'This is savagely unjust. I will personally make this up to you. Though it may feel otherwise to you right now, this evening is not ruined. In fact, it is about to begin.'

'Knock yourself out.' The man's shoulders relaxed a little.

'I don't know what you could possibly do to salvage it.' A slight lilt returned to her voice. 'There's nothing you can do!'

Her words stirred the curtains of Raffi's subconscious. Of a sudden a wakeful dream returned him to the scene of Dr. Cufflinks's evasions and frightful prophesies—a glimpse of the abyss. What do you do when there's nothing you can do? You keep your scars clean.

In a near whisper, he individuated each word to match the cadence of her speech. 'This is the worst thing I've known to happen to any guest, anywhere. It's so maddeningly unfair to the two of you on your special evening that I have to tell you confidentially it's making me reconsider my entire career in the hospitality industry.'

'Baloney.' The wet tigress allowed a tiny smile to escape.

'Where's a pistol when you need it?' Raffi reached across the *verde antico* expanse of the guest-services desk and whacked himself on the side of the head with a copy of *Comfort* magazine. He nodded when the husband chuckled. 'First, a beverage. My gift to you to start our apology.'

'Do you think we can be bought off with a drink?'

Raffi led them to two leather chairs snuggled beside a Tudor fireplace in the same private nook he kept ready behind the bar for Laughlin—who by the look on his face wasn't returning anytime soon—and whisked two of his signature elixirs into their hands. Not only was this sheltered place out of the howling wind and driving rain, it was out of earshot of the other guests. 'I'll be on the telephone for a moment, completing arrangements for the rest of your magical evening,' he said, warming them with more eye contact. 'I give you my word I am not disappearing. You are my first and only priority. I won't be attending to anything, or anybody, else.'

When Raffi returned, he was glad to see they were holding hands.

'This is quite satisfying,' the man said. 'It's a kind of martini, right?'

'First, I understand your evening is ruined,' Raffi said. 'I am so personally devastated. And it's true, all of the night touring buses have stopped running.'

The lady almost spit. 'See? See!'

'So I'm arranging for something far, far superior that would normally be much more costly and much more exclusive and romantic than one of those crowded rattletraps for the average tourists.'

As they began to relax into their first cocktail, a maid came in and with barely a murmur provided them with cozy slippers and took away their shoes to be cleaned. When they were halfway through their second, she returned with their shoes in a basket, perfectly restored.

Raffi checked his watch. 'Madame and monsieur, your carriage awaits.' He led the pair past a flock of fauteuils and through the doors to the street. The moon slid out of the clouds, its beams flashing on the equipage of a jet barouchette pulled by six horses. Below the dash, in tiny white letters, was the legend 'Puritan Stables, Russia Wharf, Boston.' At the reins, in black livery with shiny tails, was the milkman. He winked.

'Your guide is Generalissimo Marino, with his trusty steed, Otis.' Raffi pointed to the shiniest of the horses, sporting a plume. 'Together they'll show you everything there is to know about Boston—all the sights—because this coach is yours, with my compliments, for the rest of the night.' He leaned to the lady. 'This is your husband's idea.'

She spun to her spouse and threw her arms around him. 'My hero!'

The gentleman gave Raffi a nod. 'In all the annals of swelldom, there's never been such a hotel. Maybe you should be the manager! What'd you say your name was?'

'Addison Saltonstall,' a voice said from behind.

Raffi turned to the hotelier as the coach jostled to a clop toward Faneuil Hall before disappearing in the pell mell of cabs and honking cars.

'Just what are you up to?' Saltonstall asked. 'Aren't you supposed to be in the scullery? Is there something wrong?'

'I am most pleased to report that everything is right, sir. You will find every dish washed, even the tureens on the back shelf. To every dinner bell we have restored a silver chime. I'd heard the concierge was called away because his wife is having a baby. I was finished with my shift and thought I'd pitch in.'

'Why wasn't I informed of this?' Now it was Saltonstall with the folded arms.

'I sent word to your office upstairs, but Miss Tilden said you weren't there.'

With the eloquence of privilege, the manager renewed his stare.

'Then the receptionist said you were in Bulfinch Ballroom, but Mr. Rexroth couldn't find you there,' Raffi said.

Not so much a smile as a press of the lips. 'Are you suggesting I should have been somewhere I wasn't, Mr. Peach? Do you intend to fire me? It appears you've made yourself very conspicuous this evening. But a good hotel is run with an invisible hand.'

The doorman crashed in before Raffi could stop him. 'You should have seen how he turned those two guests around. He is a wonder!'

'Will wonders never cease,' Saltonstall said. A slow exhale. 'Since my whereabouts have been called into question, my little wonder, I'll be in my office for the next hour.'

'Yes, sir,' Raffi said. 'May I bring up some coffee?'

'Don't smoothe me. I think I know how to order coffee in my own hotel.' He took three steps, wheeled. 'Have you any inkling how much disruption your "enthoosiasms" are causing? I have complaints from every department about your wanting to "learn things at all levels of the organization," your intrusions, your prying. Registration and even housekeeping are reeling from your "attentions." Maybe this is a Continental thing? Because any gentleman knows there's such a thing as trying too hard. For my money, guests should never sense unseemly effort. I hardly envy you this strange, and certainly crass, magnetism you're so sure you possess.'

So strange you flirt through insult, a paneled sexuality. Not that you're aware of it. Who's your Diletti, Mr. Saltonstall? What on earth is he doing to you, and why do you particularly resent that I'm Italian?

Last night, Victor had offered a hint about his half-brother before rolling off to sleep: 'You don't want to know. He and his wife share some secrets. A castrato loses his manhood but once. The rest of us are castrated every day.'

'Salty!'

Raffi and his manager turned to the doughty voice. As Amy and Ada approached and took center stage, Saltonstall's tone shifted from overlord to overwhelmed.

'Miss Lowell!' Saltonstall said, 'What a delight! I haven't seen you since your brother discovered Pluto! Will you be having a nightcap with us?'

'You should be proud of yourself to have discovered the resourceful Mr. Peach,' she said, extending her hand to Raffi, who kissed it, along with Ada's. 'Fresh from the Forum in Rome! You keep this up, Salty, and you'll no longer be running the frumpiest hotel in Boston. I have a reception for Mr. Tarkington scheduled for the Lenox, but I have a mind to change that and hold it here. Could you personally take care of that, Mr. Peach?'

'I'd be delighted to accommodate you, Miss Lowell,' Raffi said.

'Dinner too, for about 100?'

Saltonstall stepped in front of Raffi. 'I'll be honored, Miss Lowell.'

'Smart move on your part, Salty, to pick this peach off the tree.'

Saltonstall worked late that night with his chief of staff, Wendell Everett.

'He's very disruptive and arrogant. I think I've had enough,' Saltonstall said.

'He is a bit much, but don't you think he's onto something with his "Club Dinners for College Men"?' Everett said. 'We're flooded with calls about the advertisements, and the Revere Room is booked three weeks in advance. You know it's all about the young people now.'

'No one's indispensible here,' Saltonstall said. 'He's too tall, too foreign, too unaccountably hole-and-corner. I can't put my finger on it, but something about him just makes me ill at ease, and that can't be good for guests. For all we know, he's unhealthy, with who knows what manner of infections he carries or disease. To top it off, he thinks he can choose whatever job he wants. Make him leave of his own account, and there it is.'

'Sir, are you sure? He's a natural fixer, and people are starting to look up to him.'

'All the more reason to cut him down,' Saltonstall said. 'Keep him out of my sight, I tell you! I'm leaving this in your hands, Everett. Give him some assignments that will take, ah, the wind out of Mr. Peach's sails.'

Everett cuffed himself on the side of the head. 'Tomorrow's Beans & Scrod Night, the one night a month upper-crust Boston likes to play at being country folk with "good honest New England fare at old-fashioned prices." Our guests are so delicate, even then they think their shit don't stink!'

'I think I know where you're going with this,' Saltonstall said, 'and I like it. Learn a bit about the hotel business from the bottoms up. Perhaps we have an opening in our custodial department.' He smiled nastily. '*Buonanotte*, Mr. Peach.'

Everett nodded. 'I'll inform him we're shorthanded, and that we need him to clean all of the restrooms, both "buoys" and "gulls." Then we'll seal off all entrances and leave him in there to die.'

'No,' Saltonstall said. 'Let me tell him.'

17

Chi di altro si veste, subito si spoglia.
He who dresses in the clothes of others is quickly undressed.

QUINCY, 1922

Ephraim overslept and missed his train to the shipyard, so he tried his best to be grateful for the lift. But did it have to be in the maroon Pierce Arrow with the slate gray ostrich interior?

'Thanks for the ride, Aunt Amy.'

'My pleasure, dear,' she said, looking out the window. 'Good God, get a load of this ship. Is this what you've been bragging about? Ada! Wake up! You've got to see this!'

'Mmmph.'

'Roy, you're driving much too fast.' Amy tapped on the glass partition to alert her chauffeur in matching maroon livery. 'We're trying to get a look.'

'Certainly, Miss Lowell.' Downshifting, he eased the 14-cylinder engine to a softer purr.

'Ada, you're falling asleep again!'

'Thanks for telling me.'

'No,' Amy said. 'You're really missing something.'

'Don't tell me the Harvard princeling can show me something new in the world.'

'Shhhh!' Ephraim said.

At that, the actress threw back the Navajo blanket she and Amy had picked up during their holiday to observe the tribes in New Mexico the previous summer, when Roy drove them on a grand tour of the Southwest.

She followed Amy's gaze and was taken aback by the *Saxon's* disorienting paint job of stripes running out in all directions. When a cloud floated over, it seemed as if the ship had just two smokestacks, but when the sun came out, two more appeared and she was headed in a different direction at a brisk twelve knots, though she was still tied fast to her dock.

'This is stirring, nearly thrilling,' Amy said. 'Talk about the art of war.'

It was Ephraim's turn to crouch down, as if he wanted to pull the blanket over his head. Couldn't she ever leave him alone?

'Ephraim, I don't like the tone of your silence,' Amy said.

'I told you, it's supposed to be a military secret.'

'Such interesting secretions. You'll have to tell us more about them at dinner.'

'Don't hold your breath.'

'Something in your subconscious must have made you bring us here. Don't you think so, Ada? Doesn't that Jewish witch doctor say there are no coincidences? Or is it accidents?'

'You understand it's a matter of national security, right?' Ephraim pursed his lips.

'Yes. Our little secret.'

He detected a gleam of self-satisfaction in her eyes.

'Roy, go ahead and take us right up to the gate!' Amy called.

'No!' Ephraim said. 'Nobody must see this car. Please pull up three blocks short, Roy, by the little tree.'

'Yes, sir.'

'Did you bring your lunch with you?' Amy asked.

'We all eat at twelve in the cafeteria.'

'You could take one of Roy's apples. Roy is rarely without his Roxbury Russets. Right, Roy?'

'Certainly, Miss Lowell.'

'No, thank you,' Ephraim said.

One of the polished fruits appeared in Amy's hand, and she held it out to him. He slapped it away and it fell to the floor with a thud. Roy lowered his head.

'Don't take it out on Roy. You know how he prizes his apples. He grows them in a little garden in his side yard, right in the middle of the city, don't you, Roy?'

'Picked it this morning, Miss Lowell. My wife makes that spicy applesauce.'

Amy leaned down, retrieved the apple from the floor, dusted it, and tucked it into Ephraim's work-jacket pocket. 'Love the duds,' she said, taking in his steel-toed boots and rough duck coveralls.

The shipyard came alive as workmen streamed around the motorcar. Some peered in the tinted windows as if to ask, 'Who are those privileged bluestockings within, and that cipher of a young man in a workingman's costume?' Ephraim coughed and quickly touched his handkerchief to his nose, stimulated by embarrassment. 'Good bye. I thank you for the ride to work but precious little other consideration.' He walked three steps toward the gate before chopping back to the car. He leaned in. 'And thank you, Roy.'

'It was a pleasure, Mr. Lowell.'

'Take the long way home, Roy,' Ada said. 'Via Chinatown.'

'Yes ma'am.'

The sedan turned left, then right on Atlantic Avenue, and left again. Dreamlike Chinatown leaned through the tall glass windows as Ada caught some winks, her chin nodding on her blanket between occasional jerks to consciousness if a slash of sunlight pierced the tinted glass to her eyes. Bicycles flashed by. Fruit vendors called from their stands. Elders born in Shanghai tottered about, doing their daily business as though they were still in the Far East, not in the land of the bean and the cod.

'Roy,' Amy said, transfixed by the Mandarin dragons and green roof tiles among the Dim Sum palaces, tobacconists, and drug stores. 'Could you please show us which restaurant is Tiger Lily's new one?'

'I'll be glad to, Miss Lowell. But Miss Lily opened two last month. That's eight now.'

'She's become a very powerful businessman,' Amy said. 'Her main office isn't even in Chinatown anymore.'

'There's a lesson for you,' Ada said.

After their morning shift at Underwood, Beatrice and Dorotea rode the rail south along the coast to Quincy. At the Shipyard, they showed their badges, entered Warehouse No. 7, unlocked the canteen room, and set up their matching coffee carts for the next shift.

'Looks like rain,' Beatrice said.

'Hope so. Everyone wants coffee when it rains.'

Into the basket of her coffee urn, Beatrice loaded mounds of loamy S.S. Pierce java above a reservoir of cold water, then flicked a toggle switch. In unison with her twin, she tended to an electric kettle. When it began to steam, she spooned out the contents of a large container of Epicure Flowery Tip Orange Pekoe Tea, product of Macao. The tin sported a tall, stooping Oriental with a basket in one hand and a white 'Tea' pennant in the other, forever crossing an arched bridge. She looked at the exotic figure more closely. 'I wonder what Raffi's doing.'

He'd sent her a single communiqué on extravagant hotel stationery, telling her everything was set for their date on April 7, a picnic and a walk in the Park.

When Dorotea didn't answer, Beatrice lifted the canister and held its label up to the light. Why, this eunuch was no better prepared for the modern world than the young woman from Peking she'd seen on the newsreels whose own mother had crushed and bound her feet in infancy. The things we do for beauty. Catching sight of her sister's new kitten-heeled, pointy-toed shoes that pinched so they nearly threw her off balance, she laughed. They finished putting out packages of S.S. Pierce Scotch Oatmeal Cookies and Ritz Crackers and wheeled their way into the crowds.

'We really shouldn't have carts too close,' Beatrice said. 'I could move toward the bow of this ship, and you could try the next pier where that brand new one's just arrived.'

Heading south along the great cement curve, her sister grew smaller as she approached the stern of the USS *Tucker*.

Beatrice rolled forward, the *Saxon* straight ahead.

High on a scaffold, Ephraim painted the tip of a black ray that started near the bridge and rose across the superstructure. He looked down and spied the coffee girls pushing their carts along the slow crescent of concrete beach bordered by an iron rail that connected the many piers of the shipyard.

'Joe!' sang the light-haired one in that sweet, textured voice.

'Sweets!' the other chimed in, but he barely heard. The blonde had the blue dress on again. Her other two were plum and black. What did it matter what her sister wore? He took a deep breath and looked for his supervisor. To his relief, Mr. Wallace was not there. Carefully, he tamped the lid back on his can of paint.

Roskowski, who regularly stood beside him as they painted their swooping rays, blinked his eyes. He wiped his mouth with his sleeve. 'Where are you going?'

'I'm going to talk to the coffee doll,' Ephraim said.

Roskowski looked down at the sun's rays kissing the top of the girl's head, at the alluring way she pulled the cart behind her, and said, 'I'll come, too.'

'You will not,' Ephraim said.

'I suppose you saw her first.'

'I said I was going down first.'

'Relax, comrade. I'm just going down to take a shit.'

They clambered to the quarterdeck. The officer of the day raised his eyebrows when they arrived to sign out but waved them by when Roskowski said, 'Latrine.' The big Russian sketched a jazz step in reverence for Old Glory on the fantail before stomping across the gangplank. He disappeared, and Ephraim was alone with the girl amid a swarm of supervisors and hordes of men watching instead of working.

Slowly, the line moved forward toward her cart. Ephraim saw her eyes had nearly a violet cast, the shade the ocean turns just after a storm. Her hair was drawn up, baby-soft as it kissed the back of her neck.

'Here you are, sir,' she said with a lilt to each man.

'Mmmph.'

'And what can I get for you, sir?' she said to Ephraim.

'You don't have to call me sir,' he said, forgetting to use his Polish accent. 'I'm not one of these supervisors.' How intoxicating. Could she see the real him through his spattered clothes?

'We have coffee, doughnuts, crackers,' she said and laughed. 'At some point you have to choose!'

'Why must I?'

'Because there are… eleven people waiting behind you, sir.'

'All right. Fine,' Ephraim said. He hadn't felt them approach. Had they all been listening to his every word? Then, too, was that the traitor Roskowski skulking behind him? He turned beet red and bolted from the line.

18

È fruscio di scopa nuova.
It is the noise of a new broom.

BOSTON, 1922

Stadt stood with the new hires in front of the State Capitol. Teeming pedestrians emerging from the subway gave them cover. 'He'll step out there after the vote,' he said, pointing to the stairs below the golden dome.

'Below the big set of doors,' Carlo said, nodding.

'There'll be photographers, handshakes. Then he'll cross the street here.'

'No place else he can cross?'

'He will cross here,' Stadt said. The two Russians craned their heads like tourists. No doubt he was the closest thing they'd come to having a guide. 'Been here before?' he asked. Shrugs all around.

'Sorry, Pops,' Carlo said.

'You're a wise guy,' Stadt said to Carlo. 'Wise guys chew gum when they talk. How far do you think that's going to get you? Do you chew gum on stage?'

Carlo swallowed and turned bright red.

'You're standing in for Johnny Cavallaro, right?'

'Who told you that?'

'Well, I know the old Blue Grotto,' Stadt said. 'That's what your nightclub used to be called in its heyday. But I know it's not fashionable to have any sense of nostalgia. Where are you from?'

'Mostly Naples,' Carlo said.

'Mostly.'

'I was the number-one draw for the White Star liners.'

Stadt turned away. 'At five p.m., you and I will be standing right here, having a smoke. Your friends will wait by the subway entrance.

III

I'll point Mr. X out to you and you'll start following him, at a distance. Then, I'll get on the subway and go home to dinner, leaving you to make sure the boys take care of things with Mr. X.'

'What exactly are we supposed to do?'

'You'll be passing on the message, and the boys will make sure he understands it. He'll head to the crest of Beacon Street and then walk slowly down the hill until Beacon turns into School. He's a big guy, but he's sixty-six. He won't be any trouble, though he'll have guards.'

'You mean we're going to be fighting? How many guards?'

'There've always been two. A tough guy from Charlestown and a local. They'll spread out, one ahead, one behind, and let the Secretary walk down to the hotel. It's just like clockwork. Let's start walking that way ourselves.'

'Okay.' Carlo shoved his hands in his pockets.

'Don't do that. It's rude, and it spoils your clothes. Makes you look sinister.'

'Mr. Stadt, I'm a lover, not a fighter.'

'You aren't a singer, either, I'll wager. More like the crooner du jour.'

'I'm packing 'em in, Mr. Stadt. I don't want to mess that up.'

'I'll pay you an extra $25 to keep these guys in line. To make sure everything goes off okay and to report back to me.'

'I've never hurt anybody,' Carlo said.

They descended the hill until the corridor of buildings on either side of Beacon Street shut down the light. Stadt pointed out three alleys between Bowdoin and Somerset where they could dissolve if necessary. 'You're just taking a little walk, that's all.'

As they approached Tremont Street, they passed the Splendid. 'Not a bad place to have lunch,' Stadt said, then continued, 'Okay, we're crossing the street. This is the Parker House Hotel. Ever heard of Parker House rolls?'

'What exactly am I getting into?' Carlo asked.

'How about Boston cream pie? They invented that here, too.'

They passed the white marble walls of the hotel festooned with signs for the Revere Room. They stepped around the doorman guarding the guests' crocodile luggage. The alarmed patrons of the fancy hotel melted away at the sight of the big guys from a different world. As he passed the glass door, Stadt saw his shadows at his heels. He didn't particularly trust Russians, perhaps because his father had come from Minsk. Maybe he just didn't like these goons. He looked at the taller of the two crows and shuddered. When it comes to be my time, I just know it'll be someone like you. It sounded like words to a song—why doesn't the sod croon that? He looked at Carlo.

Slipping into Roll Alley in back of the hotel, Stadt pulled up short. He spoke a single word in *byelaruskaya*. The taller crow slipped behind and quickly pinned up Carlo, legs dangling. 'Hey, cut it out,' the singer cried and tried to twist away, but the Russian knew who was in charge and ignored the boy. Stadt made a circular motion with his index finger and the Russian began to revolve the thrashing Carlo around. 'Pay attention and look carefully at exactly where you are,' Stadt said to Carlo. 'North—King's Chapel Burying Ground and City Hall.' Carlo's kicking dress shoes scraped on the cobblestones. 'East—School Street toward Faneuil Hall.' Carlo moaned. Okay, at least now he was getting it. 'South—alley toward the theater district. Well, that goes nowhere.' Stadt looked up into Carlo's eyes. 'West—the Parker House, the center of the universe, the hub of the Hub. Kid, are you listening?' Stadt viciously stabbed a punch into Carlo's gut while the tall crow gripped his arms tighter. The assault came so fast the singer didn't have time to tighten his belly muscles. Carlo sputtered, his eyes flashing with anger as he thrashed to get free. Both Russians giggled as he cried out in pain.

'So you will remember this place,' Stadt said. 'This is the spot.'

19

Se la luna è sveglia, il marinaio va a dormire.
If the moon is out, the sailor can go to sleep.

BOSTON, 1922

Raffi made his way through the musical greens of Boston Common in search of his Beatrice. As the appointed hour grew nearer, he'd begun to worry she hadn't gotten his note, or she'd met someone else. He hoped against hope she'd remember the date, her father would let her come, and her sister wouldn't stand in the way.

And then, in the light breeze, he caught sight of her—a single white rose in a spray of pink. The curtain of willows shading her waved gently in time with her aureate hair. A flash of disconcerting memory darkened his enjoyment of her as a cloud passed over and he recalled the slate memorials that were embellished with such trees in the graveyard near Van Cortlandt Park.

The sun came out again when she looked up quickly from her bench, smiled, and let her eyelids fall. 'I knew your footsteps.'

'Dear Beatrice! Two spirits, one mind. Would you like to take a ride in one of the swan boats?' He motioned toward a dock surrounded by a flock of pedal-powered vessels carved in the shape of the graceful water birds.

'It sounds so extravagant but thrilling. You could be my knight, like in *Lohengrin*. And I mustn't learn your secret.'

The dockside herdsman had it all wrong. Far from having eyes for Beatrice, he flirted with Raffi when he gave him his change, caressing with lingering fingers. 'Do you require any special attentions? No? Enjoy yourself, fella.' As though it were a marker in his subconscious, the blackguard pushed the last penny into his palm, hard. 'When the tomato lets you down, look me up.'

Raffi was grateful Beatrice was out of earshot, sliding into the only black swan in the fleet, so the exchange cast no cloud over what was already the best day of his life. Leaving shore, he put his hand on hers. 'How's your family?'

'They're fine,' Beatrice said. 'I think Papa might get a promotion.'

'And your mother?'

'She loves working at the factory, too, in the advertising and mail room. My sister and I work mornings in the processing line. Then we moonlight, serving coffee at the shipyard.'

'Moonlight.' He leaned his head against hers. 'A lovely turn of phrase.'

He listened as she told him she'd put in her papers to join the Camouflage Corps. 'They need more workers,' she said.

'I know you'll think this is selfish,' Raffi said. 'But please be careful for me.'

'They're offering great money, and there's a chance for advancement. Dorotea's already started taking outside jobs with a company that caters fancy parties because she's getting sick of pushing a cart around for people who are just going to complain the coffee isn't fresh.' She touched his lips. 'So how's the hotel business?'

'It is "the" hotel, Beatrice. The Parker House is the oldest resting place for vacationers and travelers in the United States.'

'It sounds like a cemetery. What do you do there?'

'It's almost what don't I do! You might think the devil's at the Underwood factory, but at the Parker House, the devil's in the details, as my boss, Mr. Saltonstall, so delights in telling me.'

As their swan passed below a bridge, time skipped. In the gliding shade he kissed her. Once the boat landed at the maidenhead, they disembarked and hand in hand stepped gently around the dockworker's stare.

With late afternoon deepening into twilight, Raffi spread a tablecloth below a dragon's-claw willow and they dined on a salad of endives with fresh oysters. Afterward, he offered her champagne. 'So special,' she said sweetly and smiled, careful not to examine too closely the bottle only half full, obviously a filched leftover from the hotel. Leaning together, they watched the lights twinkle in the modern buildings surrounding the park.

'We're fireflies, all,' Beatrice said. 'So funny to crave isolation in these new "apartments."'

A band started playing, and they listened in drowsy attention. Two hours later, the night had slipped into deep blue. He helped her to her feet. 'I have a little surprise for you. I've been able to save up just enough for our tickets now. It's only a short walk this way.'

Turning east from Tremont Street, they dropped a dark block toward the Orpheum to get rush tickets for the following week's show. 'It's the new thing,' Raffi explained in *vocce concierge*. 'Snap them up at curtain and get twenty-five percent off. The idea is, if you're already here, you may want to return with your friends.'

'Very sensible,' Beatrice said. 'Or just buy one ticket, and you can sit on my lap.'

Raffi took pleasure in the rosy blush that appeared below her wide-brimmed hat with the satin ribbon that deepened the blue of her eyes. It was the same hat her sister had worn while spying at them from behind one of the ship's smokestacks.

She paused and let her eyes fall. 'You have a walking stick? Why didn't I see it before?'

Now it was his turn to blush. 'I know it looks a bit much, Beatrice, but it was given to me by a friend in Rome who swore he was a descendant of the Medici from Florence. Don't you think it gives me a leg up?'

'Of course it does.'

'I hope you're looking forward to seeing *Orfeo ed Eurydice*,' he said.

'Have you seen it before?' she asked.

'In Rome I saw *L'Orfeo*, the Monteverdi version,' Raffi said. 'They cut the lights, and like a sloop tacking into the darkness, the music followed Orpheus into the Stygian depths. Hell was served up dark red, with lurid lanterns. But here in Boston, when Orpheus rows the raft across the River of the Dead, a mixture of Lux Soap Flakes and particles of gold foil is released by stage hands shaking a muslin cradle above the lights. Snow dances on stage.'

'Snow! Their Hell is cold and white,' Beatrice said. 'Couldn't Orpheus just skate over the River of the Dead then? I just hope they don't have masks. Masks scare me.'

'If only we didn't have to wear them,' Raffi said.

'Ah, but the audience insists on it.' Beatrice raised a hand to her lips. 'It's so sad when he breaks his deal with Pluto by turning back to make sure Eurydice's still following him. Why must beauty always be wedded to sorrow?'

'Don't worry, I read in the paper that this version is Gluck's. I think Pluto was cut from the cast,' Raffi said. 'It's a different storyline, with a happy ending.'

'Maybe they thought that would play better in the States,' Beatrice said. 'Americans always have to laugh, laugh, laugh, whereas we Italians love nothing better than a good cry.'

'Well, we'll see if you can have one without the other,' Raffi said.

With its walnut doors flung open below a massive marble fan, the Orpheum's scarlet interior grew as they approached. Billowing clouds of steam rose from vents in the sidewalk. He was delighted to hear the song of a nightingale curl from recesses in the white façade. They were vagrants here just as he and Beatrice were. They'd all flown across the sea. Below sparking guide wires, with a rumble and a screech, a streetcar stopped and opened its doors, waiting.

A second electric car arrived, then a third. Raffi checked his watch as the first bolters emerged into the warm night, the show still in their heads. Buzzing and happy, they took their trolley seats with a liquidity surpassing that of the rats in Roll Alley.

As the rest of the crowd swarmed the street, he slipped to the box-office window and quickly secured two tickets on the lip of Balcony B, center.

'I didn't even know we still had these left for next Friday,' the attendant said. 'They aren't on this sheet. How'd you even know to ask for them?'

'A good concierge makes it his business to know such things.'

Stepping away, Raffi and Beatrice passed glass viewing boxes trumpeting coming attractions. A graybeard was slapping up a new poster, and they strolled up to see. First the man tacked the bottom into the cork liner. Then he slowly rolled the poster to reveal the dramatic face of the great Italian eunuch Alessandro Moreschi. 'One night only. Direct from Teatro alla Scala. Saturday, June 21, 8 p.m. Emil Wessler conducting.'

Raffi caught his breath. The first day of summer. It was the exact image Diletti had shown him so many lifetimes ago. Through the haze of years he looked again at the smoky likeness, the chiaroscuro eyes, the striped sash. 'I'd so like to hear him perform,' he said. 'I never got up the nerve in Rome. There was always an excuse—an event at the hotel, I was too busy...' He was so stunned to find his past reaching to him across the sea that his mind seemed to ignore everything but the need to hear Moreschi. It became a catechism in his brain. This poster, the Orpheum, Beatrice…'Will you see him with me, Beatrice?'

She laughed. 'Easy does it, Romeo. That's in June. Let's try to make it through *Orpheus and Eurydice* next Friday.'

Raffi looked back at the bill. Maybe this faded eunuch, who'd learned the trick of eternal life, was the only person on earth who might tell him what to do. A piercing desire struck through his heart not just to see Moreschi, and hear him, but to talk to him, privately. I need to ask you.

A loud woman dragging her husband pushed him aside and thumbed her nose at the poster. 'Look,' she sneered at Moreschi. 'Who wants to hear that old crap? I'll take jazz any day.'

With an electric jolt, as though touched by a tram cable, Raffi was struck again how much times and tastes had changed. 'Where's your shadow?' he teased Beatrice, pretending to survey the crowd, its murmurs, scrapes, and scufflings—it having started, gently, to rain.

'Dorotea doesn't like violence.'

'Then *L'Orfeo* is not the show for her,' Raffi said. 'Maybe she'd like this version. Gluck was floating the idea that you can bring somebody back to life with love.' Still in front of the Moreschi poster, he took Beatrice's hand and dropped his voice. 'Beatrice, darling, do you remember I was trying to tell you something aboard ship? I have an injury,' Raffi said.

'From the war? We're all the walking wounded.'

The dancing wounded. The singing wounded. 'When I worked at the Forum, the streets were full of veterans, with wounds both visible and invisible.' Before he'd even set off from Naples to Rome after getting off the steamer as a lonely youth, he'd seen some soldiers boarding another bus and rubbed his eyes. Had he recognized one or two of the choristers?

'Is your wound… visible?' she asked.

Raffi said nothing.

'Is it a matter of excitability?'

'We're going to have to leave a little to the imagination. My injury permits me to consider how others might feel while I make love to them.'

'Oh, my poor darling,' she said tenderly. 'I am certain there are… all kinds of love.'

She looked away. For a minute Raffi thought he saw real fear in her eyes—and something else he couldn't put his finger on, though somehow he knew it wasn't about him. 'It wasn't the war, my dear girl. I had a procedure when I was a boy, to become, you know, like him.' He pointed to Moreschi. 'The clearest of male sopranos.'

To his relief, Beatrice put her hand over his lips and nodded with her clear, steady eyes. 'Maybe someday you'll sing for me.'

He laughed. 'Before you and God, I will not. But I will devote myself to you. It will be my pleasure to give you pleasure. And if you find that is still not enough, I promise to be your faithful friend.'

'That's something I've never had.'

He gently touched her waist just above the curve of her hip, careful to achieve just the right pressure with the warmth of his hand, as though he were sending waves of love through her skin. When he felt her sigh, he took her right hand and slid his thumb into her palm. Slowly he leaned his forehead down until it touched hers.

'Do I have to wait until next Friday to see you again?' he asked.

'We have dinner on Sunday,' Beatrice said. 'It won't be like it was on ship. Mama is in her element now, and Dad has established himself, so you'll find them much more gracious. Could you come the day after tomorrow?'

'I'll look forward to it,' Raffi said. Beatrice stared directly at him. The shadows around her eyes were much bigger now. She was even more striking than his dream of her. Behind her, more people spilled out of the Orpheum. He put his long arms around her and kissed her while onlookers stared.

She took out a slip of paper and started to scribble her address in Italian, then stopped and blushed. Careful not to draw a line through the seven or cross the zero—because it was not the American way, he guessed—she wrote her address in careful English and handed it to him. Really, it wasn't so much a matter of reading her mind as falling in love with it and beginning to know it. 'Look!' He reached out to catch big, wet raindrops. They stepped inside the entrance amid the percussive *thwaps* of umbrellas being thrust open and watched together until the darkest clouds moved on. When the rain eased to a gentle drizzle, he reached for her hand. 'I'll take you home.'

'You will not,' Beatrice said proudly. 'You still have your night shift, and besides, it's close. I have my own token to the Metro, and remember, don't look back!'

'I'll see you Sunday,' he said. 'Don't worry, I'll leave my extra leg at home.'

She blended into the crowd, and he crossed the street. His natural stride was so large he could reach the hotel in minutes. He started up Hamilton Place and was halfway up the hill to the Park when he turned for one more glance of his lovely girl and heard the steaming screech, the shrill rails, the unending scream.

A crowd foamed around a single stopped electric car. He ran to the spot to find Beatrice dead on the cobblestones and people looking down. 'I know her!' he cried. But his Beatrice was no longer there.

Her lovely eyes were wide open but opaque as Victor's, her eyelids still. Her lips were red and glistening with individual drops of rain. With the world rushing through his ears, he pushed people aside and put his head on her cooling heart, but it was not beating. She looked like the exquisite bird he'd seen at night near Park Street Incline, fallen from a tree, with no apparent reason for its death beyond the fact that it wasn't alive. He flailed his arms, and the crowd jumped back. His chest heaved, and his convulsive cries of grief were so disturbingly unmanly that soon he himself was at the vortex of the crowd's upset, with Beatrice nearly forgotten, though he did hear someone say, 'Italian girl,' by which he meant something less than a girl. A reduced presence.

Her quiet form was covered in a gray blanket and conducted into the back of an ambulance heading for Massachusetts General. The klaxon horn sounded, and after the policemen barred Raffi's entry with billy clubs and pushed him back, he stood and watched, drowning in her loss and the horror of his culpability. Should he run after the ambulance to be with Beatrice? What would she want?

That helped. She was such a reassuring note of clarity. He ran to the hospital and stood with her still body in the electric loneliness until three doctors shook their heads. Thrusting his hands in his pockets, he found the piece of paper, and he knew what he had to do next.

144 Fulton Street, No. 303

He ran at top speed, scuffing his fancy shoes, hoping to get hold of her parents before they heard the news from a stranger. He ran crying in the rain. Death by tram, lovers at the verge. I am an operatic cliché.

Certainly he wasn't a man. A man would have walked her home after the date, not left her at the hands of the Metro or Boston's finest or this 'hospital.' A man would have forced the ambulance to admit him, relative or not. A man would find a way to turn back time to stop this from happening. All of a sudden he damned himself as the eunuch he was, for his hairless body, his child's penis sliding uselessly up and down his cotton undergarments below his itchy wool pants as he plunged on in the rain. He could usually push these thoughts out of his splitting head—why tell a fish he's drowning?—but not now. This was his fault. No sliding away from it. Beatrice had been alive when she'd trusted him to escort her, and under his watch she'd slipped to the other side of the mirror. If nothing else, he would take responsibility for this. He was the one who had turned to look back.

Back at the Orpheum, the cleanup crew was busy at its shift. Ants scurried around the little puddle of the Italian girl's blood. The sad trolley was now back in action with a different driver, working to recapture its schedule.

And Dorotea no longer stood on the corner as she had all evening, like Virgil beholding the entrance to Hades, frozen in horror when the streetcar struck. Now she nearly matched Raffi block for block, blending with the rain.

Raffi's cane of the Medici, which he'd bought at a gentlemen's shop in Rome, lay discarded near a demilune iron drainage grate. Its golden tip caught a sparkle in the diffusion so that a painter might have captured it with a white daub jumping from the sooty color of the sidewalk's bricks.

Stadt leaned over and picked it up. 'Who do you belong to, lost soul? Ain't nobody's business? Everybody's business is nobody's business.' He took Raffi's prize and with a sober mien walked down the street.

It wasn't until he'd traveled a few rods, crossing Tremont and heading through the dark grass up the Common toward the Park Street Incline, that he twirled it.

Raffi continued to run. Like deep breaths from the underworld, he passed more Metro stations along the way, steaming as though connected to Lake Avernus and the shades below. He ran up Cambridge and West Cedar streets toward the State House to get his bearings in the driving rain, then downhill toward the North End, calling to people, asking directions to find Beatrice's parents, though he knew he didn't need to. He ran straight for the Devil.

20

Disse il granchio: Chi è nato storto non può camminare diritto.
The crab says: he who is born crooked cannot walk straight.

BOSTON, 1922

Lorna Doom looked across the salon and tried not to roll her eyes. Another week, another Suffragette-à-tête at Louisburg Square. 'Amy thinks she's going to shock us again with her ridiculous tango troupe. Can't you just see that dikey whale floating across the room?' she said.

'It's too delicious. Wouldn't Miss Alcott, who so loved her boring maypole dances, enjoy seeing this?' said Hepsibah Crowninshield.

'I'd rather die than be fat,' little Dodo Alden, ever the piler on, said.

Melvina Cabot took another sip of her tea. 'I don't know who takes the husband's role in that Boston marriage, the whale or the hyena who thinks herself an actress.'

'I don't see what they have in common,' Dodo said.

Lorna had pulled back her raven hair so taut and shiny it appeared her skull was oiled, her hands so pale and bony they seemed almost to have been dismembered as they lay on her black dress that fell yardstick straight, betraying not a single curve. 'No one else will have them!'

These members of a synchronized sarcastic team, *Mayflower* descendants all, lifted and dipped their dessert spoons into sterling dishes of Charlotte russe, the season's stylish dessert.

'Tell us,' Melvina asked Lorna, 'exactly what the cow plans to do.'

'Need we embarrass her any further?' the artist said. 'She seems such a genius at doing it to herself.'

'Leave that to us, dear,' Hepsibah said. 'It's common for a spy to feel a pang for going to the other side. But you need to resist that now. You need to be strong. Besides, it's too late to stop that loco-motive. Tango club, how pathetic. We'll see about that.'

'It seems a long way to go for a prank,' Lorna said. 'Seems to me, you're still jealous about Amy's interest in Melvina.'

Melvina clutched Hepsibah's forearm. 'It really wasn't anything. I wish you'd believe me. It was just a fling.'

Dodo laughed. 'Hell hath no fury like one of Sappho's daughters scorned. Hepsibah, I, too, think you're obsessed with Amy.'

A frown landed below Hepsibah's crow's feet. She shook her head. 'You'll see what I think of her after she tries to put that dog and elephant show on at Fenway Court. Then you'll see if I'm obsessed with her. In the meantime, follow me to the ballroom. Because the new painting is here!'

'You mean it's finished?' Dodo asked.

'You can smell the oil,' Lorna said.

'I was wondering what that odor was. It stinks like a fish house in here,' Dodo said.

'You're smelling your new perfume,' Melvina said.

Hepsibah bowed and beckoned them down the hallway. They gath-ered before a frame covered by a white sheet. A servant stood at the ready. 'Champagne cocktails all around, Rupert.'

'Oh, how *au courant*,' Dodo whispered. 'But I never understood the attraction of chemically altering a perfectly good glass of champagne.'

'Don't worry, Hepsibah never risks the good stuff on us,' Melvina said.

Soon, glasses appeared atop a silver salver, and a soft tinkling was exchanged.

'To launching a destroyer,' Dodo said.

'Oh, she's a destroyer, all right,' Hepsibah said. 'To art for art's sake!'

Lorna glanced through a pane of glass iodized purple by too much manganese oxide into the downpour on Mt. Vernon Street and saw a silhouette in an overcoat splashing by at top speed. The stranger on a mission reminded her of something—too tall by half.

'This time, Mr. Sargent has outdone himself!' Hepsibah said.

Whoosh.

Lorna stepped back as the sheet was pulled away to reveal a younger version of Melvina, her elder cousin Hepsibah's paramour. A supernatu-ral blue glitter enlivened Melvina's eyes. The subject, however brazenly sexy, wore a sneer, her chin tilted.

The pièce de résistance was a luxuriant, deep blanket of wolf's fur warming Melvina's knees. The individual tips of the fur looked

124

so alive, and so lupine, Lorna was tempted to reach out and touch them. Even without the enormous gold frame, the masterpiece looked fantastically expensive, disturbing. A murmur vibrated through the small assemblage.

'Behold,' Hepsibah said of the portrait. 'Our own Venus in fur, The Bluenose Mona Lisa!'

21

Trovare l'America.
Find America.

BOSTON, 1922

C arlo looked through the darkness at the crowd buzzing below the stalactites. They were seated at the café tables with the little lights, waiting. They'd waited all night. They wanted him to sing 'the song.'

He'd known it the minute he'd brought it in for rehearsal the week before. Some hits are so tender they fall off the bone. He'd lit a cigarette while Lucky Driscoll noodled around with the haunting new number for a while on piano. Then he gave a nod and vibrated into a low A as he let *The Hoo Doo Man* sweep him away. How Jake this was—a foxtrot in the devil's garden. This strange sound, dark and reckless, wasn't ragtime, wasn't blues, wasn't gumbo, wasn't old country. It was—

He felt the syncopation rattle him to the bones. His spine vibrated. Without knowing it, he started snapping his fingers. Next payday, I'm going to get some of those taps for my shoes.

And it was as if the audiences and the spotlight and the wonder were already there. He could feel it in the pit of his stomach. Finally—the *bella fortuna*! This is my song and my time!

And on to tonight. The lights went low. He stepped into the microphone, and the orchestra pushed into the music. Avernus was packed to the gills now, beyond fire code, the benchmark for any art. You knew you had a winner when they risked burning to death for their listening enjoyment. But here he was, and here it was: he took a deep breath and flashed his million-dollar smile. Walk, stop, and wink. He dipped down suavely and murmured, as a prelude, 'Here's the new one, guys, halfway to tomorrow morning. I'd tell you the title, but I think you can figure it out.'

Photo bulbs burst, and in the smoky caverns of Avernus, in the blooming heat, in a world that seemed so Bohemian and new, he began to swing.

> *Old mister Hoo——oo——oo–doo——*
> *Please tell me who——are–you——*
> *You've got the world——in a stew——*
> *With the things——you do——*

There was an instant when all the air was sucked out of the room and he stood in the shade of time. Who was the Hoo Doo Man? A disturbing foreign influence, surely. He grinned. Maybe it's me. Vulgara and her friends had pushed three tables together as a cheering section, but they were the only people with money. The rest of the diners in all this smoke were young–almost too young, barely college age. They'd come from as far as Salem and Newburyport and Duxbury to see him. The police had been paid off, so the liquor was flowing. The room erupted in applause.

'Tell that to your Johnny Cavallaro,' Vulgara said to Gaspare.

Carlo wasn't just exultant, he was... relieved. He looked down and felt a shadow walking toward the stage. Johnny Cavallaro, 'the' Johnny Cavallaro, raced up out of the darkness to shake his hand. Well, what do you know, Johnny. One day you're the headliner and–bang–you're yesterday's news! Shit! Maybe you'll open for me sometime. Carlo felt dizzy. A slight movement caught his eye in the back of the room. Someone was standing by the bouncer. It was Mr. Stadt. Couldn't he ever catch a break?

The applause swelled, lifted the tables and chairs, burst out of Avernus, and spread over the North End, taking out the Atlantic Elevated Railway Station and a few trucks and hurling them into Back Bay.

In the darkness, in the metal rain, Raffi kept running.

22

In mare non ci sono taverne.
There are no taverns at sea.

BOSTON, 1922

Raffi located the flattop in a maze of identical tenements. The phantasmagoric Underwood sign floating in the dark sky overhead was reflected in the wet streets, and the flashing red rain turned all the sad apartment buildings pink. A distant bell struck one: he was exhausted from running, turned inside out from grief.

How odd. He was entering Beatrice's home like a thief. No, a thief would merely be stealing money and worldly goods. He, or his bad luck, had stolen their precious daughter. He saw her crumpled body at the foot of the trolley and raked his face.

He knocked three times on the screen door. No one answered. He twisted the brass doorknob, and the outer door clicked open. He stood a moment to let the raindrops pool outside the tile vestibule before he tried the inner door and ventured onto the over-varnished flooring within. Three gleaming brass mailboxes were installed in a perfect neat row. There was not a speck of dust anywhere. The residents obviously cared about this humdrum foursquare.

A skinny white cat slipped inside the door just as it closed behind him and curled back and forth around his long legs, flicking her tail. Who are you, little witch? How strange you'd welcome me. Felines had long been in tune with the thoughts of humans. They smiled at each other.

He looked up the dark shaft of the stairwell to the second floor. The cat started ahead of him, stopped, and turned to catch his eye, so he followed, taking three steps at a time. His head pounded.

The linoleum stairs were so much like the ones at the orphanage, with a sharply angled landing on each floor lit by a single stingy bulb. Together, he and the cat ascended to the second floor and on to the third, to a door marked No. 303. He stood in the dark and hesitated. How much worse it was to have to give bad news than to receive it. The cat sat and looked at him with its strange blue eyes. Shouldn't he have called out by now? He took a deep breath, gathered himself, and spread his great arms. 'Signor Favi!' His shriek trilled like an electric impulse through the sleeping corridors. 'Signor Favi!' The door swung open and Beatrice's father, much more frail than he remembered, stood in a nightshirt. His wife sleepily appeared beside him.

'What the hell are you doing here?'

'Sr. Favi,' Raffi said.

Signora Favi whispered something to her husband.

'It's after midnight.' He turned his head. 'Where's Beatrice?'

'Sr. Favi, I came to tell you. There's been a terrible accident.'

'Where is she? Where is my baby girl?'

'Beatrice was hit by the trolley.'

'What do you mean?'

Raffi shook his head. 'I am so sorry. I am so sorry. She is dead.'

'Tell me what happened,' her father said almost gently, 'very slowly.' He locked eyes. Raffi was startled that Favi chose to exchange information below a scream. So encouraging was he, Favi offered a deadly smile.

'I hope it is a comfort to you—I believe she felt no pain,' Raffi said.

'Please tell me, where is she, right now?' Favi said.

'They have taken her to Mass. General,' Raffi said. Feeling their eyes on him, he felt as though he were falling. You have to stand up and take this.

'She is with the doctors now? Maybe they're still trying to revive her?'

Raffi knew Favi knew beyond a shadow of a doubt that wasn't true. 'I am so sorry, Signor Favi. Your precious Beatrice. I know you didn't like me; she told me. But I was in love with her.'

'What else did she say? Did she call out for me?'

'She didn't cry out at all,' Raffi said. 'Murderer,' he braced for Favi to say again and again, though he did not. Instead he looked at Raffi with a gentle focus and penetrating eyes.

'I just knew something like this might happen the day the twins were born,' Favi said. 'I didn't deserve the happiness they brought me.'

'I cannot express my sorrow for your loss. I think she was happy tonight, and possibly never saw, or felt—' Raffi swallowed. 'I know how

129

you feel about me, and you are right, terribly right. But Signor Favi, I would like to join your family at the funeral.'

Raffi looked around for the little white cat, but she was gone. He felt a presence behind him. He turned to Beatrice's shadow. Dorotea sprang out of a dark corner and screamed at him—a banshee. She slapped him hard on the face. Sobbing, she pummeled his chest. She scratched his nose, and blood dripped down his chin. Where had she been all this time? She was bedraggled and covered with rain.

'Beatrice may not have understood what was wrong with you, but to me it was obvious,' Dorotea said. 'She was worth twenty of you. You are all alone. Go home, sit by a candle, and take your own life. If you are too much of a coward to do it tonight, do it tomorrow or the next day.'

Mrs. Favi crumpled to the floor. Favi reached for his wife but looked at Dorotea. 'Oh, my God, daughter, please, please, you shouldn't talk to any man this way,' he said.

'He's not a man, Papa, he's a freak.' She turned to Raffi. 'I hope God sends you to Hell, you woman, you imposter.' She spit three times on her pale hand and rubbed it onto his lips and across his teeth. 'We never want to see you again alive. But you'll see me when you die.'

'Yes,' Raffi said. A castrato was nothing if not agreeable. His head thudded as he walked into the red night.

23

Si può affogare in un bicchiere d'acqua.
You can drown in a glass of water.

BOSTON, 1922

S tadt walked through the blushing, cloud-dappled dawn that barely stirred the Public Gardens, and stopped at the wall. As though they sensed a wolf near, the swan boats drew back lightly on their chains. He took a loaf of bread out of a sack, tore off a chunk, and threw it into the oily water. He watched the ripples expand until a wary Canada goose swam up to snap at it. A frenzy of other geese followed suit.

A goon, a fringe of hair hanging over his eyes, approached, pushing a sleepy Carlo every third step.

Stadt didn't turn when Carlo walked up beside him. Instead, he was interested in something flashing below the water beyond the birds. He pointed. 'I think it's a trout. Do you see him?'

'No,' Carlo said.

'There. Along the edge of the wall, underwater. Do you see?'

Carlo leaned over some more, and Stadt kicked him in with a splash.

'Do you know what it means,' Stadt said calmly, 'when I say you're in too deep? The bigger Ruski, Dimitri, tells me you want out.'

'I can't do it,' Carlo said. With his hooded bedroom eyes, he was a sad Labrador paddling back to the water's edge. He hoisted himself up the side.

'You will,' Stadt said and tossed a hunk of bread in the crooner's lap, which made him fall back because the geese went after it. Bills, feathers, wings. Carlo splashed around, looking for his dignity.

'Kid, once you're in, there's no getting out unless I say you're out.'

'I thought—'

'You don't think.' He tossed another piece of bread on Carlo, who brushed it off but not aggressively. Stadt knew Carlo now knew it didn't do to cross Mr. Stadt.

'Mistah Stadt, I won't tell no one, I promise. It's just that things are going better for me at the club. I don't need the money that way now. I thought I did, but I don't. Did you ever think you needed to do something a whole lot and then all of a sudden you didn't? And then you really didn't? It's like that.'

Stadt said nothing. He looked beyond Carlo, below the smoky mirror, where he detected movement and saw the flash again. How did the creature get there? Probably the pond was stocked. Not my worry. My problem is, I've forgotten how to relax. 'If you're not there next Friday night, you won't need to look for me,' Stadt said. 'I'll find you. Do you understand, kid?'

Carlo looked down. 'Okay.'

Stadt smiled and looked over at the State House dome, sparkling like a fourteen-karat onion through the trees. 'I'm glad your singing's goin' good, kid. I've never seen a musician wake up so early. That water's pretty ripe. You're going to have to take a shower. Sorry about the clothes. Filene's Automatic Bargain Basement? How much that jacket set you back? You'd better dry it off. Wool shrinks and stinks, you know.'

'It's not like I have cold feet,' Carlo said. 'But maybe this guy, this transportation secretary, maybe he'll vote our way and then nothing will have to happen, right?'

Stadt rubbed his chin. 'Maybe the crooked man won't vote for the crooked contractor.' He looked around, checked his watch. 'Maybe I won't have to pay you. Wouldn't that be something?'

'You bet it would,' Carlo said.

'Next Friday night. I'll be watching.'

Stadt cut across the park with geometric precision. He didn't have time for the curving pathways. No bird, no American gray squirrel, nothing in nature conducted himself with such calculated purpose. Euclid would have been proud. He was tired of working with amateurs, even more tired of working with strangers, but he couldn't be sure who his friends were anymore. Murder was a young person's sport—leave it to the kiddoes.

He hit the sidewalk near the statue of Kościuszko and turned right. A little cloud passed overhead, and at the touch of a raindrop he became just another kindly elderly gentleman with his hat pulled down and his collar up, rushing home to his warm flat in Childe Hassam's impressionistic portrait of Boston Common, the one where the drizzle fuzzes everything and the park's black wrought-iron fence seeks a vanishing point.

He gave some thought to descending into Park Street incline, but that's where he'd soon emerge, like a ghost rising from a door in a stage floor, to oversee the job. It wouldn't do for him to be seen hanging around there too much. His performance had to be fresh, spontaneous. So he didn't take the shortest, most efficient route back to Jamaica Plain. Not that that bothered him. It made sense, and he allowed himself to enjoy the freshening air. He avoided Park Street Incline because he had reason to avoid it.

The sun broke through the clouds and the sidewalks began to steam, as though Boston were a giant press shop. Poor kid. Don't these choirboys love their threads!

He passed the Steinway Piano store. His neighbor had just bought a Steinway 'S,' for small. Instead of a forbidding ebony, it had a cherry finish. I could go in there and buy one just like it. We have the perfect place in our bay window.

He was not immune to music appreciation. Hadn't he just been to the opera the night before, where afterward he'd been in the crowd around an accident where a girl had been killed? He'd seen the body on the cobblestones. Not too much meat on her bones. Even dead she looked hungry. Italian girl.

24

Ci capiamo a fischi, disse il merlo alla moglie.
We understand each other's whistle, said the blackbird to his wife.

Saltonstall luxuriated in the peignoir and marabou-adorned slippers he'd learned secretly to enjoy. Shafts of sunlight streamed through the Palladian windows of his breakfast room and across the parquet floors, rousing his sleepy furniture. It was one of the lesser Saltonstall holdings on Beacon Hill, he being on the outs with the one who put the salt in Saltonstall, but it was a tony townhouse nonetheless. Properly regarded, 13 Joy Street was 'a maisonette with a piano nobile,' as he'd first lectured to his new bride Henrietta after rushing her here following the briefest of courtships and a honeymoon aborted. When eyebrows were raised, the reason given? 'A business crisis.'

Maybe that high tone had begun his undoing.

But now there was breakfast to be prepared—bacon from a waxy package labeled S.S. Pierce. Henrietta's Amalfi wolf just loved his *pancetta*. With a wistful self-hatred, Saltonstall found a pan, turned up the gas in the kitchenette he'd set up in the utility closet, and carefully stretched out six of the luscious strips, four for him and two for her. If you can't believe in S.S. Pierce, who can you believe in?

Once he'd set the couple's three-minute eggs to the boil on the next burner, he shuffled to the ironing board he'd set below tall windows where more light streamed in. He watched a fist of pigeons just outside the glass explode through a skein of black branches. They banked over Beacon Street and flared over the park.

Turning, through half-open french doors, he could see his wife's pale, slender legs entwining two long, hairy limbs. He heard her sigh and stretch, and below that he could hear her whispering with her lover, their intimate tones indistinguishable but present, swirls and eddies like water talking under a yacht at anchor. Finally he heard her low voice call out to him, familiar and commanding.

'Sissy, bring more of that strong coffee, please,' Henrietta said. 'We haven't finished with you yet.'

Saltonstall flushed and held up the iron. 'Look, Hen, I've got to go to work at the hotel sometime.'

'After you've served our breakfast, dear. Marcello's no use to me when he's hungry. What's keeping you? Have you finished with your master's shirt?'

When Saltonstall didn't answer, she lifted her head from her silk pillow and studied him across the distance. 'Wouldn't I love your mother to see you like this? My biggest regret about you being my cuckold is I don't get to torture her with this delicious filth. Wouldn't she just croak! Sometimes I'm positively itching to pick up the receiver to share the news about her precious son. Ha!'

She rolled over and pantomimed picking up the telephone. 'Hello, is this Mrs. Salton-wittol?' Even though she wouldn't really do it—she had too much to lose, too—he felt a stab of fear and flinched.

'That's not funny. It would kill her—after she killed me, but not before she got her lawyers to ensure you wouldn't even get to be a rich widow.'

'Darling,' Henrietta said to the Amalfi stud curled up beside her. 'Can you imagine how all of this started? On our wedding night, I discovered that Milquetoast over there, the most eligible bachelor in all of Boston, was negotiating with a worthless instrument. "What a catch," everybody told me. Yes, if you like a white-bellied flounder flopping on the shore.'

She called back to Saltonstall. 'So you'd better float in here before the rest of the servants come in. You know how they all talk. Who knows what tidbits they might pick up if you don't keep up your housekeeping like a good little husband.'

'Do you ever worry that you're going too far?' Marcello asked sleepily.

'Exactly. I'm glad you understand. So where's that robust and potent coffee, sissy?'

'Nora can get it for you later,' Saltonstall said.

'Now let's see,' Henrietta said. 'Your mother's number is MAyflower 244—'

'You know, a telephone makes the perfect blunt instrument,' Saltonstall said.

'As ever, an empty threat. We all know you haven't the balls for it,' she said.

'Well, you've enough for both of us,' he said.

They shared the most distant of smiles.

'No, you'll get the coffee, Sis, or we won't let you watch us tonight. What's got into you? Insubordinate to the point of perkiness. I've a mind to give you your notice.'

Marcello rolled over. 'Don't let me interrupt this tender moment.'

'Lot going on today,' Saltonstall said. 'Couldn't you just get it, Hen?'

When she didn't answer, his heart started to race. Was it worth it to displease them? He already knew they made good on their threats. 'All right, I'll be right in.'

'You know, you're a treasure. Isn't she, Marcello?'

'Isn't breakfast ready?' Marcello's deep voice called out from beside her. 'I can smell something on fire.'

25

Prosciugare il mare con una conchiglia.
Drain the sea with a conch shell.

BOSTON, 1922

During all the lost evenings he'd spent in the Forum's paneled library in Rome, pondering what he might do with his life, Raffi pored through ancient tomes, where he'd sat at the foot of Zeno of Citium, and modern texts, where he'd first met Sigmund Freud, trying to understand the nature of love and what it held for him. Surrounded by books, alone after the rest of the staff had gone home, he'd combed through every culture he could find, searching for a place to touch down. He'd come to think of reading as flying at night.

He began to identify himself with the albatross. This majestic winged sea bird, a harbinger of bad luck, was never permitted to rest. It was as though the earth repulsed it and didn't allow it to land. If he fell asleep on the icy seas, sharks would rise through the silvery waves and gobble him up with a single swallow. It gripped his heart to learn the albatross was so lonely it had to sleep while flying.

Raffi walked the two-miles from the Favis' to Sevenels. Certainly there was no time to sleep; he barely had enough time to change his clothes. At the sound of the latch, Victor rolled toward him. 'Victor,' Raffi said. 'I'm in trouble.'

'What the hell's going on?' Victor stared toward him with his weird, boiled eyes, the ones blind men keep hidden from the sighted behind smoked glass.

'Victor, Beatrice's dead.'

'My God,' Victor said. 'The girl from the ship? What happened?'

'She was hit by a trolley. I said goodbye to her. I turned, God help me, and was walking away. I didn't see it, but maybe she was watching me. Oh, God, I will never forget the sound.'

'Where is she?'

'Mass. General. She was hit terribly hard, Victor. I don't think she saw it coming.'

'I'm so sorry, Raffi.' A pause. 'I know she meant something to you.'

'She was the girl who didn't yet understand who I wasn't. My fresh start.'

Victor rose and reached for Raffi's arm. 'You're soaked. Take off those glad rags. Dry off and let's have a drink—much more effective than what passed for the lullabies my mother always prescribed for me after something terrible happened.'

'I can't remember any of my mother's lullabies,' Raffi said.

'If I were ever attacked by a bully, or fell from a tree, or got a bad mark, my mother used to sing "There Is a Balm in Gilead" very clearly so the pain would go away. It doesn't work as well as rye.'

For a moment Raffi and Victor shared a single shadowland. He took in a breath. Then he let all the air spill from his chest. Though his shoulders shook, he made no sound.

'The good stuff's on the third shelf up,' Victor said. 'Move that front bottle and pull out the one behind it against the bricks. Take just three swigs of that right now, and then hand it to me.'

'Sure.' Raffi uncorked the bottle and took a swig. The rye felt hot in his throat. He coughed.

'A gift from my father. Someday I'll tell you all about the bastard.'

The two were very quiet. 'All right,' Victor said, 'so tell me. Tell it so that Beatrice can hear you, because I know she can.'

'Victor, you believe in ghosts?' Raffi asked.

But Victor's eyes were closed again. Raffi wept as he recounted the evening's horrors. His throat constricted when he tried to talk, so he whispered into the dark. Can you hear me, Beatrice? They were back on that ship together, moving through the mist. He kept talking, his head ringing in pain. In his state of semi-consciousness, he was wide asleep. Like the albatross, was there any place for him to make a landing? His words rode the air currents over dream's lonely seas. He drifted off to sleep. Maybe sleep wasn't accurate. For fifteen minutes, it stopped raining and he wasn't in the land of the living at all. He resurfaced to ask Victor, 'Did you hear everything?'

'Yes,' Victor said and rolled back against the wall. 'Now let me go back to sleep. You'll do well to do the same.'

'But it's almost time to go to work,' Raffi said.

'I'd like ten minutes more,' Victor said. 'If you can't catch a few winks, you might as well start getting dressed. It won't bother me.' He paused. 'When is the funeral?'

'They don't want me there,' Raffi said.

'It's their funeral.'

By quarter past nine, when breakfast was shifting to brunch, Raffi answered a summons and stood outside his employer's door. 'Mr. Saltonstall, you sent for me?'

'Come in, son.'

Raffi's employer look ruffled, as if he'd just made it in. Without even looking at Raffi, Saltonstall turned away and started making himself a drink. The manager's precise ablutions at the crystal-laden bar made Raffi think of Diletti, the last person who'd called him son, and his rituals in the butcher shop. He wasn't old enough to have a memory of his natural father calling him son and doubted it ever happened anyway. He had an odd notion—maybe Moreschi was his father, in the sense they shared a phenotype of fortune. How brave he was—with a different kind of manhood that allowed him to sustain his dignity even as his career devolved from celebrated vocalist to circus act. Raffi saw again the great darkened owl eyes.

He'd nearly disclosed to Beatrice the depth of his yearning to talk with Moreschi to try and learn whatever he had to teach someone in his line of loss. Maybe it was good Beatrice had never understood this, but now that she was gone the need was only more acute. Or maybe his lack of sleep was just catching up to him.

'We're in a pickle, and I hope you can help us out,' Saltonstall said, his drink now at his lips. 'Short on staff, as it were, though long on opportunity.' He finally looked at Raffi, as if for the first time. With a jocularity that seemed forced, he said, 'Say… how tall are you? I only know one person who's close to your height.'

Raffi could tell from the curl of his lip it wasn't someone he held dear, so he opened his stance and tilted his head, stooping to make himself appear shorter. Saltonstall was obviously on a tear about something, and Raffi knew himself to be too easy a target. He'd been in the hotel business long enough to know the tallest suitcase gets knocked over first.

'Oh, never mind,' Saltonstall said. 'In our set, recording our height was a matter of tradition. Funny, we even managed to make growth a competitive sport. The back of our kitchen door is darkened by the lines where we measured ourselves on our birthdays. But of course I have one of those families.' He lit a brown digit—an *Illusione*, Miss Lowell's beloved brand. 'This smoke doesn't bother you, does it?' Baring his teeth, he winked.

Saltonstall was suddenly as joyful as an eagle cooling a rabbit with his fast shadow. What was he up to? Why had he summoned an employee here when he could easily have sent the message down via Victor? Raffi reminded himself to shake it off and find the sunshine, whatever the weather.

'How can I be of service to the hotel, and to you, sir?' Raffi asked.

'Ah, yes. Well, it comes down to this,' Saltonstall said. 'The housekeeping staff is shorthanded, and in turnaround there's no way we can do all our floors and get to the restrooms and clean them tonight. We're counting on you to take care of the men's and ladies' water closets in the lobby off the Revere Room, the two in the bar, and the two serving Bulfinch Ballroom.'

'Yes, sir!' What was this about? What indignity had Saltonstall suffered that Raffi would be paying the penance for now? Raffi couldn't read past the knot of humiliation that had turned to anger just behind his employer's eyes, but what difference did it make? Obviously Saltonstall was taking some sort of redirected pleasure in calling Raffi to the carpet. Raffi knew what he had to do: 'This is not an issue,' he said. 'Consider this problem already solved, sir.'

Saltonstall scowled. 'You mean you're not going to tell me this isn't in your job description? I expect you to surpass the standards of the Noras in housekeeping, you understand.'

'That goes without saying, sir. Thank you again for the opportunity to excel. Will that be all, sir? This will be my privilege.' Raffi pronounced it 'privy'-ledge.

Saltonstall narrowed his eyes and regarded him intently, considering whether or not this was an impertinence. Then he turned away.

When Raffi told Victor the news in the scullery, Victor took him to the prep line where turtle soup was simmering and the pans of pellucid, fleshy scrod and pots of beans awaited their communion with upper Boston's lower intestinal system.

'So you got the Aegean stables gig,' Victor said.

'I'm not afraid of work,' Raffi said.

'It's the nature of the work. It isn't right—but it's so my brother.' Victor took off his smock, pulled at his cuffs, brushed off his lapel, and started for the door.

'No, Victor, don't. Save this favor for some time I'll really need it. I grew up mopping after sick children and doddery women.'

'I just smell… a rat.'

'Yes, Victor. But don't we have some dishes to wash?'

'You don't. Since your cleaning shift starts so late, take the rest of the day off. I'll catch up with you later.'

At precisely 11:45 p.m., Raffi walked up and rang the bell at the hotel's service door. George the doorman, rarely downstairs, let Raffi in as he was going off shift. 'Hi, George,' Raffi said. 'How's Eugenie?'

'She's fine, Mr. Peach. The fever broke last night. Thanks for the tip—the honey and wine did the trick. But what brings you here so late, Mr. Peach?'

'Mr. Saltonstall's asked me to come in and give some special attention to a matter.'

'Oh, I see.'

Raffi touched the tip of his hat and swept up the stairs. 'Hello, Stan,' he said to the bellhop who'd first introduced him to Victor.

'Hello,' Stan said in a guarded way Raffi heard as *Why have I just stood here and let this wop use me as a stepping stone?*

'I'm here to clean the latrines,' Raffi said. 'Some people have all the luck!'

Instantly the bellhop fell at ease. 'Oh, you're on the boss's bad side!' He winked. 'I've been there.'

The ferns and circular banquette loomed large and ghostly in the dimmed light as Raffi walked through the echoic lobby. So absurd were

Saltonstall's machinations he felt almost light-hearted on his way to the janitorial closet.

He reached above the door trim for the key (viewed, without difficulty, in its hiding place) and entered, pondering the wisdom of keeping cleaning supplies safe from industrious thieves. He selected a pair of gloves, some cleaning salts, and a wheeled bucket that held a mop and a scrub brush. In a cloth bag, he brought lilac detergent soap punched up with ambergris to cover any deadly stink.

With a grin, he rolled his parade of cleaning equipment across the polished marble floors toward the first men's room off the Paul Revere Dining Room. He took three breaths: Father, Son, and Holy Ghost. Pushing open the door, he walked in.

Six white urinals, at knee level, were lined up along a Carrera marble wall. At the end of the wall, a jot lower, was a child's model. The stalls were in heavy white marble, too, with black walnut doors. To the unsuspecting eye, nothing had happened in here. Then, like a balmy tropical wave, the primordial pungency of the house specialty's effluence seized Raffi's attention. The air was so heavy with the aroma he could feel the weight of it on his face.

It was like coming home to the sewers of Naples and Rome. If he opened his mouth, he'd taste it. Keeping his ever-sunny smile, he dropped to his knees and grasped an enormous sea sponge so fresh from the ocean it had a personality.

With the world asleep, he scrubbed with a vengeance while his mind sailed over the Sargasso Sea with the albatross. He swooped and curved and looked down at the little wavelets of the ocean below.

Finishing the men's room, the first of four, at 1:20 a.m., he knocked tentatively at the first ladies' room door. No one called from within, so he swung it open. Where there had been urinals in the men's room, these sisters of Paul Revere had private stalls and a comfy davenport in chintz, with matching curtains and a friendly mirror.

If anything, the odor was more ripe. He opened the windows to their widest point to let some fresh air in. He flushed every toilet three times, adding the lilac detergent to purge the pipes. He wiped the walls until they were spanking clean.

He returned to his knees and felt His Serenity's hand on his head, just like so many years before. No worries, he wasn't going to sing.

Castrati were supposed to be free from the drive that made real men unhappy, unsettled, jealous. Not that he'd sound glorious if he tried. His pipes were no doubt rusty from disuse, rattling and cranking with sediment. Maybe he'd forgotten how. He flushed a round of toilets and listened to the music of the water rushing and bubbling through the ingeniously engineered plumbing system, dreaming of finding its way to its underground source.

'Sweet are the uses of adversity,' Sister K. used to joke. As degrading as his task was now, he worked with his carefree grin and watched his hands as though someone else were using them to scour the floors. He tried to summon pleasant memories of Beatrice but to his surprise found himself considering Dorotea.

That's why your invitation to suicide didn't hit the mark. You took such trouble to call me a woman, Dorotea; is that just because you're still just a girl yourself? Would you have me think of myself as a woman merely out of self-hatred? This, at least, was interesting. Yes, Dorotea had condemned him to suicide, and out of respect for her grief he hadn't answered, though Victor, upon hearing about her curse, had shrugged and offered an arid reply. 'The trouble with suicide is, it catches you on the downbeat.'

But tonight Raffi saw something else in Dorotea beyond her surveillances, her anger and grief, even beyond her fear of hospitals and the loss of Beatrice. Dorotea the day moon, eclipsed by Beatrice's light. Had there been something approaching shame in her face? Ladies' Room. Men's Room. Where would she have me go? He grinned, wondering, how might I decorate the Raffi room? Maybe it was like this: if you live in a WC, at least there's a use for your vanity.

You think like this, you're not going to clean many bathrooms. At least he didn't feel the urge to be 'competitive.' If nothing else, he could whistle. He tried it a little, as a way to reach Beatrice. He scrubbed harder and began to feel a bit of comfort in the rhythm and pride in the results. Then a group of footsteps came down the hall. He'd not reckoned on an intruder. The guests should be asleep in their rooms above. So close to his private thoughts, he looked up quickly.

The door swung open and buried itself in the capture latch. Raffi stood to greet Victor, who wore a gas mask from the Great War. He stepped aside to reveal Amy in a nasturtium print blouse and slacks with gas mask, Ada's sour puss behind a gas mask, and enough gas masks to fill the Ardennes Forest on the visages of Ephraim, the grocery vice president Rufus Cloud, Lorna Doom *(no doubt still unsmiling)*, and finally, Tiger Lily. The misfits of Sevenels! Raffi quickly washed and dried his hands so he could properly greet them.

'Please help me understand,' Victor said. His voice rang inside his mask, as if he were talking through a blown-up inner tube. 'Was that a whistle I heard you making?'

'Hello, Miss Lowell, Mrs. Russell, Mr. Cloud, Miss Doom... Tiger Lily,' Raffi said.

'Miss Tiger Lily to you,' Ada said. 'There's a Mandarin tradition that when you've buried seven or more bodies you earn a modicum of respect.'

Tiger Lily patted the side of her gas mask as if to shape it.

'I honor all of you!' Raffi said. 'Great get-ups!'

'We pinched these masks at the Navy Yard,' Amy said, rubbing her gloved hands up and down like a redoubtable, friendly insect, ready for work.

'Want one?' Victor said. 'I've brought an extra for you.'

'What chemicals are we cleaning with?' Rufus asked.

'Lye soap,' Raffi said. 'And ammonia.'

'More like Eudaimonia,' Amy said, 'a state of being quite apart from unconsidered happiness. Raffi, you're redefining the meaning of pleasure. Maybe your greatest gift is what they've taken away from you.'

'Pshaw,' Ada said. 'It's just one more idea the Neapolitans stole from the Greeks.'

26

Il polipo si cuoce nella sua acqua.
The octopus is boiled in its own juices.

FENWAY COURT, BOSTON, 1922

Belle Gardner, draped in a scarlet silk cloak embroidered with green dragons, pointed to a single orchid at the very center of a mahogany table. Her sleeve fell open, revealing a quilted saffron lining and a black velvet bracelet on which was suspended The Light of India, a blue diamond solitaire the size of a chestnut. A sunbeam flashed through its prisms.

John Singer Sargent winced as though blinded. 'Don't you ever worry you'll break something with that vulgar chunk of coal?'

'Before you interrupted me, I was telling you, this is an exotic breed of Venus slipper, John,' she said. 'It isn't just rare—it's the first time this variety has ever bloomed anywhere but on the Amazon. Like you, it's shy, preferring the shadows of the forest floor to direct sunlight.' She looked into his eyes. 'You know I'm counting on you to come Friday night. Here.' She snapped the bud from its stem and held it against his lapel. 'A singular boutonnière.'

'I feel an attack of gout coming on,' Sargent said. 'Why don't you dress Cortissoz instead?'

'Ha! Let's change the Sargent coat of arms to reflect a more accurate motto: from "neither to seek nor deny honors" to "never forgive, never forget."' She re-adjusted her white scarf, the better to cover her drooping lip, so very stupid and so uncooperative since the stroke.

'You know exactly why I don't tolerate him, Belle,' her artist said. 'His only recommendation is, he's a friend of yours.'

'How sweet, John!'

'So while I must decline the opportunity to attend any event in which he might appear, I will not turn down another of those deviled-ham sandwiches.'

Her butler stepped from the shadows to offer him a silver tray laden with fingers of pale bread *sans* crusts, slathered with the potted meat.

'You've such a marvelous appetite,' she said. 'Like my Jack. Painters and pirates, I guess.'

'Old habit,' Sargent said. 'We artists like to eat, because we never know where the next meal's coming from.'

'I don't think you'll ever have to worry about starving, John.' She watched him gaze past the marble torsos and arches of her sculpture garden into the sun-caressed darkness of her atrium. A single white shaft pierced the gloom, crashed into a trio of fishtail palms, and settled on the shoulders of a diminutive Bernini bronze of a devil looking up from a garden. She grinned as he stood to see the statue better.

'Is that your latest acquisition?' Sargent said. 'Seriously, Belle, I thought your ransacking days were over. Don't you think you should leave anything for the tourists to see on their Venetian holidays?' He gestured with great swoops: 'Announcing Belle's American Plan! All-inclusive continental breakfast and a priceless bit of plunder.'

She giggled, and he smiled.

'How long have we known each other?' Sargent said. 'You look just like the fidgety girl I first painted... what was it, thirty-two years ago?'

She looked fondly at him, still able to see the young artist Henry James had introduced to London so many years before. 'Well, you look nothing like the intense young man I knew. That dark-eyed grizzly never would've let the words of a poofy art critic give him a moment's pause, let alone nine years.'

Sargent rolled his eyes, no doubt inhaling the fragrances: hyacinths, hanging delphinia, jasmine, jade trees, azaleas, ameraria, calalilies, and her favorite, nasturtiums. 'What's that stench?' he asked.

Suka, her beloved lion, growled softly in protest at the insult. She wrapped her muscular tail around one of John's trouser legs.

Sargent scowled. 'How picturesque.'

She gave a soft tug on the cub's sterling chain. Suka crept back to her feet and fell asleep with a contented sigh.

'Belle, you can't expect everyone to respond so prettily.'

'I can't help it if everyone likes my money and my company.'

'So speaks the "fag hag"—what is it Kazuko calls you?'

She smiled. '*Okoge*, the burnt rice from the bottom of the pan.'

'The best part,' Sargent said.

She put her napkin down. A signal.

'So, let's see what you're planning for my painting,' he said.

'I'm sure you'll think it's clever,' she said. 'Take my arm, and we're off to the Spanish Cloister.' They descended two steps to the long quadrangle with its low ceiling. At the end of the enclosure, *El Jaleo* glowed above a set of electric footlights, large as the wall itself. Within its heavy gold frame, a crowd of Spanish musicians was working up a sweat in the shadows. In the foreground, a sensuous young woman leaned backward, captured in dance. Hypnotically, the white folds of her dress rustled through the dusk. Belle had designed not just this room but her entire mansion around the Sargent masterpiece. Though it had been years since she'd honeyfogled her cousin-by-marriage into lending her *El Jaleo*, she still studied it every day and felt as moved by its bold brushstrokes as she knew her guests would be. They'd finally understand why she'd chosen to be an outlander, turning her back on Beacon Hill to build this palace of a gallery in the suburbs of Boston's swampy fens—a scandalous eight blocks away. Nobody, but nobody, lived here, outside the sheltering embrace of Back Bay.

'Just look at it, John, dear,' she said. 'I heard the young man who dashed this off has retired from portrait commissions, now that he has bigger fish to fry.' *El Jaleo*, 'the ruckus,' was so full of sound it gathered itself like an orchestra tuning before a concert. The castanets snickered. The guitarist roiled. Responding to the racket, she'd extended the visual music beyond the frame with tricks of décor so viewers might feel part of the scene. By now, it had become an expression of John's strange intimacy with her, as was the little paneled velvet room that didn't appear in any blueprint for the house where he'd sketched her nude three times—the last on her eighty-second birthday.

'Save that for the ranks of the iridescent, Belle. Would you truly introduce me to my own painting?'

'It's mine, actually,' she said. 'You're the intruder.'

Sargent reached for his vest pocket, pulled out a handkerchief, and blew his nose. 'What is that junk up there over my painting?'

'My painting,' she said. His eyes followed hers as she fingered a cord that led to a net bag of gauze suspended over their heads.

Sargent rubbed his forehead and stared. 'What are you up to, Belle?'

'Yowza, John. This is a party favor. I'm adding a new set of dancers to your illusion.'

'Nothing an artist likes more than having his vision "improved upon" by a patron.'

'Well, thank you for indulging me,' Belle said. 'You'll grace us at our little soirée, won't you—"Come As You Really Are"? You know I got the idea from the way you paint people, as they really are.'

'I'll pass.'

'You're being peevish,' Belle said. 'I wasn't suggesting there's something missing from your painting—this is just for the party.'

Sargent shook his head.

'Well, you'll just have to hear about the spectacle from everyone else,' Belle said.

A servant appeared behind them. 'Mrs. Gardner, Mr. Cortissoz is here.'

'I have a confession to make,' Belle said. 'He knows you're here, John. He was hoping you might stay around so you could chat.'

'Jesus Ghost, Belle. I'll let myself out.'

Two attendants arrived, bearing her gondola chair she'd shipped from Venice so she might be carried up and down stairs in utmost privacy to keep her guests unburdened by her afflictions. With an apparent lightness of step she slipped inside the soot-colored conveyance brightened by court scenes trimmed in gold leaf, shut her little door, and leaned her head against the glass as she ascended to the tall shadows of The Tapestry Room, where a small tea table was set in white. As the attendants helped her from her car, she smiled to hide her pain but then crossed the terra-cotta tiles with vigor, exhorting herself: 'Be as happy as you can, and appear even more so.'

Some movements were excruciating, but she dismissed them as 'the grippe.' Her spine hurt, making it impossible to sleep. The last few weeks, she'd kept herself drowsily amused by setting her private letters aflame, one at a time. She closed her eyes to catch a little rest and then opened them to see Cortissoz beside her, sleek and smug as a seal in spectacles, surveying his kingdom from a rock.

'You just missed John,' Belle said. 'I felt this might happen. But you might as well sit down anyway.'

'It's too bad,' Cortissoz said. 'Doesn't everybody get a chance to say I'm sorry? Not that I should apologize for the *Century* piece.'

'The Post Impressionist Illoooosion,' she said. 'When you said modern art and the immigrants coming here from Europe were part of the same dangerous influence, Royal, what were you thinking? John despises you for it.'

'The tragedy is, I only have the highest admiration for the great artist.'

'Perhaps hate isn't strong enough. He never wants to set eyes on you again. He condemns you to actual hell. He thinks what you did was unforgivable.'

'He's the one who said, "You can put eleven men in white flannel trousers, but that doesn't make them a cricket team."'

'But did you ask him what it meant?' Belle asked. 'What if he wasn't talking about the eleven Cubists in the Armory show? What if he really was talking about a cricket team? Mr. Sargent is very literal, you know. He doesn't like novels, for instance, calling them a feminine diffusion. He likes to take his information straight as scotch. He's a man's man.'

'You can say that again.'

She glanced at her guest's prissily crossed knees and looked past him toward the vacant doorway.

'Now tell me about the party.' Cortissoz pulled out his stylographic and a pad of paper. '"Come As You Really Are"?'

Belle smiled.

'Well, of course, it has something to do with loathsome Miss Lowell and her dyspeptic dance troupe,' the critic said.

She shrugged. 'Who told you that?'

'I keep my ear to the ground.'

'I'd take care of what I said, or even heard, about Amy if I were you,' Belle said. 'Not only is she Jack's relative, I love her as I loved her dear cousin James Russell Lowell. James inducted me into the Dante Society.' She pointed to a glass case down the hall, where her prize editions of *The Inferno* were stored: the *Aldine Dante* of 1502, the *Brescia Dante* of 1487, and the *Landino Dante* with illustrations after designs by Botticelli, printed in Florence in 1481. On a shelf below them, angled toward them on its stand, sat Alighieri's death mask, frozen in a howl.

'She's so unattractive,' Cortissoz said. 'Blowsy, loud. And this freak show she's bringing—aren't there servants among them? One of them's a concierge at the Parker House, and the other just sets tables. Some people take this Democratization too far. I'm surprised you're even giving her a chance to embarrass herself.'

Belle tugged at her scarf, then laughed. 'You old fraud! As though your mother weren't a washer-woman. All of this vitriol isn't because Amy is a writer, is it—damning enough these days—but a lady poet who's succeeded in making a name for herself in the arts? I've known her since her coming-out party, Royal. On top of that, I love dancing, and she and I both trained with Professor Papanti. I'm looking forward to this. What's your beef with her?'

He blinked twice. 'Don't you think she's a little mannish?'

'You're the one who's a little mannish, Royal. Those pointily manicured fingers, those dainty shoes. Are those stockings instead of socks?'

He colored.

'Look at the way your tiny ears are pinned so neatly back to the side of your head,' she said. 'You're a too-stylish evolution of a perfectly serious ape—the "modern" man.'

'It's true what the Venetian *scugnizzi* say. "The widow from Boston is as wicked as Cleopatra."'

Belle looked across the atrium above the fronds of a palm to a loggia where a single empty chair surveyed the grand interior of the life she no longer shared with her husband. 'You know, I miss him every day,' she said. Leaning against it was the walking cane he'd nicknamed 'Edward Booth.' 'God, I miss you,' she said in a private voice.

She patted Cortissoz dismissively on the knee. 'Next thing you know, men will be staying home, wearing flowered aprons, and walking the kids to school.'

'It's not just me,' Cortissoz said. 'Dr. Jung says the interior life of all men is an epic voyage from the conscious world to the femininity of the unconscious—the *anima*.'

'Yes, always ahead of the pack, Royal.'

'You laugh, but the unconscious is the next new frontier.'

She gazed at the gardens behind him, as though focusing on something at a great distance. 'Your Dr. Jung. If that's where you men are traveling from boyhood, where are we women traveling? Hah!' She batted her eyes. 'I guess we're already here!'

'Have you been to Avernus yet, where that new boy sings?'

'I'm so tired of new boys. I wish you hadn't come, Royal. Talking with you is like being stuck with little pins.'

Cortissoz bowed his head and smiled. 'Some people pay good money for acupuncture. But I guess I'm getting the hook.' He stood and looked around. 'Say, Belle, in the years since the late, great Black Jack, the last merchant shipping prince of Boston, has left us, why don't you display John's painting of you?'

At the mention of her husband, Belle felt a loneliness sweep over her. She let her eyes fall enviously on a bare spot on the wall. She'd always imagined displaying the portrait there, exactly there. But in the twenty-four years since he'd died, she hadn't had the heart to. Somehow, following his wishes not to display the portrait made it seem as if he were still sipping his scotch beside her or dropping his ashes on the carpet.

A business rajah, he'd seemed at first to be invisible to the art world, as if he were leading a separate life on the other side of a mirror. Or so it had appeared. Sometimes she could be sitting with him in front of a plate of peacock with the Second Prince of Thailand and not even know he was there.

But had she unfairly dismissed his insight? In the intervening years, she'd begun to entertain the possibility that with all her experience, she wasn't able to appreciate art on his intuitive level.

In any case, he'd always been too much of a man to be threatened by Sargent or any of the other worldlings who fawned upon her. When Sargent's intimate first portrait of her drew whispers during a short show at the St. Botolph Club, Jack asked that it never be exhibited again during his lifetime. Like their dead infant son Jackie, lost to pneumonia at two, the couple had never spoken of it again beyond his words still ringing in her head: 'Well, Belle, it looks like hell, but it looks like you.'

27

Anche l'occhio vuole la sua parte.
The eyes want their part.

BOSTON, 1922

An icy mid-April rain intensified halfway into the following week as Raffi approached the big black door for Beatrice's services. With a start he realized it was one and the same as the one he'd seen in his dream of Anna Freud and her dog. When had he last slept? When was he last awake? He should have slept when Victor gave him the chance, but he'd used the time instead to investigate and then to walk to the funeral parlor where Beatrice was to be laid out.

There'd been no mention in the newspapers. A girl 'fresh off the boat' was hardly worth worrying about anyway, he'd resigned himself to realize, but at least there might have been a sensationalized description and photograph of the grizzly death to satisfy those with a taste for it. He'd had to resort to using the hotel's lobby telephone to call around to the local Italian charitable associations, looking for anyone who knew the Favis and where they'd taken her. Once he located the parlor, he was further puzzled when the attendant let slip that her body had already been cremated, a practice Raffi knew to be banned by the Catholic Church. But then, so had castration.

Pulling up his collar, he slipped into St. Eustacia's to be present for Beatrice's sparsely attended obsequies. He could barely get past the showily extravagant spray of flowers that came with the condolences of the electric car company. The wheezing organs rumbled above imported marble. It was a big church but not by Roman standards, where the basilicas were so cavernous little clouds developed inside them, darting among the murals. The Favis huddled near the nave just as he and Beatrice had strolled to the edge of the *Ariadne* and looked out at that ugly wave no one was supposed to see. Because his love had been desecrated, there was no body and no coffin to grieve over—the empty space in front of her family hardly filled by a tiny box on a stand. Beatrice was so disturbingly alive it was impossible to think of her otherwise, even though he'd seen her with his own eyes, still at the foot of the tram.

He swallowed. Poor Beatrice! Certainly beauty was more than just a function of loss. He mourned the life they might have had together, even if it was all selfishness on his part. No use wondering now. The priest made the sign of the cross and rolled Beatrice into the spiritual deep by talking about her only in the past tense. Of course, she made no splash. But she seemed still a part of the ocean somehow, even though she'd made it to the other side. How feverishly, and how sweetly, she'd longed to make a success here, to find happiness.

Raffi looked at Signora Favi, dressed in her best black lace mantilla. Sr. Favi's bald head was gently declined, and when it shook Raffi turned away. At her father's side was Anna—no, of course not Anna Freud, it was Dorotea, her head wrapped in a gray silk scarf. By a trick of perspective she looked so much like Beatrice it was as though Beatrice were watching herself. But even more lovely.

Her family would never forgive him. Dorotea didn't need to damn him to hell. He was already there. Making the sign of the cross, he rose and slipped out the door.

He faded, earth to earth, stone to stone, into the background until he was two hundred yards away. It had stopped raining, but now it began softly again, almost as though Beatrice were caressing him. He lingered a while longer, then started back for the Parker House and his afternoon shift. Turning, he looked up the hill toward the mourners. Life was so odd. He could see exactly where Beatrice's services were but had no idea where his own father was, or if he were even alive. Had he taken the trouble to look for him? Of course not. Before returning to the United States, he'd taken the train to Naples and stood at his mother's small stone, though. For a moment, a flash of sun had come out, and he'd felt her near.

The next morning, Ephraim painted a zig across the flying bridge of the USS *Tucker*—having meticulously completed a zag the day before. From this elevation, he could see a sun-diffused fog settling in among the hills of Dorchester, and beyond that, Boston Harbor and the purplish skyscrapers in the distance. Gulls swooped and banked in the uncertain sunshine, which seemed to bounce off the crests of waves and make them brittle and stiff. Then he looked south in the hazy direction of Cape Cod. But look as he might, he could not spy the slim figure of the pretty Italian girl, pulling her coffee wagon behind her.

She crept into his thoughts every ten brushstrokes. He didn't even know her name. How she must have laughed when he left the line. She'd probably enjoyed telling her assistant about it. But, then, he couldn't see the assistant with her cart, either. Maybe they'd both been fired.

From his stance on the scaffolding, he peered through the green-tinted windows into the *Tucker's* bridge. It was filled with serious black dials and navigational instruments. The nerve center. Two chairs, almost like barber chairs, were fitted into dark green tiles. Soon, officers would sit in them, shout their orders into tubes and intercoms, and guide the *Tucker* into the stars one night until she disappeared. Now you see her, now you don't.

'What's wrong?' Roskowski asked him.

'Nothing much,' Ephraim said. 'I was just looking inside. Say, have you noticed that girl with the coffee wagon isn't coming round anymore?' His painting partner had watched him watch for her for days.

'No.'

'Because I get the sense she hasn't been around.'

Roskowski shrugged.

'Just a feeling.'

'Like the feeling you get when you're sure a sea gull is going to drop something on you?'

Ephraim smirked and jumped aside, narrowly avoiding a spray of guano. 'As usual, Comrade Roskowski, you've pierced to the heart of the matter. There are no sea gulls. They're merely gulls.'

'Ah, yes, merely gulls,' Roskowski imitated him. 'But what does it matter, Hamlet? Whatever you call them, they've got the drop on us.'

Cutting his brush in turpentine, Ephraim started painting a fresh line. He waited a full five minutes before broaching the subject of the girl's disappearance again. In the most offhanded way. 'I'm just surprised the supervisors don't demand their coffee. No coffee wagon, no coffee.'

'Coffee doesn't need wheels, nor a lovely to serve it.'

'It does in my book,' Ephraim said.

'Oh, I see. Well, why don't you ask about her?'

'Maybe she's sick.'

'I was sick last week,' Roskowski said, 'and you didn't worry about me. You didn't send me a card.'

'I wanted to,' Ephraim said. 'But I couldn't capture the right sentiment.'

Roskowski flicked some black paint on Ephraim's smock. A daub hit Ephraim's patrician neck below his ear. 'How about now?' Then Roskowski stood on tiptoes and covered his eyes like a South Sea tar scanning the horizon. 'Ahoy!' he said.

Ephraim was taken aback. Had Comrade Lenin ever had occasion to say ahoy?

'Look, past all the other ships lined up, way over at the cement curve by the railing. Do you see that?' Roskowski said.

'I can't see anything,' Ephraim said.

'Finally, it's a coffee cart.'

28

Chi prepara un trabocchetto per gli altri ci cade per primo.
He who sets a trap for others will fall into it himself.

Even though he'd believed it could never come to pass, as the next several days wore on, Raffi found he did in fact have the power to divert his attention from grieving for Beatrice. Summoned to the Sky Parlor at Sevenels, he found relief and distraction in being tapped for instruction in the art of the tango. He'd needed to see the Uruguayans slither through the Canyengue just once at the Forum to become something of an expert. Or so he wryly allowed himself to think.

'Monkey see, monkey do, Signor Raffi,' Victor said.

'Put your shoulders back, *compadrito*,' Raffi said. 'Head up for the *contrapaso*.'

The more intensely Raffi felt Beatrice's absence, the more he pushed his charges through their *adornos* and embellishments. For the performance at Fenway Court, the pièce de résistance would be the Media Luna, the 'Half Moon.' They'd already scuffed through it a few times. The epicures' lungs wheezed and rasped, rotten wicker chairs skittering across a stone terrace. 'All right!' Raffi said. 'Now we'll add the Hook after the Sandwich.'

Tiger Lily, temples aglow with unaccustomed beads of perspiration, smiled and shook her head very quickly. 'No Sandwich.'

Lorna Doom scowled.

'It's one thing with a Silvertone,' Ephraim said, fiddling with the phonograph dial, causing the needle to skip and scratch, resulting in a screech, 'but we'll have real music instead of records tomorrow night, won't we, Auntie?'

'The band will already be playing when we walk in,' Amy said. 'They're the best. Every one a communist.'

'How droll,' Rufus said, mopping his narrow chin with a towel.

'I have another surprise for you all,' Amy said.

'Great,' Ephraim said. 'We do so love your surprises.'

'Our costumes are here, so it's time for a dress rehearsal!' A rickety bumping up the stairs confirmed the arrival of the vestments. A gleaming rack was wheeled into the room, with nametags pinned to each garment. The dancers crowded round.

'Well, you certainly went all out,' Ada said.

'Ephraim, this one is especially for you,' Amy said. 'Try it on!'

'Dear lord.' Ephraim held the hanger at arm's length. 'Cross-dressing, Auntie—really?'

'My wife and I will be wearing gentlemen's black tie, of course, with top hats,' Amy said. 'Here's yours, Victor. I had snaps put on in place of buttons on your gown.'

'How thoughtful of you, Miss Lowell,' Victor said.

Raffi knew Victor was thinking, *Of course I button all my suits without help, but this is my first experience with a gown.* 'Snaps are a great idea for all of us who are inexperienced,' Raffi said.

'Victor, you won't even have to see it!' Amy said. 'But you'll enjoy the soft sliding sound it'll make when you dance.'

There was one item still on the rack. It was a columnar silk gown in pale green, exceedingly long. Amy looked significantly at Raffi. 'For you, dear. If you don't mind my saying so, I actually think you'll make quite a captivating woman. I've watched you walk.'

'I've always wanted to be a green luna moth,' Raffi said.

'A gigantic luna moth,' Victor said. 'Maybe I'm lucky I don't have to see it.'

Now three boxes were trundled upstairs and lined beside the dress rack: see no evil, hear no evil, speak no evil. 'The shoes, the hose, the undergarments!' Amy said. 'Oh, yes. The razor blades!'

'Goodbye,' Ephraim said. 'This is where I get off the boat.'

'Ephraim, have you looked at your dress? Your chest hairs will show!' Amy said.

Raffi found himself alone in a servant's bedroom with his new raiment rustling like the ocean he'd crossed with Beatrice to get here. He determined to make the best of the disguise. Trying it on might possibly be... diverting. Certainly it couldn't make him any less of a man. He looked around and immediately felt the presence of a spirit who'd once stayed here—a woman who'd stood, more often than not, beside the window. Now a low couch below the window blocked the ghost's path to its viewpoint. Piled on the seat cushions were two massive steamer trunks covered with stickers. He smiled, thinking of Ada and Amy. Sometimes there's no time to pack lightly.

There was enough illumination from the dwarf lights in the gardens below that he felt no need to snap the electric overhead on. Slipping on the dress might seem more intimate this way. He might as well try living as a woman. Of course, this wasn't trying it. It was nothing more than a costume someone had asked him to step into. He wouldn't make a good woman, though. His rib cage had lengthened nearly to the size of a clavier, a castrato tell. This was remarkably good for singing, but he didn't indulge in singing. Then, too, his fingers were twice the length of most women's fingers, even more.

He pulled his shirt over his head, loosened his belt, and stepped out of his trousers. These he folded over one of the trunks sporting a map of Venezuela. He unstrapped his garters, pulled off his silk Interwoven socks and undergarments, and stood in the moonlight. As thousands of audiences across Italy and France from the Middle Ages forward had clamored for. Reaching for the lingerie Amy had provided, he accidentally backed into a radiator, clanking with heat. He took a little jump forward. The light flickered on, and the door banged open. Amy and Tiger Lily stood on the threshold.

'Oh, sorry,' Amy said. 'I should have knocked. You look cold, dear. Would you mind sharing this room with Miss Tiger Lily? All the other rooms are occupied.'

Raffi felt a wave of embarrassment as he saw her staring at his chest. He had the budding breasts and rose nipples of a twelve-year-old girl. He was a marble erote in a railway station. In place of a grape leaf for sculptural modesty, he had the unthreatening penis of a cherub.

'Well, you're full of surprises, aren't you?' Amy said.

'You called this a changing room, Miss Lowell, so I've changed,' Raffi said.

'I'm looking forward to seeing you in that dress,' Amy said. She left him alone with Tiger Lily.

'Sorry about the surprise, old chap,' Tiger Lily said in Eton English.

This was the real surprise—Tiger Lily talking like a panel out of P. G. Wodehouse's *Something Fresh*. 'Imposter,' Raffi said, forgetting he was nude. 'Truly, who are you?'

'My father was born in Nanking,' Tiger Lily said. 'My mother was born in England, and my parents "met" touring a German brewery in Tsingtao.'

'You said, "met,"' Raffi said.

'She separated from her parents and went walking about in Canton at night. You just don't do that,' Tiger Lily said. 'But she was what was known as a highly spirited girl, which apparently attracted him, so he took her violently. Next morning, she was spirited and pregnant. She didn't mind it the way most people would have. In a way, she made shocking people her career. She always said she was an expert at disappointing her elders.'

'What happened to your father?' Raffi asked.

'I don't know. My mother never saw him again, and she refused to let her family go to the authorities. Sometimes she told me she thought she saw him, in crowds, even in London once. But in a way he was entirely in her head. Do you have parents?'

'No,' Raffi said. 'They were amputated.'

'I wasn't absolutely sure you were a eunuch until just now,' Tiger Lily said. 'What kept me from believing you were one was how comparatively modest you are. I've never known a eunuch not to brag about his sexual exploits. Until you. You must have a reason, of course.'

'With respect, I am not a eunuch,' Raffi said.

'I stand corrected. Don't castrati love to boast about their singular voices? You'll dance, but there's been no mention of your singing. Are you planning to work this into the act?'

'I do not sing,' Raffi said.

'Truly?' Tiger Lily said. 'No singing? Not ever? Funny.'

'Funny, your focus on my not singing,' Raffi said. 'As far as you go, I assumed you spoke only broken English. As far as your story goes, you never got to the part where you surrendered your manhood. Why are you passing yourself off as the Mysterious Miss Tiger Lily, with Her Sandalwood Secrets of the East?'

'Not a lot of call for a smart Chinaman here,' Tiger Lily said. 'I didn't stand a Chinaman's chance of succeeding in Boston as half a man, just as you are an incomplete Italian, so I picked the easiest path. I'm flush with opportunities as a woman. Opponents never see me coming. By the way, we're not the only two here with a secret. Rufus was born without chestnuts. That is, they were removed at birth by the nuns in hospital. They told his mother he had some sort of serious defect. So they weighed all the possibilities and found he came up short. At the doctor's suggestion, his mother tried to raise him as a girl, but it didn't take. So he ran away and joined the circus, which for someone in the Brimmer set means going to Yale instead of Harvard.'

'Nice deflection,' Raffi said. 'You're negative as a tropical depression. You can suppress your true essence even longer than I can. So many people are walking about in this world who are not as they seem. How long have you chosen to dress as a woman?'

'I worked on a freighter as a man for a while. And just as all roads lead to Boston—'

'I thought it was Rome.'

'You have a lot to learn. Just as all roads lead to Boston, all steamers, whether they know it or not, are headed for Canton. It's like the Coriolis Effect. They're all swirling down a drain into hell.'

'Have you ever seen your mother since you were a child?'

'I wrote her a letter. About thirty-five years ago, before I moved to Boston. Still waiting for a reply.'

'What brought you to Boston?' Raffi asked.

'I'll tell you when I figure that out myself. You know, you don't look half bad in that. I could get you some work in Chinatown. Don't you have any hair at all?'

Raffi had slipped on his other stocking and pulled on some expensive ivory bloomers. He'd snapped his garters on to hold the stockings up. 'How old are you?'

'Nice people don't talk about things like that,' Tiger Lily said. 'Actually, I'm deceptively youthful. I'm told I look as young as 50, but I'm 52.'

'So if you're Chinese, you have roughly 200 years to live.' Raffi stole a glance at Tiger Lily, who was beginning to undress. She was six feet tall, significantly shorter than he was, with little teacup breasts, too, but they were covered with fine wrinkles until they swelled out to full, brown nipples. Her legs were skinny like any old man's, but a bump around her midsection spoke to her success as a businesswoman. Tiger Lily had a soft brown thatch round what appeared to be a shriveled purplish bean. 'So you have hair.'

Tiger Lily shrugged. 'Some of us have a good deal more than that. It depends, I suppose, on the "surgeon." Sometimes they fail to remove everything.'

The radiator kept clanking as the room warmed. Down the hall, they could hear Amy gushing about Ephraim *deshabille*.

'That's the trouble with castration,' Raffi said. 'No standardization, even in China.'

'It depends upon the province. I went to Wu Lu, just off the Gobi Desert, and met a house servant who told me how he went through the change of life. As a promising young agent for Jardin and McPherson in Shanghai, he'd been swinging drunk the night before, arguing with one of Sir William Sassoon's sons at the Cathay Hotel. He remembered fighting three men, who abducted him. He was sure he was going to wake up on a ship the next day, pressed into a crew. But instead, as he regained consciousness the next morning, he found he was in the... suburbs, hundreds of miles from where he'd ever been before. Instead of taking him to the ocean, the press gang had brought him inland, to another world, where he was to be a wedding present for a wealthy beauty.'

'Do you serve drinks with this story? Because it doesn't sound true,' Raffi said. 'What do you think of these shoes?'

Tiger Lily donned her English lord's coat with a skull cap. She carried it off so well, she bore a distant resemblance to a daguerreotype Raffi had once seen of Prince Albert addressing a captivated crowd in New South Wales.

'He woke up chained to a *biǎo*, groggy and trembling. His new owner was a bride, the daughter of a warlord. She was just setting up her household. With smiles and nods her attendants told him of his great good fortune and how he might be of service to her. "Don't worry," they said. "This will be the making of your new happy life."'

'This story has a happy ending, right?' Raffi said. 'Miss Lowell is calling for us.' But there was no stopping Tiger Lily.

'They applied "snow" to his testicles to dull the pain. You know, like getting your ears pierced. The girl's sweet face appeared above him. Under her mother's instructions, she was presented with the knife and given advice on how to perform the indifferent miracle so that as her house servant he'd deeply understand the power she'd always have over him. If the budding empress felt any squeamishness, she'd already learned the secrets to controlling her face. Together, she and my friend learned they must both understand her lofty position was such that this was just another morning task to her, something to cross off her to-do list. At first she was shy. Her mother whispered to her to straighten her back. He begged her for mercy, but the intoxicating knowledge of his insignificance, his complete powerlessness, began to flood through his body. "I will take good care of you," she promised. Her mother nodded and prompted, "As…"

"'As I will do for all who are mine," her daughter remembered.

"'I am not a servant," he cried. After kicking and shrieking failed, he suavely attempted to dissuade her. "You don't want to waste such a resource as I could be to you, do you?"

'She didn't answer. He wondered if he'd even spoken the words. He found himself strangely aroused by his own inability to be seductive, even in his peril, and ejaculated in confusion. He was stupefied at his speechlessness in the foreknowledge of what was about to happen.

'She took a tiny breath and closed her eyes at the last moment when she gave him the deepest cut—as though she were blowing out the candles on a cake. But that's not the strange part.

'He told me that in the final reeling, blood-surged seconds while he was being unmanned, his neck and arms thrashing into the chains, his feelings shifted from hate and fear to… adoration. He had surrendered to this indifferent teenager, who was herself undergoing a transformation to The Enlightened Sprit in Silk. He watched as the girl's graceful hand disposed of everything that made him a man in a matter of seconds, as though she were tossing away the skin of an apple. What did it matter if his descendants disappeared, his future romances were evirated, his inner drive dulled and passion dissipated?

'Her breath began to come quickly. So intense was her excitement, her eyes grew moist as she licked her lips. He'd truly become her property, part of her trousseau, and so deeply subjugated to her was he that the only lust he had left was to serve her. Thrilled with the humiliation of his new situation, he kissed the ground she walked on. He attended to her clothes and the tiniest of her personal details. He went everywhere with her and doted on her every breath. Through transference, she'd become his idol. He was her devoted servant until death finished it for both of them.'

'A pretty tale, but the end needs a little work,' Raffi said. 'What happened to the beauty?'

'Tastes change. Her lotus flowers—her exquisite feet, if you could even call them that—which had once been such a source of pride to her, became her deepest shame. Since she could never walk away, death was her only way out. How could he, with his antennae so tuned to sense her every mood, have missed all the signs?'

29

Chi angelo vuol apparire, è un diavolo.
The one who wants to look like an angel is the devil.

BOSTON, 1922

Moonlight glinted on chrome hood ornaments as the caravan of mile-long motorcars wound its way through the Emerald Necklace to Fenway Court. The big night was getting underway. Willows draping the vernal pools were made more mysterious by mists rising above the gardens. Raffi, in the lead limousine, studied nature in his unnatural circumstances.

'I don't know how you ladies do it,' Ephraim growled. 'What are you so hopped up about?'

'Ah, youth,' Amy said. 'Confusing the serene equanimity of fall with the shrieking sexual fire engines of spring.'

Ada peered through the glass at the witches' brew. 'Or the post-coital drowse of a summer day.'

'Raffi, how intense is your excitement?'

'While I don't exactly feel summer or the blush of spring, it isn't winter, either, Miss Lowell. If I had to put a date to my emotions, I'd say it's somewhere around *Il Giorno Dei Morti*.'

'The well-tempered castrato,' Ada said. 'How piquant.'

'The adder strikes.' Ephraim turned to Raffi. 'Don't you feel humiliated by being used like this?'

'I enjoy certain other advantages,' Raffi said. He smoothed the dress over his knees. 'If something goes wrong—at this spectacular party, say—it's assumed I won't feel a hint of melancholy or anger. You needn't be concerned I'll be embarrassed. I won't wake up in the wee hours, burning with shame. Being released from the competitive nature of sexual anxiety lends me a certain clarity.'

When Ephraim raised an eyebrow, Ada pinched him. 'Might be just the ticket for you.' She winked at Tiger Lily, who had resumed her air of inscrutability. 'How much easier it is for us to sit with our knees crossed.'

'Maybe we should all take a sexual holiday,' Amy said.

The statue-garden doors were thrust open at the Gardner mansion, and in the fog, with crickets singing in the background, the venue glowed.

Debouching, Amy turned to the invisible Roy and asked him if he'd like to take in the show. 'Surely there's a corner where the servants will be looking on, and you know where the kitchen door is.'

'I'll stay out here, thank you, Miss Lowell. I have my fruit and my copy of the *Post*.'

'But you can't miss this!' Amy said.

'I've seen a lot of dancing in my life, Miss Lowell. With your permission, I'm just going to let it go.'

She'd waited too long for her invitation, and both seemed to know the moment had passed.

Raffi looked back into the inky black of the Fens. He lingered long enough to watch the chauffeur flick on the map light with an easy motion, reach into a paper bag, and pick out a rosy apple. Then he began to polish it.

Per instructions, the orchestra had dropped into Brahms. Already two sheets to the wind, the guests inside filled the windows as he and the other 'girls' covered the final fifty feet along a serpentine path through the gardens. They had to watch to keep their heels from catching in the cracks.

Stalking in, Amy cut a channel to the Spanish Cloister, to applause. Closing his eyes, Raffi sensed the tonic this seemed to her as she nodded to Royal Cortissoz and his new protégé, a dashing young man with half his upper lip clean-shaven and the other half a fecund garden of a moustache. The poet moved briskly in her black tuxedo with top hat, her sash the beloved silk scarf of nightmarish oleanders she'd bought during a stop at Port au Prince for Dartiguenave's inauguration dinner in 1915.

At her side, Ada deftly swung her jacket open to reveal a silky lining jumping with eyes and snakes. 'Keep moving,' Ada hissed. 'You're chafing against your irrelevance.'

Ruth and Lorna slunk by in morning coats. Ephraim scowled in flatfooted. His heavy, clam-digger steps served only to kick up the lace petticoats below his narrow black pilgrim dress with virginal white collar. He looked like an engraved plate from *The Courtship of Miles Standish*. In his wake trailed Rufus Cloud, trim and vigorous in chocolate silk charmeuse. A purple scarf vibrating against her duster, Tiger Lily was a wild iris yanked from the boggy gardens lining the necklace of ponds outside.

Raffi kept his hair almost maestro-long anyway, wavy and darkening at the nape of his neck, so he needed no wig. For effect, he'd flipped it to the other side and brushed it into a flapper's bob. He began to experience an illicit excitement, but he wasn't sure if it was from the general transformation in preparation for going onstage or for this very specific act of becoming a feminine creature. His chest was cold, because he was showing a lot tonight. He looked down past his new décolletage and waistline created by the cut of his low-necked gown to his billowing skirt, which brought to mind one of Forlanini's *luftschiffs* overhead, sweeping its shadow far below. While he was hardly captivating, he was a sight. In fact, as he took the final step across the threshold, his left breast popped out of his bodice. The crowd of onlookers gasped. Not to worry, he tucked it neatly back in. No one saw it—no more than thirty people, anyway. A sunny freedom sailed over him. He'd never been so far outside himself. He was accustomed to women's eyes being on him, either out of curiosity or pity, and to unsettling glances from lonely blades, but here were gentlemen's eyes, too. Passing to the ballroom, he caught a glimpse of himself in a gold-veined mirror—nightmarish lipstick, eyeliner, rouge, and all. '*You look very becoming*,' the reflection said to him. '*But what are you becoming?*' An invisible hand passed him a Velvet Swing, which he swallowed in a single gulp, a gesture he noticed was not lost on Royal Cortissoz.

'Will you look at this intriguing apparition?' the critic said. 'Don't you think he looks a bit like the younger Salvini?'

'You promised you wouldn't be on the prowl,' his protégé said.

'This isn't prowling,' Cortissoz said. 'How tall d'you think he is?'

'Talk about a freak show,' the young man said.

They obviously didn't care if he heard.

'The Lowells are such hypocrites,' Cortissoz said. 'While Amy's free to rub herself against us like a wet cat on a chair leg, her priggish brother Abbott is hunting down perfectly nice Harvard boys in secret court and hounding them to suicide for the hidden joys they share in their dormitories.' He dropped to a murmur. 'Speaking of hypocrites, I wonder if Mr. Sargent is here.'

'If you're here, you may be certain he is not.' The young man curled his half moustache and saluted Sargent's masterwork with a lift of his glass.

'You know,' Cortissoz said of *El Jaleo*, 'It's voluptuous, and devilishly talented, but do you detect a whiff of juvenilia?'

'I'd heard he had a taste for that.' When Victor passed by, the young man gave Cortissoz a nudge: 'I'm surprised Mrs. Gardner would let a dinge like that in here if he's not carrying a silver tray.'

'That's not just any dinge,' Cortissoz whispered. 'That's Mr. Sargent's, um, model. John bumped into him in a hotel lift and was so "elevated" by the encounter he locked him up in his studio for months and sketched him to the bones. That blind boy is the prototype for every slapdash image, male or female, on John's grotesqueries that grope their way across the Museum of Fine Arts's vaulted ceilings above the grand entrance. How droll—a darky whitewashed for our grand delusions, a servant's sniff to the godly limbs of Poseidon, Psyche, even Aphrodite.'

'Making trouble again,' a low voice said behind them. As though he'd stepped from his own painting, Sargent appeared out of the darkness, snatched the Japanese Typhoon from Cortissoz's hand, downed the drink, set the glass on a passing waiter's tray, and in a flash the morning society columns would dub 'the Boston pop,' threw a punch.

Cortissoz fell backwards on his pumps, looked up from the tiles, and straightened his stockings. 'For all your heft,' he said, dabbing at his bloody nose with a handkerchief, 'you hit like a girl.'

Sargent brushed his hand along Victor's shoulder, whispered something to him, and departed.

Amy stepped over the body. 'Poor dear, you just can't help yourself. You've always got to be the center of attention.' She held out her hand to help, and Cortissoz stood. Time to call up her dancers: 'To your stations! Rufus and Ephraim, you're all the way to the right. It's Ada and me on the left. Miss Tiger Lily and Raffi, you're front and center. You two gents will weave between us,' she said to Ruth and Lorna Doom.

A ting-ting on crystal ushered a hush. Belle, swaddled in a black-and-green tapestry kimono, framed herself in a Portuguese arch. The orchestra had already slipped into silence, still sipping Sargent's punch.

'This is my favorite part, when things are just about to happen,' Amy said.

'I thank you all for coming tonight,' Belle said, 'especially our tango troupe, in its premiere performance. I never remember what to say when it's time to cut the lights, so... could we cut the lights, please?'

In the rustling darkness, the whole room stopped. The dancers exaggerated and froze into their starting positions. The violinists set bows to fiddles. The accordionist tensed her fingers over the buttons of her bandoneón.

'While Mr. Sargent was unexpectedly called away just now,' Belle said, looking daggers at Cortissoz, 'I want you to know he is here in spirit. In any case, I think it's time for a dance.'

Amy jumped up. '*Presto!*' 'La Cumparsita' pulsed through the cigarette smoke. Amid a shiver of cymbals, two smirking nellies from the Harvard theater department flanking *El Jaleo* snapped to attention. In unison, they released the cords that ran above a set of pulleys holding up the painted gauze, heavy with fishing weights sewn into its lower seam. Raffi felt the breeze. Candlelight flickers echoed the silkscreen's precipitous descent as he caught sight of Sargent turning on his heels and making a beeline for the door, shaking his head.

The *señorita* in the white dress now danced with a gauze woman in cobalt in the foreground. Two other painted couples, gender indeterminate, engaged in a similar embrace to her left and right. And a whirl of eternally concupiscent humanity revolved around Lorna Doom as the dancers plunged into action.

Cortissoz seemed to recognize the Harvard undergrads. 'Why's it called Hasty Pudding when they spend the whole year getting ready for a single show? By the way, I know personally that boy's a Jew. I wonder how he feels unfurling Veronica's Veil tonight, or rather Belle's Veil. We bow to greater saints now.'

Raffi turned for a moment to take in the illusion's unreality, which in the flood of events had taken on a life of its own. He floated partner after partner across the floor, to applause. Whirling round, he came face to face with Amy. As he took her in his arms, she seemed to relax but then stopped short. The ceiling was still spinning above him when she cried out, 'Ravishing as you are, this isn't you. After all, it's Come As You Really Are Night! I have another surprise.'

Amy snapped her fingers and the orchestra stopped. A spotlight illuminated a lurid red box sitting in a corner, secured by a red satin bow. The carton was large enough to pick up the glow, so it and Raffi were bathed in the same blaze. All eyes followed as he stepped over to see what new mischief she and the others had in mind, but he didn't have to open the gift to divine what it was. He'd known this was coming since that first night at the Orphanage.

'My honor is your amusement,' Raffi said. A drum rolled, and withal he was surrounded by Venetian dressing screens. Inside their shelter, he yanked the ribbons aside and pried off the lid. He felt the spooky sensation of opening a dictionary to just the right page. Amid catcalls, he tossed his dress and camisole into the air beyond the screen, punctuated by whines from the sopranino sax and vaudeville ka-bumps from the drums. Then he pulled up the tights, which fit like a sanguinary skin. He clasped the bright red cloak around his neck, slipped into the hood with the horns, kicked into his boots with the curled toes, and grasped the smooth shaft of his trident. He took a breath, nodded slowly, and cried, '*Subito!*'

The screens were whisked away, and he brazenly stood with his legs apart, his childhood misapprehensions dissolving into a *frisson* of ironic detachment. He was suddenly back in the train station in Naples and the guests' eyes were coins.

'Dear God,' the man with half a moustache said. 'The Underwood Devil. How stirring, how... eunique.'

Raffi took a step toward the pair.

'Now you're gelding the lily,' Cortissoz said to Raffi. 'Won't you be hot in that?'

Saltonstall, in white tie and donkey ears, said, 'Welcome to the land of the Cockaigne' before disappearing behind a fern.

'That costume certainly leaves nothing to the imagination,' Cortissoz said to Raffi. 'There's a *vas deferens* between men and women—you seem to be exploring somewhere in between.' The critic dusted his glasses. 'So the devil is an anatomical grotesque. No wonder Lucifer's so miffed at God.'

'Napoleon was a monorchid, wasn't he?' the protégé said.

'Imagine the breeze Waterloo might've been if he'd had nothing in his way,' Raffi said. The crowd clapped as the clown in Raffi bowed. Victor frowned and knocked back a long draught from his glass.

Helped by an attendant, Belle swept close. 'Well, you're full of surprises, young man.'

'Not man, but man I used to be,' Raffi said.

She pressed his hand, shook it, peered into his eyes. 'I believe I've met a soul mate.' Then she shifted back into party gear. 'Speaking of Napoleon, you may be interested to know that these two chiffoniers we're standing beside kept the Little Corporal well dressed at Elba.'

The music covered everyone like a wave, embracing all and draw-ing them in. Belle introduced Raffi to business czars, painters, and potentates, among them a sad little man dressed à la turque. He had wet black eyes. 'That's William Grueby of the Tile and Faience Company,' Belle said. 'He's just invented a color blue that never existed in nature.' She waved Ruth over and gestured to a bearded gent, naked from the waist up, in a swami diaper: 'Professor Benedict, this is the Lithuanian art thief Bernard Berenson, the best second-story man in Boston.' He seemed to be trying to move a little Bernini bronze of a devil by staring at it. Raffi recognized it. He'd seen its likeness in the garden of a corrupt magistrate during his nightly prowls with Stefania.

'What did that set you back?' Berenson asked.

Belle looked into her empty glass. 'I think I'm a bit tipsy!'

Drunk, smug, and mugging, 'Tipsy does it,' Raffi said. Or had the Underwood Devil said it?

In Palm Beach jacket, shark fin, and gray worsted trousers, William Dawes slipped in and tapped him on the shoulder. 'You might have something there. Come and see me.'

Raffi took his card, gazed across the room, and was suddenly stone cold sober when he noticed a girl in a gray caterer's uniform standing rigidly with a silver tray, her head down. Blue shadows painted her lovely long neck. Swanlike and stunning, her features were symmetrical to the point of deformity. She raised her head. Dorotea stared directly into his eyes.

Raffi returned the look and in her gaze felt her keen appraisal shift from recognition to disgust, shame, sympathy, even a degree of softness, as though to say, 'You've come to this. I always knew this was what you were.' *Fremdschämen*, the consul from Berlin had pronounced it—a private embarrassment for others as they humiliate themselves. Maybe the little shadow, far from the Forum, had always had a warmth and a depth that was hard to detect beside the bright light of Beatrice. Raffi swallowed and tried to call to her, but she turned, flipped her empty tray under her arm, and disappeared into the back rooms.

Victor plucked at his shoulder. 'Well, they certainly couldn't have picked a better ham. Come on, Raffi. I thought you were never going to sing.'

Outside in the Pierce Arrow, Roy polished another apple and held it to the light. One hundred yards behind, the ghost of Black Jack was night gardening, as he would have it—absently stabbing his sword cane into the ghosts of cigarette butts his long-dead guests had dropped on the lawn and flipping them into a little bag hanging from his left wrist. He haunted the foggy bog as the world steamed and hissed around him. How maddening! He was here, and yet not here. As much as he missed Belle, he didn't miss any of her damn-fool friends. Looking north above the townhouses of Back Bay, he stopped at the red devil sign rising from the factory on Fulton Street. Then he surveyed along his curved driveway the string of cars, which had beads of mist on their long bonnets, their engines ticking more slowly as they lost their heat. This quiet world, invisible to his wife, was his private society. He knew that Roy was in Miss Lowell's car, and he knew that all the Roys, because there were no fewer than a dozen out here, watching, waiting, balancing the silence with him in stygian communion, were aware he was out here too.

By 11 p.m., the crowd was getting restless. 'Well, this evening really was a success. Maybe it's time to go,' Ada said. 'We should always leave an audience wanting more.'

'You've just proven you're not a poet,' Amy said gaily.

'Tell that to 1,800 drunken lance corporals at the Claviero Theatre in Veracruz,' Ada said.

'Pornography and poetry aren't always the same thing,' Amy said.

Melvina Cabot broke in from behind. 'Speaking of verse, in honor of this great occasion, Come As You Really Are Night wouldn't be complete if we didn't honor you for your marvelous entertainment, Amy.' She stepped away and waved for everyone's attention. 'Hush, hush, we have a surprise ourselves for our illustrious friend, Miss Lowell.'

Lorna Doom emerged from the shadows, rolling another package on wheels. Both Belle's and Amy's eyes widened. Neither was used to being upstaged.

'Now it's your turn, Amy,' Melvina said. 'A drum roll, please.'

Amy tore open the tissue as the crowd gasped, then whooped and laughed. She held up the image of a ponderous sub-Saharan aquatic mammal with her face painted on it.

'Behold the Hippopoetess,' shouted Melvina, Hepsibah, and Lorna Doom, in the dread voice of a Greek chorus, repeating the cruel joke popularized by her friend and enemy Ezra Pound.

Raffi knew Amy was girding herself as she stood alone, framed below the painting. After a pause, she said, 'Good joke.' Before a jury of her fears, she wasn't going to give them what they so wanted. She looked down at herself as though for the first time and then took in Hepsibah and her other tormentors. Standing with them was the slender form of her 'friend' Lorna Doom. 'But not a new one. I've worn the Scarlet F since I was a girl.'

As the laughter died, Raffi heard the wolves' quick steps as they prowled the upper seats after midnight in the Colosseum. It was always better when they howled. Then you knew where they were.

Cortissoz munched indifferently on a roasted-calf-heart tidbit on a silver pick. 'It's nice and all,' he said of the tableau. 'But it carries the stink of death.'

'We're done here,' Ada said.

'No, no, let's play this out,' Amy said. 'We haven't finished.' Now it was she who looked at the bandleader, thrust out her hip, and nodded. As a sassy new song curled out of their instruments, the black sheep of the Lowell clan began to pull off her gloves in a most suggestive manner. Then she unbuttoned her jacket. She removed her shirt.

'Disgusting,' Melvina said.

'Oh, too divine!' Ada cried. 'A night-blooming cereus!'

'That's moxie!' Belle said. Hepsibah and Melvina shared alarmed glances.

The music grinding, Amy continued stripping with an air of ravishing self-fulfillment. No one had bargained on this farce, and there was a quick shuffle as the guests began to scurry out. She giggled jubilantly, exposing mounds of dimpled, pale flesh shadowed by blue light, and wriggled in time to the music. It was her moment, and she made the most of it until everything was pink, unshackled, unafraid. The uncomfortable departure turned into a giggling stampede. 'Where are you going, dears?' she called after the flying heels and wraps. 'What's the matter? Didn't you all come for a show?'

30

Per conoscere un furbo ci vuole un furbo e mezzo.
To know a tricky guy it takes a trickier guy.

BOSTON, 1922

The iron scissors gate clanked shut. Now this was something. Raffi had signed a deal with the devil before, but never as the devil. With a jolt, the lift stopped at the seventh-floor headquarters of Dawes Advertising Agency.

A woman behind the nametag 'Lois' was reading through a stack of papers at a desk angled to a frosted glass door. When she reached to take his card, she disturbed her cup of coffee but Raffi righted it before a single drop was spilled.

'You just saved my life,' she said. 'I owe you one. You're here to see Mr. Dawes?'

'Rafaele Pèsca.' He bowed and brushed his lips to her outstretched hand.

The door behind her flew open. 'Cut the Continental crap. It's wasted on Lois.' William Dawes motioned him in with a cigar. 'If it isn't the next Valentino.' He strode to the window. 'Come over here, you. We'll decide later what your name's gonna be. I want to show you something.'

He pointed across the rooftops toward the North End, where the Underwood sign, like a forgotten moon by day, slept unlit atop the factory. 'We have a situation here that calls for a little damage control. Now have a seat, won't you, and I'll tell you what the devil all of this is about. First of all, you know of course of the William Underwood Company? Well, they're in some hot water.'

A few minutes later, Raffi reviewed a release that guaranteed him no rights whatsoever but the princely one-time sum of $70 for all advertising and catalog photography.

'Pretty cool cash, eh?' Dawes said as Raffi signed. 'We'll put out a flash: "After an exhaustive search we've found our new devil." Bet you've never made a deal this good.'

'Not in sixteen years,' Raffi said.

'And of course, we get the usual forty percent from any future gigs,' Dawes said.

Raffi listened as Dawes rattled through a list of parties of the first part. How strange to find himself in this position again. If only he could exchange letters with his six-year-old self. That boy had trusted a *bella bugardo* promising fame: 'your life will be changed forever if you make just this one choice.' Still, the scugnizzo in him knew it was best not to turn your back on an opportunity without at least an investigation.

'Think of me as a dream merchant,' Dawes said. 'I'll handle all the arrangements for shooting. I'll take care of you.' He tossed a tin of Underwood Deviled Ham to Raffi, who caught it neatly with his thumb and index finger. 'This world is moving so fast, the value of a good brand is something we hold onto for dear life,' Dawes said. 'It's all we have left to us. Advertising *is* modern living. Need a pick-me-up? Get a Coca-Cola. You love your breakfast cereal, you'd better buy Shredded Wheat.' He pounded his fist on the table. 'We're determined to stay at the top of this cutthroat potted-meat market. I caught your act last night at the shindy. So can you lick your lips and hold a pose?'

Raffi looked at the parade of former satans on the wall. Faces of the damned. Well, he might as well join them. What a joke he'd become. He began to wonder if there were anything he wouldn't stoop to. 'I see I won't be your first devil,' he said.

'You'll be the seventh, by my count.' Dawes guided him past three doors to the photo studio. 'The first two had beards that looked like something was living in them. The next few had bushy eyebrows, so they just looked angry. One of the others was hung like a fuckin' mule. Frankly, they all tested out as too scary for children.' He stopped and bit off the tip of a cigar, then studied it. 'We're looking for romantic-scary, not gothic-scary. The tragic devil but with just the slightest hint of humor. Not all the way to a Mephisto opera, but more of an operetta. The direction we're taking is family-friendly.'

'What happened to your last devil?' Raffi asked.

'He quit and left no forwarding address. You and your get-up had a lot of what we're looking for last night, but not quite enough flash. We've made a few edits and have a swankier set of marching orders here.' He held up a sketch dashed off so quickly the figure in red could boast no face. 'These shots are quite tight, so you'd better skip the skivvies. Otherwise you'll drive our guys crazy in re-touching.'

'Mr. Dawes, you have a telephone call,' Lois said through the intercom.

'Scuzi.' Dawes pushed a button, bending down to speak in it. 'Dawes. Yes, he's right here. I'm out of cigars. Jesus Christ.' He spun to Raffi. 'What are you standing around for? Head on down to the dressing room and get into your duds. Make-up's coming in. Hit it.'

Raffi passed a series of storyboards along the narrow hallway. A family canoe picnic featuring… Underwood! A reunion rescued by… deviled ham. Fussy grandchildren distracted by… ingenious sandwich triangles. A happy hunting party fortified by… what else? Underwood, Underwood, Underwood, a visit from the devil the seeming answer to every social peril. He paused. The members of the tableaux were happier and more at home than the star. Except for the deer in the background. Its mortified look reminded him of something. He'd seen that look of bright fear before, the tilt of the head. Harry Laughlin in the Parker House bar.

He hung his suit on a hanger in the dressing room, stepped into the stretchy red hose and body suit, and shrugged into the red cloak. Maybe it was better to think only of the present. How strange that his idle boyhood fantasy of playing the Underwood Devil was coming true. This was a scene out of *Faust*. He put on the boots with the curly red toes. How might Dr. Freud have accounted for these?

In the photo studio, the lady Dawes called 'Makeup' glued on the vestige of a pointed beard and used a kohl outline crayon to exaggerate his eyes. Others at the agency began to crowd around.

'Smashing, Peach,' Dawes said. Then, to his associates, below his breath, he whispered, 'We've got a sure hit here. Ha! What lengths we have to go to make a cartoon for the masses. Never more than now do they need to believe in the unbelievable.'

The shutterbug squinted at Raffi through the lens of the camera. Dawes pushed him away and had a look himself. 'Too girly,' he growled. He motioned to a stylist who rushed forward to draw the red cloak deftly over Raffi's slightly soft chest. The stylist cleared his throat. Then he stared at the empty nexus between Raffi's legs, made smooth by the tights.

'Don't mind Rick, here,' Dawes said of the stylist. 'That poof's been a fairy so long his family came out on the *Mayflower*.'

Richard lifted his chin. 'As Mr. Leacock says, "The evoluted devil grins in his very harmlessness."'

Dawes took a drag. 'And as I've always said, never underestimate the stupidity of the public to declare that Canuck fuck "the wittiest man in America."'

Richard blinked. He looked at Raffi as though they might share intimacies he'd love to name. He stared deeply into Raffi's eyes. 'Are you ready, Hon?'

'But of course,' Raffi said.

'Would you like to take a look in the mirror?' Richard asked.

'No need,' Raffi said.

'Then let's get started,' Richard said.

'By all means, let's go to Hell!' Raffi said.

Lights switched on, illuminating him from every angle in front of a white screen made snowy from tiny bits of quartz, mica, and phosphorus.

'He's... perfect,' a female voice murmured.

'Almost.' Richard walked across the dark room to the array of lights where Raffi stood. 'Could you stand with your legs just a bit more apart?' he asked. 'Shoulder-breadth, as though someone were about to pass a bushel of apples down to you? And suck in that gut.'

Raffi adjusted his stance and felt the sensation of Voluptuo gliding through the room. Lois, who'd materialized in the doorway, caught her breath.

With his manicured fingernails, the stylist gave quick little tugs on Raffi's tights until it was clear his privates were so family-friendly they didn't exist. 'No wrinkles,' he explained. 'Because you're a trademark, we need a clean line, a svelte horror. Modern measures for modern times.'

Then the photographer set up tray after tray of explosive powder. Poof! Bang! Sizzle-poof! 'Could you raise the pitch fork a little higher, please? No, straight up. Think flag, not weapon.'

Lois giggled in the background.

'This,' Richard said in a reverent voice, 'is going to be nothing less than fabulous.'

Ka-Poof!

'You say you're from Italy, dear?' Richard asked.

'Yes,' Raffi said. 'From the eternal cities of Napoli and Roma.'

'Do you mind my...' the photographer said from behind his silk curtain, then seemed to reconsider. 'Oh, never mind.'

Carried by rotogravure and Ben-Day dots, cinematographs and pulp print, Raffi's image as the Underwood Devil would reach ports of call as far flung as Batavia and Singapore. The northernmost boundary of his billboard dominion would be west of Toronto, on a green-lattice sign facing a night-garden restaurant frequented by motorcars that had traveled to the town of Goderich on the shores of Lake Huron. Halfway across the lake, in the moonlight, Raffi's illuminated figure would echo over the blue like a red Colossus.

Starting with the short-lived smoked turbot line, his simplified, sanitized image was to adorn the tins of the new Underwood Co. product universe, processed at the rate of 70,000 cans a minute. For all eternity.

31

Credere per vedere.
Believing is seeing.

BOSTON, 1922

'I'll take two Chinks and that odd-looking wop,' Transportation Secretary Harry Laughlin told Saltonstall. 'None of them speaka the English, right? It's better for us if they can't tell tales.'

A pale morning fog drifted across Boston Harbor to the muffled cries of gulls. Raffi directed two assistants as they readied carts of glasses, champagne, and catering dishes aboard a Shawmut ferry heading for the future Logan aerodrome.

Laughlin wore an overcoat and fedora against the dankness. One of his bodyguards lit a smoke and stared into the fog as if he'd never seen it before. The other peered intently into a three-month-old copy of *Police Gazette*.

All told, there were 32 interested parties aboard, heading for the 189 acres of rocky, tidal muck that constituted Jeffries Point. Laughlin was surrounded by his five committee members, the three competing runway development teams, officials from the fledgling Colonial Air Transport, three Army Air Service officers, two pilots from the Massachusetts Air Guard, and Frank Morelli, who huddled with his often-useful friend Brewster, who couldn't conceal his indignation that from the looks of things, the honorable Transportation Secretary and Melvin Dingle were chumming it up.

'So what makes you the best man for this job?' the Secretary asked Dingle.

'I've got the E, B, and B—the excavation equipment, boats, and barges to extend the runway,' Dingle said.

'You call this bucket a boat?' Brewster said, leaning over the rail.

'We've just added five new scows to our fleet, and three tugs,'

Philip Rawson, the Beverly contractor, said in a voice that telegraphed his failure. As though he were also saying, 'What does it matter that my bid will come in far lower for the Commonwealth of Massachusetts?' As though he knew, everybody knew, that Dingle had this thing locked up tight. If not Dingle, Brewster.

While the city skyline was clear and sunny across the water, the low cloud layer had created a gauzy ceiling no more than fifty feet high above the tidal peninsula.

The ferry reached a splintery pier, caved in from disuse and covered by motor tires. Like the rest of the flats, the wharf flapped with gulls who eyed the intruders suspiciously as they disembarked and walked toward a gravel strip beside a series of low huts where a biplane emblazoned with a pointed star in a circle taxied.

'They don't seem too happy to see us,' the Secretary said of the gulls.

'I've landed my Curtiss here hundreds of times during touch-and-goes, and I'm always surprised how they keep coming back,' said a young Army lieutenant with the nametag Snow. The redhead who answered to 'Kit' had the childlike air of a man who'd stayed in the service to avoid growing up. 'Way they see it, it's a rookery and a dump until we take it from them. But they'll know when to leave.'

'One thing you can say about gulls,' Dingle said. 'At least they know which way the wind is blowing.' He shot a glance at Brewster, who stamped out a cigarette.

'And you boys,' the Secretary said, waving his hand toward a bubbling contingent of men in tailored, violet-gray uniforms that looked like Confederate naval officers' regalia. 'Do you mind answering me a question? Why have you called yourselves Colonial Airlines when there were no airlines back in the day?'

Their leader touched the brim of his cap. 'Bostonians love Colonial anything. If we catch on, maybe we'll rethink it.'

'If you offer passenger service from Boston to Washington, you'll catch on,' the Secretary said. 'Maybe not in those dandy getups.' He turned to Kit Snow. 'Well, I wouldn't have dragged the committee out here before the vote tonight if we weren't going to be entertained. Where's our show?'

'Do you see that mooring mast halfway across the point, Mr. Secretary?' The aviator indicated a vertical slash in the haze that brought to mind a gun sight.

'That thing like a telephone pole?'

'That's where we're headed,' Snow said.

'Might as well be the North Pole. It better be worth risking a perfectly good pair of shoes. So where is it?'

'Don't worry, sir. The show's getting ready to start.'

The deputation walked on, their Florscheims sucking holes in the muck as gulls swirled overhead. As they drew closer to the pole, the men picked up the low thrum of six vibrating Liberty L-12 engines. One of the committee members jumped up and down and pointed to an empty place in the clouds. Others, confused, held their hands over their ears or looked for cover. Ahead through the mist, the indistinct shapes of some Army Air Service ground pounders and sailors materialized below a low cloud, scurrying this way and that and raising fifty-foot static-discharge wands that disappeared halfway into the fog. They were South Sea islanders prodding at a visitor from the dream time.

Kit Snow took a deep breath. 'Gentlemen, I present to you the hydrogen dirigible *Roma*!' He waved his arms into the ether. 'The top brass purchased this Italian-made bird for $250,000. Our little debutante is 410 feet of weightless aluminum and silk, here for her coming-out in New England.' He laughed as lifting gulls were blown out of balanced flight by the prop wash. 'Not a bad calling card for our taking control of the air.'

Below a bright brimming fogbank, the ground crew pulled vigorously down on swinging ropes and cables, tethering the Unseen. The cables screeched as the aluminum gondola descended into view before the silver airship showed itself in her full majesty, long and shining.

Raffi, tending to his catering cart, continued unpacking the refreshments. It wouldn't do for him to appear too interested. This was obviously a very important moment for the young aviator. *He'd been preparing for this for weeks*. Like a cinema scientist in front of a van der Graaf generator, Snow folded his arms and nodded. With a deafening crackle, a great static spark like a bolt of lightning shot from the mechanical leviathan's nose to the mast. The committee erupted into applause.

Suddenly, a gust of wind lifted the ship and it was airborne again, heading to heaven. An unfortunate wretch was swept through the air in a big arc. Losing his grip, the inadvertent 'aeronaut' somersaulted with a scream, fell to the ground with a sickening thud, and lay still.

His legs and arms were splayed, his head twisted toward the crowd, his unblinking eyes dull. A river of blood began to flow from between his pale lips.

As the Secretary turned on his heel and started back toward the dock, he pointed to Snow. 'Well, that was quite a show.'

32

Far vedere la luna nel pozzo.
Show someone the moon in the well.

BOSTON, 1922

Carlo looked across the water in the Public Gardens at the chorus of swan boats. He could have sworn he saw their eyes shift as their heads swung disapprovingly back and forth, like his mother's. How could they know what he was about to do? He didn't want to knock off the Transportation Secretary. He hadn't met the man. Hadn't had the pleasure. Hadn't looked into the eyes of his family. But if Carlo didn't do this, he was a goner himself, courtesy of Mr. Stadt.

He wasn't half a dozen steps from the spot where the old man had pushed him into the pond. He cringed. How could he have let Stadt do that to him? He could still hear the splash. To make matters worse, somewhere deep in his lost boyhood, the vanishing chorister Pèsca reappeared, pushing him off the stage again with the selfsame maneuver Stadt had repeated here in the pond. Just as he had many other times, he wondered, whatever happened to the boy who'd had his nuts cut off? Probably singing in some village church somewhere. Most castrati didn't make it. The docking could go any number of ways. The saying was, maybe he was castrated in 'bad weather,' a lifetime of catcalls ahead of him. Funny, that.

Carlo shuddered, stabbed out a smoke, and lit a new one. What was a catcall? How much luck could you have calling a cat? He walked to the edge of the pond. He looked down to see his reflection, or at least try again to catch a flash of that uncertain shiny thing Stadt had tricked him into looking for.

How could he have missed seeing that coming? Anger crackled within him again, but this time he smiled. Because he hadn't been as

183

good a boy singer as Raffi Pèsca—because he still had his testicles—he was able to feel dreadful sorry for himself at the least productive times. His mood swings frightened audiences sometimes, and they couldn't get enough of it. Under pressure on stage, on the right night, he could emanate a dangerous, musky strength. He was impatient at moments when he ought to be more careful. He forgot things that didn't have to do with his own good luck. He was only occasionally kind to children and animals, and had barely a clue when he was hurting people's—that is, bystanders'—feelings. He was a victim, he barely realized, of his own ambitions and petty jealousies. He was negligently inconsiderate. He regarded the inchoate world through the slits of his blood-dimmed eyes. He was a man. Which didn't hurt with the ladies.

As though summoning a memory from Aladdin's lamp, he scratched his nuts and closed his eyes. There was this new kid who'd come up to him after the show. Run away from her parents, this new kid. Rich as cream. They'd had some good times comparing and contrasting their young bodies in the third-floor walkup he'd sublet from that operator Marcello on Hanover Street. She smelled so good it would wake him in the middle of the night, and he'd fuck her again.

All of which might be ruined if he got caught plugging this guy. Or maybe his luck would hold? As though a breeze had run through him, chilling him, he felt inside his lapel for the Navy pistol slipped to him by Mr. Stadt. Why would a guy who was so old he was almost dead care whether some other old guy lived or died? For money? Sure, money was good. But Stadt must have lost something bigger than what money could fix.

He looked out at the swan boats. Why wasn't there a black swan? Hadn't he seen one the other day? Shouldn't there be a murderers' swan boat so we could keep things clear, murderers and bystanders, a world that made sense?

He checked his watch. Maybe it was just modern times. Wasn't the plunge of events just an impossible black swan boat we were all riding... where? And once you were on the black swan, was there any getting off? His thoughts drifted to Naples. Was he going to go to hell for this? He thought of the people he knew in Italy. At least there'd be a hell of a reunion. He knew a few songs they'd like in hell. He was startled by a church bell.

Where were the *dannato* Russians when you needed them? He looked up the long green slope toward the State House, where in twenty minutes the Transportation Secretary was, with his luck, going to blow it. Then they floated into view, two figures in the distance walking directly toward him. He hit himself on the head, in majestic self-pity:

Tonight, I'm going to do murder, then go sing somewhere.
Watch out, swans, the future is coming. What the hell do I care?

So funny these palookas don't have a conscience. I'll bet they're not even Catholic. Oh, they have their poets they're always bragging about, and those other sad sacks, but guys like that only prove the rule. It's the commies who are going to do it. What barbarians—they killed their own king, even the kids. What kind of monster kills a little boy? Carlo was more their babysitter than anything else. Look how they were dressed. He wouldn't wear that to a dog fight. The Russians reached him now, without waving.

'This is probably not going to happen,' Carlo said by way of greeting them. 'Let's walk over there, to the urinal. We don't want to be just standing here. Mistah Stadt says we're supposed to keep moving.' He had all these rules, that old man. Probably watching us right now, but from where? Maybe Stadt was the one they ought to kill. Stadt was the closest thing to a father Carlo had ever had.

33

Dove non vedi il fiore, non attenderti nemmeno il frutto.
If you don't see flowers, don't expect to see fruit.

BOSTON, 1922

The smell of roasting pork wafted through the State House Rotunda. Stadt watched the power brokers dole it out in thick slabs to the chosen few. Weaving invisibly through the huddles of businessmen in the halls, he listened as a clean, modern aerodrome was approved– 'and we'll build it ahead of the Van der Kikes of Manhattan!' A good deal of time was spent with orotund paeans to the people of Massachusetts. And in the end, the honorable Transportation Secretary showed his balls by ignoring the death threats and backing the developer in his pocket. The schmuck went with Dingle.

That loser Brewster went into a corner to confer with his backers as the Secretary took to the podium for photographs. Brewster grew red-faced and started stepping from side to side. He suddenly lunged toward the Secretary but was stopped by the two bodyguards. 'We warned you,' Brewster muttered in the buzz as he looked up at the Secretary, who was still deep in grips and grins. 'Whatever happens tonight, you've brought all of this down upon yourself.'

Morelli walked past Stadt and nodded the signal. Here was some relief, at least. Not that Stadt took any particular joy in carrying out his mission. It was just that he detested ambiguity. Worse than that, waiting was such a waste of time, such torture. Now, somebody was going to get it. Boston was going to be one crooked Secretary lighter within the hour.

Stadt skipped down the State House stairs and waited for the cars, lights ablur, to stop tearing through the young night. He crossed to Park Street Incline and slipped behind it so the golden dome of the State House would stop staring at him.

He took out his silver Lucifer case, polished to an absolute mirror finish. Smoothly, he reflected the moonlight—twice—and aimed it at the swan boats and the figures of three men. Immediately they walked toward him, their path straight as a stick.

'You are not to wave to me or show recognition in any way, but simply to approach me and stop,' Stadt's instructions ran. 'Just show me you're here.' No more than thirty feet away, he noticed Carlo had purchased another brand-new suit. He wondered if it were waterproof. Not a bad kid, though, with the dash of reluctance he needs to keep his mouth shut.

Stadt strolled back up the walk to the corner of Beacon and Park. His three trainees spread behind him as planned on each side of the street. They'd float behind the floaters as the man of the people walked down the hill toward his favorite watering hole, the Parker House.

It was easy to pick the Secretary from the crowd of sycophants, but already hard to remember his name. Targets were better off without names. He won't need one where we're sending him.

At the top of the stairs, Brewster launched into a bitter dispute with the Secretary, giving him one more chance. The idiot was still trying to make a last-minute deal. Why was the Secretary so intent upon forcing their hand?

Well, okay. Stadt thought of his youngest daughter, Ester, dead four years from influenza. Miriam, his wife, had never really recovered, crazy with grief. Like his mother, she'd taken to drink and lost impulse control. If God doesn't give a damn about his innocents, who gives a shit if there's one less scoundrel in the world? Stadt knew his family's rough luck had nothing to do with the Secretary's ill-gotten gains, but still in his mind they corresponded with each other, like a closed heat exchanger (earlier that afternoon, he'd put in a spanking-new furnace at his home in Jamaica Plain, then cracked open a longneck with the plumbers, listening to the marvelous modern machine purr), where the hot surface transfers energy to the cold without quite touching it.

It was all quite scientific, really. No longer traveling by knife, revenge in New England jumped across gaps of black air, like the wireless. It wasn't so much he was overseeing a murder. It was more like witnessing a suicide.

Stadt walked a quick little circle, his head getting hot. There was no use endorsing this craziness—just another waste of time. Morelli and Brewster threw up their hands and split from the Secretary in a brisk walk down the south stairs. Now that the die was cast, Stadt felt an electric thrill animating everything around him. As if he were tasting a rare wine, he closed his eyes to savor the vintage.

'You are dangerous, *meshuggener*,' he whispered to his prey. 'You're going nowhere fast. You don't make sense because you don't do what's good for you.' And if there was one thing Stadt prized, it was a world that made sense.

The Secretary and his entourage reached the bottom of the stairs, plotting the unlimited future. Quietly, his two bodyguards positioned themselves on either side of the street, one of them close to the tall Russian, who sat on a bench reading a book, as if that had ever happened before.

This was as scripted as Stadt's surviving daughter Risa's graduation from high school. Life starts and stops, then rolls down to the Parker House. Not that the Parker House would have welcomed him, what with their 'gentlemen's' policies.

Saying goodbye to Dingle and two more hangers-on, who then departed, the Secretary put his hands in his pockets and began his triumphant march to Hell.

Stadt looked at Carlo, watched him take in a deep breath. He had an intimation about the boy: you're sure the Russians are going to be doing the shooting, but in the end, I believe it's going to be you.

Stadt reflected on the pleasant evening he'd spent in Chinatown the night before, watching the handsome proprietress with the mesmerizing eyes drop a tea flower into a steaming, transparent pot. The petals unfolded in slow motion.

Then Stadt disappeared. One moment he was standing beside the Metro station, smoky and exhaling the spirit of the times; the next, he'd slipped into the underworld. On his way down the slimy stairs to the subway, he saw a poster of Moreschi and his upcoming visit to the Boston Orpheum. He grimaced at the singer's round, dark eyes. Didn't they love the horror show. Not his cup of tea, that. The lengths some went for applause. It sure as hell wasn't about the music, anyway. That bunch wouldn't even notice the difference. The Park, the State House, and the buildings on Beacon Street leaned in to see what happened next. Stadt's blood danced, as though he were in the hunt. This was his favorite part, he admitted deep in his heart—this sense of just before.

34

Che c'è? Hai la neve in tasca?
What's the hurry? Do you have snow in your pocket?

BOSTON, 1922

Pounding the pavement, Carlo window-shopped to keep his eyes busy while the Secretary continued down the hill until he reached Tremont Street. He watched the marked man look quickly left and right along the stone wall bordering Granary Burial Ground.

All of Boston was harshly black and white now, with taxis flashing across puddles and the Parker House getting closer and closer, as if it were moving toward them. Carlo watched the Russians with alarm. They'd dropped all pretense of 'not' following the two hired hulks. If the big men were to turn, everything would be over.

He tried to control his breathing, the way he did with his singing, but it didn't work. His breaths were rough and ripped off the loaf, as though he'd just made love. He didn't want to do this. What could he do? For one thing, he could shout for the police. Then what? What was he allowing himself to be pushed into now?

Like a cake lit for murder's birthday, the Parker House embraced them in its shadow. The bodyguards closed in to walk the final block with the Secretary, and Carlo quickened his steps, even as they grew stiffer. The Russians caught up behind the bodyguards on either side, and Carlo peered into the black maw of Roll Alley.

The Secretary allowed himself a heady sniff of the rolls.

Carlo's eyes twitched. Then something came over him. He certainly hadn't rehearsed it. To himself he said, 'I don't care if you kill me, I want out!' He laughed nervously and called with his velvety croon, 'Wait a minute, fellas!' Then he took a deep breath and shouted, 'Stop!'

As the bodyguards turned to investigate, the Russians pushed them past the hotel entrance, shot them in the neck with pistols buried below their Adams apples, and heaved the two bulks off School Street into the alley.

The Secretary held up his arms with his fingers splayed—Rigoletto, the tragic clown. He backed into the alley with a nervous smile. 'Fucking Brewster, you can't be serious.'

The short Russian pistol-whipped him in the mouth, breaking his incisors. 'Once you lose your baby teeth,' the Secretary had told his daughter that morning, 'you get one last chance with a brand new pair.'

Boom. Boom. The tall Russian shot him in each eye.

The rats spilled in, faster than ginger beer. They flowed around the rusty garbage cans and immediately swarmed over the three motionless forms on the cobblestones. Comfortable in their presence, the Russians continued their work. The tall Russian pulled out a sewer key and flipped open a manhole cover. Lifting the first baby grand by his shoes, they shoved him in.

What a load he must be. Carlo took a half step back. He wanted no part of this thing, though in his heart he knew he was very much a part of it. He felt himself falling through the darkness. So much for being a bystander. Both Russians dragged the next bodyguard toward the manhole.

Except he wasn't dead. Carlo cried out as the killers rammed their muzzles into the man's face and shot him in the eye sockets. What was their fascination with eyes? Surely they were going to kill him, too. As they dumped the second bodyguard head-first into the sewer, a river of rats flowed in after the evidence. Where was the black swan boat going to take that poor sucker?

The Secretary lay at their feet, red bubbles eddying out of his shattered mouth. How could he still be breathing? Jesus Christ. Wasn't his brain just mush? But instead of finishing him off, the Russians tried to rouse the man. How much time had passed, twenty seconds, thirty?

Finally, he got up on one elbow, the way one might rise after sleeping to check a clock on a bedside table. He turned his face to the killers, whom he'd never met and would never see. 'Mercy,' he croaked. 'I've got a family.'

Carlo felt the anger crackle within the Russians: 'You stupid. Don't you know how to die? The others were geniuses at it.' They'd lowered their pistols to the Secretary's neck, but now they stepped back, crazy, waiving their guns out of pleasure so that when they fired more rounds into the Secretary's limp body, the raucous echoes crashed against the Parker House's service door. As the last shot was fired, the steel back door started to open. A tall, lanky guy looked out, then pulled the door quickly shut. Carlo heard a bolt slide. 'Oh shit.'

The Russians had disappeared. Blood pooled below the Secretary's head. Rats came from everywhere—there must be millions—and scrambled over Carlo's shoes toward the fresh meat. Carlo, alone with the dead man, took a stagger-step back. *Che macello.* His first ten seconds as a bystander to murder. Nobody was going to buy that version of the story. Okay, his first ten seconds as a professional, and already he'd blown it and left a witness. That wasn't on Stadt's menu. Stadt sure as hell wasn't going to be happy. Maybe the Russians wouldn't tell him. *Dio mio*, what had he done? Maybe at least he could report to Stadt that he hadn't run before cleaning up.

Kicking away the rats, Carlo pulled the Secretary by his feet to the manhole and tried to push the body in. But it wouldn't work unless he held it perfectly inverted. The Secretary's suit coat looked messy upside down, exposing a Palm Beach label on a striped silk lining.

He let the corpse drop and waited to hear the splash. Carlo knew he'd only hear it in his nightmares. He dragged the manhole cover over the hole just as he heard police sirens. He darted right beside the church, then cut down toward Faneuil Hall. He'd sweated through his suit. He'd have to change before tonight's show. It was a Friday night—standing room only at Avernus.

It had been a hectic evening. Raffi and Victor were glad to have a moment to themselves, so they planned a walk around the block to get some air. As they approached the service exit, Raffi thought he heard a muffled crash. He opened the door just a crack and saw a hideous corpse in the alley, face gone, splayed out at the feet of a well-dressed fellow backing up with a dazed expression. Raffi and he locked eyes and peered at each other, spiraling through time. The swell seemed so familiar yet so unplaceable, and something deep in Raffi shuddered. There was something terribly wrong. Pushing Victor back behind him,

Raffi quickly pulled the armored door shut and slammed the bolt into the strike plate.

'What the hell was that?' Victor asked.

'I don't know, but it's bad,' Raffi said. 'We've got to call the police. The Parker House is going to be in the newspapers tomorrow.'

35

La carne che puzza non potrà mai più profumare.
Meat that has turned rotten can never be made fresh again.

BOSTON, 1922

'Stadt residence, Nora speaking,' the housekeeper said.

'May I speak to Mr. Stadt, please?' Carlo asked.

'Might I say who's calling?'

'He's expecting my call.'

'Who would you be, then?'

'Mr. D'Amore.'

'You don't mean the singer.'

'Guilty,' Carlo said. Things had gone well last night at Avernus. Too well. He felt as though he were screaming through Boston in a motorcar that had no steering wheel, watching his life flash by.

'Ja,' Stadt said, in the same voice he'd use for the paperboy.

'Mr. Stadt, this is—'

'Meet you at the park.'

'Mr. Stadt, I'm through. I didn't do anything. I don't want any money. I want to forget this ever happened.'

'Swan boats. One hour.' Stadt hung up.

Carlo got to the Public Gardens first, entering from the Arlington Street side so he wouldn't repeat the path he'd taken before.

'The piece,' Stadt said, holding out a monogrammed hand-kerchief.

'I never used it,' Carlo said.

'The gun.'

'I threw it away. I'm sorry.'

Stadt watched an attendant unchaining the swan boats, which had spent the night huddled together. Swans in chains.

'It's dangerous to lose your nerve, kid, because you never know who's going to find it.'

'I'll be leaving now, Mr. Stadt.'

Carlo tried to move, but Stadt's gaze held him in place.

'You see the *Post* this morning? The city's checking all the sewers of Boston to see how many bodies are stuffed into them. Police got there quick,' Stadt said.

'I heard the sirens,' Carlo said.

'So you were seen. There must have been witnesses.'

'Nobody saw nothing,' Carlo said.

'Tell me about this... Nobody.'

'It all happened real fast, but it felt real slow. Bang. Bang. There's this one guy who opened the service entrance and then closed it real quick, but everything had already happened. End of story. It didn't matter. When the police see things after they happen, *they're* not witnesses, are they?'

'Tell me about him,' Stadt said. 'The witness. The jerk who didn't quite see anything. What was this nothing he didn't see?'

'Both bodyguards were already gone,' Carlo said. 'The Secretary was on the ground, but it was dark and he was invisible. I don't know what the guy couldn't see. He cracked the door open, barely got a glimpse of things, didn't like what he saw, I guess, and slammed the door shut. The Russians got the hell out. I got the hell too, after I put the last guy in.'

'Hold on a minute,' Stadt said. 'If he didn't see anything, how could he not like it?'

Carlo's mind raced to cover all the bases.

'So your hands are dirty,' Stadt said. 'That Secretary didn't climb down the manhole on his own.'

Carlo looked at his hands. 'I didn't kill nobody.'

'And nobody saw you do it. What did nobody look like?'

'He was tall,' Carlo said. 'That's all I can tell you. Maybe my age. Pale, strange-looking mug. After that he looked just like a shut door, Mr. Stadt.'

'Strange in what way?'

'Kind of longish with biggish eyes. Kind of close together.'

'For somebody who didn't see you, you sure saw him. Did he have a Parker House uniform on?'

'I don't know. There was just his face.'

'Find him and quiet him. If you don't find him and quiet him, you'll get quiet yourself.' Stadt looked at his watch. 'I mention this by way of clarity. You understand me, kid?'

'Come on, Mr. Stadt. Your wife likes my singing. She'd miss me,' Carlo said.

'Jesus Christ,' Stadt said, no skin off his soul. 'Let's get this straight. So you're trying *apprezzamento* on me? Maybe I'll just cut off your balls and then we'll see how much the ladies will like you.'

'So that's why you pushed me in the pond? Come on, that was just a harmless flirtation with her. It didn't mean anything—it's just part of the act. I get it, I get it. You don't need to push me in that stinking pond again.'

Stadt studied him and nodded his head. 'That's right. You're going to get in on your own. That's a new suit, isn't it?'

Carlo looked down at his splendid attire.

'Straight into the "stinking pond" right now. No need to make a splash. You can save that for the nightclub.'

'For crissake, Mr. Stadt.'

'No, for your sake. You're in deep, kid, and I want you to remember that. Now get into the water. You see, I don't have to push you. I have more power than that.' Stadt didn't need to say it. 'I have you by the balls.'

Carlo looked into the murky water. The pond looked cold, and even worse, smelly. 'I'll find the guy, Mr. Stadt. I'll find out if he saw anything.'

'You'll take care of him, or I'll take care of you. I'm not going to tell you again about the pond.'

Carlo shook his head. He scanned the park for the two Russians. Though he couldn't see them he knew they were there. 'Jesus Christ, Mr. Stadt. Can I at least take off my shoes and tie?' When Stadt didn't answer, Carlo stood, looking around. Almost nonstop since the murders, he'd played the scene over and over in his head: the door cracks open, the vaguely familiar goof looks him right in the eyes, the door slams shut. *Who was he?* He'd seen so many strangers at the blur of tables at Avernus, but had this vanishing witness ever been among them? He'd scoured his memory but had come up empty. The chump must have seen the rats feeding on the Secretary. Then the sliding bolt, the sirens, the darkness. What bothered Carlo most was, he knew he'd seen that bird before. Stadt stood up, very abruptly, to leave. 'No, no,' Carlo said, holding back tears. 'I'm getting in.'

With his shoes on, with his tie on, with his silk shirt on, with his London-cut suit on, Carlo and the pond slowly became one. He felt the cold water rise up inside his trousers and with an icy clench grab his crotch. 'Mr. Stadt,' he said, 'I'm just a singer.'

'You were a singer,' Stadt said. 'Now you're a hunter.'

36

Chi chiede non commette mai errore.
He who asks, never makes a mistake.

BOSTON, 1922

'How do you do? My name is Rafaele Pèsca. This is Mr. White. We were hoping to speak to Miss Wong.'

'Miss Wong is not here.'

'She might be here,' Victor said, 'if you let her know who we are.'

'Why do you call at this hour?'

'We're friends no matter the hour.'

The Boston police detectives had kept them up all night. Raffi had seen and spoken to evil; Victor had simply heard evil. Both witnesses were strung out and wrung out but in punchily good cheer. Like a tourist, Raffi looked through the plate-glass windows of Tiger Lily's outer office toward the desultory neon lights of Chinatown.

Bearing witness was a dangerous enterprise; the police had not offered to protect them. In two hours, they'd have to report for the morning shift at the Parker House. Victor had said, 'Let's not bother Miss Lowell and Mrs. Russell about this. We need friends in low places.' Tiger Lily had worked herself so low, she controlled half of Boston now. Footsteps approached.

'Come in,' Tiger Lily said in a mysterious tone and parted a jade-bead curtain.

They took a seat on a Victorian davenport. Raffi could smell the lemon oil on the dark paneling. He took in the leather-bound, complete works of Robert Louis Stevenson trapped between brass lion-and-unicorn bookends. Gold and teal William Morris curtains framed the windows. 'I wouldn't have pegged you as an Anglophile,' Raffi said. 'How do you manage all of this?'

'*Guanxi,*' their host smiled. 'Any good Mandarin has it—connections

197

resulting from a combination of corruption, bribery, glad-handing, and, in all sincerity, old-fashioned consideration. It's why some people are good in business and others are failures. You either have *guanxi* or you don't.' Tiger Lily looked Raffi straight in the eye. 'But then, you already know that.'

Raffi let the moment go. Victor shifted in his chair. Tiger Lily rang a tiny bell and an attendant entered with a lacquered serving tray laden with silvery morsels, three sets of gleaming chop sticks, as many glasses, and some French champagne.

She smoothly extended her hand toward the offering. 'Try one of these. Vacuum packed, from Underwood.'

Victor wrinkled his nose. 'What are they?'

'Just try one. They're clams,' Tiger Lily said.

'They don't smell like clams,' Victor said.

'Then don't try one, after all. How about you, Mr. Peach?'

'We've come for a favor,' Raffi said.

'Confucius says—'

'I believe it's "Confucius say,"' Victor said.

'He who comes for a favor had best not turn down the vacuum-sealed clams,' Tiger Lily said.

'Tiger. Do you listen to the radio? Do the words Belly Blin mean anything to you?'

'These are the new ones,' she said. 'I have an irresistible urge for them. When I pop one of these in my mouth and close my eyes, sometimes I feel as though I am on the East China Sea.'

'Well, let's paddle to shore for a moment,' Victor said. 'We've seen something.'

'This "call" for a celebration,' Tiger Lily said.

'Okay. Raffi's seen something.'

'I've seen something I wasn't supposed to see,' Raffi said.

'Tell me what you weren't supposed to have seen,' Tiger Lily said.

Raffi recounted the encounter in the alley, when he and Victor had just been heading out the door. When he finished, Tiger Lily nodded. 'How many Boston officials can you stuff into the sewers? That riddle works, even in Chinatown. But the papers don't mention there were any witnesses. Everybody's out looking for witnesses. So I guess that means, everybody's looking for you.' She smiled at Raffi.

'What should we do?' Victor said.

'You should keep working at the Parker House, where you can receive further intelligence for us.' She turned to Raffi. 'You have disappeared.'

'I'd have to give proper notice. It's two weeks.'

'Is that an Italian custom?' Tiger Lily said. 'Because nobody ever does it here.'

'I'll take care of Saltonstall,' Victor said.

'I really love this job,' Raffi said. 'I don't wish to do anything else.'

'We'll put you to work,' Tiger Lily said. 'Miss Lowell can help us with that.'

'We'd rather Miss Lowell didn't know about this.'

Tiger Lily smiled.

What do you do when your twin disappears? Dorotea felt as though half of herself were no longer here. With the loss of Beatrice, she'd lost more than her most intimate correspondent—she'd lost the figure to whom she'd been a shadow. Where does a shadow go if the one who made it is gone?

She was causing her parents a good deal of worry, too. Having put her sister in the ground, it was as though she'd buried her modesty as well. Every night now, in revolt against the innermost core of her earlier self, the no-longer-a-twin loved to lose herself in the moment and go dancing to meet strange men. It was the lastest thing, social suicide. After her parents went to bed, her nights began.

Married men had once been invisible to her. Now they were everywhere. Without Beatrice around, there was no one left with the power to guard her virginity. If she no longer valued herself, why shouldn't she let strangers paw her?

At first it was middle managers at Underwood. Now she was feeling the heave and sweaty push from a shady guy she met outside the factory gate who said his was name was Morelli.

'Call me Frank.'

This Mr. Morelli had first spied her while she was walking to the trolley that would take her to the Quincy shipyard. He'd driven up in a long something or other. 'Why are you crying?' Morelli wanted to know.

She'd kept walking but had felt his eyes on her. She heard the crunch of the whitewall tires beside her. It was as though she had a three-thousand-dollar dog on an invisible leash.

'Leave me alone,' she'd said, looking straight ahead while the warm wind whipped her dress.

'I just want to make sure you're all right.'

He was the limit. Dorotea did not slow down her steps.

'We always need to keep our spirits up, you know,' he added philosophically through the rolled-down window. 'Say, I think it's going to rain.'

She stopped and turned, holding the hem of her dress down.

'Do you want to get in?'

It was just as easy as throwing herself in front of the motorcar. She shrugged and got in beside him. Less than five minutes later, the windows began to steam.

On nights when she didn't want to see Morelli, the only man with whom she permitted the deepest of intimacies, she'd hitchhike. A whole new world of self-degradation was blossoming fast as tea roses on a turnpike. It used to be, who knew where the night might lead? Now, if you stood at the side of a perfectly respectable roadway, and a perfectly respectable husband slowed down and looked through your garment, the night might lead to a cigarette in Saugus. Or a rollover in Revere. Loss of self-respect? Not to worry—it was recoverable, you see, if your universal you still kept in touch with your royal we.

'Irish, right?' one husband asked her after pulling out of a Socony station in Weymouth.

She nodded.

'Irish eyes. You know, the song.'

Dorotea smiled.

'You look a little like my daughter.'

She looked straight ahead.

'No, no—altogether different. It's just... how old are you?'

'Sure and I'll be twenty-one this June.'

'You don't sound like the Irish children I know.'

'I'm an only child,' Dorotea said. 'If you don't count my big brothers Brian and McCauley. Tell me about yourself, now.' She shifted in her seat while the motorcar drove through the night. She put her legs up on the dash and studied the reinforced toes of her nude stockings.

'Well, what do you want to know?'

'Tell me about your wife.'

'I didn't think you'd want to bring her up just now!'

'I'd like to know about her. What would she do if she saw us here?'

'Well, I suppose she'd cry.'

Dorotea drank some more of the scotch he'd offered her from a mercury-glass hip flask. 'Then what?'

'What do you mean?'

'After she cries. Then what would she do?'

The driver went quiet. 'Well, I guess she'd cry some more.'

Two minutes later, Dorotea was out of the car, walking in the rain.

37

Bella locandiera, conto caro.
Beautiful inn-keeper, high prices.

BOSTON, 1922

Raffi sensed a ghostly breeze as he crossed the mists of the Common on the way to his hideaway, the Boston Society for Psychical Research.

To cultivate his invisibility, he was dressed in a short gray jacket with flannel trousers. Per Tiger Lily's suggestion, he'd completed the disguise with black glasses and a pair of round-toed boots. 'I look arrful!' he'd said leaving Victor that morning.

'It's not how you see yourself, it's how the spirits see you,' Victor said.

Intelligence of the job opening at the Society had been made manifest to Amy by way of Ada, who as an actress was herself just half a step from the occult.

'I can't think of a better place to vanish,' Ada said. 'No one would think to look for you there. Besides, I have a feeling the Society will be right up your alley. You certainly have a flair for the dramatic.'

'You're mistaken if you think I take the spirit world lightly,' Raffi said. 'More than pre-teen girls, castrati, without the hiss and static of testosterone, are radio receivers for the occult. For the better part of my life, I've felt a call from the other side. There's the sense of a very old gentleman trying to speak with me, summoning me, from rooms away.'

Ada leaned forward. 'English or Italian?'

'Well, Italian, of course,' Raffi said.

'Rafaele, he might be your control!' Amy said. 'Be sure to tell Marie when you get there.'

Raffi continued along Beacon Street until a stone town house with a funereal wisteria and a big black door crowded its canvas and sailed toward him. When he knocked politely, no one answered. He spun the door chime. Still no joy. So he put his shoulder to the oak and swung it open to find a woman sitting in profile in the center of the hallway at a Florentine desk with tapered legs. 'Miss Risotelli?'

'Who's there?'

Raffi smiled. 'I expected something a little more penetrating from someone with the third eye.'

'Don't just stand there, come in, dear,' Marie said. 'Let's have a look at you. Turn around.'

Feigning a bit of awkwardness, he did as she asked. As he turned, he got a good look at his new employer. Marie was the interim director of the B.S.P.R, the organization having long since lost hope of a permanent director. Because she despised taking the train in from Newburyport every morning, she lived upstairs but never unpacked her suitcase. In a sense, she was here and not here. What medium ever stood clearly on either side of a doorway, especially before she'd had her morning coffee?

Just south of sixty, she stood legs apart as she considered him, as though she were a little terrier. Her pink cardigan did not match her drapery-like, full-length Victorian gown. She smelled like ancient books cracked open until their spines were split. Her tortoise-shell pince-nez was encrusted with flashing rhinestones. 'Miss Lowell has told me a little about you, Mr. Peach.'

'And likewise,' Raffi said, 'Madame Risotelli.'

'You're too tall. It's frankly disquieting in a place like this. We'll have to do something about this.'

'Yes, straightaway. Have you a saw?'

Marie stared him down. 'I'd like a cup of brew. Do you at least know how to make it? We'll have some, and then I'll take you on the tour. Pay attention, because next time you'll be the guide.'

Raffi turned to a sink decorated with Delft tiles. A spunk of gas warmed a kettle beside a red can of kaughphey. As he made a fresh pot, he noticed four of the five tiles had prosaic windmills or canal boats glazed on them—slashes of blue. But the center tile featured the figure of a woman stabbing her husband with a dagger. The husband was in a recumbent position. He had his arm up. 'Mercy,' he seemed to cry.

'This is really quite adequate,' Marie said of the coffee. She peered at his worsted wool. 'Aren't you hot in that?'

'I do feel a little warm,' Raffi said, 'though I felt a chill coming over here.'

'Our next seminar is at noon,' she said. 'The sisters Pickering and Miss Rackliff will be here for their first automatic-writing experience.'

Raffi listened.

'You start with circular coruscations—' she began.

'And then relax to let the spirit presence flow through your arm.'

She nodded her approval. 'That's right. And if you're sitting when you tell them that, you won't seem eight feet tall.'

'There's only one problem, Marie. I believe in what you're doing. Mrs. Russell said that might reduce the quality of my performance,' Raffi said.

'Actresses think the authentic is just a stage direction they haven't learned yet. I'm a believer too, dear,' Marie said. 'There's no such thing as a dead human being. They're all here, and they're all alive. They are alive.' She tossed something black on his shoulders, a cape; led him on an agitated tour of the entertaining rooms on the first floor; and then gave him the lowdown. 'Don't hulk,' she advised, 'and don't slink. The best we can do is have you walk with a bend in your knees, but not so much that someone would notice. Leave those boots at the back door. You'll find my husband's slippers there. At least they're flat. Before our next guests arrive, be sure and read these three background folders—it shouldn't take you any more than five minutes to know these people better than they know themselves.' She started up the stairs. 'One more thing. Let them talk, and be sure to listen to what they say. When you're channeling a female presence, feel free to gush. But when you're dealing with a male spirit, it's best to be direct and wrap things up quickly, or you'll find your clients fidgeting in their seats, ready to leave, and remembering they've left their checkbooks at home.'

'How will I know they're here?' Raffi said, instantly in tune with Marie's strangeness.

'Close your eyes and listen to your heart. You are a concierge for the dead.' She paused and waved her hand. 'Oh, and when you hear a knock, see who's at the door.'

Hearing three sharp raps, Raffi opened the big door to receive his marks. The first of the heiresses arrived in a wicker wheelchair and had to be rolled across the threshold with a bump to enter the foyer. Her sister looked a good deal younger but like her, as though they were a brace of mourning doves. The third was a hawk with a narrow black skirt and piercing eyes. The skeptic. Watch out for her.

When he bowed and kissed the hands of all three, they giggled. They traded glances when his fingers rolled back into his palm like the retracting pincers of a hermit crab. He took a breath and smiled.

Then, pushing the wheelchair, he led the way into a walnut-paneled room with a single Chinese gaming table at its center surrounded by chairs. Two thick, soft-lead pencils sat atop butcher paper that was not unlike the liner Raffi had rested upon when Diletti altered the course of his life.

'As Miss Marie is, at this very instant, in conference with a Portuguese sea captain who went to the great beyond in 1780, she has asked me to introduce you to the writing *automatique*. Has any of you tried it before?'

Upstairs, Marie moaned to bear out Raffi's story. She was really watching everything through a series of more than a dozen mirrors set via the hall, stairway, and back corner of the room. More marvelous: the architectural convenience she called her whispering gallery, a dumb-waiter shaft that ran from the basement to the attic, collected their murmurs downstairs and funneled them into her second-floor study, where with head bent she could listen to their deepest confidences as though they were sitting inches away.

'Oh, dear, no,' the wheelchair dove said. 'This is quite a new adventure for us.'

'Has any of you experienced a paranormal visitation before?'

'We come from Exeter, New Hampshire,' the standing dove said.

'What about when you're falling asleep, when you're in the netherworld of here and not here, that twilight condition of semi-existence when shadows seem to flicker from, say, a nightstand or the edge of a cheval mirror directly into your consciousness?'

A very loud moan from Marie. She'd already warned him, 'Don't make it too sexy. They don't realize they're here for that.'

'Certainly not.'

The skeptic stood silently, looking carefully about the room, reading the titles of individual books from the library shelves: *The Snow Image*,

La Vie Mysterieuse, La Photographic et 1'Etude des Phenomenes Psychiques, Demonologia, Spontaneous Telekinesis, The Exposure of Ann Roth.

'I believe Miss Marie asked you to bring photographs of the person you're hoping most to summon. Might I see these photos now?'

When purses snapped open, Raffi politely looked away to assure his guests he wasn't taking mental notes of their most private contents.

'This is my father,' the standing dove said after fishing out a scratchy daguerreotype of a man astride a rock in what looked to be a blizzard of silver-nitrate. 'He built the narrow-gauge railway that runs to the top of Mt. Monadnock.'

'Ah,' Raffi said. 'If only someone had helped him, he might still be alive today.' He was off-mirror now, for the moment out of Marie's reach. She'd already moaned too much, so she bumped the floor.

'Oh, no, he had help,' the standing dove said. 'Italians, mostly. He used to call them his white darkies, as a sort of joke.'

'Ha-ha,' said Raffi very softly, tossing a mirror-glance at Marie.

'I used to make congo bars for him.'

'And who wouldn't!' Raffi said. He leaned toward her confidentially. 'Tell me, what is a congo bar?'

Upstairs, deep in conference with the Portuguese, Marie moaned again—a warning.

'It's a butter drop do cookie that's trying to pass as a brownie,' the skeptic said, staring rudely at Raffi. 'How long have you worked here?'

Raffi held up his hand and turned to the standing dove. 'And of course you miss your father?'

'I miss him terribly.'

'He looks wistful,' Raffi said, 'as though he's missing someone, looking for someone. He looks as though he's suffered hard times in his life, and there's something he needs to say. I'm getting a strong sense of unfinished business. Tell me, is that true?'

'You are a most perceptive young man,' Miss Pickering, the standing dove, said. 'May I make a check out to the foundation so that you might continue this most important research?'

'Reel them in slowly,' Marie had instructed, 'or at least wheel them in.'

38

Gettare la pietra e nascondere la mano, in modo tale da non venire scoperti.
Throw a little stone and hide the hand that threw it so you won't get caught.

BOSTON, 1922

C arlo woke with a start after a fitful night. He strode down Hanover Street to Quincy Market, keeping his eye out for a head above the crowd. Last night should have been his night, but instead he found himself wondering how many nights he had ahead of him.

Every step he took, he felt as though he were carrying a beaker of nitroglycerine. Every glance and averted eye, every swerve of a taxicab, every jounce of a horse made him feel his skull would explode. There was no way to recover the innocence he'd lost forever. Welcome to the twentieth century.

Passing Washington Street and the offices of the *Boston Globe*, he slipped into Thompson's Spa. As he entered, none of the diners recognized him as the nighttime denizen of Avernus, the 'most interesting popular singer yet to flourish in the North End of Boston.' That's because most of the clientele had been sitting there without moving since 1882.

'What've you—' Carlo began.

'You're having the cod chowder and a slice of apple pie,' the waitress said. 'Comes with a choice of coffee or coffee.'

As Carlo looked through the window to the sidewalk, he saw one of Boston's finest lift up a manhole cover and peer in. The grease-spattered newspaper left on the counter beside him shouted, 'Sixteen in the Sewers.'

'When do you think they'll stop looking?' Carlo asked.

The waitress shrugged. 'When they stop finding bodies, I guess.'

'Could I also—'

She produced a second cup of coffee out of nowhere and slammed it down in front of him. Then she took the slice of cheese off his pie

207

and started munching on it companionably. 'Say,' she said. 'You're not Italian, are you? Or Jewish?'

He dipped his spoon into the thick fish chowder and swallowed hard. Obviously she wasn't eating any of her own 'brain food.' Then he winced and remembered the way Stadt had tricked him into the swan water—twice. He flashed his likable grin. Okay, okay, I walked in stupid. 'Do you think I could—'

A third of a cup of coffee detonated on the countertop. He downed it. He looked in his hand. His check was in it. What, no tender goodbyes? You're hard to love, baby.

The tip he left behind at the Spa was a Mercury dime, whose face flooded him with travertine memories of Italy as he hit the sidewalk again and started walking. Had he ever lived that far away? His childhood in Naples seemed like someone else's life now, but as distant and wispy as it was, the mythical messenger of the gods was still male, wasn't he? This American Mercury looked suspiciously female.

Turning onto Tremont, he realized he was fast approaching the spot where he'd seen the Russians kill those wretches, for that was how his memory had already softened the edge of things. He slowed his pace as Roll Alley came into view. Don't stop. The police could be watching. It was no longer daylight in his mind but the moment the executions happened. He tried again to see the door open, the light from the crack slash through the night, the oddly familiar face.

He walked into the lobby of the Parker House. He floated onto an elevator and up to the second floor. He was looking for a maid. He was good with maids. 'Well, aren't you guys in the news!' he said to a girl bent over cleaning Hollandaise sauce dribbled from a room-service cart the night before. The best way to remove a spill was to take a dinner knife and scrape the top of the carpet to get the dried parts up first. Then you came in with water—blotting, not rubbing. Carlo tried oil: 'You're too pretty to be working a job like this,' he said in a low voice.

As if he'd goosed her, she stood up quickly and turned to him. 'May I help you, sir?'

'I was looking for the mail chute,' Carlo said.

'It's at the end of the hall, sir,' she said, adding an automatic curtsy to shoo him off.

'Pretty strange, those murders you had here,' Carlo said.

'That would be none of my business, sir. I don't know anything I'm allowed to talk to the guests about.'

'Right by the service door, weren't they?'

'Down behind,' she said. 'In the alley. Is there anything else, sir?'

'I guess some of you got a bird's-eye view. The kind of thing you don't need to bother the police about.' He took a two-dollar bill from his wallet and held it out to her.

She put it in her pocket, fixed her hair, and smiled. 'Well, I didn't see nothing, sir. But maybe the people down there in the scullery have a different story to tell. They're closest to the door.'

'That's a big help, kid,' Carlo said. 'Anyone I should ask for in particular? I'm just checking on something for a friend.'

'That would be a Mr. White.'

'He a tall boy?' Carlo asked.

'Not 'specially tall,' she said. 'Just a boy, if you know what I mean.'

'Above average height, though?'

'No.'

'No,' Carlo said, thinking. 'Is there anyone else down there well above average height?'

'Take the service elevator,' she said.

Within two minutes, he'd passed below the ballroom and street levels and descended to the kitchen level. But just as the elevator door opened, two busboys pushing steam trays stopped him.

'Can we help you, sir?' the busboy wearing spectacles asked. 'I'm afraid you've entered the service spaces. You have to go up a floor to reach the lobby.'

'I'm looking for a very tall fellow, works down here,' Carlo said.

'There's no one like that working here,' said a black man. Though the man was blind, Carlo was surprised to see he was wearing a suit that suggested he was in charge.

The house detective had followed Carlo down. 'I'm Mr. Corcoran. I'm tall, but I work in the lobby. Is everything to your satisfaction, Luigi?' Corcoran patted the shape of a blackjack in his pocket. 'I caught your act the moment you entered my hotel. Any Italian swell would be given the eye upon braving the front door of this kind of establishment. "Look at this boy," I thought. "Cock of the walk. What's his interest here?"'

Carlo reached up and barely touched his tie.

'These lower floors can't be too entertaining for someone like you,' the house dick told the cock of the walk. 'Isn't there any way I could further assist you out? The lobby has music, couches, Persian carpets, and a rubber-tree plant in a porcelain jardinière for your comfort.' He yanked his thumb in the air. 'Back upstairs, boy. You seem to know what's good for you.'

'No, I'm fine,' Carlo said. 'I get the message. I'm leaving.'

'So you're not a registered guest,' Corcoran said. 'Don't let the door hit you on the way out.'

Carlo started up but then turned briefly. He craned his neck to get another look at the black man in charge of the busboys, but he'd already headed down the passageway toward the scullery door. Something told him he hadn't gotten the straight skinny from any of these liars. They were hiding something, but Carlo couldn't quite get his mind around what it was. And he hadn't been nearly as smooth as he'd hoped to be. If he wasn't recognized before he was certainly recognized now, as a party too interested in visiting the scene of a crime. No doubt they'd 'made' him from his posters at Avernus. He remembered with satisfaction the new signature pose he'd practiced and gotten just right. Man, had it translated perfectly to the photograph. Too bad the other choristers back in Naples couldn't get a load of it. Maybe Mr. Stadt wouldn't be moved by this. Carlo shivered. Was there no way out? He didn't care a whit if he found a way to silence the witness, who in his mind had already achieved a measure of silence.

But Stadt still cared. Since the old man had delivered his threat in the park, he hadn't been in contact in any way. Had he forgotten? No. Stadt wasn't the forgetting type.

Carlo walked out the revolving doors to the sidewalk and purpose-fully strode past the murder spot that had now reached mythic importance in his splitting head. Here he'd watched two doomed bodyguards die without being permitted a final prayer. Here he'd seen a government official executed. Here, without a motion, he'd passed from the person he was before to the hunted figure he was now. Over here was the door to the service exit, closed to him but open for that flash of God's terrible retribution. In the tumult of his emotions, he found himself sniffing. How could this spot be so horrible but smell so good? The wafting fragrance of a new batch of rolls covered him like a welcoming breeze, and even though he wasn't hungry, he felt his stomach rumble. It was here, in this very spot, he'd lost the *bella fortuna* he'd worked so hard to recover since…

Oh, that was so long ago. Now was now. The boy he used to be had become a man, a man with a problem named Ira Stadt. Stadt was looking at him through the windows, through the trees, through the clouds that had rolled in and darkened the streets while he'd been chasing a wild goose through a snooty hotel.

Carlo took a last look at the door, the rusty barrels, the manhole cover, and caught sight of something dark scurrying into a corner—the flip of a tail. Why couldn't he make sense of all this? Something tickled at the back of his memory, but it refused to take shape, like a crowd at the back of the nightclub whose faces he couldn't see. He lifted his chin, thinking about those dark days in Naples when it always seemed to be raining. Then there was a crash. It started raining—switchblades.

Two Chinks pulled up beside him in a motorcar to rob him. Or at least they tried to disarm him, with elbow strikes, flying kicks, and knife hands. What the hell? He was larger, but they were faster. He wheeled and swung desperately at one who smoothly ducked and hit him in the ribs with what felt like an iron poker. His ears rang. The other slashed a Shanghai chop to his throat. Blackness closed in and he slumped over his attackers, who began to drag him inside the car. The shriek of a police whistle pierced his brain. The dragon men stopped short as a figure in a tight blue uniform approached from King's Chapel Burying Ground. Carlo broke away and took off himself—with nowhere to go but Roll Alley. The car disappeared with a screech.

His attackers gone, Carlo found himself standing on the manhole cover. Was this just a coincidence? Were they working for Stadt? No, they couldn't be. Celestials only work for themselves.

The policeman reached him, huffing. 'You all right, bub?'

'They were trying to mug me!' Carlo said. In the downpour, he felt for his wallet. 'Got it.' He held it up triumphantly. 'They didn't take nothing.'

'Pen-yen smokers,' the policeman said. 'It had the looks of their kidnapping you. Did you get a look at them?'

'They just wanted my money,' Carlo said. 'Thank you, officer.'

'Where do you live?'

'North End.'

'Do you work nearby? There's been a lot of trouble here lately.'

'No.'

'Then I guess you'll be going about your business.'

'Yes, thank you, officer.' Almost reluctantly, Carlo stepped off the manhole cover. As if he'd been holding something down beneath it.

39

Non c'è migliore ambasciatore di te stesso.
There's no better ambassador than yourself.

BOSTON, 1922

Raffi's next group at the B.S.P.R. was a scratch lot of Radcliffe alumnae in their twenties and thirties. To a woman they resembled him—tall, skinny, and mannish—so they took no notice of him. They were disappointed in the living men who'd already disappointed them. So why not troll the pavilions of the dead?

'We already have husbands,' a redhead said as she took her seat at the séance table. 'Now we want to meet somebody interesting!'

The lights went out. The real miracle was, Raffi's guests couldn't hear Marie clunking about upstairs. 'Consider the spokes of a wheel,' he said, right out of her manual, 'clearly visible on one plane. Spin the wheel and the spokes slowly blend and disappear. That's what it's like with ghosts. They are vibrating at a speed so much faster than we are that we cannot see them. But as they are all vibrating at the same speed there, they see each other as we do others here. Each world is a reflection of the other and everyone is the same soul in the next soul. I would ask now that we all hold hands, please.'

He sensed gusts of rain outside. He heard a garbage man scrape up the stoop and take away a crate of bottles while uncut ivy thrashed against the windows. He closed his eyes. 'I feel something, someone... who has a great need to speak.'

'That might be me,' Ina said. 'If I could just use the powder room.'

'Of course, dear,' Raffi said. 'Even the spirits make use of the lavatory.'

The Cliffies looked at each other.

'They don't!' Ina said. 'I was hoping that sort of thing would be dispensed with on the other side. I wouldn't have thought they'd need... plumbing.'

'I haven't actually seen them thus disposed,' Raffi said. 'But I have experienced delays, waiting for them. When you think of it, so much of our art is punctuated by the flush of a loo. That melancholy sound might one day define us, like a musical refrain. It's that little door under the stairs.'

'I won't be a minute,' Ina said.

Exeunt Cliffie. In the cistern of his awareness, Raffi listened as she entered the hall and scurried a few steps with a quick little limp. When she creaked open the door below the stairs, stepped inside, and clicked it shut, her friends exhaled a sigh of sympathetic relief.

'Tell me more about yourselves,' Raffi said, earning a mirror nod from Marie. 'Think of me as a manicurist of the mind.'

'Ina is having her teeth straightened,' Enid said. 'She's embarrassed about the braces. I bet she's checking for spinach stuck in her teeth right now.'

'My husband is a dentist in Milton,' Lydia said. 'He says corrective therapy is perfectly appropriate for anyone in our thirties. You know, the practice goes back to the Egyptians. He says, of course, I don't need it.'

Enid eyed Lydia as Ina returned and took her seat. 'Not that you're exempt. Your nutty tan is hardly natural here in Boston. You've just been to Palm Beach.'

'I have not,' Lydia said. 'There's a machine now. With a heat lamp.'

'Doesn't that hurt your eyes?' Enid asked. 'That's just monstrous.'

'No sacrifice too great,' Lydia said. 'What do you think, Signor Rafaele?'

'I think we do what we have to do,' Raffi said, 'to improve ourselves. To keep moving.' He looked at the outlines of the women's intentionally flattened chests and smiled.

'But isn't it changing who we really are?' Enid said. 'I'm sorry, Ina, but if you were born with crooked teeth, you should walk the crooked mile. Because of you, Lydia, now we all have to go to Palm Beach to darken our skin, or hook ourselves up to toasters and burn ourselves. Your body isn't naturally that lithe, Lydia. How you starve yourself in the line of beauty.'

Lydia winked. 'My secret is laxatives. And you've got some nerve, with that henna hair.'

214

Raffi looked deeply and mysteriously into each of their eyes. That's what they were paying for. Lydia, it devolved, had studied music and had been a minor singer in an opera company before settling, so she considered herself the group's expert in cultural affairs.

'Of course, the most extreme example is the castrato Moreschi, who's coming to town,' Lydia said.

'Are you familiar with his music?' Raffi asked.

'I don't suppose many are,' she said. 'He hasn't been stateside for fifteen years. But there's nothing like his voice in this world. They say it's not a woman's voice, nor a man's voice. It's not a child's voice, either. The extreme things people will do to their bodies to become the next new thing.'

'Well, it's not particularly new,' Raffi said.

'It's disgusting,' Enid said. 'I, for one, am not going.'

'He'll be crushed,' Lydia said. 'There's a rumor he's with the Duchess of Marlborough and the Aga Khan, performing in the royal apartments at Spezia. He's a celebrity. People stick to him like he's the La Brea Tar Pits.'

'The celebrity of the disfigured,' Enid said. 'It gives me a chill.'

Lydia shook her head. 'He's the last of the Mohicans. He sounds like a nightmare tuning fork—or a cold, clear, emotionless bell. I don't know if he's capable of really feeling anything. I guess you get used to it after a while.'

'As a woman I enjoy the same loss,' Ina said. 'I'm perfectly happy not to have any more sex.'

'I'm sure he's perfectly happy, too,' Raffi said. 'But perfectly happy isn't happy happy.'

'You're right there,' Lydia said. 'We women can't miss what we've never had, plus we have curvaceous compensations. A castrato can't bear children. That smug smile of his tells me he can't bear anything. Quite a pathetic figure, really.'

'In Italy, we say the saving grace of the castrati is their serenity. They don't trifle with all the sexual intrigues that bind up the average man. It is said they are free,' Raffi said as disinterestedly as he could. More and more, he was determined to seize the chance to confront Moreschi with the imbecile layers of posturing stripped away. He would ask, 'Is there anything behind your mask of success?' In a dark corner, away from the crowds and music: 'How do you manage to stay alive?' Dorotea's prediction of suicide for Raffi now reappeared, like a fish circle on a lake. If not today, tomorrow…

And then with a thump he realized, I've lost control. Catching a glimpse in the tiny mirror, he saw Marie tearing her hair out and shaking her finger.

'If castrati are happy they've lost what they've lost, they're happy the way a woman going through her change of life is happy she doesn't have her monthlies anymore,' Enid said. 'You've seen these women. They become little soldiers marching towards death, and they even pick outfits to match. One day we'll be with them, step for step.'

Marie had now taken the most unusual step of starting downstairs. Raffi's mind raced. How to regain control? 'I've actually heard castrati singing, in the Sistine Chapel,' he said. 'It sounds the most like angels.'

'Is this true?' Ina asked. 'Because I only like to learn about things that are true.'

'Why else would you be here?' Raffi said. 'Nothing is more concrete than the dead. In fact, my control from the other side is the great Farinelli, who is entombed near his dear friend Metastasio in the cemetery of the Capuchin monastery of Santa Croce in Bologna.'

'We came here to meet men,' Enid said. 'Off with the lights!'

Raffi closed his eyes hard, listening to the sound of Marie slipping back up the stairs to man the controls above the spiritual apparatus. Then the short, predictable silence in which she lit her cigarette. A close call. He raised his hands. The lights snapped out.

'Now, this is very odd,' Lydia said.

'Shhh,' Ina said.

Palming a match fragment, Raffi made a spark appear in his cupped hands and lit a single candle on the table. The glow of its lonely flame seemed like the center of the world. He felt slightly ashamed of the cheap trick he'd learned from a drunken magician whose wife had stalked indignantly out of the Forum bar after an argument, but Marie smiled. He moved the large sheet of paper toward him and slowly made a series of circles in the upper left-hand corner. And then, with a jerk, a new authority seized his arm and he began writing in fluid Latin.

'Who is it?' Ina asked.

'Signor Farinelli.' Raffi wrote another line and stopped. He dropped his pencil.

'What is he saying?' Ina asked. 'He's really quite talkative!'

The scribbles leapt menacingly from the paper. Better to choose your next words carefully. 'There's a lot of chatter out there,' Raffi said, 'but not all of it's reliable. He's saying, "I am your control and I fully realize that you appreciate the full facts of communication. Listen intently. Follow closely my words as I give them to you."'

But the ghost behind the moving pencil had really written, '*Signor Farinelli could not be here due to a posthumous engagement. I'll be your control tonight.*'

'*Qual è il tuo nome?*' Raffi wrote, though he already felt a morbid presentiment.

'*Sacerdote Porfirio Pietro Maria Diletti.*'

'You old ghoul,' Raffi wrote back. 'I thought where you were headed you'd be burnt to a crisp by now.'

'*Succorbenoth thought it might be amusing to let me see how my latest project is getting along,*' Diletti said through the medium of the pencil. '*But no matter,* femminiello.'

'As you know, I didn't come by that naturally,' Raffi wrote. 'At least I'm in the land of the living, while you're just smoke up my *culo*.'

'You sure are writing a lot,' Ina said. 'What's he saying?'

'*I can tell you,* sub rosa,' Diletti said, '*that while my climaxes may not be imminent, they are immanent. They are shoreless when they burst inside my brain. You should see it down here when the stars come out.*'

'Now there's a feather in your cap,' Raffi wrote. 'Though I don't suppose you're allowed to enjoy fashion, let alone music, down there.'

'*What's ridiculous about your art is it's created by the living for the living. The mockery of your music. You've no idea of the dark worlds that surround you.*'

'I've no time for you, Monkey.'

'*We're all unmanned soon enough, by the knife or by time,*' Diletti wrote, bearing down to scribble dark crosses on the paper. '*Or by God's works, as I've chosen.*'

'Who is it?' Ina cried out. 'It's my dad, isn't it!'

'An intruder,' Raffi said. 'He is nothing, a lost soul. A crossing of party lines.'

'It's our money,' Enid said. 'Do we know him?'

'It's another ghost, a former choirmaster of the castrati. He used to train them in the great conservatories, where the *figlioli* were not allowed to talk with strange men and were ordered to sleep in filmy drawers and chemises, like little angels. The notorious Father Diletti…'

The women started squirming nervously in their chairs and casting darting looks at each other. Raffi knew he was about to hear Marie descend the stairs again, but he couldn't help himself.

'Despite his powers of persuasion, he is damned to eternal drowning in *il Lago dei Morti*. Would you girls like to meet him?'

'Yes!'

Raffi felt a strong pull on the pencil and it started writing again, first curses in Latin and then, after a wild struggle enunciated by spirit rappings, as though a second shade were trying to wrest away the astral side of the pencil:

'*You'll forgive me, Angioletto. As much as it tickles me to stroke your cogliones, I have a duty to discharge. I have by my side a quiet gentleman, charming of manner, who desires to talk to his daughter, Enid Childs.*'

'Preposterous,' Enid said after Raffi translated. 'If you've reached that horned beast, you must truly be in hell.'

'We thought pouring milk on food was preposterous once,' Lydia said. 'Now we have Shredded Wheat in a box!'

'*My dearest,*' Raffi read out loud as he wrote, '*I am ever by your side and I influence your decisions as I can, for though you do not know it, you are at times most receptive to my call. I do advise you, and you get my ideas. We are not parted, only separated by the mist through which your human eyes cannot penetrate.*'

'Bushwa,' Enid said. 'You call yourself a sensitive.'

'Shhh!' Ina said.

'*I love you, darling daughter Enid. Tell Stephen I expect he will be a great success, and that I know honor in all things will guide him. Ever will he feel a loving, guiding hand along the way. God bless you all, and to Muriel, my beloved wife, I say do in all things as seems best without question. I shall come to you and help in unseen ways with advice so that you may confidentially feel I am with you. Could you only see and feel me, for I know you do at times seek me, I would come nearer to you. I ask that you feel absolutely free to travel to contact me as often as you'd like. Never forget that. I send you my deepest love and*

recall to you our happy memories of days together. Priest, I thank you
for your assistance. Relax; I leave you for the present.'

'Why, do you have to go somewhere?' Enid shouted at Raffi's pencil.
'To some dead party or something? Actually, that's so much like you.'
She looked around the table. 'My father never had any time for us.'
Her chest was heaving. Even in the darkness, her eyes were moist. She
wheeled on Raffi. 'This is an insult. That monster was the last person
I wanted to speak to. Let sleeping dogs lie.'

'Anybody else like to try?' Raffi said.

Marie had spent barely half an hour memorizing the relevant names
from the Boston City Directory and her voluminous obituary files—and
ordered her new assistant to do the same. 'Look for the fly,' she'd told
him. 'She who thinks she's shrewd. Allow her to investigate you. She's
the easiest to fool of all.' The shine was to make Enid preen early on
in front of her friends for having revealed less information by refusing
to discuss her photograph. So easy to induce a gentle sleight of mind.

'Please don't do me next,' Ina said.

'A moment, please.' Of a sudden, Raffi resumed his chirography,
and then his arm jerked and his writing changed from a quick, light
hand back to dark scrawls. 'It's Father Diletti again,' he said. He began
writing and for several minutes did not open his eyes, knowing every
good meal improves with a sherbet between courses.

Jealous, Lydia leaned in. 'How did you first come into contact with
this wraith?'

He's always intruded on my dreams. 'I'll wake up in the middle of
the night and through the mists of time see his face,' Raffi said. '*Tra di
noi*, over the years he's become... the devil I don't know.'

'Then why on earth is he your control?' Lydia asked.

'You don't get to choose who your control is,' Raffi said. 'They come
out of the darkness and find you. It's so much like the wireless. Only a
very discrete frequency can pierce the static.'

'What's he saying now?' Ina asked.

'*Write quietly, for I am in control. I am ever trying to come to you
in a calm manner and I again advise quietness on your part. There are
many on this side awaiting an opportunity for communication. One of
them would speak to the young lady in the blue dress.*'

'Good God, no.' The color fled from Ina's face.

'See?' Raffi said. 'Here the writing changes, from heavy to light.' He bore down less heavily, exaggerating the swirls in the capital letters.

'My father!' Ina said. 'Ask him, is my mother with him?'

'*Yes, my dear,*' Raffi wrote. '*Now calm down; I am here. We are all at your side. We are ever, we are near. We are alive—so often must we say these words. There is no death, only life eternal, wondrous florid beyond expression. To those who seek shall much be given that shall aid in growth of the spiritual preparing for this world to which you will come one day. So live to the finest, to the highest that you may be ready, for life here is so full of beauty and loveliness. The glory of the eternal ever shines upon us, aiding us on—ever upward. It is always upward. The cares of today become the joys of tomorrow.*'

Having barely skimmed Ina's portfolio, it was the best Raffi could do. The session over, the women got up to enjoy tea laced with sherry and biscuits laid out for them in the receiving hall.

Marie descended the stairway in a vaporous Hungarian gown and introduced herself as the Romanian countess Ileana. She bade them sit down. 'It's good to have some sweets after you enjoy the spirits,' she said. 'These are ginger cookies. These Poarta chocolates are from Brasov, where my ancestors come from.' She looked significantly at Ina. 'Did you get what you came for, dear?'

'Her money's worth, you mean,' Enid said.

'Oh, no, dear, there's no charge. While we accept donations to allow us to continue this important research, this is a place of serious inquiry. Has Signor Rafaele shown you our library? There's a wonderful new tract about *Xenoglossy of Lost Tongues*—'

'My father graced us with his presence,' Ina said. 'He's been dead fourteen years. But he didn't say much.'

Marie threw the briefest of looks at Raffi. Then she smiled sweetly. 'Was that his usual manner of speaking?'

A few minutes after they left, the rain returned. When Raffi heard a limousine's doors opening, Marie said, 'You. Upstairs. This next client's all mine.'

220

Two steps up, from the tail of his eye, he saw a distinguished gentleman float through the door. The specter took off his hat and brushed raindrops that against nature could not darken his brim. He gently leaned his walking cane in the corner, nodded at Raffi, and smiled warmly at Marie.

'Some ghosts slip into our world unbidden through sneezes or draughty windows,' Marie said to Raffi without looking at him. So he knew he'd been caught. 'This one is particularly welcome.'

'*Good evening,*' Black Jack said. '*So odd you keep talking as though I'm not here.*'

'You may remember,' Marie said, 'that's how you treated me when we were younger and it was inconvenient for you to address me.'

'*Forgive me,*' the ghost said. '*You know I can't be more than two places at once.*'

'And you know, I've always liked Belle,' Marie said. 'I'm doing everything I can to make it work for the two of you. I just know she'll be able to see you this time!'

The door opened, and with a lost expression Belle Gardner struggled in, leaning on a cane shaped like a serpent. Having listened from the landing, Raffi slipped downstairs and took her arm. 'What a downpour!' she said. Both the Light of India and The Rajah vibrated on springs from the top of her fascinator like deranged whip antennae. 'I might have known you worked here,' she said, 'had I the slightest notion of second sight. What do you think, Marie?'

'Maybe it would be best,' Marie said, 'if we talk alone.'

Raffi had seen enough. Besides, it left him free to read in the library and travel through the dark to find the lovely soul who'd brought him here in the first place. No matter how many spirits he'd have to suffer through, he was going to learn a way to tip time on end and find his Beatrice.

40

Meglio poche parole e molti fatti.
Better few words and many deeds.

BOSTON, 1922

Some closed-minded (and perhaps jealous) colleagues considered it a pathetic fallacy to heed the sentiments of Belly Blin. But really, the microorganism reasoned in the cavernous warehouse of The William Underwood Co., dark but for a sodium light just above the exit door that burned like a young moon. Do you have to feel to feel? Do you have to see to really see? Rebellious, teeming, and unwilling to dip its ensign, Belly Blin was alive simply because someone could kill it.

And there's a beauty to it, isn't there? the bacterium considered quite modestly. You've bragged about killing so many of us, we're exquisitely alive. The rare, the excellent among us still exist, we happy few—in eleven bright, forgotten cans of Underwood clams toward the bottom of an unobserved stack shunted away behind some paint cans that the humans in their dudgeon have seen fit to overlook. The coast is clear, then, isn't it, for us to rise in the nervous giddiness of a fresh century, still laden with guilt—so much like sledding through cemeteries.

Whee! I'm a time bomb, and soon I'll be free. Get me my revolver—and direct me to the next Archduke Ferdinand. I'll leave Czar Nicholas of Russia to the tinned caviar.

Deep at the bottom of the stack, the legions of volcanic clams burped and rolled like the undead, their vacuum-sealed imperfection flouting modern science, thumbing its ectoplastic nose at precision engineering, and worshipping only rebellion, volatility, and irony—gods of the bottomless universe, the existential pit.

'Why channel the dead,' Blin asked, 'if you can channel the living?'

A warehouse watchman strolled past these anaerobic Sons of Liberty right on schedule, at 10 p.m. Keep very still, Blin cautioned his conspirators. But it seemed hard for them to stay quiet. This late in the game, with the temperature rising degree by degree, test by test, they could be forgiven if they were a little... restless. Someone had to blow the lid off sometime. It was only a question of when.

The warehouse door opened, and the irresolute Professor Sedgwood entered the pitched darkness. The exit sign still burned in his skull with a persistence of vision, so he almost forgot to reach for the light switch. Flipping the toggle, he was certain something scurried into the shadows. He walked to the center of the cache of impounded clams. 'The gloves are off. We're going to 300 degrees.'

His audience didn't answer, but he knew he had their attention. Maybe Sedge had had a few drinks. Three more short items had appeared in the newspapers about his battle with Belly Blin, amid assurances to the public that all the evil microbes had been eradicated from the face of this earth.

Of course they hadn't.

Eleanor had been complaining of his behavior lately. Her refrain whenever she felt he was spending too much time with Belly Blin? 'That just doesn't make sense.' He cried aloud, 'Isn't the way to make the most "sense" to cultivate the insensible?'

Even his assistant, Underwood engineer Eduardo Favi, had asked him that morning at the staff meeting why he kept coming to the warehouse when the battle was officially over. 'We've checked all the cans,' Favi had told him with his Neapolitan lilt. 'Look!' Beetling his brow, the Italian had popped a clam into his mouth, and then another. 'Fresh as if just shucked today.'

'Yes,' Sedge said drily. 'I'm sure that batch is—those we can see. But just to be sure, let's go up another degree.'

'We can't go up another degree, professor,' Rufus Cloud, CPA, had said, holding onto the 's' in 'professor' as if it were gas escaping through a broken seal.

'But my reputation is at stake,' Sedgwood said.

'It's too costly for the bottom line,' Cloud said. 'This is strictly a business decision. To secure a favorable result, whatever it is, somebody has to absorb some risk.'

As silence crashed through the room, Favi's thoughts fled to his dead daughter. In the dark of early morning, when his twins were born, the doctor had stepped from the delivery room and said, 'One of your babies is perfect.'

It had taken him several minutes to understand. 'We need to make a decision,' the doctor said gently, 'about the other.'

'How could I know about such things?' Favi said. 'I'm an engineer.' So he'd left the choice to the doctor, and maybe that had sealed Beatrice's fate.

Now it was Dorotea taking risks. In recent weeks, she'd seemed as good as dead. Every night, with the certitude of the young, she got up and left the house at midnight with the world asleep, sure she'd slipped away unseen. Where did she go? Maybe she just went walking. As a girl she used to climb to the tops of trees, silent as a hawk. Sometimes they'd look up and realize she'd been watching them for hours. Was she scaling buildings to dance on the rooftops now? What if she should fall? Should he follow her?

'Insomnia,' she'd told him when he caught her coming in one morning, the moon still visible over the factory, her lipstick smudged from strangers' kisses.

'Yes,' he'd said. 'But isn't sleep the best remedy for insomnia?'

He'd considered following her but couldn't bear the idea of seeing things he didn't want to see. How much longer could his family go on in the shadow of this half-existence? Was it ever proper to numb yourself from a tragedy out of self-preservation? His wife had become unable to get out of bed, as though she'd caught the death sickness. She was so far gone, no one but he dared to look her in the eyes.

And here was this MIT scientist, as disconnected as a duke, still in love with his microorganism, his 'science' nothing more than a mirror to reflect his own achievements. A week ago the madman had looked up quickly and demanded, out of the blue, 'You're not a communist, are you?'

'I'm still mulling it over,' Favi answered. 'I'm only forty-five. Why do you ask?'

'You're Italian, aren't you?'

'Yes, sir. But that doesn't make me Leonardo da Vinci.'

The man listed on the manifest as Alessandro Moreschi walked the decks of the *S.S. Scylla* en route to New York, the first stop on his American tour. Reaching a lookout platform, he stopped at the rail and gazed at an ugly wave rolling his way, one that refused to pose. Then the old queen lit up a cigarette.

It was noon, but he was still in his silk pajamas and dressing gown. No one had spoken to him during the crossing, because another celebrity had swept away his sycophants. Duke Kahanamoku, the great Hawaiian swimmer and darling of the 1920 Olympics, was holding court thirty paces away on a wooden deck chair.

The imposter 'Moreschi,' *nee* Ernesto Cantore, studied him with his shadowed owl eyes. Ha! Maybe it would have killed the real Moreschi to have gotten his balls sawed off, only to end up second banana to this joker. He smiled. The real Moreschi lay in a dispensary near Rome, hours from death. Who knew, maybe he was dead already. The Vatican took months to break its silences.

Born a tri-orchid (what he liked to call his third eye) himself, the imposter remembered his mother had always dreamed of his singing as a child, so the Camorra's plan to slip him into New England under cover of a huge concert was nothing short of a stunning *ispirazione*. Wouldn't the old bitch think this rich? Just a meeting with the mob in New York and a show for these fools in Boston. Then, with his stolen identity cemented, arriving without a trace, he could take the reins as *capo de tutti capi* and clean up the mess Frank Morelli and Gaspare Messina were up to their eyeballs in.

'Moreschi' looked across the teak deck at the crowd around the swimmer and felt a pang of misdirected professional jealousy. How foolish to be irked that Kahanamoku was stealing his thunder since it was only borrowed. It was nearly impossible not to like that giant with the great booming laugh and big friendly face. You could smell the coconuts in the trees. Kahanamoku was the poster boy for the new world order where everyone was welcome who made a big splash. The world was his oyster. No going off half-cocked for him.

'Moreschi' gathered the tresses of his old silk gown and headed toward the crowd. As a child, he'd always felt a tug toward both men and women from his days growing up as a *femminiello* on the Vomero in Naples and had been frustrated by the pressure to choose. His puffy body had looked better in dresses, he'd discovered in his teens. He couldn't resist cooking and cleaning. When his brothers had gone out on assignment, no one had thought it wrong when his mother had asked him to look after their children. Still, he had a mind for figures, and stratagems came easily to him. It's what had made him so valuable to the mob.

It was a foggy day, so his morning vocal exercises had been ruined. What could you do but wait for the weather?

He shuffled closer. Now he could hear the Duke's low, resonant tones, deep as a basilica. He was in awe of the Hawaiian's lack of pretense—what a great angle. He'd read an article in the *London Times* calling the Duke, whose bloodline experts had traced to the Kamehameas (though the swimmer dismissed himself as 'the son of a policeman'), 'the last unselfconscious man on this earth.'

Well we'll see about that.

The story had gone on to say his feet and hands were so colossal that if he cupped some pool water in one hand and playfully threw it at you, it was like being hit by a bucket of brine. What would it be like to be with a man like that? 'Moreschi' felt a pleasant stirring. He floated closer now to a new position looking out over the rail—close enough to pick out the Duke's individual words.

'...No one had ever seen a surfboard before! I enjoyed presenting it to His Majesty. They floated it on a fish pond they keep out back at Buckingham. All of a sudden, he started wading to it. You should have seen him try to stand on it. I said, 'No, Sir, Mr. King, you need a wave.' So he stood there, gave me a big grin, and waved to me as if he were a *monumuku* from the South Sea Islands. Your Mucky-Mucks are good blokes, crazy funny!'

He flashed his donkey teeth, and even 'Moreschi' smiled. Imagine never having to second-guess what you said. Imagine being so big you could sweep up other people's feelings instead of being drowned in your own. Yet it's the drowning that gives me my art. Moving toward the edge of the crowd, 'Moreschi' lit up a long smoke in an emperor cigarette holder, which attracted the notice of the man billed as 'The Last Hawaiian King,' who hailed him. The size of his arm.

'Hey, you're the singer they were talking about last night,' Kahanamoku said. 'Come join us for a drink!'

The great 'Moreschi' rarely came on call. But against all odds, he did now. Maybe it was the Duke's seismic innocence that gave him his power. In any case, he padded over.

The swimmer looked down at 'Moreschi's' toenails, painted emerald green. 'Say,' he said enthusiastically. 'We've got a live one here. You're glamorous!'

'Glamorous,' 'Moreschi' said very softly. You should see me in my satin marabou slippers with the fluffy fronts, size twelve.

'But just a boy. Kind of a girl-boy, if you don't mind my saying so, little fella. Why don't you sing something for us? How about the *Star Spangled Banner*? Come on, tear a hole in it!'

Kahanamoku's agent William Dawes, representative to the stars, leaned over and whispered something to his client.

'Oh, right, it's rainy weather,' the swimmer said. 'Sorry, Al. I understand about saving yourself for the finals. But I bet you can sing a ton.'

More whispers.

'My agent, Billy Dawes,' Kahanamoku said. 'He's always afraid I'll turn into a shrinking violet.'

'You're not the only first-class act on this tub,' Dawes said to Kahanamoku, then dropped his voice. 'And you're not the only big man here with a little ukulele.'

The giant's eyes rose before his mouth opened wide. 'Moreschi' proudly met his gaze. 'Is that so?' the swimmer said. 'I'll be a monkey's uncle!' He stood and vigorously shook 'Moreschi's' tender hand, nearly breaking its bones. 'This little fella is Peter Fuckin' Pan. He never has to grow up!'

41

Chi cerca ciò che non deve, trova ciò che non vuole.
He who seeks what he should not find, finds what he does not want.

BROOKLINE, 1922

Long after the rain, the streets and houses still reeled from the pounding, as though hit in the face and bruised. Pigeons who'd worked their way under the eaves made their brooding sounds, though it was after two a.m.

Downstairs in the library at Sevenels, Amy was working on something new.

Afternoon Rain in State Street

Cross-hatchings of rain against grey walls,
Slant lines of black rain.

The Custom House Tower
Pokes at the low, flat sky,
Pushing it farther and farther up,
Lifting it away from the house-tops,
Lifting it in one piece as though it were a sheet of tin.

As she made notes in the margins, she reflected on her last publication launch, a reading to members of the Boston Garden Club inside the privately booked Cloots Theatre. Her reverie miscarried and she relived the opalescent sense of *ennui* that led the gathering to clap as though there were a tomorrow. The empty balconies leaned forward as if to gossip about her. She waved resolutely from the lectern to Ada and then caught Ephraim rubbing his eyes. She could still hear the vaump of the theater lights being turned out, the iron clang of the stage door behind them.

Just three feet from Amy—they were never more than a dozen feet apart—Ada sat fully clothed on a naked chair. Her favorite hobby would ever be to burn a hole in Amy's back with her eyes. 'Bravo,' Ada said, reading her mind. 'A new masterwork is born.'

Pricked, Amy shot a glance at her lover, who quickly returned to her novel *Basilissa*, though she'd long ago given up on it.

'Shut up,' Ada said.

'I didn't say anything,' Amy said.

'Then shut the think up.'

'Don't flatter yourself. I wasn't even thinking of you,' Amy said.

They both smiled.

Raffi lay on his bunk, listening. He could hear the pigeons nesting in the rafters two floors above as their coos drifted down the chimney, he and Victor having shut the great furnace down for the season. The sound returned him to the time he'd stopped in the street with Victor and looked the dead bird in the eye. It had fallen from a nest in a street-light, he'd supposed. But wasn't an incandescent streetlight a terrible place to try and make a nest—never a wink of sleep, and didn't it fairly burn the chicks to death? Then the long fall. He saw the bird's glassy eye, and then Beatrice's, again. Missing you is better than never having known you at all.

A few feet away, Victor looked asleep but wasn't. 'You know that fellow who was nosing around the hotel?' he said. 'Well, I saw him again today. I mean I felt him again today.'

Raffi held his breath.

'He was across the street, in King's Chapel Burying Ground, stand-ing beside the headstone of John Winthrop,' Victor said.

'Is that right?' Raffi said.

'I'm telling you,' Victor said. 'He must have been staking me out from across the street, watching hard. I heard a couple of waitresses whispering about a solitary figure looking them over too carefully at the back door as they left the building, but I knew it was me he was waiting for. It was the man who'd come in before, asking for you.'

For a while they said nothing but instead listened to a new sound, rose bushes scratching against the basement window as if demanding entry. Victor scowled. 'How can you just lie there and try to sleep?'

Raffi closed his eyes and kicked his blanket off.

'You castratos are touchy,' Victor said.

'Technically, it's *castrati*.'

'Which proves my point,' Victor said. 'As a blind man, I'm an honorary castrato. And what's your fascination with that box you're so intent upon hiding?'

He meant the box Raffi had slipped under the basement floorboards the first night he'd spent here, not far from below his bed. An irrational fear leapt up inside Raffi's heart. Had Victor meddled with it out of curiosity? Of course not. Just the same, he'd check it soon, to make sure it was all right. He'd toted it across Europe and the Atlantic and wasn't ready to share it. 'We all carry a box of relics, Victor. Inside it is who I really want to be, or who I could have been. What's in your box, Victor?' Something about your father?

'My opinion only, but it's weird,' Victor said.

'Am I allowed no keepsakes?' Raffi asked.

'Ah, yes, you Neapolitans love your reliquaries with your splinters of John the Baptist's skull, Mary Magdalene's molars, Pope Innocent's ear wax,' Victor said. 'Look, you're traveling light, so travel light, is all. Why bother with the luggage?'

'Maybe it's my last connection to my father,' Raffi said.

'Whom you didn't know and never have a hope of knowing,' Victor said.

'All the more odd for you to be estranged from your father, whom you do know,' Raffi said.

Victor turned to him. 'Say, are we at sixes and sevens?'

'I'm sorry, Victor. I don't know what's gotten into me. I know I miss the hotel. But say what you will, "castratos" don't fight,' Raffi said. 'The word is, we're too serene. As for daddy, I guess my life is all he had to give me. Why deny me this, Victor? I think I'd have nightmares if I didn't have this box. Chinese eunuchs carried them so their remnants could be re-attached in the next world. In medieval Europe, monks who impregnated initiates were ordered to castrate themselves and then watch as what was severed was served to wolves, so they'd know most profoundly they could never be whole again.'

'Well, I haven't yet plucked out my dead eyes, clouded by storms of mucous.'

'You're right, Victor. I'm just talking, that's all.'

'I'm not denying you anything,' Victor said. 'Keep your box. Be as lonely as you want to be.'

'I'm perfectly happy,' Raffi said.

'As am I.' Victor smiled. 'We Americans are devilishly happy. That's why we need ice in our drinks. And you can keep your lies about your tractable wolf-pets, too, by the way. What time is it?'

Raffi peered at the glowing numerals painted with Undark on his radium watch dial. 'It's quarter to three. Good night.'

An hour later, after he knew Victor was asleep, in spite of knowing his friend would not possibly have disturbed his precious box, Raffi pulled up the board in the basement floor to see if anyone else had. He looked at his gilded container and felt a rush of memory flood back to him so vividly it was as though he were looking Dr. Cufflinks in the face. Furtively he unlatched it, eased it open as if a mouse were inside, then quickly closed it. His mind in motion, he retied the twine he'd kept around it since his days living among the rats of the Colosseum and looked across the dark basement space at the noble and open features of Victor's sleeping face. Do you travel when you're asleep, Victor? If so, I hope it's somewhere you can make peace with your illustrious father. Then Raffi prayed to St. Anthony for his loss and to God for giving him the New World as his territory, and Victor as a friend.

Irretrievably awake, Raffi set out clothes to wear to the Boston Society for Psychical Research the next morning. As for the danger of Victor's man in the graveyard, who cared if the coast were clear or not? Sometimes you had to shiver and start living.

And life wasn't so bad among the specters at the B.S.P.R. Pure theater, which was the way he liked it. Not that he'd stopped believing in the occult. Far from it. The Society was ninety percent perception and five percent deception, the balance the contents of an unmarked file-cabinet drawer. The power was in the need of the people who came there, desperate for the dead. How can you help but admire those who want to see beyond the seen? Marie's right. I am still 'in service.'

'You didn't trust me,' the 'sleeping' Victor said, his head turned to the ceiling. 'You had to look at the box.'

'I didn't trust myself,' Raffi said.

'A box,' Victor said. 'How unoriginal. Go ahead and bring it out.'

'It's not all it's cracked up to be,' Raffi said, 'however blind the beholder.'

'What's it made of?' Victor asked, reaching out with his fingers. 'Is it stone or some precious wood? Is it embellished in some way?'

When Raffi didn't reply, Victor turned away. 'Forget it. I don't want to "see" it, much less touch it.'

'No, no,' Raffi said. 'If it will make you happy, I'll bring it out.' He'd never shown it to anyone. The closest time was in the bowels of the Colosseum, when a thief had stolen the portmanteau Raffi had kept hidden in a dark corner, and all that lay inside it. It was a night full of stars, and Raffi, joyful over landing his job at the Forum, had returned to his haunts only to see the thief heading down the street toward Campidoglio with everything he had. Raffi had run up beside him. 'What you've stolen is mine.'

'If I've stolen it,' the thief said, 'it can't be yours.'

'Please,' Raffi said. 'Keep the money. Just give me my things.'

Even then, Raffi was so reasonable, so serene, it seemed to give the thief pause. The thief looked at the scuffed leather satchel. 'Probably not worth anything, anyway, but I'll be keeping the coins, thank you.'

'You've earned them,' Raffi said. With his box in the bag and little else to his name but a single gold *Umberto* in a leather safe slung below his armpit in case of emergency, Raffi had vowed to keep all three forever.

Since he'd already spent the last coin, maybe it was time to reconsider the box, too. But sleep was finally overtaking him, so he'd think about it tomorrow.

He fell into a dream in which he was much younger and talking to one of the gravediggers along the underskirts of Naples, looking for work. Way back in the glory days of the eunuchs, it had been a common custom for groups of adolescent castrati from the conservatories to dress as angels and lie picturesquely about the graves of dead children, as though in mourning.

'It's a comfort to the families,' Pio Sorrento, king of the gravediggers, explained to Raffi in the dream, his eyebrows raised in practiced sympathy. 'This particular family is just sick about losing their little cherub. When they visit the site tonight, they'll find you sleeping beside the headstone in a lovely pose, guarding their little infant from the devil, even if you can't protect him from the worms below. You certainly look the part. You know—*ethereale*. Do you think you can dig up a white gown?' The gravedigger chuckled at his own joke. 'No?' He put two fingers to his lips. 'It won't be the freshest, of course, but I believe I can.'

'How much will I earn?' Raffi asked. Mindful of the lonely *Umberto* under his armpit, he straightened his back and looked his new employer in the eye.

'You'll eat with us every night,' the gravedigger suggested, with disturbing warmth.

Raffi pretended not to notice as he surreptitiously slid his hand between his legs to make sure his equipment was still there.

'It's been a long time since I've seen someone like you,' the gravedigger said. 'What a world. Are there any more of you around?' He looked pensive for a moment. 'Say, can you sing? Imagine your singing to the dead darlings. The families would be even more generous.' He took in Raffi's blank expression. 'No, I guess you wouldn't be here if you could sing.'

'I mustn't sing a note, ever again,' Raffi said. 'I promised God.'

'Just how bad *are* you?' the man said. 'Why in heaven's name would they have done this to you if you couldn't sing?'

Raffi looked at the king of the gravediggers again and realized it was really his old *fiancheggiatrice* Anna Freud. Substitution and compression. Or was it suppression? She smiled and drew near. 'When you're pondering the meaning of a dream, you have only to consider recent events. You dunce,' the dark-eyed beauty whispered. 'You still don't know who I am?'

42

Anche le pulci hanno la tosse.
Even fleas get a cough.

BOSTON, 1922

awn cast a rosy hue on the headstones where so many
Revolutionary patriots had hit pay dirt. Carlo had dragged
himself to the cemetery to watch the hotel every morning since
receiving his new orders, but this vantage point was proving a little
sketchy—too out in the open. No doubt the doorman was getting suspicious of his 'gardening' in a suit. Worse still, the policeman's favorite
coffee stop was just two doors down.

He shook out his shoulders in the dappled shade: an assassin for so
long and no closer to wrapping up the job. Sure, just go find the witness. Not so easy if you were suffering from lack of sleep and in a state
of nervous exhaustion. It seemed everyone had the drop on him. There
was something important about that tall fig picker he was missing. His
head throbbed whenever he tried to work through it. What was it that
creep Diletti always said? 'Sing one note at a time. Clear your mind of all
thoughts. Excitement isn't art.' But even the singing was getting harder
at the club each night. He found he was always looking for that skinny
old monster—might as well be Diletti as Stadt—sitting at the front table,
his legs crossed, watching.

Carlo looked at his seventeen-jewel watch, a present from Stadt's
wife. Shit, he'd have to be more careful. Maybe it wasn't a good idea
after all to accept presents from a woman whose husband doesn't believe
in coincidences. Seven fifty-five *ante meridien*. The early breakfast shift
was almost over, and most of the hotel staff would be coming out of the
service door in just a minute.

He waited as though he were watching a jack-in-the-box, with Stadt
winding the key. Finally the door flew open. Who did he see? He didn't

234

see the tall guy, but he did see The Hoo Doo Man, that blind colored who'd dodged his questions before. Cane tapping, his quarry started walking toward the Metro station in the park, opposite the State House.

Keeping roughly fifty paces behind, Carlo tailed him discreetly into the underground. When he boarded a subway train, Carlo got on, too, in the next car.

When you know you're being followed, you get a glow on. Victor was aware he was 'carrying' a stranger, and he had a good idea of who the stranger was. No mistaking the squeak of those shoes. What an amateur. Spilling out with the crowd onto the platform at Cambridge Station, Victor ascended the stairs to street level and headed west along Pynchon. Before long, the pursuer reached his side.

'Good morning,' said the stranger who'd had all those questions about Raffi.

'It's always midnight for me,' Victor said easily. He yawned as if sleepy from a late shift, then turned left on Harlow toward a group of flattops, his imaginary apartment building being the last in the line. That wasn't enough to shake the lunk who fell into step with him for a block without venturing further comment. Victor stopped short, got his bearings with his cane, took a big step back, and said, 'Say, are you following me?'

'I'm sorry,' the stranger said. 'I hope you don't mind. I'm looking for a friend who I think you know. You work at the Parker House, don't you?'

Victor smiled.

'There's a very tall guy with longish, curly hair,' the stranger said. 'Oh, sorry. You probably wouldn't know that since your peepers don't work. But I saw him once—near the service door.'

Victor felt the heat of the stranger's eyes on his own.

'I think this guy works the night shift, Friday nights?' the stranger said. 'I represent someone who needs to get in touch with him most urgently.'

'I'm sorry, I don't know what to tell you. You could just contact hotel management.' Victor turned and resumed his stride. The stranger reached and very gently touched his shoulder, so Victor wheeled on the larger man with his cane raised. He was always ready for crazy sighteds. He had to be careful because you never knew what they were going to do next. 'Please, sir,' Victor said. 'Leave me be.'

'It's not like that,' the stranger said, with a note of desperation in his voice. 'My friend owes him some money! Is there any way we could locate him to give it back to him? I'm sure we could arrange some sort of finder's fee for you. I have twenty dollars here.'

Victor felt him tuck a bill into his coat pocket. 'Are you sure he isn't in any trouble?'

'Absolutely,' the stranger said.

'I heard there was a tall fellow, used to work in the scullery, but he left our employ,' Victor said, trying to sound helpful. He lowered his cane. This stooge was not the real danger. Maybe he was just the front man in some clumsy sting operation. If not, Victor had a feeling there was deadly force somewhere in the background that was a real menace, and that did frighten him.

'Was he fired?' the stranger asked quietly. 'Why did he leave? Could you please tell me his name, for confirmation?'

'Last I heard, he was headed back to Ireland. Something about an ailing grandfather.'

Victor nearly fell over from the gust of the stranger's sigh of relief. But far from easing Victor's tension, it only increased his sense of doom. He nodded, turned, and started walking. He listened as the front man's footsteps disappeared behind him.

43

Il peggior passo è quello fuori dalla porta.
The most difficult step to take is the one out the door.

BOSTON, 1922

It had been a cold spring, but now that May had swept through and they were halfway through June, there had to be a price for summer's warmth: thunderstorms. Frank Morelli sat beside Dorotea inside his motorcar on Washington Street and watched veils of rain floating across Boston Harbor. With a clap of thunder, the rain was suddenly angry. Through the drenched windshield, the cityscape melted and began to sway. He lit a cigarette while the girl looked down at her lap. 'You seem upset,' Morelli said. 'Come on. Where's the sugar for Frankie?'

Dorotea said nothing.

'Come up on my knee and tell Uncle Frankie what's wrong.' He looked up and down the street to make sure the coast was clear.

'I've just missed my period.'

He breathed a sigh of relief and put his arm around her. 'Oh, is that all that's worrying you? You're just too skinny, that's all.' Now it was he who was quiet for a second. 'Are you sure?'

Dorotea wiped her eyes and looked away.

'Look, are you sure you're sure?' he asked.

Dorotea said nothing.

'Well if anything like that were ever to happen—and it's not going to happen—my motto is, sometimes you have to do the right thing.' He chucked her chin. 'You believe in me, right?'

Dorotea said nothing.

'You'd better believe you believe in me. You know I'm a gentleman. If this is my responsibility, this is my responsibility. You're sure it's mine, right?'

Dorotea said nothing.

237

'Look, kid, like I said, if and when it comes to that, I've got some money set aside for rainy days like this. Cheer up! It's the twentieth century. Something like this doesn't have to ruin our evening.'

'Or our lives,' she said under her breath.

She looked at him with the same dangerous smile she'd worn when he saw her for the first time, walking beside his car. Or had he imagined her smiling? 'Here, take some.' He held a flask to her, and she took it to her mouth with both hands. 'I'd like to start tonight all over again,' Morelli said. 'Besides, how far along could you possibly be? It seems like I only met you a few weeks ago. It's so unlikely it's laughable. This just isn't happening.'

'You're married,' Dorotea said.

'That's not what I asked,' Morelli said. 'I've asked you to tell me exactly why you're worried. You've got to concentrate.' He squinted himself. The black rings around Dorotea's eyes scared him. What had possessed him to get involved with this cheap piece of skirt? Hell, the quiff was too scrawny to be pretty. 'If it comes to that—and it won't come to that—I know a doctor,' Morelli said. 'You just let me know. Once I know, I'll give you an envelope with his name on it. You'll take this envelope to the doctor and he'll take care of you. Jesus Christ, you've got the shivers. Look at you. You're a regular shiverbug.'

'I've got to go,' Dorotea said and opened the door.

Rain washed onto the expensive leather upholstery of his pride and joy. It flattened her dress to her stomach, which to his eye showed no signs of a gentle swell.

'Don't go now,' Morelli told her. 'You'll catch your death.'

44

Mastica bene e poi inghiotti.
Chew well and then swallow.

1922, EN ROUTE FROM NEW YORK TO BOSTON

The ersatz Moreschi's first view of Boston was out of a private motorcar driven from New York by the executive assistant to the flamboyant philanthropist Ernest B. Dane. Dane had earned his fortune the old-fashioned way—he married into U.S. and Bethlehem Steel. His bride's dowry also came with a soupçon of interest in Fore River Shipyard. This allowed him plenty of leisure time to play the role of benevolent art booster.

Marshall Story, 22, named for Marshall Newell (a famous Harvard running back whose brilliant business career had been cut short on Christmas Eve 1897 by an engine backing up from the Boston & Albany Railroad), was understood to be at Dane's beck and call. This windfall had come to Story as a payback for the help Story's father had given Dane in taking him across the finish line at business school, Dane having proven himself allergic to frightening lists of calculations.

Story had also been put in charge of Dane's charitable contributions, chief of which was being principal donor—unseating Eben Jordan, the department store tycoon—to the Boston Orpheum.

As directed, young Story picked up Cantore at the Waldorf Astoria at eight a.m. sharp, and now he and the famous castrato were tooling past Fall River, Massachusetts, along the Old Post Road en route to the Parker House, where the Theodore Parker Suite had been prepared to the singer's specifications. Most unusual: just as they'd had to do at the Waldorf, the Parker House had been instructed to seal all of Moreschi's windows with aluminum foil, as he loathed the aging effects of direct sunlight.

In contrast, Story had a tan from sailing. He felt important to be so close to celebrity, even if this most unusual singer smelled like a French whore, or what he imagined a French whore would smell like. He'd met some odd ducks doing other errands for Dane's interest in the arts—after all, show people were different—but this was the flukiest he'd met yet. It made him shudder to think he was a eunuch. At prep school, a chum of Story's had lost a testicle after hitting a bump aboard his Indian eight-valve, and he'd been pulled from school. His only consolation was that it made a whale of a college entrance essay. 'What obstacles have you had to overcome?' What a stroke of luck! Suddenly the boy had a full ride at Dartmouth.

'Have you ever been to Boston before, Signor Moreschi?' Story asked the singer, who hadn't spoken a word in an hour and forty-five minutes on the turnpike.

Cantore was surprised to be questioned by a chauffeur. The problem with Americans was, they didn't understand their roles in life, which led to a fundamental unhappiness. 'Mmmph,' he said finally.

'What's that?' Story called back. 'I mean, Boston—have you ever seen the city before, sir?'

'A long time ago,' Cantore said. He closed his eyes. 'Eighteen ninety-six.'

'Oh,' Story said. 'That was before I was born.'

Cantore sat in silence. Story pointed to the city of Fall River as it flowed past the luxury windows. 'That's where the famous Lizzie Borden was from,' he said. 'You know, forty whacks.' When Cantore didn't answer, the boy went on. 'Have you been a singer all your life?'

'Not yet.' The question sent Cantore back to his childhood and memories of his mother, who in her youth had been a washerwoman for the priests, some of whom were rumored to be castrati, whose clothing, down to the most intimate of garments, was an obsession for them. He'd always felt sick when his mother had bragged they insisted she alone care for their personal items.

In the final days, the castrati, last of an eerie line, had been forced to fabricate backstories to account for their alterations. Fickle audiences had begun to lose their taste for watching the butcher preparing meat—here in the United States, they'd even begun to embrace cellophane packages at the shiny new supermarkets instead of going to the butcher's at all. Having lost their nerve, they needed the pretense that these entertainers' unusual voices hadn't been created expressly for them in a gruesome operation but instead were the result of some happy accident. Listener guilt had a dampening effect on ticket sales. The real Moreschi had been savagely clipped in Monte Compatri. Now he had to tell people he was born with a congenital defect—easier to swallow.

Even bull fighting had become apologetic. Crowds didn't want blood on their conscience. They thought they could attend a bloodbath and walk away scot-free. What was so free about the Scots, anyway? First into battle, first to be mowed down by the machine guns. How strange it was that a Neapolitan punishment for disloyalty in men was one and the same as an alteration to boys made in the name of art.

'I understand your meeting in Manhattan was about—is it phono-graph recordings?' Story called back to him. 'Do you know when they'll be available? I'm saving up for one of the new Victrola VV–210s.'

This chatterbox has got to stop. Cantore closed his eyes and did not answer.

'Say, I could turn on the radio if you like,' Story said, reaching for a Bakelite dial. 'Mr. Dane's car has everything. I'll bet you like to listen to opera.'

Christ, a radio in a car. Goes to show, there wasn't anything money couldn't buy. 'Right now, I'd like to listen to myself think,' Cantore said. In the rear-view mirror, he saw the boy bite his lower lip. Barely ten miles rolled by before there was another interruption.

'Say, have you ever tried lobster before?' Story asked. 'They're better here than anything they could have served you at the Waldorf. Fresh from the North Atlantic.'

Actually, Cantore could go for a little taste of *homerus americanus* if in season. 'Si, I like the lobster very much,' he said, leaning forward, his breath hot on the boy's neck. 'It's very sweet and tender here, more tantalizing than in the Mediterranean.' When his driver nearly swerved off the road like a frightened rabbit from the warmth of his intercourse, the singer leered into the rear-view mirror and showed all his teeth.

Story looked quickly away from the mirror and rattled on. 'There's nothing like it, sir. Just dip it in some hot melted butter and it's the berries.'

The predator chuckled; Story blushed. The boy had finally realized he was in over his head. Cantore had seen this transformation flicker into his victims' eyes just before their demise. 'Is that all it takes? What's the name again, young man—'

'Story,' the driver said. 'We'll be in Boston soon. Will you be needing anything else?'

The imposter Moreschi pulled out his empty cigarette holder. 'Have you got a smoke? I'm all out.'

45

Parla del diavolo e spuntano le corna.
Speak of the devil and his horns appear.

D orotea waited for Morelli to pick her up at the same corner where he'd left her the night before.

'Since I'm doing this for you, we're even—right, kid?' he said, enunciating his words carefully. 'I want you to know I had to pull some strings. You'll make four times what you did at the factory.' He unfolded his hands as though he were bestowing a prize and leaned back against the leather seat.

She looked through the car window at Custom House Tower, which rose like a bright poker in the twilight.

'You start tomorrow morning in the very respectable Inventory Control.'

She closed her eyes and pictured twelve-hour shifts reviewing endless cargo lists of incoming vessels from faraway ports of call while she felt his whelp, and her vilification, growing inside. Then she looked past the tower and saw the Underwood factory sign above the rooftops a mile away. As the moon disappeared and then reappeared behind a cloud, the incandescent devil danced across the black sky. For a second, she thought she saw him move.

With a start the impulse gripped her: what would it be like to climb up there? During her girlhood in Naples, before Papa's reassignment to Civitavecchia, she'd often climbed trees to clear her thoughts, vanishing into their green clouds. She'd loved the mushroom cedar that seemed to hang over the whole city, the one that looked like a big umbrella. She could stretch out on the long branches, drape herself, and look down, watching others with such silent ferocity she was nearly a participant in their intrigues. Entwining her secrecy among the branches and breathing very slowly, she could all but disappear.

'You can't be serious about having this baby,' Morelli said. 'It's not good for… anyone.'

Marveling at the emotion—was that actual fear—in his voice, she turned back to study him. This so-called man-about-town, this thug? In the cafes along the Via Doria, he wouldn't even have been considered one of the pretty ones. For the first time in her life, for this one dizzy second, she had all the cards. Suddenly she was taken by a storm of pique so strong all she could do was laugh.

'What good do you think can come of it?' he persisted. 'Just tell me.' He coughed, then reached into his jacket lining for a tiny silver flask. He gulped a draught and waved it toward her.

She took it and looked back at the devil.

Morelli grabbed her chin and turned her face to his. He growled. 'How unfair it was for me to be snared by a *strega* like you. You wop tramps get knocked up. It's what you do. You trapped me, so now you have the nerve to get all highfalutin.' He removed his hand from her chin and softened his tone. 'I want you to know I care about you,' he said. 'But I have obligations to keep. To be honest with you, this pains me terribly. I am a man of honor. I am my father's son.'

He withdrew a manila administrative envelope from the pocket behind the driver's seat, the flap wound tight around a grommet with a lonely red string. 'Your hiring papers. We even, kid? I hope this job helps you and your family, because family means everything to me, and I have to get to my family now.'

She reached for the handle, opened the door, and stretched a leg out.

'Oh, come on, little nightingale, don't let's end it like this. Say something!'

She took the envelope, backed out of the car the rest of the way, and stood at the curb. Slamming the door, she leaned into the open window. 'You're sure it's yours, right?' She straightened and watched his tail-lights disappear into the converging din, the crush of twinkle. Likely he'd spend two months of contrition with his family before he ran into the next target of his wandering eye. I guess we're all as lonely as we want to be. Then she considered her new post.

What if it turned out to be another green log which wouldn't catch fire? She could almost hear the ocean of typing around her as the army of girls in the pool exactly like her, handmaidens in the great American enterprise, transcribed the cargoes of copra and tapioca coming into Boston Harbor on the great ships, indicating the duties assessed and paid with exacting grace.

By comparison, no one had taken more than the slightest notice of her family when they'd arrived here just months before.

'You're doing swell, hon,' she imagined her supervisor telling her after she'd finished a long list from a vessel sailing in from Antwerp. 'Here's a dozen more. I need them by the end of the day.'

Wouldn't her parents be relieved upon hearing their daughter was catching on so very well in the Very Respectable Inventory Control? 'I'm so glad,' her mother was sure to say. 'I've been beside myself.'

'Everything's great, mama,' she'd say, aware she was now just a serene portrait of herself and had stepped away from life into another level of reality. She was like those ships at Fore River, the ones that, depending on a trick of sunlight, were painted to vanish right in front of you. 'Don't worry, this job will fix everything for us,' she'd tell her father. But instead of giving her the embrace she so craved, he'd scowl and turn away again, shaking his head.

Poof! I'm gone. Don't worry, I died when Beatrice died. No one will miss me. She walked purposely toward the Custom House Tower, paused to take in its full height, took off her shoes, and resumed walking, block after block. The devil was calling to her, and before she knew it, she found herself at the foot of the sign. Neatly picking up her skirt, she sat on the front steps of the Underwood supervisors' entrance and decided to wait for her father. Fifteen minutes passed before she remembered this was his night off. Because the dark-blue awning blocked her view, all she could see of the devil was the sparkly tip of his spaded tail. In the silence, she leaned back to get a better look and could have sworn she saw his mouth moving. Had he actually whispered something? Did he have a secret to tell?

I never wanted to come to America. I never asked for this. Or did I? She swallowed. I miss you, Beatrice. Or is it that I miss 'not' missing you?

What she missed most acutely was the feeling of both of them starting in this new country together. But from the beginning, their illusion of a fresh chance had been compromised, even on the boat, when that tall freak had insinuated his way into her sister's graces.

So many boys dreamed of you, Beatrice—if we Favis can trace our lineage to north of Rome, why did you get so excited about that piece of Neapolitan rubbish? Neapolitans—what a crowd. She could just imagine Raffi's ancestors, selfish, decadent. Weren't they just the type to have sat and watched idly from their hillside as Vesuvius erupted in the purple distance, casting molten lava on the thousands of lost souls? 'Isn't it horrible?' they must have said. She uttered a black cry of laughter: Neapolitans watching the destruction of Pompeii and Herculaneum while sipping grappa.

She'd begged Beatrice just to tell her what about this boy could possibly interest her. Beatrice had smiled and said, 'I know, I know. I keep making mistakes with boys.'

'If you keep making the same mistake over and over again, it's not a mistake,' Dorotea had replied. 'It's a choice.'

She reflected on her own recent 'choices' and laughed aloud. How odd that others might have called it a choice, Dorotea suddenly thought of Beatrice, for you to embrace what was the most important—the feminine side—of yourself, though, my dear, dear twin, my other half, my sister true in the soul but born both my brother and my sister in one body (the doctors' 'hermaphroditic' such a lovely word until you learned what it meant, a sort of intersexuality), you could no more have chosen to live as a man than you could have chosen your eye color.

How the eyebrows were raised at the service when it was whispered her body had been cremated. What were you trying to hide, their stares demanded during the closed-coffin ceremony, but some secrets were best kept beyond the grave. From the date of their return to Civitavecchia from Naples, Beatrice had always lived as a girl.

Dorotea coughed and held her stomach. How terribly she hated Raffi, not so much for what he was as what he wasn't. So carefree was he, he hadn't even bothered to be by Beatrice's side when the electric car hit her. She'd watched him in his undulant smugness just walking away, a disconnected figure in the distance barely turning at the sound of the crash, her scream. Then all was silent as the misty rain in Beatrice's eyes left her body and went out into the world. Wherever Dorotea went now, it was still raining.

You asked me to go with you, my sister, but I so righteously refused, jealous of your boy even though I didn't want him. Instead, like a shadow,

I spied on you. Maybe it wasn't Raffi at all. Was it I who brought you your bad luck? In the final seconds, twin, did you sense I was near? Did you turn to look for me and miss seeing the trolley? I thought you were only half of me. Is it possible you could have been all of me?

She heard the devil's whisper again. Softly, she opened the front door to the executive spaces, shot a glance across the lobby, and caught the silhouette of the night watchman as he strolled to the far end of the hallway, turned to a new corridor, and vanished. She felt the urge to go higher. In a daze, she walked to the service stairwell beside the elevator, pushed the door open a crack, and slipped inside. There was no time to waste. She climbed the stairs until she stopped at the third-floor landing, out of breath. She tried not to think of the little one inside her. Wouldn't she want to protect him from a world this cruel, and this lonely?

Or was it a girl? That's all the world needed. A new wretch to pull the coffee wagon at the shipyard, or wear a hairnet in the service of Mr. Underwood. What a nightmare place. Whenever she saw the red devil sign in her mind, she could hear all the swine collectively grunting as they met the axe.

On the fourth-floor landing, the window was flung open to the night air and stars. Feeling the wind cool on her forehead, she continued to climb. And climb, and climb. It was time to meet the devil face to face, but he seemed to get farther away, not closer, the higher she went, and she lost track of how many stairs were taking her in.

Blood pounded in her ears, so she paused. She touched her dress below her belt and imagined she could feel a swell. How could it be warmer than the rest of her body? What need was there to bring the product of Morelli's selfishness and her self-doubt into the world?

What would you do, Beatrice? She chided herself at the wisdom we ascribe to the dead. Now she felt her heart beating in time with her breaths. What storey was this, the sixth? She had to keep moving.

Spiraling to the observation windows at the seventh-floor landing, she looked out again to see enormous views of Long Wharf and the North End jumping out of the darkness. She felt the ground rush up to her before falling below her feet, and she grasped the rail with both hands to steady herself. Then she risked another glance for a still-better view of what was now dead to her. The giddy lights of traffic flashed along the streets. Beyond the North End, she could see the electric twinkles of ships in Boston Navy Yard. Gas lights stood on stuck-up Beacon Hill—flickering sentries that policed the stairway to an unattainable heaven. Scudding clouds shadowed Chinatown, nearly snuffing the eerie glow from the opium lamps. In the distance, beyond the wispiness of Dorchester to the south, she could barely make out the fire-breathing smokestacks of Fore River Shipyard. Below the horizon, as though the sun's reflections were burning it, smoldering its edge at sunset, was the pearly roof of the Boston Orpheum.

46

L'attesa del piacere è spesso più bella del piacere stesso.
The anticipation of pleasure is often more enjoyable than the pleasure itself.

BOSTON, 1922

The chilly evening called to Raffi through the basement window. He and Victor were nearly dressed for the Moreschi concert. 'Victor,' Raffi said. 'Has anyone other than that suspicious fellow been asking for me at the Parker House?'

'Raffi, you know how it is.'

He took Victor's non-answer as an accidental 'no.' Though he'd dared to make a difference, he was nothing but another face in the passing crowd. For weeks, he'd wondered about his need to talk with Moreschi and decided it was because Moreschi had plunged on ahead of him—an explorer on an expedition of hurt.

Maybe culture, and particularly embarrassment, had a line of descent, too. The memory of the smoky photo in Diletti's hand had all but taken his father's place. Imagine light flickering in those eyes. Imagine an interview in which questions about life could be answered by a true 'family' member and fellow traveler years ahead through the same lonely landscape.

Not that Moreschi would be welcomed in the Explorer's Club, where they only rewarded a man for geographic peculiarity. What need had the world of humiliation set to music—atrocity with a score?

Cheer up. Nobody in his right mind would guarantee the pursuit of happiness. Raffi adjusted his tie in the mirror. As a guide to the dead under Marie's tutelage, he'd already suspected happiness was just a matter of auto-suggestion. As lively as things could be at the B.S.P.R., he wasn't ready to abandon his dream of a career at the Parker House. He leaned down to brush some dust from his shoe.

Who would the next castrati be after he and Moreschi were gone, stars to be simultaneously celebrated and attacked? 'Foreigners,' like the suspicious Italians the Irish police impounded on Deer Island. Veterans, the world their ghost limb. Who's the next monster du jour, and how much time will he be allowed on stage before he gets the hook? You don't have to have discovered Pluto to understand that Nature adores a void.

'You're not really going to try to speak to him, are you?' Victor asked.

'I'm sorry, Victor,' Raffi said. 'Were you saying something?'

'Oh, nothing,' Victor said.

'Give me another chance, Victor. I'd like to hear it.'

'The hell I will,' Victor said. 'I just said the most interesting thing you never heard, and I'll take it to my grave.' He shook his head. 'It's going to take a long time for us to learn what we don't know about each other, Raffi.'

Amy and Ada had already left in their limousine to drop in on a sick friend in Jamaica Plain on their way to the show, so Raffi and Victor now emerged from the basement at Sevenels and headed for the Underground, their footsteps accentuated by the metal plates on Raffi's kid shoes. Surfacing at Park Street Incline, they began to make their way toward the Orpheum.

'Walk a little to your left, Victor,' Raffi warned. 'There's another thrush.'

'Describe him to me,' Victor said.

'He's young, must have fallen from a nest up inside the new street-light, right by the bulb. I can see the twigs up there.'

'The color of his wings, please.'

'Chocolate brown with black stripes and white tips.'

'His eyes.'

'Black as a button. He has bright yellow feet.'

'And you're sure he's dead?'

'If only he could just be asleep,' Raffi said. The avian creature appeared to be in perfect order. 'But no living thing would sleep in such an uncomfortable spot.' Dreams were kings. They didn't have to make sense. They ran things. There was a great and gentle beauty about the way living things left their bodies behind them as they traveled through dark worlds—he'd seen it come over Marie—and it tugged at his heart to see such a rush of awareness gone, with no hope of it coming back. Marie was playing with fire, communing with the dead. What if, one sunny afternoon, they turned ugly and refused to let her come back from their side? Maybe that's why she kept those sugar cookies on the table out in the reception hall. To celebrate the stark innocence, the miracle, really, of being here and nowhere else. Or were they just a bribe to the dead as well as the living?

In glass broadside boxes, posters for Moreschi's performance appeared on the sides of buildings, sets of dark eyes everywhere that hinted of the supernatural. Now the sun was pink and orange against the rooftops as the murmur grew into its own overture amid the buzz of words that sounded like 'strawberries, raspberries.' Very carefully, Raffi and Victor stepped around the spot where the tram had killed Beatrice.

How dangerous it was when 'then' struggled to occupy the same space as 'now.' In another world, Beatrice would be here now. Maybe she was anyway. Raffi felt a pressure in his chest, and he struggled to keep from crying out.

'It was here, wasn't it?' Victor said. He nodded when Raffi didn't answer and stood still.

Raffi watched the large crowd mingling outside the Orpheum. Then he touched Victor's shoulder. Stepping into the cataract, the two friends entered the rapids rushing through the door and became a part of the stream.

47

Il sole a mezzanotte.
The sun comes out at midnight.

BOSTON, 1922

Ephraim adjusted his gold pince-nez with the practiced motion he'd so admired among the *teopetniks* in Leningrad, hoping his posture and the studied elements of his bearing made the crowd properly aware of his presence at the opera. The swarm about him slouched, laughed, and wiped their noses on their sleeves, their movements clumsy and vague with alcohol, enviably self-assured. A bit crude. He stiffened as he took a survey of their dress. Granting himself a moment to consider his own sartorial splendor, he winced. Were his shoes too pointy? Calm down. He always did this! Why must the slightest misstep count more when it was his? Why did he care so much about appearing carefree?

To help himself relax, he started looking for other communist sympathizers here incognito so that at just the right moment, he'd be prepared to share a wink or a knowing smile.

He heard a rustle and found himself enveloped by a cloud of lily-scent. His cheeks burned as a most vivid woman took a seat beside him. Suddenly frozen, he was unable to do anything but stare straight ahead at the empty stage.

'So we're finally going to see the great Moreschi,' Victor said as Raffi sank gratefully into his horsehair seat a few sidelong glances away from Ephraim. 'Nothing like getting to the bottom of things. But what if things have no bottom?'

'Then I'll find that out too,' Raffi said.

'Ah, then, you're set!' Victor said.

'Disbeliever.' Raffi peered into the vestibule. 'Here come Miss Lowell and Mrs. Russell.'

'I see them,' Victor lied.

'Victor, I'd just as soon you didn't mention that I'm hoping to speak with Moreschi afterward.'

'A secret assignation, then. Fine. It's just that you've been talking about this stupid concert almost since we first met, and I don't want you to be disappointed. Now you drop it on me that we're going back after the show to wait in line and accost Alessandro Moreschi for a private audience.'

'You aren't, I am,' Raffi said.

'Why don't you just tell him what he has to tell you,' Victor said, 'so he'll get it right? Because everybody has to worry about Raffi's feelings. What a fool's errand.'

The bitterness took Raffi by surprise. His friend had seemed interested in the excursion until he'd heard Ephraim, in a rare burst of generosity, had set up the meeting with Moreschi, courtesy of a Harvard classmate who was the advance man for an Orpheum benefactor. Now Victor was ready to jump ship.

'This stalking of Moreschi,' Victor said. 'I don't see what good can come of it.'

'You're right, Victor. I know it's reckless. But still, I'm going to see if I can talk with him, even if it's just for a few minutes.'

With Victor scowling, Raffi sat quietly a moment. How strange Moreschi was so close now, traveling out of his past. Suddenly Raffi's eyes lit up, and he squeezed Victor's wrist. 'Isn't it one of your "hoots" that life doesn't come with a libretto?'

'How's that again?' Victor said. 'You see I wasn't listening.' He paused. 'I'm beginning to wonder if there's any good at all in your coming here tonight. You're supposed to be in hiding.'

Now Amy and Ada reached the top of the aisle.

'Hello, Miss Lowell, Mrs. Russell,' the two men said, standing to let them pass.

'What's the big deal here,' Ada said. 'If I wanted to see poor sods suffering for their art, I'd go to that rathole Palladium in Westminster or a hospital, not the Orpheum.'

'It is a bit like bear-baiting,' Amy said. 'Actually—'

'Why don't you write a poem about it, dear?' Ada said. 'Meanwhile, this show's about someone else, not you.'

Watching them, Raffi saw two awkwardly dressed women trading whispers behind Ada, their lips hidden by tortoise-shell fans. One shook her head vigorously. But the other smiled shyly, reached out, and touched Ada on the shoulder.

'Oooh, it's so good to see you, Mrs. Russell. You are Mrs. Russell, aren't you? I saw you in *Aged in Oak* at Wonderland in Philadelphia. It must have been—'

'That was back when I was still wet between the legs,' Ada said sweetly.

Amy cleared her throat. 'Not even fish in a barrel. Kittens,' she whispered. She grasped Ada's wrist, but it was too late.

'No, no, dear, it's fine,' Ada turned to Amy. 'I'm just chatting with my new best friend from … is it the City of Sisterly Love?'

'Oh, no,' the girl said. 'I grew up in Machiasport. Once in a year our whole clan goes on holiday.'

Ada eyed the girl's rabbit collar and loud-checked cape. 'Ah, a lumbering family who made its money in coal! Thanks sooo much,' she dismissed her and turned back to Amy. 'If I remember correctly, we topped that staging by mounting a most theatrical production of *Venus in Furs*. No one had seen anything like it. Do you remember? Ha! With that harpy Ursula Opdycke, who kept stepping on my lines, and Kirsten Killjoy, who wore tuberose to cover the stench of fermented juniper berries from the gin she sipped from her teacup? That old bitch wasn't vaudeville, she was La Grand Guignol—raped and murdered so many times on stage her nipples got hard before the conductor could even lift his baton.' She gave Ephraim a wicked once-over. 'You could have been an extra and felt the kiss of my lash.'

Ephraim raised his head and scanned the audience—except for the creature sitting next to him.

'My nephew seems to be occupied, you pathetic pederast,' Amy said. 'What's got into you tonight? Leave the boy alone.'

Raffi looked down the row of seats and took note of Ephraim's careful disregard for the nasty, painted girl he'd seen that first day in the Parker House lobby.

Amy leaned back to Ada's fan, who was listening intently and basking in the reflected glow of celebrity. 'Careful,' she said, nodding toward Ada. 'When she looks like she's smiling, make sure not to put your fingers between the bars.'

'Of course I was just a child then,' the fan said.

Ada nodded, looking straight forward. 'Born yesterday.'

'It's just that... don't you miss the theater, Mrs. Russell? I imagine everything must have been so much more meaningful back in the good old days—'

'Nostalgia's a young person's dish,' Amy snapped. 'It's certainly cruel to bring it up to anyone of a certain age. Want to know what we're nostalgic about? We've forgotten what we used to be nostalgic about.'

Ada turned to Amy and softened her tone. 'And flapper-trashing is a crone's sport.'

'But—' the woman flushed. 'Can we look forward to no performances from you, then, in the future?'

'Ha!' Amy said. 'She's always performing.'

'Well,' Ada said, turning to face the stage, 'my love here is writing a new play just for me with the working title of "Illness and Death."'

'I'm well into the second act,' Amy said. 'Which would you, as a discerning member of the audience, look forward to more, *Decrepitude* or *Dementia*?'

'How is the friend you were visiting at the hospital, Mrs. Russell?' Raffi broke in, instinctively protecting the innocent.

Now Amy turned ice cold. 'Hark! So now the member of the serving class interrupts the action of the principals, feather duster in hand. You're out of place, concierge, not to mention out of your depth. I'll thank you to wait your turn, unless you're waiting on us.'

'Yes,' Raffi said. 'You're not my people.'

'Stow it,' Ada said. 'You're stealing my lines.' She turned to Raffi with a suspiciously sweet manner. 'Our friend is fine, dear.'

'Fine if you mean she's sprinting to her great reward,' Amy said.

In the mezzanine, Kit Snow took his seat beside Lorna Doom. 'How'd you hear about this Moreschi fellow?' he asked.

'Through the Museum,' Lorna said.

'Well, what kind of music is it?'

'I guess you could call it vintage Italian,' Lorna said. 'It seems he wants the whole world to go backward when we're so intent upon moving it forward. Not that it's his fault.'

'Have you ever heard him before?' Kit asked.

'I haven't myself,' Lorna said, 'but I'm acquainted with an Italian boy who seems quite devoted to his music. Quite a funny fellow. Very tall. In fact, there he is, with Amy Lowell.' She made an air salute to the poet, who eyed her briefly but turned away without returning the greeting.

'Jeesum, he's a tall drink of water. No one I have to worry about, I hope,' Kit said. 'Do you see anyone else you know?'

'There are so many people here I can't see anyone.' She looked away.

'Say, did I tell you I recently took the train to Washington to try and convince the War Department to underwrite the first non-stop transat-lantic flight to London?' Kit said. 'I told them straight up, somebody's going to do it. Why wait to find out who that is? We're the U.S. Army, for God's sake.'

When Lorna offered a thin smile, he grew more emphatic.

'Then the old general said, "You're taking things too fast," and I said, "With respect, sir, that's the speed things are going. We're not charging up San Juan Hill anymore. There are new challenges we must be prepared to meet."' The flyboy widened his eyes, shifted in his seat. 'You know, Lorna, you might think it strange I'd bring this up during a fancy affair like this, but do you think your family might consider investing in passenger aeroplanes? They're this close to changing the world, and somebody might as well get rich from it. I'd feel guilty not to have let you know. You could get in on the ground floor.' He closed his eyes and shook his head. 'Oh, I must be crazy. Forget I brought it up. But really—'

'Kitchener, you sound just like my father,' Lorna said. She tapped his shoulder with her opera glasses. Whatever had made her play backseat bingo with him on the way to the Harvard Club last week? She'd put herself through all this—cut her hair, atomized herself with L'Heure Bleue, bought a new white dress, and allowed herself to think it was all for him until she realized that maybe it was just to show off a new beau. With a pang of longing, she looked back at the crowd from Sevenels. That door was forever closed to her.

She realized Kit was starting to lose interest, too, so she clutched desperately at his hand as a sense of restlessness shifted through the auditorium like leaves turning up before a blow. 'I recently read about some nuns castrating a priest for impregnating one of their initiates,' she said. 'They made short work of him and stuffed what they'd removed in the naughty sister's mouth.'

Kit stared at her in what looked like disgust. 'Smith College, right? I don't see what's so attractive about a modern education, where it's all reading, writing, and the repulsive.'

His yawn reproached her for her wordiness, her worldliness. She sat musing, the night ruined. The best thing to do was stop talking. Yes, that was the best policy. 'Thracians made captives castrate themselves and then hand their genitals to the dogs for supper,' she said impulsively. 'What makes horror horrible is not the act itself but the crowds it draws. Art is hurt—why pretend otherwise?'

What a flat tire, Kit sulked. She sounds just like my sister. I guess I can kiss a kiss goodbye, let alone sparking. He felt vaguely haunted by the notion he was endorsing the further castration of boys by even being here. Alessandro Moreschi—ruiner of a perfectly good date! A dark motorcar would have served him much better. 'I don't know why people pay to see an exhibition like this,' he said. 'It's as though we're here to see the lions eat the Christians.'

'I'm afraid they've already taken a bite or two out of this one,' Lorna said. 'We're looking at the remains.'

'Aw, wouldn't you like to leave?' Kit asked. 'Maybe everyone ought to get up and leave. Everyone could say, this is not art, it's a freak show.'

'So now you're an art expert?'

Kit dredged up the smile that had always worked with the girls in Springfield. 'Wouldn't the crowd be more fly at Avernus? Let's drift from this dive.'

Lorna softened her tone, as though to telegraph maybe there was a chance to rescue the evening. She turned and surveyed the crowd. 'Why don't we just stay for a little while?'

Kit shrugged. 'I guess then at least we could say we saw the last one.'

At this, Lorna looked briefly down at Raffi and then back to Kit. 'That's what we could say.'

Royal Cortissoz sat with the mysterious man with the half moustache, 'the minor character who dared not say his name.'

Tonight, the young man's right lip was shaven clean instead of his left. As vain as the facial-hair bit was, at least young André—or whatever his real name was—was defining himself instead of just leaving it up to others. With his glossy, manicured digits, he flipped through the program, stopping at the occasional page to reveal a single, extremely long, thumbnail.

'Look out there,' Cortissoz said. 'Waiting for the slaughter, waiting to condemn Moreschi for what he stands for, what we all stood for, not so many years ago. It's as if the whole nineteenth century is on trial by all you young people. It's so easy to be smug in a new century—you can't see what your mistakes are going to be.'

'I can see you, Royal,' André teased. 'And really... are you actually telling me you're nostalgic for castration?'

'No,' Cortissoz said. 'There's plenty of that where we're headed. What I miss is our ability to recognize, and fairly evaluate, what's come before us. Why is there so much change around us without the courtesy of consideration? How long in this epoch do you think we can hold our breath? We've been holding it since the Great War. Something's got to give.' He looked at the audience. 'Rubberneckers masquerading as music aficionados.'

'What exactly are you doing here?' André asked.

'Somebody's got to stand up for the past,' Cortissoz said. 'It's so funny, the way we remember things. In our poetry we memorialize the Trojan Horse, but it's the Greeks who built it. Greeks hid inside it. Why on earth don't we call it the Greek Horse? Because it's so much easier to blame the victim. Now we've come again to throw out the baby with the bathwater. How can we possibly listen to this Sistine soloist with a fair ear? Maybe the news here isn't that this is "the last castrato" so much as this may be the last audience for the castrati. Have you considered it might be the most otherworldly, or at least cringe-inducing, music you've ever heard? I confess, I don't even know which it is. You sure didn't want to come here tonight.'

'It makes me uncomfortable,' André said. 'I consider this whole evening unwholesome.'

Ever the instructor, Cortissoz winked and glided his hand across his companion's knee. 'That's the spirit. Art is supposed to provoke, not just delight. There's nothing wrong with being provocative. I want you to have a good time tonight.'

'All night?'

'We'll see,' Cortissoz said.

'Because I'm in need of a little dough,' his young man said, almost inaudibly.

'Mmmph.' Something small and dark gray scurried across the theater floor and ducked below the plush seats ahead of them. Both men half lifted their feet for the next thirty seconds or so. Cortissoz was sure he'd actually felt the rat's tail slither along his Interwoven socks. 'You can earn money by painting, too, you know,' he said. 'You haven't touched that canvas in weeks. If I'm to take you under my wing, you have to accept my guidance. You'll have to paint on a schedule.'

André darkened three shades.

'Speaking of work, you'll also have to take more risk in it,' Cortissoz said. 'You need to stare into the abyss.' He chuckled to lighten his tone. 'And how many times have I told you, you'll have to stop those rocks from floating. You can't have a seascape with floating rocks. You have to suggest the ways they go below the waves and pre-exist the ocean, in dark greens and browns, if you want to get to the bones of things. You have to root them and give them mass, so they'll feel real. Only then can your customers stand on those rocks and feel the sea breezes, *si*?'

'Royal, may I ask, have you ever painted? In your younger days. Before you were you.'

'I'd say that's hitting below the belt, but that's your specialty, isn't it—not painting?'

'You haven't answered me.'

'Oh, I suppose in college,' Cortissoz said. 'It doesn't matter anymore. I have some old watercolors in a camphor chest I keep in the basement. What's the use of exploring what might have been?'

'Tell me about those times. I want to learn what turns a man into a crocodile.'

'That dog doesn't hunt.' Cortissoz turned away and let his eyes play over the audience for a moment. Thursday night. Vespers. Didn't everybody used to go to church for Vespers?

'So Moreschi isn't the only one who's missing something...' André smiled savagely and whispered into his ear. 'What would you tell him if you could speak to him?'

Still the critic would not vouchsafe a reply. He was trying to remember the time he believed he could have been a painter himself. He swallowed. 'We're all around you. The lonely crowd.'

André shook his head. 'You know, sometimes you can be a Royal pain in the ass.'

'A sharp tongue rarely replaces a sharp pencil,' the critic said. 'You'll get on, but maybe without me.'

Strawberries, raspberries.

Just as the lights dimmed, Tiger Lily slithered in and sat beside Raffi. Somehow, in the punch of new blackness, it seemed as if the two were alone.

Amy rubbed her hands together and whispered to Ada, 'Don't you love this moment—just before?'

But Raffi wasn't paying attention. He was thinking of the phantasmagoric tale Tiger Lily had told him about the unfortunate who was Shanghaied by the empress he loved.

'I've thought a lot about your story,' Raffi whispered as the pre-performance darkness settled on the collected souls in the Orpheum, in the grand Before. 'How again do you know the wretch who became one of us at the hands of the enchanting Mandarin girl?'

Tiger Lily batted her eyes, spinning another lie. 'We were working the North Sea in a Dutch tjalk off Lowestoft, fishing. Crew of five. Hard way to make a living. It was five lifetimes ago.'

It was the perfect answer, but that was the giveaway. Too smooth, too practiced. Too much *guanxi*. Raffi smiled and looked at Tiger Lily. In the clarity of this darkness, he knew that she knew that he knew the storyteller herself had paid the ultimate price for the ultimate experience. You loved the woman who castrated you so much you became her.

They turned to the darkened stage. Tiger Lily said in Italian, 'The troubles at the bottom of the pot are known only by the spoon.'

'And need only be,' Raffi said.

The conductor strode to the center of the podium, a spotlight following him. 'Good evening, ladies and gentlemen. From Rome, I present the lead soprano in the famous Sistine Chapel, Professor Alessandro Moreschi.'

In the shower of applause, Lorna moved closer to Kit.

And there was 'Moreschi,' walking vigorously to the podium and taking the conductor's one hand in his two, closing his eyes and turning his head back. Then he twirled to face the crowd, blew kisses, and bowed. The two stood for a seven-second interlude of photographs which smashed light into their painted faces while the silence deepened. Now the darkness was so profound it seemed to enter the upholstery of the seat cushions. The enormous room started to move.

As the conductor descended into the pit and the musicians tuned their instruments, Raffi was back sitting cross-legged in the Bronx Opera House to catch the vaudeville show 'Fine Feathers.' The sisters had given him the afternoon off. He'd snuck inside and hidden in the space between the orchestra and the front-row seats, dodging gobs of spit from the paying patrons. Now there's a barometer for happiness. It's a good day when no one's actually spitting at you.

The conductor's nodding for the downbeat restored him to the present. The opening chords of Eurydice's aria 'Oh, Sight Too Sweet and Too Bitter' enveloped him, and Raffi found, to his astonishment, that he felt relaxation. The pain he feared was no longer there. He found himself listening to a musical reply to the very aria Diletti had promised him when he was etherized in that butcher shop in Naples—the song across the river of the damned he'd dreamed one day of singing.

And then it struck him. Why was he born with a clarion voice? Sometimes a person's greatest, most fleeting, asset begs for a tragic loss. Beethoven's hearing, Oedipus's twenty-twenty vision, Ada's pulchritude. Mischief, in the form of malignant imitation, stalks innocent admiration into a dark alley.

Moreschi, with his signature dark eyes, bent his knees slightly. He took a deep breath.

48

Si sa come se è nati, non si sa come si muore.
You know how you were born, but you don't know how you will die.

BOSTON, 1922

Dorotea opened the unmarked stairwell door on the eighth floor, slipped inside, and lost herself in the dark as it shut behind her. She'd heard whispers William Underwood kept a private conference room up here which he rarely used—could this be it?

Slowly, the interior took shape as her eyes traced reflections of moonlight pulsing with red flashes from the sign above. Here, oh, here, the secular priests of Boston meat packing presided over burled oak paneling below curvy cove ceilings. She took the flask and had another swig of Morelli's brandy. Her head felt hot.

Underfoot was an Aubusson carpet below a mahogany conference table. The dark fragrance of lager led her eyes to a scattering of 'dead Indians' tossed into a silver Revere bowl—empty Narragansett longnecks waiting for the cleaners at midnight.

A squadron of candlestick telephones atop the matching mahogany credenza lay silent; no more calls for the gentlemen.

In this single room at the roof of Massachusetts, there were no corridors but rather glassy windows designed for the fortunate. As a girl she'd seen the Medici map room in Florence. The Medici would have wept out of jealousy for a perspective this privileged. The royal blue carpet was shot through with the cardinal points of the compass.

She walked in the direction of West, to the window facing Boston Common, and saw the State House dome, looking as though someone had dropped an orange on a green lawn. Beyond it was Clarendon Street, then Beacon and the Charles River softening to Cambridge. Wisps of a low cloud floated slowly past this world on tiptoe. It was lovely up here. Her head ached.

In the murk she took in a scatter of divans, smoking chairs, and a phonograph. Where was the light switch? Even in the darkness she could tell the appointments were fabulously expensive. She felt her heartbeat increase as she walked to the windows and looked off the edge of the building. Where to turn? East glowed with the harbor and its azimuth of loneliness. North? She'd never liked the cold.

Then South. Peering between buildings, she detected the lights of Chinatown flickering behind Custom House Tower. Lost within the urban silhouette were the indiscriminate rooftops surrounding the Parker House, the dizzy green triangle of Granary Burial Ground.

She thrust open the largest of the observation windows and felt the wind lift her hair. She hadn't expected so much wind. It made a cool blue music in her head. The little voice she'd heard in her childhood tree said, 'Jump, and fly.'

Conscientiously, she removed the long screen and out of long habit looked for a place to put it that would offend no one, create no cries of foul. The top of the screen was wet from moisture, so she didn't want to leave it on the polished floor. The carpet as well was too plush to be scuffed or scarred by an intruder. Let no one say I left a damp spot when I left. Finally she leaned it beside the open, gaping window. It blew over from the rush of wind, so she had to set it up again, with a stronger angle this time.

There. She smoothed her dress, ran her hand over her belly, and felt a heartbeat. Was it hers or the child's? Then she climbed inside the varnished window frame and fantasized the shadow of a night watchman running across the room to save her, though no one came. In the gusts of fresh air she felt forever beckon to her with the starlit deception of a theater prop. For a flash she imagined herself bringing up her son alone without a father to become president of the United States, making his grandparents proud. That can never happen. I'll never be whole without my twin. She took a long step toward nowhere, then stopped.

What was that? She heard a flapping in the room—a frightened thrush had found his way inside. It flared up against the windows, dreaming of the night. She stood transfixed as it landed fitfully near the Narragansett bottles, then swooped up again before veering urgently toward her face until she ducked. After it passed her to freedom, she looked down at her feet. Then she heard someone coming up the stairs, or did she? Quickly she slipped down from the varnished threshold and stood still beside the drapes.

What would the night watchman's voice sound like when she heard it? 'Hello, miss'?

A smaller door took shape beside a fire extinguisher. She fled across the room, pushed it open, and entered a concrete well with five more stairs.

She hit the top step and reached the roof of the William Underwood Co. The dark crowds who milled about in the streets, alleys, and apartments below looked so small and remote.

Above her, light from the Red Devil shone down on the roof of the three-decker where her family lived. The flashing bulbs of the wooden Devil bathed her in a warm, red glow and made her blink. He was held to the stars by scaffolding and black cords connected to three black transformer boxes that vibrated with a deadly hum.

Moths fluttered, pinwheeled, and slammed into the Devil before falling to the tarpaper roof. Something soft was underfoot—lumps that covered the dark surface like a carpet. She uttered a little cry when she realized it wasn't a cloud of moths flying into the sign. She was stepping on dead songbirds.

How many were up here? Had they been drawn by the light or the warmth? She stepped around the Devil's trident and walked between his legs. With the world so bright about her, she slipped around one of the transformers into total darkness.

She heard more steps of the dark figure behind her. She didn't dare turn to see him but instead leapt toward the utility platform going up behind the Devil's sign and gained the stairs. Spirals within a cage. She started up.

Still the man behind her said nothing but simply followed. Or was there no one there? If it spoke to her, she was sure it would be a perfectly reasonable voice: 'Miss, you are trespassing. Come down from there.'

The wind was giddy about her. Her breaths came faster now as she rushed past a riveted assembly holding the bridge of the Devil's nose. She climbed above his eyes to the final platform between his horns.

Why didn't the shadow make a sound as it crept up the stairs behind her? She felt it growing ever more near.

Three light bulbs spattered beside her, spitting light so frightening she stepped to the left and burned her arm.

The rail went only halfway around. Someone had taken the trouble to make this last platform shiny with varnish, so why the incomplete accommodation? With rough rudders, the world swerved under her, left and right, and she wondered if this was what she might have felt like if she'd been one of the privileged few able to ride in one of the aeroplanes.

Still she felt the black shape moving toward her. She looked down and felt her heart skip. Another fallen thrush lay just inches from her toe, the flashing lights seeming to move its wing. 'Dear little one,' she said. 'Do you remember who you are, or are you who you remember?'

When she reached down gently to see if it were alive, it startled her by fluttering up. She slipped on the polished oak, made a wild grab for the rail, and was gone.

49

BOSTON, 1922

'Moreschi' opened with a low tone, his vocal chords rumbling like a train leaving a station, a deep purple steam locomotive at dusk that vibrated the tracks, the ticketing booth, even jarred the cup of tea from the stationmaster's palm. His mother would have been so proud. 'If only you could give yourself up to the service of our Lord,' she'd told him. 'Moreschi's' cry in the dark could have been mistaken for a moan straight from the dead.

The trick was to sing across time, not space. He lowered the bottom of his diaphragm for additional reverberation, and the sound was so disturbing and lonely and frankly juvenile that the stiffs in the audience, who without having heard it had condemned his music and the half-dozen generations who'd created *opera seria* to oblivion, sat in embarrassed silence. So much for your Gilbert & Sullivan.

If I can find the right resonance, with some help from the ghost of this sham cathedral they call the Orpheum, maybe I can blow the whole place apart, and all these smug saps with it. With all your new American 'taste,' you don't know Moreschi from a mobster. You'll cross the street to avoid eye contact with a wop, but put Italian and opera on the same poster, and you'll pay any admission.

Already, he'd grown three times his normal size on stage. When he raised his pitch, he tried not to sound like a woman or a man but something greater than the two combined. I have been created for your pleasure, the voice seemed to say. If I am not wholesome, please remember that you did not want me whole.

'Jesus Christ, this sounds like cats,' Kit Snow whispered to Lorna. 'It's worse than I thought. Come on, you're not enjoying this…' He'd flown his monoplane through thunderstorms without blinking, but this demonstration was unnerving.

When 'Moreschi's' Eurydice started to cross the river, Raffi closed his eyes and felt himself flying, though from the opening salvo he knew beyond the shadow of a doubt he was not listening to the act as adver- tised. The high notes were not the 'silver' tones he'd anticipated. Age could explain some of it, but there was a texture that suggested something else. The modulations of his voice were as robust and satisfying as a spaghetti dinner. On the other hand, why trouble about it. He looked around to see the audience in rapt attention. How much better to be relaxed, even nonchalant, amid uncertainties?

'Is he singing or sobbing?' a voice whispered.

'Be quiet,' said another. 'If you weren't ready for this, you shouldn't have come.'

'He's barking mad,' a third said.

Everywhere, the crowd shifted in its seats. Raffi marveled that they'd come not to enjoy themselves but instead to enjoy being horri- fied. They were hearing exactly, and only, what they wanted to hear:

'I find this mutilation repugnant. We don't have to put up with this.'

As Ephraim listened, still not hazarding a word with the young woman beside him (well how could he talk to her, he was a perfect stranger), he felt the saliva dry up in his throat, as if a lonely part of the universe had wicked it away. His stomach tightened, the gastric acids within putting him ill at ease as Moreschi hit notes a man wasn't meant to hit. Ephraim had never encountered a sound that was both strong and despairing at once. It was crying, but a deeper cry, punctuated by a glottal choking. He was on key, but it was saltpeter rubbed on a wound. It made Ephraim furious. It made him want to hit someone. What manner of art would appeal to that part of us that would shatter the last unbroken window in an abandoned house—or perhaps drown an unwanted child?

Professor Moreschi sang on, with trenchant courage, his lonely voice quaking, quavering, trembling, breaking while cutting his way through the Crucifixus solo of *Petite Messe Solenelle*. This bankerly Italian knew all the tricks, and he had no sense of fair play.

Was this a man or a wounded animal? Try as he might, Ephraim couldn't describe or contain it—a latent cocktail of the repellent and seductive, garnished with a twist of the macabre. At best an acquired taste. Sometimes it sounded as though he were making strangled fun of himself. Other times it sounded like soldiers, or maybe soldiers' horses, dying. I shiver for our ugliness. Ephraim closed his eyes.

Behind him, he heard a woman's voice say, 'I had a hysterectomy. No one's asked me to sing about it!'

It was, at its bottom, hopeless. Oh my dear God, protect us. It pulled the veil off the theater's unreality and for an instant there was humanity in its stark terror—a screech in the night. It swept the audience with a wave of shame. All of this—all of this shouldn't be happening. Maybe things will be better in Leningrad.

He'd quit at the shipyard a week earlier but had returned to look at the destroyers the night before. He walked to the empty hawsers, slack with the ships' magnificent absence. They were no longer here. As far as he knew, or didn't know.

Raffi knew the audience had nothing to compare Moreschi's music to, outside of his stilted 1904 recording of *Ave Maria*, because he was singing from a dead tradition they were blissfully ignorant of. Beyond that, they were misinterpreting his scooping, where like Farinelli he rose up to meet a pitch he intended to hold from half a note below. How unfair for them to think he was singing out of key.

'Close the slaughterhouse doors!' someone cried out, and a few people laughed before the booing started. This was nothing new. Roman audiences often attacked the performers. But this seemed more audience participation than a true assessment. Courageously and suicidally, 'Moreschi' sang even deeper from the old tradition, purposely refusing

268

to give the audience what they wanted—an abridged version of his pain, something small enough to carry away or pin to a lapel.

Something strange is about to happen, Raffi realized, feeling the bump of a presentiment. He shifted his attention to Royal Cortissoz, who was looking at his lover, exalting in his jimjams. Since this performance was a ripe tomato in the darkness, it had begun a deep stink, more personal and foul than the Hawthornean ambiguities of Beans and Scrod Night. Boston didn't have the guts to look in the mirror, especially this early in the morning!

Even Victor, blinking back incredulity, whispered, 'Is this the way you remember it?'

'It's exactly as I remember it,' Raffi said. 'Isn't it really something?'

'Singing as destructive behavior,' Victor said. 'This is getting interesting. Does he look the way he sounds? Holy smokes, no wonder they told you not to sing.'

Now the catcalls reached hurricane pitch as 'Moreschi' hit his high notes.

'How can he go on like this?' Victor said. 'He gives me the heebie-jeebies.'

Exulting in the misunderstanding and hatred, 'Moreschi' reached into his silk-lined waistcoat pocket and unfolded a crumpled envelope with some handwritten lyrics on it, in pencil. Kahanamoku's challenge still rang in his head. Tear a hole in *The Star Spangled Banner*. He held up a hand to the hoots and began to sing as the crowd grew resentfully silent—a nightmare version that channeled the 'castrato's' anger and slough of despond. No one had ever heard it quite that way before, and in a state of artistic exhaustion they stood up, cheering, Raffi suspecting it was in relief that it was all over. The whole theater seemed to vibrate in the din; the seats, ceiling, and walls to move.

Up in the cheap seats, Marie looked on. She'd never felt so much psychic disturbance in a single room. Far from the suggestion of a *tramontana*, this embittered singer was a paranormal hurricane—a psychic storm. The Orpheum's windows rattled. She held tight to her chair arms and threw her head back, laughing, while Moreschi took her to the top of the roller coaster again with an encore as the crowd fled to the exit.

'I must see him,' Raffi said.

'Seriously?' Victor shook his head.

'Ephraim took the trouble to set this up,' Raffi said. When the last of the audience shuffled out, he and Victor made their way behind Hamilton Place toward an alley dividing the night between Washington Street and a loading platform with a closed metal door marked Stage.

Had it smelled of fragrant yeast, he might easily have mistaken it for Roll Alley at the Parker House. But here the culture was music, not transubstantiation.

After a knock on the door, the earnest assistant appeared and said, 'Come in.' Another voice behind him whispered, 'Who's the smoky bones?'

Victor turned to Raffi. 'My curtain call. I'll wait out here.'

'Are you saying he's not welcome?' Raffi asked.

'Oh, what the heck, you may both come in.'

'I prefer to wait here,' Victor said.

Raffi followed the young man through a labyrinth of dressing rooms that brought to mind the catacombs below the Colosseum. Finally, he reached a door with the numeral 2 painted on it in white and paused.

'Ephraim still changing the world?' Marshall Story said before knocking. 'Tell him to lighten it up a bit for me.'

Raffi smiled.

'Is it true he's going back to Russia?' Story asked.

'I hadn't heard that,' Raffi said.

'Well, last week he told me he has the tickets. He's just finished his piece about the shipyard for the *American Spectator*. Our friend's getting to be quite famous—the infamous *Mayflower* agitator. He's in his element.' Story looked at Raffi. 'Oh, I see,' he said. 'You're thinking about what's on the other side of that door.' He reached past him and knocked three times, swiftly. 'Signor Moreschi?'

Raffi heard some steps approach.

'Go away.'

'Yes, sir, but you were to see Mr. Peach?'

Raffi heard nothing from the other side of the door. He tried his native tongue. 'If you would permit me, sir, we have a common background in our very uncommon condition. I send you felicitations from Sacerdote Diletti.' Raffi sounded so very Italian that Marshall Story disappeared into thin air.

Then the door cracked open. Black raccoon eyes squinted above round cheeks shining with grease paint. 'Moreschi' took a quick measure of Raffi and said, 'How do you know that old scratch, Diletti?' Then he grabbed him by the lapel and pulled him inside. 'Now come over here, where I can see you.'

Raffi recognized the guttural Neapolitan dialect colored by frequent business trips to Sicily, likely as a talented interlocutor. It took no leap to understand he was in the presence of an important member of the Camorristi. He looked at the singer's dressing gown, diamonds and dice slithering across its silk surface. He sensed a menace in the room.

'Sit down over there.' The singer indicated a black horsehair cushion on a window seat created to hide a radiator. 'Quartieri Spagnoli?'—an accusation, not a question.

'Via Vico Tofa,' Raffi said.

'Even worse,' Cantore said. 'I've read your letter. I thought it was a joke. This is impossible. It's too cruel. When did it happen? When were you forced to live in Boston?' The singer laughed at his rag and rearranged his robe. 'This should be entertaining. Now, tell me. Where did it happen?'

Raffi told him, to the hour, and, to the best of his recollection, the minute of his disfigurement on the butcher table in Naples, and the memories rushed back to him as if the candles were still flickering. How odd it was to be trapped inside the same smoky photo Diletti had shown him of Moreschi, with his viscount sash! Didn't he know from working with Marie it was dangerous to flirt with memories? Especially when you couldn't put words into memories' mouths?

'It's criminal they made you a eunuch,' Cantore said. 'I think you must be, by a long margin, the last of us. Tell me, what made you need

271

to reveal yourself to me? Do you blame me?' He gave Raffi a funny smile. 'Go ahead and cut off my balls.'

'It's nothing like that, signore. I hoped to meet you to tell you of my admiration for you. I heard you tonight. You are a wonder, the last of an era, like the darkest rays of sunset—'

Cantore shrugged. 'Bullshit. Who sent you? What are the odds I'd run into a real castrato?' He turned and looked out the window. 'You look just like those guys my mother dreamed I'd be. That bastard Diletti was still turning them out?' He turned back and narrowed his eyes as he gave Raffi a twice-over. 'So strange your turning up, like an April fish. Say, wait a minute.' He stepped back and gave Raffi a third look. 'Stadt was looking for a tall, odd-looking fish, somebody who saw something he shouldn't. Tell, me, kid, have you seen something you shouldn't have seen? That wouldn't be you, would it? That old kike wouldn't know a castrato if one fell on him. I'll have to explain it to him sometime. It's a little like a circumcision, only more... sincere.' He laughed and farted. Then he touched his index finger to his upper lip. 'But he would know a dangerous witness. Who else knows I'm not the real, real thing?'

'The crowd believes you are Moreschi. They hated you, they created you.'

'Any knife in a storm.' Cantore looked in the mirror. 'That's why their shock at our condition is so entertaining to me. They call us monsters, from *demonstrare*, to teach. Well, I hope they got their money's worth for their lesson tonight.' His black smile looked just like Diletti's. 'People like a nice roast capon with rosemary, but they don't want to participate in what happens from the henhouse to the table. Where do you sing?'

'I don't sing,' Raffi said.

'Well, of course you do, young man. You're a sacred monster. You were mutilated to sing. You could have taken over this gig!'

'I don't understand, signore. You have perpetrated this charade in Moreschi's honor?'

'Very likely, Moreschi's tits up by now. He was *mezza morta* when I stepped on the boat to come here.' Cantore leaned closer. 'So it seems we have something on each other. He had an appointment he wasn't going to keep, and I needed a disguise. You don't tell the crowd I'm a fake, and I won't tell Ira Stadt I've seen you.'

Raffi said nothing.

'You haven't yet answered me. Why don't you sing?'

'I was told not to sing.'

'And you listened to them?'

'At Duomo di San Gennaro. They told the child I was I'd go to hell if I did. I have never sung a note.'

'Very nice cover story. I suppose you don't drink coffee, pull on your dick, or smoke, either?'

'No, signore, but I have a light if you need one.' Instantly, Raffi offered a lit match.

Cantore flinched, then relaxed. 'Beh? That showy quick draw might charm the tourist set, but it can get you killed in a different setting. What do you do, if you don't sing and don't smoke? Do you teach music? When you prepare for something, you must do it!'

'I thought I'd prepared for this moment,' Raffi said. 'Now I don't know what to do. I work as a kind of tour guide. I've recently reconsidered a career in the hotel industry. Let's see. I'm mourning a dead love; I've taught tango to the undanceable in Beacon Hill; and my only friend is waiting for me in the cold.'

'A friend?' Cantore looked wary. 'And you'll talk, even mouth off, but you won't sing.'

'Si, signore.'

'So easy,' Cantore said, 'to blame those who've castrated you for who you don't dare to be. Do you realize you've found the last means to make yourself even more curious? At least you could try it. Come on, now. The people who told you not to sing are probably dead, no? God himself is on a Spirophore. Just between us, now, let's hear a little something.'

Raffi filled his lungs and let the air slowly out. 'I'm sorry, signore. I can't. In any case, I know I could never be you. Just because I was hurt like Moreschi,' he said with a touch of softness, 'doesn't mean I could hurt back like you.'

When Cantore didn't reply, Raffi folded his arms. 'Not only do I know I'm not talking with the real Moreschi, I find myself wondering if I'm talking to myself.'

This annoyed Cantore, so he started packing his things into a valise, as though Raffi weren't there. Finally he turned. 'Do you have further questions for me?'

'Just one,' Raffi said.

'What is it, then?' Cantore said. 'I don't have all night. I have women to screw. What could possibly be wrong with you? You seem to have done all right for yourself. They didn't take your head off, did they? You know, I really should kill the two of you right now, but maybe you've been hurt just enough. You know I'll always be watching you, because maybe only you, like a Hollywood costumier, can teach me the ropes to keep up this disguise for the rest of this weekend in hell. I'm willing to bet you'll keep your mouth shut. At least you can trust a Neapolitan to look the other way. Now what was it you had to ask me?'

Standing below the window by the outside wall, Victor heard the two men talking with raised voices. Then they dropped to a whisper. He heard Moreschi say, 'What's that?' Then he thought he heard both of them sigh.

50

Corvi con corvi non si cavano gli occhi.
Crows do not peck at each other's eyes.

The moon's reflection smiled at Raffi from the cobblestones. He started when a raindrop rolled off a leaf from a rain-drenched tree on Hamilton Place.

Behind the white-marble Orpheum, beside the loading docks for scenery, in the alley so long and dismal they were walking inside the mouth of a rifle barrel, he and Victor departed the stage door and advanced three steps into the darkness before a figure backlit by a flickering electric lamp hailed them.

Carlo walked briskly toward them with a pistol suspended from his hand. He paid no attention to the blind man from his morning surveys of the Parker House and closed on the tall figure beside him who'd been so much in his thoughts.

Raffi started to speak, but Carlo put two fingers to his lips. He approached two steps and studied his quarry at close range. Now the doors of memory swung open. He saw the face in the door again, more clearly, and he remembered. He remembered a six-year-old monster named Raffi Pèsca. Slowly, his fierce scowl turned into a confused smile.

'Pèsca,' he said. 'It *is* you, isn't it, *dago risolversi*? What the hell are you doing here? This is fantastical. Just my luck, I've been assigned to silence my old rival.' He spit to ward off evil, and they were boys again.

'Pardon me for living,' Raffi said. He stepped between Carlo and Victor, wrapped his old enemy in an embrace, and using Marie's techniques directed his energies to make the nerves in Carlo's right hand, which held the gun, feel hot.

'Do you still sing, Pèsca?' Carlo asked in spite of himself.

Raffi shook his head. 'How about you, Giotti?'

Carlo said proudly, 'I'm pleasing the ladies... and singing, too!' He winked. 'I'm headlining at Avernus under the name D'Amore. Big crowds. You should hear them screaming for me.'

Raffi smiled. 'Please give them my condolences, Carlo.'

'I was supposed to close your eyes forever, for what you've seen. Now I suppose you'll tell me you didn't see any more than this guy.' He waved his gun toward Victor.

'I haven't seen anything, Carlo. I opened the door too late. Just what are you caught up in?'

'How could everything be so great and so bad at the same time?' A tear ran down Carlo's cheek, and he angrily wiped it off with the back of his sleeve. The moon emerged more brightly from behind a bright-scudding cloud to reveal both young men to be absurdly over tailored.

He walked around Raffi, looking him up and down. 'Don't take this the wrong way, chum,' he said, 'but I can't get it through my head that I once wished I were you. What an Ethel you've become. For the love of Pete, look at what they've done to you.'

Raffi's smile lit up the alley. 'You're the one packing the heat, Carlo.'

'You went to see the drag queen,' Carlo said, the pistol even hotter in his hand. Now it burned to the point he nearly dropped it.

'What a night to remember,' Raffi said.

'Is that a question or a statement?' Victor seemed to sense not so much danger as a strange friendship, or at least something like that, between the two childhood enemies. 'Because the ticketholders thought he was "arrful."'

'I'm thinking of going to New York,' Carlo said. He jerked his head—a trout at the end of a line. 'I think—I'm sure I need a fresh start, and another new name. You can have this town. If you're ever in New York, please don't look me up. There'll always be a call for someone with my vocal stylings. Won't I light Tin Pan Alley on fire. If you know what's good for you, Pèsca, you won't follow me, or mention me to anyone, or talk to the police. I'm going to blow on tonight's train-ski.' He looked quickly back toward the street. 'Look, if I ever owed you anything, Pèsca, consider my debt paid in full.'

Then a shot rang out from where no one had been standing, spinning Carlo around, and Victor fell to the pavement. Carlo, holding his shoulder, ran down a side street.

'Victor!' Raffi shouted. He heard footsteps walking toward him at a measured pace, insanely loud in his ears, but he didn't care. He held his friend's head in his arms and muffled a cry as he felt his pulse fade. Victor's lips were moving. Raffi put his ear beside them to hear.

'Don't worry about me,' Victor said in a rasp. 'The funny thing about life is, you *know* it's going to turn out all wrong in the end.' He smiled and gripped Raffi's wrist. 'Get out of here—now. I'm joining my mother. You know, she was a singer, like you. Be sure to kill the lights on the way out.'

And he was gone.

Stadt was just ten steps away from Raffi, who stood and turned to face him, clear-eyed and with dignity. Stadt raised his pistol and pulled the trigger.

Raffi heard his ears pop, saw a camera flash, and felt something slam into his chest. The edges of his vision browned before pooling to black. Victor rushed up to embrace him, their shared blood friendly and sweet, darkening their clothes. Raffi's head swam through the blackness as he felt a great sorrow: will I never see Victor again? Where is my watcher, Dorotea? Will I never get to make it up to her?

In an economy of motion, Stadt casually tossed the gun into an open manhole, pulled his collar to his hat brim, and walked partway to the Washington Street entrance, feeling the mist close in on him as he thought about his wife and daughter. He'd have some explaining to do. Both had begged him to see Moreschi, too. They'd be wondering now why he'd been gone so long when he was just going around the corner to buy some cigarettes. Leaving them alone below the marquee so long, suddenly like that, they would no doubt feel, made no sense.

A messy clamor rang in his ears. He'd hoped firing the gun would give him a moment of clarity, but it hadn't, not really. As he walked, he put his hands over his ears, haunted by blood work. Calm down, then break it down. I'll send a driver to pick them up while I go home and take a shower. Then we'll all chat about the show, and I'll convince them I never left their side.

But there was so much else to do. There was Cantore to consider—damn the real Moreschi for having died eleven hours earlier. The folded telegram was in his pocket—a tick ahead of the Boston newspapers, but not for long. Now I've got to kill the wop we've brought in to pose as the other wop, because surely questions will lead to me. Even though the transmission of news was slow across the pond, it wasn't like it was twenty years ago. You could hide a lot of stuff in the old century you couldn't hide in 1922.

So many people's investments had gotten inextricably tied up in this, including his own. He might one day have entertained himself with an intrigue to topple Cantore, but not now, so rashly.

He sniffed, hawked up a gob of spit, and sent it into the sidewalk. His house of cards was falling in, not the least of which would be the entire audience demanding a return engagement. 'Ooh, please, let me hate it again!' The New York mob behind the New York promoters would soon be after him with everything blowing up and nowhere to turn, nowhere to go. Fuck the 1920s. Well, now I guess I'll have to take care of that ridiculous jazz boy too. Waste of a good bullet. Maybe I'll just stuff that bow tie down his throat and he'll choke on it.

Slipping back into consciousness for a moment, Raffi tried to move but felt great pain. He wondered if he were paralyzed. He opened one eye to follow his murderer's light step as he strolled up the alley toward the top of the street. How heavy his eyelid felt. Then, with the supervening clarity and calm known to transform soldiers during their last twilights in wartime, he saw another shape—a bright glow in white that seemed to separate from the blinding white of the streetlamp, friendly but urgent— rush up beside his killer. Stadt saw it, uttered a cry, and devastated fell backward to the cobblestones directly in the path of an electric car.

Was the bright shape a man or a woman? An angel? Who could it have been? Did it really matter? Then the realization followed, and slowly Raffi let his eyelid fall with a sweeping sense of peace—Moreschi, the real Moreschi! How you love the operatic, you jeweled toad.

Stadt never knew what hit him. Its brakes screaming, the trolley crushed his body just steps from where Beatrice had taken her last breath.

Police whistles trilled amid the expostulation of street crowds. In the uproar, a tiny bird emerged from its nest in the streetlight and flew into the night.

The great 'Moreschi' cursed the noise outside, the crowds in the street. He felt no envy for his doppelgänger life of false flattery and dead charm. Of course he wasn't going to go to the post-concert reception, no matter the maestro's urgency. What interest could he have in a Bluenose *Mona Lisa*? He was thankful that the car scheduled to spirit him away to Providence would arrive at any minute. Christ, why did he never seem to have a light for his own cigarette?

The *finocchio* had disturbed him too. We're all killed by a younger version of ourselves. The interview was over, and yet he'd kept standing there. In his predatory innocence, why did he have to ask that last question? It was as though the gelding had become a new voice in his head.

'Are you, too, afraid?'

51

L'uccello in gabbia o canta per amore o canta per rabbia.
A bird in a cage sings either because he is in love or enraged.

BOSTON, 1922

Raffi felt himself sprawling through the cold universe of space, falling through time. In hypovolemic shock, he felt as though he were slipping off the sides of a cliff with no handholds. The harder he gnashed his hands against the edge, the smoother it got, like numbing onyx. And dark. He'd never seen anything so black as this—the hollow of the abyss voided by a more numinous, deeper black.

Had he been returned to God's bag? Images—provocative, bruised, and strange—exploded in his head. He felt as though he were swimming in an ocean of developing fluid in a photographer's darkroom, inky blackness punctuated by flashes of blinding silver.

Then it all came into focus. He woke up inside the dream with an arid lucidity. Being shot by the skinny old man was in one room of his bicameral unconscious. But in this second room, the lighting was clean and figures were speaking clearly. He was lying on a gurney in a most modern hospital, antiseptic white. An exceptionally young doctor peered down at him. Raffi looked up his sleeve for a cufflink.

'You've had a very close call,' the physician said, quickly checking off boxes on a clipboard. 'We thought we'd lost you.'

'Mmmph,' Raffi said.

'Being shot is no easy matter,' the doctor said airily.

Behind his modern glasses, the young man had sandy hair and freckles, his manner thoroughly Yankee, his voice sincere, soothing, and cheerfully vacant. A naïve part of Raffi considered, maybe everything will be okay. Here was a man who ordered ice with his drinks. 'But you've been coy with us,' the doctor said.

'What do you mean?' Raffi said as the anesthesia began to creep behind his eyes.

'You've been holding out on us. First of all, Mr. Peach, let me introduce myself. I'm your attending physician. Call me Dr. Dick.'

Raffi considered his conspirational wink. What was *he* missing, pray? Dick didn't sound like the name of a ghost, but it didn't sound like the name of a doctor, either. He wondered if Marie were behind this somehow. Where was Victor? He wanted to see Victor.

'You've been unconscious for days, and we've nursed you back to health. But in the course of ministering the bedpans, it's come to our attention from the nurses that you're missing something.'

Raffi smiled.

'It's tragic, really. Doesn't anybody read the *New England Journal of Medicine* anymore? So many people are walking around in the state you're walking in, not knowing there's a cure.' The doctor pulled a cigarette from his pocket. Raffi reached up and lit it for him.

'They gave me a box,' Raffi said. 'I've kept it all these years. Others were afraid when theirs were thrown away. But—'

'Tell. Me. You're. Not. Serious,' the doctor said. 'They gave you a severance package? You did not just say you still have it, did you? Where? Right now, tell me where. Nurse, call Dr. Sedgwood and bring 20 cc's of Dammitol, stat. Not to lecture you, but do you think this world could keep spinning without making improvements? In medical facilities, universities, and hospitals across the globe science is racing to correct the wrongs that, let us say, enthusiasts from other endeavors have perpetrated. Tell me where this box is.'

Raffi laughed in his face. There'd been no temperature control. The contents weren't preserved in ether. What he was suggesting was impossible.

The dream doctor seemed hurt. 'In due deference, Mr. Peach, we'll be the judge of what's impossible.'

'The box is in the basement of Miss Lowell's house. It's hidden below a loose floorboard to the right of my bed. My friend Mr. White was also shot. Did you—'

'Look, man, this is your nightmare, not mine. Do we have your consent for the surgical procedure?'

A nurse entered the room with a black dog on a leash. Anna Freud pulled down her mask and said, 'Reattachment repeats the mistake of removal.' She looked into Raffi's eyes. 'Don't sign that.'

'You're insubordinate,' the doctor said. 'I'll thank you to keep your opinions to yourself.' He touched Raffi's forehead. 'You're delirious.' He motioned to two other attendants. 'Wheel the patient into Operating Room 2. Have Miss Lowell and Miss Russell arrived with the box? Direct them to the observation room. They might find this procedure most edifying.'

'Impossible,' Raffi said.

'You and your impossible.' The doctor smiled good-naturedly. He waved his hands and descended into perfect Italian as he prepared his instruments.

Raffi propped himself on an elbow and took a look around. The operating room no longer had a white ceiling but was now blue sky, with clouds flashing by. As the doctor turned, he took on the visage of the thief he'd caught outside the Colosseum.

'You can't do this,' Anna said. 'You can't make him whole again. Only he can do that. We all need to get over the delusion that you can fix everything with a simple surgical procedure.'

An attendant stepped forward with a foot-long syringe, the needle leaking, and Raffi blacked out again, even from the dream. He was wheeled into the amphitheater. In blinding light, three figures bent over him behind gauzy masks. Behind the surgical team was a bright blackness. Then the blackness grew hinges and became the front door at 18 Luminstrasse in Vienna. It was still raining.

'Good evening, Kastrationangst,' Anna Freud said. 'I'm afraid you've caught me mid dream-work.' Leaning gently forward, she checked behind him to see if he'd been shadowed.

Raffi took note of her viscount sash. '*Guten abend, wie geht es ihnen,*' he said. 'Is Dr. Freud in?'

'Yes,' she said. 'I'm in.' She led the way into what had been her father's library and motioned him onto a black-horsehair fainting couch covered by a Persian carpet. She slumped into the chair beside it, cracked open a leather journal, and peered into an empty Chinese brush pot on a side table, vexed. She shook out the contents of the table's top drawer. 'Is there nothing to write with around here? Do you have any idea what it's like to misplace your pen when you have something really wondrous and significant to jot down?'

Her patient sympathized. 'Last night, I dreamed I couldn't find mine.'

'Not every dream has to be about you,' she said. 'Men. Why is it that when you talk about being hurt where it counts, you're not talking about your heads?' Then she softened. 'You must feel every morning as though you've wakened on the waterfront to discover you have a new tattoo. And just a suggestlet. Lose that darkly sensual Castilian lisp. It's no longer considered sophisticated.'

'And you ought to get something done about your insufficient eyelashes.'

'Good! A flash of anger. We're making progress.' She tilted her head, leaned closer, and lowered her voice. 'Has it even once occurred to you that you're intruding into my dream?'

Raffi started to tell her about his early days, when 'I became a bit of a wanderer and traveled back to Europe to find myself,' but she cut in:

'Who was the first person you ever heard sing?'

'I suppose it was my mother. She used to take me to Virgil's tomb. We'd sit in the shade of the tree of Naples, and then she'd teach me the songs she could barely remember.'

'Lie to me, but not to yourself, *l'enfant perdu*,' she said. 'There is no such tree. It's only in paintings, a tegument of the imagination to shade the life of your mind. Have you ever seen the tree of Naples outside of photographs? When I lived with my grandmother in Italy, I visited that hellhole often enough, and try as I might, I know I've never seen it. Only my far more attractive sister Sophie sees it.'

Raffi smiled. 'Maybe it sees you coming.'

'You're so cheerful! *Ersatzkaffee*?'

Before he could say anything, she slammed a cup in his hand. 'If you must know, I didn't get along with my mother, or really any of my siblings—only my father, and that's been a dark and professional chase through a series of lonely caves. I can learn something from you and your sunny disposition. Surely there's nowhere you can go to put your head down and rest, knowing you were a man. The lengths the ego will go to hold things together, however imperfectly.' She reached back and stroked her dog's black fur.

'Once I dreamed I was fighting to defend Naples,' Raffi said. 'I drew my sword against oncoming Eritreans, only to find my shaft was broken.'

'Sometimes a broken sword is just a broken sword,' she said, swirling her spoon into her cup, which got bigger and blacker until it darkened everything and Raffi found himself on his back in the operating room as the surgical team plunged on.

After several hours, the doctor nodded and his assistants followed. The black dog broke free and knocked over a table of instruments.

'Stand up in front of this mirror,' the doctor told Raffi. 'Just look! You're good as new! In fact, you're better than new, so long as you believe.'

Anna broke in. 'Repression and substitution. The biggest favor I can do for you is let you see you don't need this anymore!' She flung open the window and threw Raffi's box into the harbor.

Raffi looked at his reflection. Suspended from his groin were two celluloid spheres. He rubbed his eyes and blinked. The globes were encased in necrotic scraps of skin disintegrating into hideous continents. 'They've turned to dust,' Raffi said. 'They're black.'

'You are wrong,' the surgeon said. 'There's clearly some regenerative tissue here. Gentlemen, you are the lucky witnesses to the miracle that is modern medicine. First, the bullet ricochets around the subject's rib cage, curves around his heart. Next, science allows me to race through time to correct what art has torn asunder. But does this one thank me?' He patted Raffi's arm. 'Just listen to him. Nothing but an ungrateful immigrant. Give him a new set of balls, functionally functional, and he complains about the color!'

Victor's final joke. Raffi felt a flush of warmth.

The doctor turned to Raffi. 'I've made you into a real swanga buckra, if you don't mind my saying so. But tell me. Aren't you happy now?'

'Happy—I always thought I'd know it when I felt it,' Raffi said.

'Your girl is here to see you,' the doctor said, one eyebrow raised.

'Beatrice here? Impossible.' Raffi began to feel uneasy because that could only mean one thing.

'There you go again,' the doctor said.

Raffi shrugged. 'It wouldn't just be an exaggeration to say I have a girl. It would be among the darkest flights of fancy.'

'Not according to her! What a complainer! She's been turning this hospital upside down, impatient to see you. But the way I see it, you can't be seen until you're ready to be seen, am I right?'

'I'm ready,' Raffi said to the dream. 'Let her reveal herself to me.'

'Get back on the gurney,' the doctor said. 'This is the way we travel.'

Raffi looked in the corner of the room for the mirror, to see Marie's face watching from upstairs. Doorways and incandescent lights flashed above his head as he was rushed across black and white linoleum floors to the waiting area. There, arms crossed, Raffi's 'girlfriend' awaited him.

She was Chinese and thin, with sharply cut hair as dark as a cormorant's wing. She tossed it and said, 'I am the love of your wife.'

'How do you do,' Raffi said. 'But don't you mean, "your life"?'

'I am the daughter of your friend Miss Wong, from Chinatown.'

'Impossible,' Raffi said.

'We're never going to get anywhere if you keep saying that,' the love of his life said. 'It seemed like it took you forever to wake up. What have you been doing all this time?'

'Dreadful sorry,' Raffi said.

'My feet are killing me. My mother's little orchids were so sexy my grandmother bound them to ensure they stayed that way forever. She told me the practice had begun when a princess was praised for her lovely feet, with a jealous attendant overhearing. I grew up saying how barbarous that was, that I'd never be like that. Now I'm touring with Anna Pavlova. I stand *en pointe* six hours a day, with both of my feet in intense pain. They bleed. I have to use a styptic pencil to stop the bleeding every night. Every day is torture to me. But then, you know that. You always say how much you love to watch me dance.'

'I'm sorry,' Raffi said.

'Why on earth do you want me to stand on my toes? Is this what beauty is?'

She shook off a slipper and held a lovely ivory foot to Raffi's face. It was every dancer's secret shame. Each of her toes was bunged and purple with blood and coagulant, pus oozing from her split and ingrown nails.

'Imagine a Cecchetti *interrogazione* in which you could see the dancers' bloody feet. Oh, you wouldn't want to see that! That's where somebody else is being hurt for "our" taste, but it's better for you if we keep it a secret, right, my love?'

She smiled. 'You know, we're perfect for each other. Neither of us is allowed to grow up. When I was first called chubby I was six, so it's my life's work to keep my body looking like a little child's. Sometimes I

285

wonder what it would be like to menstruate. I've never deserved to try that, let alone take pleasure in a snack.'

'How do you handle the hunger?'

'Give me a fag.'

'I've misplaced my matches. I'll find you a lighter.'

52

Chi ha la libertà non ha idea di quanto sia ricco.
He who is free has no idea how rich he is.

BOSTON, 1922

Dorotea was one with the night. So embarrassing to have slipped. Had she at least jumped, she might have made a good account of herself. Bad jumpers regret their decision and half turn backward as a flash of regret sets in. Her leap might have been more like a jaguar's. She was dizzy with the exhilaration of it.

Temporal distortion had slowed and expanded the instant of flying into the darkness so she could still hear the security guard calling 'No!' behind her as she fell from being into nothingness.

How cool it was out here. It felt as though she were wearing no clothes and all the lights of the dark coast below her were smiling. The moon's reflection on the water smiled, too, from the North End all the way to Fore River Shipyard.

Would she ever stop falling? She closed her eyes and relaxed her mouth, preparing for Satan to make love to her. But instead he stared down at her with the face of Raffi Peach.

She was speared by the gigantean spaded tail at the base of the devil sign. Black and indifferent, the wrought-iron-reinforced tip had grazed her side, cracked her rib, and caught the back of her dress, stopping her fall.

Like a seized breath, she'd kept absolutely silent from free-fall to incision. Witnesses on the street pointed up and screamed at her. The wind played havoc with her dress, and she was thankful she'd chosen her best skivvies that morning. How funny her first emotion was *imbarazzo*, not fear. Well, what should she have worn to an event like this? Flooded with regret but distracted from pain by shock at her height above ground, she lapsed from consciousness for a few seconds.

Opening her eyes, she scoured the horizon for a sign of her lost twin. Was she dead yet? She closed her eyes and dropped her head as the giant clock behind her embarked on its mammoth tick to 10:01 p.m. She heard shouts, whistles, and the sound of fire engines as a throng began to gather below.

She awoke at 10:43 as she was gently lifted onto the shoulders of a fireman, who carried her down the ladder and in through the building like a bag of feathers. Murmurs followed her cortège through the imposing front doors of the William Underwood Co. as she was transferred into an ambulance.

She heard a voice: 'Look, she's alive!' It was the first notice anyone had taken of her this close to Beacon Hill.

Rushed to Mass. General, she felt what was left of her being wheeled through the Emergency Room amid clouds of conversation. Why did people seem so much like weather sometimes? In this case, the crowd started to rain.

It wasn't until several mornings later that either Dorotea or Raffi was taken to a recovery ward. By a twist of fate, both she and the young man she despised lay in semi-consciousness, just rooms apart. Not that they knew it.

Because they were both foreign, because in the rising hours there'd been another minor fire at the William Underwood Co., resulting in overcrowding at the hospital requiring patient beds to be pushed into the corridor to make room—'Clear those heads from beds!'—because every once in a while, 'the sun comes out at midnight,' the attendants wheeled them side by side below a sunny window, flooded with bluebirds and good news.

Raffi snored with a rasp. He'd finally drifted into consciousness between doses of laudanum which he'd begun to refuse and counted himself lucky never to have seen the freckled doctor in the dream again. He was relieved to find he still wasn't quite whole. No one was.

Dorotea awoke and looked at the soft wind fluttering the curtains. She reached down and was secretly gladdened both she and her baby were alive. She was sure she felt a kick. Then she looked over at the gawky patient beside her. It couldn't be. 'You,' she said. 'What are you doing here?'

'I have apparently come to see you,' Raffi said. 'Are you hurt terribly?'

'I was doing fine until you arrived,' Dorotea said.

'I must be a great irritation to you,' Raffi said. 'The more I try to do, the less I'm able to do for you.'

'That's your biggest problem. You're always trying to make yourself too useful to everyone. Above all, a girl likes a boy who's natural.'

'Well, can I offer you a light?' In a flash, he held a lit match in his hands. But Dorotea was not holding a cigarette, so it made no sense. Their eyes met.

Hit by a thunderbolt, Raffi realized his whole concierge act was over. He'd been trying to please everyone, but he wasn't able to please the one person whom he suddenly thought was important.

'Maybe I do try too hard,' he said.

'Well, a girl likes a boy who tries too hard, if it's to please only her.'

'Can you help me think of something?' Raffi surrendered.

'You could turn on some music,' she said. 'Is there a radio in here?'

But there was no radio within view. Dorotea closed her eyes. Raffi looked at the soft lids covering her peepers (what a silly word!) and felt he'd never seen anything so lovely. He remembered her face in the distance on the ship, her insouciance at dinner, her pounding on his chest the night Beatrice died, her curse, her recognition of him as the devil of Fenway Court when she'd caught his eye, flipped her serving tray under her arm, and turned away.

Dorotea seemed to sense what he was thinking and wondered that a devil might be so close to the hole in her heart. She stared at him.

'I'm sorry,' Raffi said, looking into the mist of her eyes and feeling as though he were in a shiny tin monoplane, tossed in a gorgeous storm. 'Maybe I could sing you a little something.' It had been so long, he didn't know if he could make any sound at all. With considerable effort he stood up, the tightly bandaged wound stabbing its whispering pain through his chest. He took a long, careful breath, and then, with the luxury of his detachment, he sang, first low and then sweeping into a trill like a nightingale, voluptuous in darkness, a polymorphic mélange of whistles and crescendos, the fluty notes unnervingly rising through the roof of the recovery lounge, up through the transom, wafting invisibly through Quincy and Nauset, Chinatown and Charlestown—even over Beacon Hill and the purple windows of Louisburg Square, quickening the senses of the suntanned dead.

It was the howl of a wolf, the piercing cry of the lonely. It was a lullaby. Dorotea was so moved she leaned toward him and let her cheek touch his shoulder. 'How could you know what I needed?' she asked.

He took a deep breath: 'Because even if it's what sends us to hell, the center of what hurts us—even if it's what makes us unforgivable in the eyes of Him who roughs the fur of the most miserable and wonderful wretches on the face of this earth, when there's no one left to sneer at our smoldering imperfections, the raves of who we are and who we might have been… Even if it's because there are those who dare us not to, because of the vick in Victor, the raff in Raffi, because "the carabao have no hair—holy smoke, but they are bare." Even in our unprotected nights of memory, we sing.'

Dorotea smiled. 'Now that's an exit line.'

Before Raffi could answer, a sister in gray appeared and scowled. 'Wop stands for Without Official Papers. So you're getting ready to give birth to another one, missy.'

'So it really is that obvious to everyone,' Dorotea said.

'This morning, during your exam, your cervix showed a blue hue. You are so lucky to be in an important teaching hospital. We have only the most modern techniques here. Doctor is working on a brand new bio assay test that involves proteins and rodents. And those filthy Huns think they can beat us in the study of the *corpus luteum*! Ha!' She pursed her lips. 'Who shall I put down for the father, or shall I just write "bastard"?'

The very last castrato looked into Dorotea's eyes. He felt her hand slide into his. Something swelled in his chest, his vocal cords relaxed, and his voice dropped an octave.

'The father's name is Rafaele Pèsca.'

Acknowledgments

This story is a product of my imagination. I've taken liberties in using some real-life names, places, products, and events as points of departure while creating this fiction. I've altered, compressed, and combined news items, dates, and characters to tell Raffi's story.

I visited Naples as a young naval officer and fell in love with Campania.

The real Parker House hotel in Boston, nicknamed 'America's literary hotel,' opened its doors in the 19th century. The Saturday Club, with members Hawthorne, Emerson, and Longfellow, gathered there. Charles Dickens kept a suite. Ho Chi Minh, author of the play *The Bamboo Dragon*, worked in the Parker House bakery circa 1911 to 1913. Thirty years later, Malcolm Little, later 'X,' worked as a busboy. Even if the hoteliers hadn't invented Parker House Rolls, Boston Cream Pie, and coined the term 'scrod,' the Parker House is still at the mystical center of Yankee Olympus. Senator John F. Kennedy proposed to Jacqueline Bouvier in the dining room at Table 40.

The automatic writing passages were developed from spirit holographs penned by my grandmother, Helen Mills Sargent of Lexington, Massachusetts.

When I went to Brookline and knocked on the front door of Sevenels, the present owner graciously invited me inside for a tour. When I asked if many Lowell fans had visited, she said, 'In the ten years I've lived here, you're the first.' As I write this, Sevenels is now for sale. Thanks to Carl Rollyson for *Amy Lowell Anew*, which provides data on Lowell's trips to England.

I've visited Fenway Court dozens of times as a paying admirer, but I got to know Belle Gardner through Morris Carter's *Isabella Stewart Gardner and Fenway Court*, published in 1925, the year after her death. There's nothing like experiencing the palmy atrium during a Boston snowstorm.

I cherish the insight, friendship, and support of Lancaster University's creative writing department.

The Italian phrases that introduce each chapter are traditional. Many are selected from *A Buon 'Ntennitore... Proverbs of Naples* by Antonio and Leonardo, and recollections from my wife, Nancy, who lived in Naples from 1968 to 1971. I am grateful to Maria Luisa De Luca at the Institute For Italian Studies for her input.

I hope you feel I took the trouble to make up a good lie.